THESE FEATHERED
FLAMES

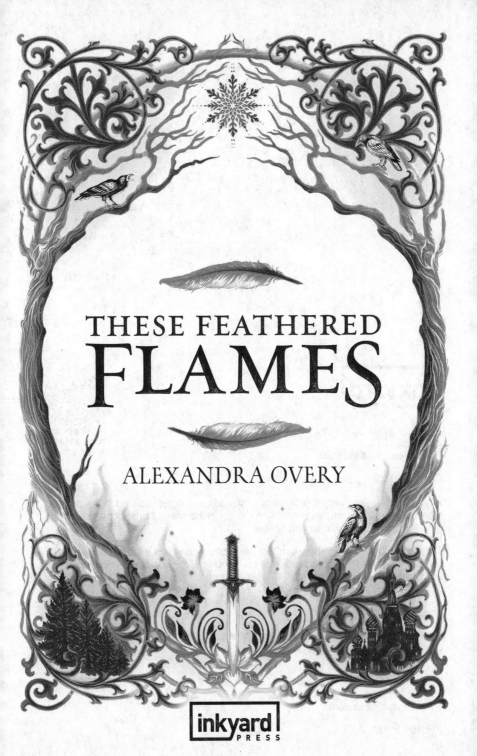

THESE FEATHERED
FLAMES

ALEXANDRA OVERY

inkyard
PRESS

ISBN-13: 978-1-335-14796-7

These Feathered Flames

This edition published by arrangement with Harlequin Books S.A.

For questions and comments about the quality of this book, please contact us at CustomerService@Harlequin.com.

Inkyard Press
22 Adelaide St. West, 40th Floor
Toronto, Ontario M5H 4E3, Canada
www.InkyardPress.com

Printed in U.S.A.

Recycling programs
for this product may
not exist in your area.

For my sister, who creates magical worlds with me, and for my mum,
who always makes them feel possible.

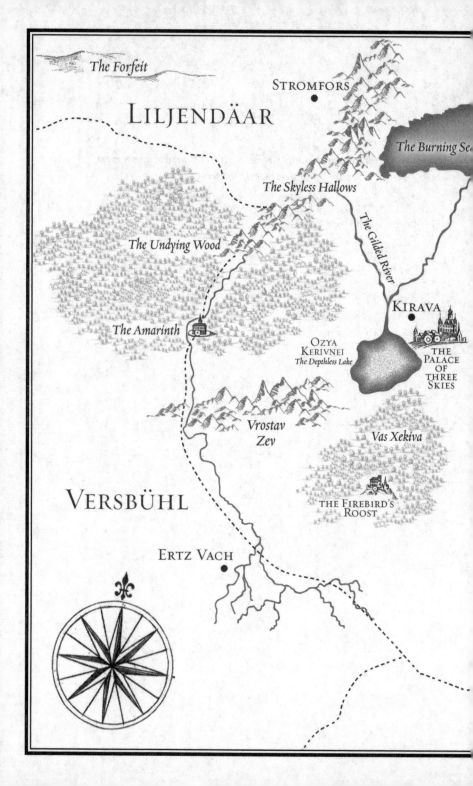

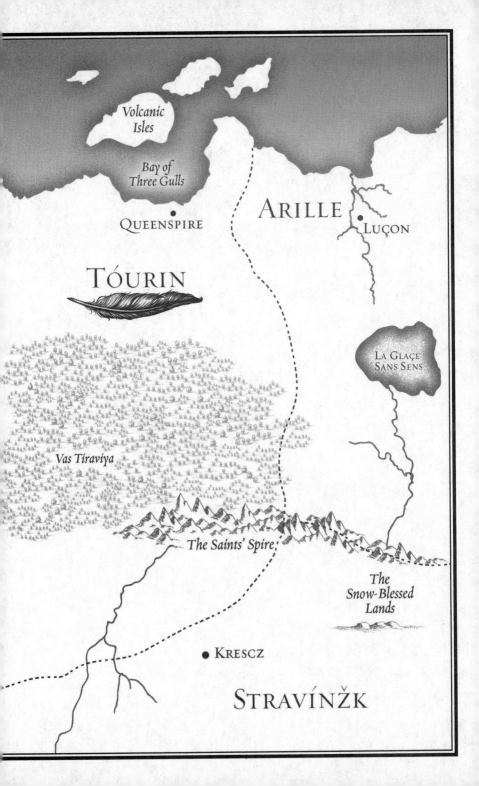

PART ONE:

THE GIRL WHO GREW CLAWS

Once, in Tóurin, two princesses were born
Of mortal blood, but divinely sworn.
When monsters of chaos prowled the night,
To protect a queendom, the girls took flight
To the old hallowed lands, where they first swore an oath
To pay the greatest price and sever them both,
So there the merciless earth took its claim,
Binding one to the throne, and one to the flame.

—"The Queen and the Firebird"

CHAPTER ONE

The prey wasn't meant to be a child.

When Asya had smelled the sharp tang of magic—strong even before she emerged from the tree line—that possibility hadn't so much as fluttered across her mind. It was never meant to be a child.

But the scent of magic was undeniable. That indistinguishable combination of damp overturned earth and the metallic copper of blood, cut through with the acrid burn of power. It was overlaid with the cloying sweetness of waterose, as if someone had tried to mask it.

A futile attempt.

And Asya was sure this time. The person they were looking for had to be here.

The comfort of the forest stood at her back, the dark canopy of trees stretching behind her in every direction. The fading sunlight could not break through the writhing tangle of branches, so in the shadow of the trunks, it was dark as twilight.

Most people feared the forest. Stories of monsters that lurked in its depths, witches who lured unsuspecting children in and tore out their hearts. But to Asya it had always felt safe, the gnarled trunks and rustling leaves were like old friends.

"This is it," Asya said, inclining her head toward the clearing in front of them.

A slight smile tugged at her lips. Two years ago, when her great-aunt had first deemed Asya ready to try tracking—to follow the magic with only her mortal senses once they were close enough to the source—she'd found it impossible. More often than not, she just led them in circles until Tarya gave up on her. But today, Asya had managed it.

She might not be as unwavering as her aunt, as strong or as dutiful, but at least Asya had succeeded in this.

She glanced over at Tarya, waiting for her reaction. But her aunt stood stiller than the trees, an immovable presence in their midst. The shadowed light filtering through the leaves cast her face in stark relief, carving deep hollows into her snow-white cheeks and emphasizing the wrinkles at her brow. She could have been a painting—one of the old oil portraits of the gods, soft brushstrokes of light adding an ethereal glow to her stern face.

It made her look otherworldly. *Inhuman.*

Which she was. One of the creatures that prowled these trees.

While Asya, or any other mortal, could smell the residual magic, her aunt could *feel* it. No amount of waterose or burned sage—or any of the other tricks people tried—could hide magic from Tarya.

Her dark eyes flickered to Asya. "Correct," her aunt murmured, a hint of satisfaction in her soft voice.

In front of them, the comforting trees gave way to an open paddock. It had been allowed to run wild, chamomile glinting yellow in the long grass, like sun spots on water. Purple-capped mushrooms pushed their way through the weeds, intertwining with the soft lilac of scattered crocuses.

The tinge of pride in Asya's chest melted away, replaced by a thrumming anticipation. The paddock could have been beautiful, she supposed. But the cold apprehension burning in her stomach overshadowed it, darkening the flowers to poisonous thorns and muting the colors like fog. It was always like this. Ever since the first time Tarya had taken her on a hunt. Once she was left without a task to complete— a distraction—Asya couldn't pretend to forget what came next. She'd hoped it would get better, but she still couldn't shake the lingering fear.

She shifted her feet, trying to ignore the erratic rhythm of her heart. She hated waiting. Each frantic beat stretching out into an eternity.

She just wanted this to be over.

After all, her sister had always been the brave one.

But that was why Asya was here. Why she had to follow this path, no matter how she wavered. She owed it to her sister. They were the two sides of a coin, and if Asya failed, then her sister would too.

Tarya's words—the words Asya had to live by—pounded through her. *This is our duty. Not a question of right or wrong, but balance.*

Her aunt stepped forward. She moved silently, slipping

like a shadow untethered from its owner, from the gnarled trees and out into the overgrown paddock beyond. She didn't speak—she rarely did when she felt a Calling—but Asya knew she was meant to follow.

Asya took a shaky breath, touching one finger to the wooden icon around her neck. An unspoken prayer. She could do this.

Far less quietly, she followed Tarya into the uneven grass, wincing at the snapping twigs beneath her boots.

The paddock led to a small cottage, surrounded by more soft crocuses. Their purple seeped out from the house like a bruise. The building's thatched roof had clearly been recently repaired, and the gray stone was all but consumed by creeping moss. The stench of magic grew with each step. Wateroses lay scattered on the ground, interspersed with dried rosemary sprigs. The too-sweet scent, cut through with the burn of magic, made Asya's stomach turn.

Tarya stopped by the wooden door. Marks of various saints had been daubed across it in stark black paint, uneven and still wet. Acts of desperation. They felt out of place in the idyllic scene. The sight sent a prickle of unease through Asya's gut.

"Your weapon," Tarya prompted, her voice as low as the rustle of grass behind them.

Asya's fingers jumped to the curved bronze shashka at her waist. A careless mistake. She should have drawn the short blade long before. She couldn't let the apprehension clawing at the edge of her mind overwhelm her. Not this time.

She had to be sure. Uncompromising. She had to be like Tarya.

Asya unsheathed the weapon, the bronze glinting in the fading light, and forced her hand to steady.

Her aunt gave her a long look, one that said she knew just how Asya's heart roiled beneath the surface. But Tarya just nodded, turning back to the freshly marked door. Sparks already danced behind her eyes—deep red and burnished-gold flames swallowing her dark irises. It transformed her from ethereal into something powerful.

Monstrous.

Asya pushed that thought away. Her aunt wasn't a monster.

Tarya reached out and pressed her palm to the wood. Heat rolled from her in a great wave, making Asya's eyes water. A low splintering noise fractured the air, followed by the snap of the metal bolt. The door swung open. All that was left of the painted sigils was a scorched handprint. Asya's mouth went dry. She couldn't help but feel that breaking the saints' signs was violating some ancient covenant.

But Tarya just stepped inside. Asya tightened her grip on the blade, trying to shake off the sense of foreboding nipping at her heels, and followed.

The cottage comprised a single small room. Heavy fabric hung over the windows, leaving them half in shadow. As Asya's vision adjusted, she took in the shapes of furniture—all overturned or smashed against the cracked walls. Clothes were strewn across the floor in a whirl, along with a few shattered plates and even a broken viila, its strings snapped and useless. A statue of Saint Meshnik lay on its side, their head several paces from their armored body. The room looked like it had been ransacked, perhaps set upon by thieves.

Or like someone wanted it to seem that way.

Tarya turned slowly, her sparking eyes taking in the room. Then her gaze fixed on a spot to her left, and flames reared across her irises again. Asya couldn't see anything. But she knew her aunt was not really looking at the wall, she was *feeling*—reaching for those intangible threads that bound the world and using them to narrow in on her prey.

Asya waited, her breath caught in her chest.

Tarya moved in a flash, as though Vetviya herself had looked down and granted her secret passage through the In-Between. One moment beside Asya, the next in front of the wall. Flames, golden and bright as sunlight, sputtered from her wrists, licking along her forearms. She put her hands on the wall, and the flames eagerly reached out to devour.

They burned away what must have been a false panel, revealing a tight crevice behind. Three faces stared out, eyes wide and afraid. Two children, a boy and a girl, clutching on to a man with ash-white hair, now covered in a faint sheen of soot.

"Oryaze," he breathed, terror rising on his face like waves over a hapless ship. *Firebird.*

Bile burned in Asya's throat. She took a halting step back, staring at the huddled family. *It's the man*, she told herself. It had to be. The thought murmured through her, a desperate prayer to any god or saint who might be listening.

The man leaped forward, spreading his arms as though hiding the children from view might protect them. As though anything he did would make a difference. "I won't let you touch her!" he cried, grabbing one of the broken chair legs and brandishing it like a sword.

Asya clenched her teeth, a sharp jab of pity shooting through her. It would be no use. Nothing would.

The flames coiled lazily around Tarya's wrists as she watched the man with a detached curiosity. "The price must be paid."

He let out a low sob, the chair leg clattering uselessly to the ground as he clasped his hands together as if in prayer. "Please, take it from me. She didn't know what she was doing."

The room was too hot, the flames scorching the very air in Asya's lungs. *This is what has to be done*, she intoned. *This is our duty.* The same words her aunt had hammered into her. Asya's knuckles shone white on the hilt of her shashka, the cool metal tethering her to the ground, to this moment, and not the rising guilt in the back of her mind. A panic that threatened to crush her.

"I cannot," Tarya said, her voice hollow. "The price must be taken from the one who cast the spell." With a casual flick of her wrist, a burst of fire sprang at the man. He dived aside, toppling into an overturned table.

The little boy was crying now, soft whimpers barely louder than the spitting flames. But the girl did not cry, even as Tarya wrapped an elegant hand around her arm and dragged her forward.

Asya saw the stratsviye clearly against the milk-white skin of the girl's wrist. A mass of black lines that coalesced to form a burning feather, seared into her flesh like a brand. The mark of the Firebird. The mark that meant a debt had to be paid.

"Please," the man said again, pulling himself from the collapsed table. "Please, she didn't mean to—"

"Asya," her aunt said, without looking up from the mark.

Asya knew what she was meant to do, but her legs took a moment to obey. Muscles protesting though her mind could not. But she moved forward anyway, placing herself between the man and the little girl, shashka raised in warning.

No one could interfere with the price.

The man scrambled for the chair leg again, leveling it at Asya with trembling hands. "She only did it to save her brother," he pleaded, emotion cracking through his voice like summer ice. "He was sick. She didn't know the consequences."

Asya's gaze slid to the little girl. To the determined set of her jaw, her defiantly dry eyes. That look wrenched something in Asya's chest. The resolve she'd so carefully built crumbled around her. She knew what is was like to have a sibling you would do anything—*risk* anything—for.

But Tarya was unmoved. "Now she will know—magic always comes with a price."

He lunged. He was clumsy, fueled by fear and desperation. Asya should have been able to stop him easily, but she hesitated. A single thought caught in her mind: *Is it so wrong of him to want to protect his daughter?*

That one, faltering breath cost her. The man swung the chair leg at her, catching the side of her head. Bright lights danced in front of her eyes. She stumbled into the wall as the man let out a fractured cry and threw himself toward Tarya.

Tarya did not hesitate.

Another tongue of flame reared from her, forcing the man back. This one was more than a warning. The acrid smell of burnt flesh sliced through the scent of magic. A low, broken sob trembled in the air as the man clutched his now-scorched left side.

Tarya's head snapped to Asya, flames flashing bloodred.

Ignoring the throbbing pain in her head, Asya darted forward. She grabbed the man's arm and twisted, sending the chair leg tumbling to the ground again. It was painfully easy. The injury made his attempt to swing back at her fly wide, and her hands fastened on him again. She spun him, one arm wrapping around him, the other holding the shashka to his throat. Her chest heaved, and her head reeled. But she didn't move.

He let out a low whimper, still trying to struggle free. Asya pressed the blade deeper, almost wincing as a trickle of blood ran down his throat. "Don't," she said, half command, half plea. "You'll just make it worse."

Tarya had already turned back to her prey. Her gleaming eyes, still threaded with flame, stared down at the girl. There was no malice on her face, just a cold emptiness. Asya wasn't sure if that made it better or worse.

"You must understand, child," Tarya said. "The price has to be paid."

And in a breath, she transformed.

Flames devoured her eyes, spreading from the pupils until they were no more than luminous orbs. Twin suns, captured in a face. But the fire did not end there. It rose up out of her like a living thing. Glinting golds and burnt oranges twisted with deepest crimson to form hooked wings, spread behind her like a blazing cape. Another head loomed above her own, a vicious, living mask. It formed a sharp beak, feathered flames rising from it to forge the great bird's plumage. They arched up into an expression of cruel indifference, mirroring the human features below. The very walls of the cottage trembled.

The Firebird.

Asya felt her hand go slack. A deep, instinctual fear sank into her bones. She had seen her aunt transform before, more times than she could count. But that primal fear never went away. The mortal instinct that she should run from this creature.

She was eleven when she'd first seen her aunt exact a price. Asya had been naive and desperate to shirk her new responsibility, to run back to her sister. Tarya had brought her on a hunt to see—to truly understand—the weight of this duty.

It had terrified Asya then. It still terrified her now, six years later.

Everything about the flaming creature exuded power. Not the simple spells mortals toyed with, but the kind of power drawn from the depths of the earth, ancient and deadly.

The girl could not hide her fear now. It shone in her dark eyes like a beacon as she tried to back away, but Tarya's curled fingers held her tight. The boy was screaming. The sound rose in Asya's ears to a high keening, writhing through her insides.

The creature—*Tarya*—looked down at the girl, head cocked to one side. Considering.

Asya wanted to close her eyes. To pretend she was somewhere far away, safe beneath a canopy of trees. But she couldn't.

She had to do this. This was the duty the gods had chosen her for. The burden she had accepted.

And looking away would feel like abandoning the little girl.

Asya tried to take a breath to steady her whirling thoughts, but the very air was bitter and scorched. *Please be something small*, she thought. *Not her heart.*

She couldn't stand back and watch that. Or, perhaps, she didn't want to believe that she *would* just stand aside as this monster tore the girl's heart from her body.

Because Asya knew she would. Knew she had to. That was her price.

The flames spread down Tarya's left arm, coiling like a great serpent as they bridged across her fingers to the girl. A cry tore through the air, raw and achingly human. The greedy, blazing tendrils wrapped around the girl's arm, as unmoved by the screams as their master. They consumed the flesh as if it were nothing more than parchment.

In only a few frantic beats of Asya's heart, the girl's left arm was gone. Not just burned, but *gone*. No trace of it remained. No charred bone, not even a scattering of ashes.

The price had been paid.

The flames receded, the creature folding back in on itself until it was no more than a spark in Tarya's eyes. All that was left was a heavy smoke in the air, thick and choking.

Asya let her hand holding the shashka fall. The man threw himself forward—though Asya had a feeling he would have moved even if her blade had still been at his throat—and clutched the little girl, who was still half-frozen in shock. The boy flung himself at his sister too, his screams reduced to gasping cries.

Asya's stomach curled as she stared down at the huddled family, enclosed in a grief she had helped cause.

She backed away. It was suddenly all too much. The suffocating smoke. The man's ragged sobs. The blistered stump that had been the girl's arm. Her aunt's impassive face, as empty as the carved saint's head on the ground.

Asya whirled around, pushing back through the broken door. She doubled over as she stumbled across the threshold, leaning a hand against the moss-eaten stone to keep upright. Bile rose in her throat.

It had never been a child before. Despite all the hunts Tarya had taken her on, all the training lessons, Asya hadn't thought of that possibility—that it could be a little girl desperate to save her brother.

Something wet trickled from the wound on Asya's head, but she barely felt it. Her insides had been hollowed out.

All she could see were the little girl's eyes. The ghastly reflection of the Firebird in them, looming and monstrous. A creature of legend.

A creature that, one day, Asya would become.

CHAPTER TWO

As they left the claustrophobic sorrow of the small cottage behind, Asya couldn't shake the image of the little girl. The blazing, instinctual terror of the Firebird had seared into her mind like a brand.

Night was falling now. The clouds darkened from a forlorn gray to a soft purple, the last of the sunlight spilling across the horizon like blood. A chill wind came with it, biting against Asya's exposed skin. She welcomed the cold. Anything to chase away the last embers of the Firebird's flames.

Her aunt walked ahead. Some of the color had drained from her face in the aftermath, but Asya knew that had more to do with the power receding than with any guilt. Tarya was unwavering in her task. For a moment, Asya wondered what her aunt had been like at her age. When she had been just the apprentice to the former Firebird.

Had she questioned too? Had she wondered if their dark duty was the right thing to do? Somehow, Asya couldn't imagine it. Her aunt had likely accepted the gods' choice with the same unrelenting determination she did now.

Unlike Asya, who had hesitated. Who had almost ruined their hunt again because of her doubts. Who had cried the night of the ceremony. They'd been only ten, she and her sister, but that was the age their paths were to be determined. That was the magic of this land. Twin heirs, one destined to be queen, one destined to be the Firebird. Both needed for the queendom to survive.

That day was etched into Asya's mind, as indelible as a stratsviye. The cloying incense of the cathedral, the weight of the hundreds of eyes pressing down on her. The stinging bite of the ceremonial knife on her palm as her blood spilled onto the altar. The burst of deep red flame, so bright it seared into the back of her lids, signaling that she was to be the Firebird. The shower of gold that chose Izaveta to be queen.

Asya and Izaveta had tried to argue against it. To claim that even if history and tradition dictated they must be separated, they would be the exceptions.

It was no use. That night, when Asya had known she would have to leave the palace with the aunt she had never met to become something she wasn't sure she could be, she'd been unable to hold back her tears. Izaveta hadn't cried—she never did—but the two of them stayed huddled together until the sun rose. Izaveta came up with increasingly far-fetched schemes to keep them together, while Asya let herself be swept up in the comfort of pretending that might be possible.

But there was no escaping it. No running from their fates. The next morning Asya left, with the new weight of this duty heavy on her shoulders. A duty she still wasn't sure she was strong enough to fulfill.

She pulled herself back into the present, running her fingers along the faint scar on her left palm. The only remnant of that day.

"Do you ever wonder," she said suddenly, unable to keep the bursting question in her head any longer. The question that always lingered just beneath the surface. "If we are doing the right thing?"

Tarya stopped. For a long moment, she said nothing. So long, Asya was sure she would not get a reply. But then her aunt turned, a last sliver of sunlight reflected in her eyes like flames. "It is not a question of right or wrong," she said. "It is about balance. We are not judge and executioner. We merely ensure the scales remain equally weighted."

That was Tarya's answer to everything. The reason Asya and Izaveta had to be separated, the reason this duty was vital. It was the same thing Asya'd told herself many times over. That the Firebird never sought to hurt—to kill—but merely to ensure the price was paid to keep the world in balance.

The Firebird didn't always have to intervene. Only when the caster had not paid the price did it awaken a deep Calling in her aunt, drawing her toward the magic. A soothsayer could summon a dove without worrying about the Firebird, provided they threw several hairs or a vial of their blood into the flame. But the problem with magic was that it was rarely as simple as that. It ebbed and flowed with the winds, its whims just as changeable. While one day a healing spell might require a finger, today it had demanded that girl's arm. And many times, the caster would only realize they had not paid the full price when a stratsviye appeared on their wrist. And then the Firebird came calling.

Asya swallowed, wishing her aunt's unshakable belief that they were doing the right thing would be enough for her. But she kept coming back to the same uncertainty, and mere words would not relieve it. Words did nothing to erase the terror on that girl's face, or the desperation in her father's screams. "But the girl just wanted to save her brother," Asya pressed. "She didn't deserve to lose her arm for trying to help."

Tarya's knifelike gaze pierced through her. "It is not for us to decide who deserves what. Without balance, the world would fall to chaos. Monsters would roam free, and unbound magic would devour our very essence. The queen herself would fall. Would you consider that *right*?"

Asya looked away, her eyes trailing along the coiling roots at her feet. It sounded so simple when her aunt put it like that. So why didn't it feel simple?

"You should not pity them," Tarya said, barely louder than the biting breeze. "Those who try to evade the price."

Asya focused on the roots, as tangled up as her insides felt.

"They do not see the necessity—the *kindness*—in this duty. To them, you will never be more than a monster that lurks in the night." Tarya paused, and Asya felt her aunt's eyes sweep over her, sharp and all seeing as the Firebird's. "The sooner you accept that, the sooner you will find peace with this responsibility."

Asya clenched her fingers. There was no hesitation in Tarya's voice, no flicker of uncertainty. Because her aunt was right. To those people she would never be more than a monster in the shadows.

"It does get easier."

Asya glanced over, surprised. That was the closest to sympathy she'd ever heard from Tarya. To admitting that it was not as simple as accepting her duty and acting on it.

"Over time," her aunt went on, "you will come to understand it."

Asya wasn't sure that made her feel any better. Her aunt was close to a century in age, though she did not look it. The Firebird was immortal until a new one rose, kept alive by the burning power inside her. Since Asya's mother had not been a twin, meaning no new Firebird could rise, Tarya had not aged. One ancient Firebird had lived nearly three centuries before a new set of twins was born to relieve her of the obligation.

That possibility scared Asya more than anything. The idea that she could remain trapped in this body, becoming less human and more monster with each passing year.

But she had time still. Time before the power of the Firebird passed down to her. More and more, she found herself clutching on to those slipping days as if they were a lifeline. Which, in some ways, they were.

"You will not have the luxury of indecision—of doubt— much longer," Tarya said. Her gaze lingered on the blood darkening Asya's crimson hair.

Asya looked away. Her aunt had not said anything about her injury when they left the cottage, had not mentioned how Asya's hesitation could have resulted in something far worse.

But she also hadn't offered to help her bandage it. Asya had torn a scrap from her cloak, pressing it against the still-bleeding wound herself.

That indifference—no anger or concern, not even a glance of sympathy—was almost as painful as the cut.

Tarya turned, any hint of emotion gone from her lined face. "It is high time you prepared yourself fully. Immersed yourself in your role."

Asya took a long breath, sucking in the scent of the forest. The fresh earth and sweet leaves. She could do that. She could help her aunt hunt those marked by magic. That was her responsibility, the mantle that would pass down to her.

But no matter how much she told herself that, she couldn't stave off the ache of guilt nestled inside her.

Tarya began to walk on, then paused, her head snapping up to the sky.

Asya squinted into the gathering dark but saw nothing. "What is it?"

"Falcons."

Asya froze. A chill spread through her that had nothing to do with the wind. Something stirred inside her, as if the earth had just shifted beneath her feet, setting her on a new path without her knowledge.

"Are you sure?" she asked. But then she spotted them. Three dark silhouettes, like forgotten blots of ink, blacker than the night sky behind them.

"We must hurry," her aunt said, already darting on through the trees.

Asya followed, nearly tripping in her haste. Birds had their own meanings in Tóurin. Soothsayers used them to cast fortunes, reading them from the sky or their cards crafted from feathers. Swallows swooping low at night signified a clear day. A gathering of six crows meant trouble was afoot.

But three falcons together… Asya had never seen that. The falcon was the bird of the ancient sorcerer Koschei. In the old fairy tales he'd sent his falcons out to steal children from their beds, using their blood to feed his growing power.

One falcon foretold misfortune, but three were a grave warning. A portent of calamity and ruin.

Chapter Three

This was one of those rare moments when Izaveta wished she were proficient in some projectile-based weaponry. Perhaps throwing knives. A blade slamming into the solid wood of the door would certainly be a satisfying way to wipe Strashevsta Orlov's smug expression off his face.

Not that she would actually act on the inclination, even if she were able. But fantasizing about it took the edge off her irritation.

"My orders were very clear," the strashevsta finished. "I'm not to let anyone in until the meeting is over."

Izaveta smiled, a smile as carefully crafted as the delicate silk of her dress. "I'm sure there has been a mistake."

The strashevsta raised an eyebrow. "I very much doubt that."

Izaveta clenched her teeth. Her late-night meetings with her mother were often the only times she saw the queen. Even if they were occasionally canceled when more important matters arose, her mother would always let her know. *Always.*

But even inside her head, that thought was tinged with bitter uncertainty.

"The queen will send for you if she needs you."

Izaveta swallowed, ignoring the faint sting. She had become well practiced in brushing off those slights, the barbs from her mother. But no matter how hard she tried, she couldn't quite make herself immune to them. Not when it came to the queen.

Her mother was likely just meeting with the spymaster. Izaveta was never privy to those conversations. This was not a change, not a hint that her mother was pushing her away or playing some new game.

Perhaps if Izaveta told herself that enough, she would believe it.

"It's no matter," she said, smile firmly in place. "I shall wait."

She stepped back to one of the swirling pillars that lined the passageway, eyeing the guard. Anything to distract from the curling knots in her stomach, the cloying fear that her mother was shutting her out on purpose.

Orlov's uniform was crisp, the double bars that denoted his rank as captain gleaming on his right shoulder. Not so much as a hair out of place. But he'd missed something. Slight black smudges wisped along his hairline, disappearing into his ink-black hair. Some kind of root oil, Izaveta guessed, to hide any gray. Signs of aging in someone supposed to protect the queen would likely not be well received—though the dye might have been vanity more than anything else.

Her eyes flicked down, searching for any other details. His weight was not quite balanced. Though his back stood straight as the stone pillar, he listed a little to the left. Not his dominant side, judging by the saber also strapped there.

She smoothed her skirts, reaching for her own weapons. The only ones she had. "I am glad to see you're on duty tonight."

"And why is that?" The strashevsta's mouth still had a self-satisfied set to it—no doubt pleased at his small victory over her.

Izaveta widened her eyes, the picture of innocence. "Your injury, of course."

A muscle in his jaw twitched—the slightest movement, but enough to confirm her suspicions.

She allowed a small curl of her lips. Finding the weaknesses, the openings in someone else's armor, was always calming. To know that even if she had a vulnerability, everyone else in court did too—and most wore them far more plainly than she did.

Orlov's brow creased, hands folding in front of him—defensive. "My injury?"

Izaveta shot him a look, appraising. He had only been made commander of the strashe because of some dealing between the queen and his family, too long ago for Izaveta to remember the details—likely the Crown receiving land or troops in exchange for this position. It was all a part of the game, not a true display of devotion to the queen. That was all anything was in court, an elaborate game of exploitation where loyalty was no more than another card to play.

People like him, who barely hid their desire to grasp any dregs of power they could, were all too easy to manipulate.

"Mother told me all about it," Izaveta went on, apparently

oblivious to his confusion. "A pity too, as you would have been the ideal candidate."

His voice took on an edge—a flash of that jealousy, that desire for power. "An ideal candidate for what, my lady?"

She waved a hand. "It's nothing important."

His jaw tightened, shoulders tensing as he drew himself up to his full height. "There must be some confusion, my lady. I am quite well."

"I thought—" She broke off, as if suddenly realizing something may be afoot. She glanced over her shoulder, making an exaggerated performance of backtracking. "Perhaps I misunderstood. Think nothing of it. I'm certain there will be other opportunities for someone of your experience."

She let the emphasis hang on the final word, the implication clear. Rumors of an injury, on top of his evident worries about his graying hair, would be plenty to cause some discomfort for the smug man. If Izaveta had to wait out here—no more important to the queen than a visiting dignitary—at least she'd succeeded in sowing some seeds of discord. It would be no more than a minor irritation to her mother, but it was a small victory.

A tiny way Izaveta could pretend she had an effect on the queen.

Before the strashevsta could respond, the carved birch door swung open. Izaveta snapped to attention, all thoughts of her trivial games forgotten. She raised her chin as she prepared to face the spymaster. To glean any hint as to what she and her mother had spoken about from Zvezda's posture, the fluid lines of her face.

But it wasn't the lithe figure of the spymaster who stepped

through the doorway. It was Vibishop Sanislav, still in his heavy church robes, spiderlike hands clasped in front of him, looking as if he had every right to be there.

Her insides went cold. Of all the members of her mother's cabinet, the vibishop was Izaveta's least favorite. All of them spoke in half-truths, eager to advance their own agendas, but she was sure nearly every word out of the vibishop's mouth was a lie. He spun them as easily as breathing, all while his pale lips twisted into that simpering, pious smile.

But that was not what caught Izaveta off guard, what knocked the air from her lungs.

Why would the queen have met with the vibishop in private? And more than that, why hadn't her mother told her? They'd discussed the Crown's stance on Sanislav's ludicrous theories on the Fading only a few days before, and her mother had agreed that they were not to be entertained. *They* had agreed.

The magic flowing through this land was one of the few things her mother trusted her with—listened to her input as she did only her most trusted advisors'. Or at least, that was what Izaveta had thought.

"My lady," Sanislav said, with a triumphant set to his mouth that did nothing to alleviate the doubt coiling in her stomach.

Izaveta inclined her head, forcing her smile to remain in place. "Vibishop Sanislav. Lovely evening, is it not?"

His thin lips quirked. "Indeed."

He disappeared down the passage without another word. She watched him go, trying to extract anything more from his posture or movements. Information was the most powerful weapon in the court, and when facing her mother, Izaveta needed to be well armed.

She gave herself three breaths to recover from the surprise, to ensure her mask was back in place. If she let her mother see her rattled, the queen would pounce.

Izaveta shot the strashevsta a winning smile. "As always, thank you for your unwavering dedication to your post."

She slipped through the doorway, allowing it to fall shut behind her before he could catch her hint of sarcasm.

The queen sat by a great stained glass window that stretched at least three times her height, tapping her finger against the edge of a zvess board. The window depicted one of the former queens, the Firebird at her right-hand side shown in all her flaming glory. Beyond, the palace gardens stretched into the distance, the colored glass adding unnatural hues to the carefully tended lawns. The moons were rising over the forest, barely more than glimmers against the darkening skies.

From this height, Izaveta could see all the way down to the gnarled queenstrees of the sacred lands that rimmed the palace and, beyond that, the soft glow of Ozya Kerivnei. The Depthless Lake.

Despite rumors to the contrary in the neighboring countries, the lake did still gleam with power. It used to be known as the Fourth Moon, the crowning jewel of Tóurin. Magic flowed freely then, pulsing through the land like blood and bending to a person's will as easily as breathing. The price for a simple spell was low, so the Firebird rarely had to intervene. It made Tóurin powerful—*feared*. Even its militaristic neighbors in Versbühl could not hope to combat that magic, no matter how many weapons they forged.

But now the lake shone less like a full moon and more like a waning crescent on a clouded night. *The Fading* people called it, as if naming the thing might make them able to control it. And since the lake had begun to dim, so had the magic of the land.

Already it made Tóurin vulnerable, unable to defend its borders with enchantments and rituals as it once had. But the queendom had not lost its advantage yet, not fully. And Izaveta was going to make sure they never did, even if she had to scour every corner of the lands for a solution.

And she was certainly not going to let someone as foolish as Vibishop Sanislav stand in the way of that.

Izaveta pulled her gaze away from the fading lake, focusing in on her mother. On the matter at hand. The queen sat in a high-backed chair carved in glinting metal to resemble burning wings. Her hair, pale as moonlight—the mirror of Izaveta's own—was twined on top of her head, artfully arranged around the barbed points of her crown. The shards of twisted glass and silver curled up toward the vaulted ceiling, light glinting off their edges like a halo. Queen Adilena had an easy authority to her posture, a surety in the sharp lines of her face that said she was not to be questioned.

Izaveta approached her slowly, glancing down at the zvess board, the pieces still spread out midgame. She and her mother had been playing this particular round for a little over a week. Their games were always drawn out, with only a few moves played out on the evenings her mother called for her.

The queen always won, though. No matter how many times Izaveta thought she had found a way to outthink her, the queen was always two moves ahead.

Usually when she wanted something from her mother, Iza-veta would plan out her strategy in the same minute detail as a zvess game. But she had not expected the vibishop, and the question slipped out involuntarily as soon as she met her mother's gaze. "What was he doing here?"

The queen tapped her carved Firebird piece against the edge of the board, her expression unmoved. "Are you going to play, or are you going to interrogate me?"

For a moment, Izaveta wavered, torn between standing her ground and bowing to her mother. As she always did. When Izaveta was younger—after her sister had left—she used to play a game where she would see if she could get her mother to put the mask away, to break through the queen to the woman beyond. She had never succeeded.

As she grew older, she started to realize there might not *be* a woman behind the mask. Her mother was regal and queen-like to the core.

Izaveta sank into the opposite chair. Not a defeat, she told herself, but a change of tactic. Subtlety was always the an-swer with her mother.

The queen nodded to the board. "Your move."

Izaveta looked down at the pieces, grasping for the strat-egy she'd been honing the night before. Her stomach plum-meted as she saw her mother had already moved her queen three spaces to the left, successfully evading the trap Izaveta had been trying to lay.

She leaned forward, as if considering the game—though her mind was still consumed with what that meeting had been about. "Strashevsta Orlov is certainly taking his position seriously this evening," she said, forcing a casual voice. "At first, he would not even allow me in to see you."

The queen did not look at Izaveta as she replied, staring out at the sprawling gardens instead. "He does as he is ordered."

Izaveta's hand froze, fingers hovering above her carved banewolf piece, though she tried to keep her face blank. She couldn't ignore that jab. But she would not let her mother rattle her. Wouldn't let a few well-placed words reduce Izaveta to a hurt child, making careless mistakes in both of the games they were playing.

She settled on the soothsayer piece, moving it to counter one of her mother's strashe. A safe move, more to distract herself than anything else.

Her mother slid her own soothsayer piece forward with an elegant flick of her hand. "You were right about the lands in the foothills of Vrostav Zev." She glanced up, pale blue eyes piercing into Izaveta. "Once I reminded the archbishop that they had been tithed to the Crown as an act of solidarity during wartime, they could not refuse the payment. It is certainly fortuitous that you thought to reexamine the original document."

From anyone else, it might have sounded like a compliment, perhaps even fleeting pride, but her mother's words were never that simple. They twined together like tangled thorns, and trying to break free would merely get Izaveta caught on their spines.

From the queen, a comment like that was closer to a gauntlet. Thrown on the ground for the unsuspecting challenger to take up.

But Izaveta had learned long ago that she was not yet a worthy opponent.

"It's your move," the queen prompted.

Izaveta's stomach contracted, the double meaning of those words prickling through her.

Her fingers drifted to the Firebird piece, moving it two squares to stand opposite her mother's queen. She glanced up, hoping to discern something from the slightest flicker on her mother's expression. But no matter how long she studied the shifting lines of the queen's face, she had never been able to determine what was real and what was an act.

Her mother sat forward, cool eyes sweeping over the pieces.

Izaveta smoothed her skirts, trying to expel those weaknesses with the movement. "And I trust the Church was satisfied with the outcome?"

Once, the Church had been irrelevant to the politics and movements of the court. But almost fifty years ago, in the wake of a failed coup, Izaveta's grandmother had opted to consolidate power where she could before another attempt was made. She'd offered the Church a position in the queen's cabinet in exchange for the sway they held over the general populace, and the gold that lined their pockets. Now the Crown and the Church were inseparable, the queen's power as dependent on the Church's support as the dwindling magic that flowed through the earth.

Her mother believed she could leverage the Church's beliefs against them, bending even the gods to her will. But Izaveta had never been so sure. To her, the Church was as ephemeral as magic—and just as likely to turn on the user.

"For now," her mother replied, moving her queen to capture one of Izaveta's banewolves.

Svedye, she shouldn't have missed that.

Swallowing, Izaveta examined the board. Her eyes snagged on her mother's soothsayer, and a thought crept into her mind, momentarily banishing the vibishop. A thrill of anticipation jolted through her—that same cool satisfaction of finding the weakness in someone's armor.

Izaveta's mistake in losing a piece might have given her an opportunity. If she had planned it, she doubted her mother would have fallen for the trap. She would have been able to read it on Izaveta's face, in her purposeful maneuvering of the pieces. But in capturing the banewolf, the queen had left a vulnerability in her carefully laid lines of defense.

Three moves. That was all it would take for Izaveta to win, provided the queen did not realize her own error.

Trying to sound casual, as though it were a natural progression in the conversation, Izaveta said, "Then Vibishop Sanislav was not here to further plead the Church's case?" At the same time, she slid her queen two spaces back, away from the center of the board.

Her mother sat back, folding her hands in her lap. She fixed Izaveta with a look—the look that used to make her want to hide under the table. But now she held her mother's gaze. Izaveta was no longer the scared little girl she had once been, and she would not show the queen any of the apprehension that churned inside her.

"No," her mother said finally, moving her clergyman as she spoke. "He was here to further discuss a theory of his."

Her mother's move did nothing to protect the vulnerability.

Izaveta's eyes swept over the pieces, her heartbeat picking up. It seemed almost impossible that the queen had not noticed. Had Izaveta missed something?

But she hadn't. This time, the queen was one step behind.

Izaveta fought not to let the excitement bleed onto her face and give her away. She moved her strashe into position. It was a weak piece, one most people ignored. And that would be to Izaveta's advantage.

One move. Just one more move, and she would beat her mother. That tantalizing possibility was almost more enticing than the information. "And which theory is that?"

She still could feel her mother's eyes on her, piercing into her bowed head. "His theory on the Fading. On how to restore magic," her mother went on. "The same one we deliberated on before."

Izaveta's hand jerked, knocking over the elegantly carved Firebird piece. She barely noticed. "You are not seriously considering that."

The queen pursed her lips, a warning sign that Izaveta was bordering on insolence. "I am more than considering it."

Cold dread trickled into Izaveta's stomach, icy and foreboding as midwinter snow. This had to be another of her mother's games, a ploy or trick to leverage something she wanted.

The queen seemed to read Izaveta's thoughts on her face. "The plan is to be set in motion this week, once all the pieces are in place."

Izaveta took a deep breath, trying to form her racing thoughts into something coherent. "This *plan*—" she laced as much contempt into that one word as she could "—would leave us vulnerable. It could destroy our country."

The queen tilted her head, face as blank as the stained glass woman behind her. "It is a calculated risk."

"A calculated risk?" Izaveta repeated, momentarily dumbfounded. "His plan to use the Firebird's blood and bones as his own personal source of magic is a *calculated risk*?"

"Yes," her mother replied simply, as if that were all the explanation required.

Izaveta reached for her nearest zvess piece—a frowning witch—and wrapped her fingers tightly around it. She needed an outlet for the frustration flaring inside her. Digging the carved edge of the witch's cloak into her palm, she forced her tone to remain even. "There are other steps we could take before going to this extreme. There are already rumors in Versbühl that our magic is growing weak. Without the Firebird—"

"This is not a discussion," her mother cut across. "The decision has been made."

Izaveta stood, abandoning her zvess piece with a resonating clatter. "What did Sanislav say? What did he offer that could make you agree to this?"

The queen rose to her feet as well, a dangerous glint in her eyes. "I am not required to explain myself to you, daughter."

"Mother," Izaveta pressed on, her frustration bubbling through in her voice, giving away too much. "You have to see that he has no evidence for his belief that the Firebird is behind the Fading. That her magic grows as ours dwindles. No reasoning beyond his supposed divine knowledge and a distrust of power he cannot control. Sanislav is a fanatical fool, and you would hand him the very weapon that could destroy Tóurin."

Izaveta froze. She shouldn't have said that, should not have so directly attacked the queen's plans. But it was too late now. There was no taking it back. Izaveta raised her chin. She would not back away, not cower in front of her mother as she once had.

The queen met her gaze, a terrible quiet solidifying around her. The moment before a predator pounced. "You would do well to remember, Izaveta, that Vibishop Sanislav is a respected member of my cabinet. Moreover, I agree with his theories, and, as such, to insult his intelligence is to also insult mine. The vibishop is making preparations as we speak. I shall be overseeing them myself tonight. In this matter you should trust that far wiser heads are seeing to it."

Izaveta's breath hitched. She knew she was pushing too far, overstepping her bounds, but she couldn't stop herself from adding, "Have you thought about what this would mean? What it could mean for Asya?" She threw the name out almost without meaning to. A last desperate push for something to get through. It tasted odd on her tongue, so rarely was it spoken aloud. "Do you think he'll stop when he's drained the magic from Tarya's bones?"

But instead of any crack in her mother's face—any hint of emotion beneath the regal mask—she just smiled.

Her mother had perfected that expression. A devastating smile that made one feel like they were special until she cast them aside. Another way she gave and withheld affection like a game.

The queen took a step forward, her expression fracturing into something far less kind. "So now you care about your sister? What brought on this sudden rush of affection?"

Izaveta opened her mouth, trying to find words. "I—" she started, then trailed off when she realized she had none. No answers that would sway her mother. No way for her to win this battle. Because her mother didn't care. Words were Izaveta's only weapon, and they were useless against the one who had trained her to wield them.

The queen let out a low laugh, hollow and tinkling. "We both know you have no concern for anyone else—least of all your sister. You wanted to find the solution, and it pains you that someone else might have reached it first. Don't pretend this is a noble cause. You are interested in your own power and position, no more."

Izaveta reeled back as if her mother had slapped her. Those words tugged at some deep part of her. The part she tried not to examine too closely as she worked to mimic her mother's cool indifference. Her twisting manipulations. The way she used and discarded people as she saw fit.

After all these years, Izaveta had learned to emulate her mother so well she couldn't always tell where the imitation ended and she began.

"Don't look like that," her mother snapped with a dismissive wave of her hand. She turned to the zvess game, moving her Firebird piece with an expression of supreme disinterest. "It's one of the qualities I actually admire in you."

Izaveta stared at the board. Her mother's ornately carved Firebird had reached the bright silver square in the center, and now Izaveta's own queen was too far to pose a challenge. She'd missed it, too caught up in her own strategy to remember her mother always had a plan of her own.

And her mother *always* won.

A weight pressed on Izaveta's chest, too heavy to draw breath. Why did she let her mother get under her skin like this? Anyone else she could brush off or cut down with a barbed remark of her own. But her mother knew how to slip a blade through her armor like no one else.

She swallowed, pushing down the traitorous lump rising in her throat, grasping for words again. Her only weapons. "Mother, this is a dangerous plan. It could weaken us irreversibly."

The queen's smile vanished, and with it her patience. "I will discuss this no further."

The familiar tone of dismissal, icy and impossible to argue with. For a moment, Izaveta teetered. She hated to back down, to slink away and admit defeat. But she had no more words.

Nothing that would move the immovable.

She turned on her heel. As she swept out of the room, a cold realization spread through her. A deep chill that seeped into her bones. Her mother would always win these games when she set all the parameters. So if Izaveta wanted to outmaneuver her, she would have to find a way to change the rules.

CHAPTER FOUR

It was not far to reach the Roost. The small cottage was the closest thing Asya had to a home. It sat at the heart of Vas Xekiva, the sprawling forest they'd walked through to find the girl. It was unusual the mark had been so close; plenty of Tarya's Callings took her much farther away. More times than she could count, Asya had spent days alone with no idea when her aunt might return.

Night had closed in by the time they neared the Roost, the three moons already high in the sky. The western moon— the one belonging to Vetviya, god of the In-Between—was barely more than a sliver on the horizon. Of all the moons, Vetviya's was rarely full, shrouded as she was in mysterious dark. The other two, though, were both near-perfect orbs. They stared down at Asya as though watching, waiting for something to happen.

The sight sent a prickle of misgiving through her. What would the gods be watching for?

She touched a finger to the icon around her throat—the

miniscule wooden portrait of the bear god, Dveda—sending a quick, desperate prayer to him. What exactly for, she wasn't sure. But Dveda had always held a special meaning for her. As protector of the earth, he felt so present in this forest. As near and comforting as the branches of the trees.

Her left foot touched the softer earth of the clearing when it happened. She had just opened her mouth to ask her aunt if she had seen anything, or perhaps felt the stirring of a new Calling, but the words would not come.

Asya stopped, suspended in that instant. Where had her voice gone?

Then pain—blinding hot and blistering—cleaved through her. She fell to her knees. Flames clawed their way down her throat, bursting into her lungs. Her chest felt like it was caving in from the pressure. At any moment, surely the fire would tear through her rib cage, devouring skin and bone.

She thought she was screaming, but she couldn't hear anything through the rush of blood in her ears. Her very bones were on fire, marrow replaced with an agonizing heat. Tears streamed from her eyes, her vision blurring in and out of focus. Her veins twisted inside her, contorting and re-forming like metal in a forge.

Distantly, Asya felt hands on her. She recoiled, their icy cold as painful against her skin as the fire inside. The fingers tightened. Asya tried to pull away, but her body wouldn't obey. The pain ripping through her stole her motion, all control of her limbs.

Surely the flames would burn out soon. The fire must have turned her innards to ash by now, leaving her a shell filled only with that piercing agony.

Shadows shivered behind her lids like embers. They contorted into people, there and gone too quickly to recognize. But she thought she caught a glimpse of her mother—older than she had ever known her—and an unfamiliar man.

She blinked tears from her eyes, and the odd shadows dissolved. The night sky loomed above her, tilting as her stomach rolled. The moons seemed to stare down at her, too bright. They grinned, mouths stretched wide with monstrous fangs.

That was the last thing Asya saw before the fire claimed her for its own.

Asya felt heavy. As though the fire had burned away her blood to replace it with stone, weighing her down.

For a moment, she lay still. She didn't want to open her eyes to see what those flames might mean. The pain was gone now. She should be relieved, but a whisper of misgiving ignited in the back of her mind. She remembered the scorching fire, devouring her from the inside out. If she was alive, she *should* still be in pain.

And that meant only one thing.

A noise to her right—like the flutter of a bird's wings against leaves—finally forced her eyes open. She was inside the Roost. The familiar, slightly askew wooden beams rose over her head, and the warm scent of cloves wafted around her.

She sat up, her stomach lurching at the movement. It was still night, the room lit only by the soft glow of the hearth. Asya shifted, pushing herself along the bed and away from the flames. She knew they were contained—that they couldn't be moving—but the tendrils seemed to reach toward her, begging her to join them.

She shuddered. The memory of that scorching pain lurked behind her like a new shadow. She couldn't shake the feeling that it might rise up to consume her again.

The fluttering sound continued. Asya's eyes found her aunt, bent over the small wooden table with a leather pack. Not a bird's wings, but papers. Everything in Asya still moved slowly, so slowly she couldn't get her thoughts to catch up with what had happened.

"Good, you're awake." Tarya set down the pack, scanning the small room as if deciding what else they might need.

Asya blinked. Her aunt looked dimmed, some of the color stolen from her vibrancy. Her edges blurred, no longer sharp and in focus. Though that could have been Asya's swimming head.

"What're you doing?" The words came out a little slurred, her throat still choked with phantom smoke—or at least she hoped it was phantom.

It wasn't time yet. She still had time.

"Preparing," her aunt replied, as if it should have been obvious. "We must return to the palace."

"The palace," Asya repeated. That word was so out of place in this cramped room that it struggled to sink into her mind. The Palace of Three Skies felt so far away now, like something Asya had heard of in a story, even though she had spent her first ten years within its walls. The dense smoke curled through her head, remnants of the fire within her. Why would they need to return there?

Asya stood, and the room swayed with her. She steadied herself against the headboard, drawing in a shuddering breath. Something knocked against her chest, and she looked down to see a heavy stone pendant hanging around her neck. It was rough, some sort of uncut mineral. The surface was dark and writhing as the forest at night, with veins of something else threaded through it. A deep red that pulsed like blood.

She put her fingers to it, almost jumping at the slight tingle of power that flickered from it. "What is this?"

Tarya paused in her work, looking up at Asya with a shrewd expression. Asya knew that look—it said she was deciding how much Asya was worthy of knowing.

"It's an amyeva," her aunt said finally. "A firestone from the heart of the Volcanic Isles."

Asya blinked at her. Tarya had a particular way of answering questions with information that somehow made it all the more confusing. "Why am I wearing it?"

"It dampens the Firebird's power." Her aunt's voice was even, as steady as ever, but it ricocheted through Asya. Her mind did not want to process that. Did not want to string the words together and find their meaning.

She was meant to have more time.

"Then why do I need it?" It was a foolish question. A last, desperate grasp at the fleeting hope that this wasn't real.

Tarya turned her dark eyes on her. No flames flickered there now. Even the faint reflection of the hearth seemed hollow. "Because a new Firebird has risen."

"That isn't possible."

Her aunt let out an empty sound, something that could not quite be called a laugh. "It is more than possible, Asya. It is inevitable."

Asya reached for the headboard again, digging her nails

into the soft wood. She wanted to close her eyes. To sink back into not knowing.

"But not yet," she said, her voice small as a lost child in the wood. "Only when…" Asya trailed off, the rest of that dark thought echoing through her mind.

"Precisely." Tarya nodded, as if she could read Asya's unspoken words on her face. "The power transferring to you can only mean one thing."

Asya thought she could feel it then. Roiling under the weight of the firestone, the flames that had burst through her. Not devouring, she now realized, but remaking. Melding with her and forging her into something new. A creature that now lived beneath her skin.

Tarya turned her attention back to the assembled supplies. "Dawn is approaching. If we leave with the sun, we will make good time to the palace."

One last, obstinate part of Asya wanted to ask why. Wanted to still cling to that pretense.

But she couldn't force the words out. There was no point, not when the truth seared through her bones.

Her aunt was no longer the Firebird. And there was only one reason that power would transfer to Asya now. Only one reason for that creature to rear up inside her.

Her mother was dead, and a new queen had to be crowned.

PART TWO:

THE CAGED BIRD'S CRY

A creature forged in flames and wrought of shadows,
Unrelenting as the scorching sun that devours the dark,
The Firebird knows all things come with a price
And that price must always be paid.

—THE CALL OF THE FIREBIRD
from the writings of Kirava,
the first Firebird

CHAPTER FIVE

The walls of the cathedral clung to the cold like it was the last embers of a fire in the cruelest winter. The woven prayer cushion she knelt on was the only protection from the unforgiving floor. The chill crept over her as though desperate to claim her for its own, to turn her to merciless stone to join the saints' statues lining the walls.

But Izaveta might be stone already. Where she knew emotions should be bubbling, each clamoring for attention, all she felt was hollow. Cold and empty as the statues.

She's just in shock, the voye had assured each other when Izaveta had not spoken, had not been able to react to the news.

Perhaps they were right. Or perhaps the queen had carved out Izaveta's heart and taken it with her when she'd died. Now the fluttering veil of the In-Between stood between Izaveta and what she *should* be feeling. And she didn't want to pull that veil back.

The great altar rose up in front of her, guarded by statues of the three gods. Her mother was laid out atop the marble structure, already covered in her shroud. It was made of finest Araïse silk, intricately embroidered in a whirling pattern of stars and trees.

Vaguely, Izaveta wondered how they could have had that made so quickly. Or perhaps it came with being a ruler. One had to be prepared for every eventuality.

Izaveta kept her eyes carefully averted from the glittering shroud as she knelt before the statue of Zmenya, god of the skies. She stood in all her glory, part woman, part vulture with a hooked beak and swooping wings. While beneath the earth spoke of comfort and safety, the skies were loneliness and loss. *Death.*

Izaveta thought she could see that in the way the artist had rendered the god's face. It was not a cruel expression but one of emptiness. One that said she knew of this inevitability.

As daughter, Izaveta was afforded this prized spot. Zmenya's calming presence was meant to soothe the grieving princess. Izaveta could not forgo this display of pious mourning, even though she held little faith in the gods or saints. There was no comfort for her in the idea of cruel masters who smiled at their subjects' pain. An empty world offered more consolation than that.

And besides, *grief* was not quite the right word. Izaveta could not call the ache in her rib cage grief for her mother, or even sadness at the loss of her queen. It was absence. A constant, certain presence now torn away.

She couldn't shake their last conversation from her mind. It clung there like a resilient cobweb, tangling all her thoughts in its strands.

We both know you have no concern for anyone else. You are inter-

ested in your own power and position, no more. The echoing memory sliced through her empty chest. The bitter edge to her mother's voice. The zvess pieces left scattered like gravestones. The looming promise of her mother's scheme with Sanislav.

And the next morning she was dead.

It seemed impossible for someone who had been as constant as sunlight—more so, as there were no clouded winters to hide her—to be gone. A fever, the voye medics had said upon examination. A rare but powerful one, coursing through her in less than twelve tolls of the bell.

Izaveta wasn't sure anyone really believed that.

She'd heard the whispers, even as she walked to the cathedral this morning. The courtiers were hardly trying to hide them, perhaps hoping they could guess the truth from her reaction. Some were unimaginative, claiming the intervention of a foreign power—most likely Versbühl, though some of the more creative theories imagined the involvement of their southern neighbor, Stravínžk, as well. Others muttered about the Church's discontent, or the way the eastern commanders had been scheming.

But the ones that cut into Izaveta, threatening to shatter her carefully composed mask, were those who whispered that the princess had done it, eager to be queen and ruthless in her quest for power.

Izaveta clasped her hands in her lap, eyes firmly on the trailing feathers of Zmenya's carved wings. Whispers didn't matter.

A voice, so very like her mother's, floated into her mind as unbidden as storm clouds. *Whispers are enough to bring down a queendom.*

She tightened her grip, digging her nails into the smooth

scar on her left palm, prominent even through the fabric of her gloves. The mark from that fateful day, seven years ago. The one that had set her on this path. She'd sat in almost this exact spot as she waited for the archbishop to complete the ritual, watched as her own blood ran onto the altar and chose her path. The moment that had trapped her in the palace.

She gritted her teeth. She had endured enough to reach this position—*lost* enough—and it would take more than whispers for anyone to wrench it away from her.

Touching a finger to the hollow of her throat as a sign of respect, more because she knew people were watching than because she felt moved to do so, she rose to her feet. She smoothed the silk of her dress, the palest blue of empty skies— the color of mourning—and turned to face the pews.

She adjusted her thin gloves as she cast her eyes around the high, vaulted room. The elaborate wooden pews were lined with mourners—most of them acting the part more than anything else, all wonderful players on this elaborate stage of grief.

Conze Bazin, who likely spent more time in the cathedral than out of it, sat before the towering statue of Saint Korona, murmuring prayers under his breath. Several more of her mother's cabinet members were scattered around, faces drawn—planets unmoored from their orbit. Vada Tsvestov, their head bowed, sat in the front row. Even the pragmatic and elusive Vada Nisova had made an appearance.

The most powerful people in Tóurin, all on their knees for a dead queen. Her mother would have loved that, Izaveta thought bitterly. Even if their grief was only for show.

Slowly, steeling herself to return to the mutterings and

stares, she walked back along the central aisle. Rather than look at the arranged mourners, she kept her chin high, focusing on the nine saints who stood spread out along the two sides. Their larger-than-life statues gazed down at the worshippers with a calculated air. Izaveta's gaze caught on the serene face of Saint Lyoza, the girl who'd made a bargain with a witch to grow claws and then gouged out the eyes of those who wronged her. A woman who refused to crumble beneath what people expected. Izaveta might not hold much faith in the saints, but she had always liked the story of Lyoza.

Izaveta touched the hollow of her throat with her right forefinger as she passed under Lyoza's statue. If any of the saints deserved her reverence, it was Lyoza. *May I be as steadfast as you*, Izaveta thought. *And care as little about what others think.*

That second part was a fruitless prayer. Izaveta could not simply grow claws and attack outright; she had to hide her fangs behind smiles and manipulation.

A princess could not ignore what others thought.

A queen, she amended.

The word sat awkwardly on her, a new language she was trying on her tongue. But she would need to get used to it. There would be twelve days of mourning following her mother's death—one day for each of the three gods and nine saints—and on the thirteenth day, Izaveta was to be crowned.

Thirteen days was not long to wait, but each one stretched out in front of her like the looming shadow of a saber. It would not be a smooth path to the coronation. Not with courtiers already flocking like vultures to a body, eager to grab any scraps of power they could. The queen should be an untouchable figure, above those petty squabbles. But this day had proved even a queen could fall, without so much as a culprit to string up in the name of justice.

It showed the queen for what she truly was: mortal, just like everyone else. And that made her vulnerable.

Izaveta turned past a group of courtiers eager to share their condolences, nodding her head in a look that she hoped spoke of a child too grief stricken to stop, when a figure blocked her path.

The vibishop wore his full regalia this morning. He may not be the official head of the Church, but the archbishop was frail, rarely seen beyond the confines of the cloisters. Vibishop Sanislav had all but assumed the role, right down to his gold-edged robes and embroidered kokoshnik—designed to resemble a crown. He'd claimed the three points were representative of the gods, and well within the established history of the Church. Her mother had conceded the matter, but the way the vibishop stood now beneath the shadow of Saint Restov, chin raised and metal points glittering, Izaveta wondered if that might have been a mistake. This cathedral was his kingdom, and he'd all but fashioned himself as king.

He had at least replaced his usual deep black sash with one of pale blue, though that was his only nod to the late queen.

"My lady," he said, tilting his head in a passable impression of a bow. Izaveta didn't miss his emphasis on her title, the slight reminder that she was not yet queen. "May you find comfort in the earth and solace in the skies," he intoned, with little more emotion than if he were reciting from his prayer book. Something in his glittering eyes unsettled her. A flicker of complacency that set him apart from the other mourners, as though he knew something they did not.

The vibishop was not as simple to dissect as many of the courtiers. He wasn't merely grasping for shreds of power like Orlov. No, Sanislav held true convictions, a fervent belief in his divine right to steer Tóurin. It made him all the more dangerous.

Izaveta forced her mouth into a wan smile, a careful balance between grieving daughter and grateful acceptance of his sympathies. She was well practiced at manipulating her mask. The rest of the court might be accomplished in their acting, but she'd learned the art at the hand of her mother. And the queen had been the most accomplished of them all.

"Thank you, Vibishop Sanislav," Izaveta said, her voice cultivated into a deliberate mix of determination and sadness. "May she rest in the earth under the protection of Dveda." The vibishop wasn't the only one who could recite from a prayer book.

He glanced around the pews, nodding to a few of the gathered mourners in a display of shared grief, before turning his watery eyes back on Izaveta. "In the aftermath of this terrible tragedy—" she ground her teeth, keeping her face serene as he spouted his false sincerity "—there are many matters we shall need to revisit. You know the Fading has always been of the utmost importance to the clergy, and with this great change, the Church is eager to begin working with you, my lady. We believe our divine knowledge will be of great use. Perhaps this afternoon we should call a meeting of the cabinet?"

She almost had to bite her tongue to hold back a sharp retort. The only reason Sanislav wanted to discuss *anything* with her now was because he wanted to exploit her delicate position. Not princess, but not yet queen. Without her full authority, he would happily press his advantage.

"Forgive me," she said, managing to keep her irritation from her tone. "But this is a time of mourning, Vibishop, not a time to discuss policy."

A muscle in his quivering jaw twitched, anger briefly creasing his features before he settled back to contrived sincerity. "Of course, my lady. Though these matters must not be left untended, lest we be remiss in our duty. Especially with such a young queen, we are eager to share our guidance."

She refused to rise to his bait, even with his false civility grating against her skin like stone. She wanted to throw decorum aside—to ask him the question burning in her veins. What deal did he have with her mother? What had they spoken about last night?

But she could never be so direct. Not in this game of smiles and manipulations.

So she kept her expression frozen in a forced calm—the picture of *duty*—as she replied, "I'm sure the Church, and all the people, would not expect great change during the mourning days." She lowered her gaze, bringing a hand to her heart as if the mere discussion was too much. "We must pay our respects to the queen."

The vibishop's thin lips curled into a smile. He probably intended for it to be sympathetic, but the pretense shone from his eyes. "We shall return to the matter another time, when you are more composed." He held her gaze, lowering his voice a fraction. "But you would do well to remember, my lady, queens who ignore the counsel of the Church rarely survive long."

Chapter Six

The firestone beat a steady pulse against Asya's chest, matching the solid pace of her bear. His easy rhythm was usually enough to soothe any nerves, but this morning her mind was too knotted up for even his warm presence to unravel it.

Mishka was one of the few things that had come with her from her old life. The Firebird was to have no attachments, no personal connections to sway her from her path, so almost everything else she cared about had been left behind. But Mishka was practical, and if there was one thing Tarya valued, it was pragmatism.

Though if she had realized how much Asya doted on the bear, she would probably have made her get rid of him. The fact that he was a little on the small side for a brown bear, and had a perennially confused expression, was almost enough in itself.

Tarya's bear, Lyev, was as steadfast as her, with its sleek black coat and astute, all-seeing eyes. It stood at least three hands taller than Mishka, an imposing presence. Fit for the Firebird.

Except, Tarya was no longer the Firebird.

Asya curled her fingers in Mishka's fur, her ribs constricting with them. Even with the heavy weight of the firestone and the sensation of power crawling beneath her skin, it didn't feel real.

"Why have I never seen a firestone before?" she asked to distract from the twitching anxiety in her stomach. The sudden sound of her voice blared too loudly in the silence of the forest. The sun was already high in the sky, but there were no birds calling, no distant fluttering wings. Even the trees seemed to stand eerily still. As if the falcons from the previous night had driven all the life away.

Tarya kept her head forward, back straight, as she replied, "It's a closely guarded secret. One you could only know when the time was right."

Asya dropped her eyes to the cracked leather of the great saddle, a quiver of hurt echoing through her. What else had been kept from her? She had been forced onto this path and had dedicated herself to this duty, but she was still not trusted with everything.

She was still not enough.

You did hesitate, said a nasty voice in the back of her head. A voice that sounded like a contorted version of her aunt's detached disappointment.

Asya swallowed her guilt. She didn't want to sink into those thoughts now, not when everything inside her already felt raw and liable to break. "Did you wear one when your powers awakened?"

"No." Tarya's tone held no emotion, but Asya thought her hands tightened on the looping reins. "I did not."

Asya looked away, down at the pulsing stone. Of course, her aunt had managed without it.

The glow of the Depthless Lake reached them first, soft as the earliest rays of sunlight. Splintering through the branches, it bathed the landscape in an ethereal hue, tempering the colors of the forest to pale phantoms of their vibrant greens and rich browns.

Then the trees melted away and the Palace of Three Skies rose up in front of them.

It consumed the skyline. A mass of pale stone, interspersed with the glittering marble and veined silver trozye that decorated the facade in swooping whorls like falling stars. Three turrets loomed higher than the rest, with onion domes in whirling reds and golds, topped with gleaming spires that stretched up toward the clouds. Pointed arched windows ran along the palace walls, some larger than the rest and sparkling with multicolored hues of stained glass.

The sight tugged at something in Asya's chest. It had been seven years since she'd seen these towers. They were still achingly familiar, but they weren't home. Not anymore. Not like the soaring canopy of the forest, with its comforting blanket of leaves—a stark contrast to the severe colors of the palace.

Suddenly, she was ten years old again. Her face tearstained as her aunt led her away, carving out the chasm that would forever divide her from her sister.

And her mother.

The queen was as much a character from a fairy tale as the palace. Someone Asya had read about long ago, but not someone she truly knew.

Even before the ceremony, Queen Adilena had never been a

mother in the way Asya imagined mothers should be. She and Izaveta had been raised mostly by their nursemaid, a woman who'd been almost as stern as Tarya. She'd been stringent in their lessons and less than amused by the twins' antics.

Asya had seen her mother, of course. She'd spent time with her during formal occasions and various dinners, but she always felt like she was standing on ceremony. Pushed into the roles of daughter and princess, and never sure how to fulfill either of them.

Though none of that lessened the hollow pain that had nestled in Asya's chest since realizing her mother was dead. The grief of losing what could have been.

But, beneath that, Asya couldn't ignore a flicker of excitement, as delicate as a flame against a storm. Because returning to the palace also meant seeing her sister again. Seven years they had been apart. It felt longer. Being severed from Izaveta—from her other half—had been like losing a limb. A phantom ache that always hovered in the back of her mind, the distinct feeling of something lacking.

But after so long, the idea of recovering that lost limb was almost as unnerving as losing it had been.

How would her sister, the person Asya had once known better than herself, have changed? Her stomach twisted as another question trembled through her: How might Izaveta think Asya had changed?

Asya was no longer the child who had lived in this palace, who'd raced bears around the lake with her sister. She hardly even remembered that girl anymore.

She and Tarya came to a halt at the base of the great marble staircase that led to the palace's arched entranceway. Two bearkeepers waited at the bottom, reaching out for Mishka's harness before he'd even come to a full stop.

Asya's hands tightened reflexively. She didn't want to dismount. Dismounting meant leaving behind the isolation she'd grown accustomed to and moving back into the realm of the court.

Not only that. It would mean all this was real. Her mother was really gone, her sister would be crowned queen. And Asya was now the Firebird.

She took a deep breath. She could do this.

She slid from Mishka's saddle, holding on to his harness a split second longer as she eyed the bearkeeper. This palace had a way of taking things she loved and never giving them back. She knew it was a foolish notion, yet she couldn't help but feel it would try to take Mishka too.

But in the next moment, all thoughts of her bear slid from her mind. The great doors of the palace swung open silently, and a small procession stepped out. A line of royal guards, all dressed in their fur-lined formal uniforms of molten silver, as colorless as the clouded skies above.

And at the forefront was a figure with palest blond hair. A figure that was both achingly familiar and agonizingly foreign.

She looked like their mother—or how Asya remembered their mother.

Izaveta had the same hair as the queen, falling in silvery waves to her waist like ripples on the Depthless Lake. Her face was pointed, all carefully honed edges. She was paler than Asya, though that might just have been the lightness of Izaveta's hair draining the color from her skin. A bejeweled silver chain hung down over her forehead, the glittering blue gemstone falling just above her eyes. Not a crown, not yet.

She wore a light blue dress that swept behind her in an elegant whirl, as if she'd carved out a piece of sky and sewn it to the garment. Only a delicate fur cape and thin silk gloves served to protect her from the incoming chill.

Asya was suddenly very aware of the simplicity of her own clothes, all designed for practicality. How her flame-red curls were falling out of their plait in a mess of tangles and leaves. Her hair used to be the same pale silver, but the Firebird had darkened it after the ceremony. Staining her with the blood on its hands.

A hand touched her side, and she glanced over to see Tarya's expectant face. She nudged Asya again—not a gesture of affection, but one to remind her to keep her head.

Swallowing her anticipation, Asya ascended the sparkling staircase. She couldn't draw her gaze from Izaveta, as if she were the first hint of clearer skies in a turbulent storm. Despite everything, a lightness bloomed inside Asya. She was back with her sister. Reunited in a way that made her feel more whole than she had in years.

Asya reached out instinctively as she drew level with her sister. She wanted to hug her, to draw her close and pretend they were those little girls again. Back when everything was easy and they were inseparable.

But the remnants of her formal training in the ways of court warned her that this was not the place. She lowered her hand to worry at a loose thread in her sleeve. "I, uh—" She broke off, unsure what the correct greeting was. How was one supposed to greet a long-lost sister who was about to be crowned queen?

Before she found the answer, she blurted, "You've gotten taller."

Izaveta's lips twitched, threatening to break into the smile Asya remembered. "You haven't."

In that brief moment, those seven years melted away. It was just the two of them, sharing a secret world where no one else mattered. As Asya drank in Izaveta, her sister's eyes roved over her in turn. The twins were not identical as they had once been, but now warped reflections, with points where their images converged and then veered away.

"Your hair—" For an instant, it looked like Izaveta would reach out to touch it. Then something shifted. Izaveta's eyes were the same deep brown as Asya's, but there was a coldness to them. As if a veil had been drawn across.

Izaveta's mouth pulled into a smile—but not the one Asya remembered. A false, twisting thing that left her eyes flat. Wary. "Welcome, sister." As easily as that, she slid back into stiff decorum and those years came crashing down between them like rubble.

Izaveta turned her head to Tarya, who was as unreadable as ever. "And Conze Tarya."

Asya winced. She knew it was customary for the former Firebird to be afforded land and the new title of conze, but hearing it aloud was a sharp reminder of Tarya's shift from Firebird back to mortal.

And Asya's transformation from mortal to something else entirely.

"We are so pleased to see you both return to the palace," Izaveta continued. "Even for this tragic occasion."

Izaveta's voice echoed through Asya. She had always imagined Izaveta would end up closer to their mother, trained at her side. Sharing this unfamiliar world.

But she spoke of the tragedy as if it were something far-off, something that hadn't touched them at all.

Asya scrambled to match her sister's formality. "Thank you," she said. "It's been far too long."

Izaveta tilted her head a little, as if considering her. "Indeed, it has."

There was a long pause as Asya searched desperately for something to say. She'd pictured this moment so many times, but she'd never imagined it like this. It had always been a joyful reunion in her head. They had been so close before Asya left, so inseparable that they had to be pried apart the day after the ceremony.

But even if she wanted to, Asya couldn't shift the changes those seven years had wrought.

"I'm sure you are tired from your journey," Izaveta said. She stepped back, inclining her head to the guards. "We have rooms prepared for you. The strashe will take you there to allow you time to recover. Food is being sent up. Stroganov, like we used to have."

"I—" Asya swallowed, not wanting to sour the moment. "I don't eat meat anymore." It was a concession she'd made to her guilt, a way of keeping her life her own after the Firebird's burden had been forced upon her. Tarya had disapproved, as Tarya tended to, but Asya had clung to it. A piece of humanity she wouldn't relinquish.

Izaveta stared at her. Asya saw her own feelings reflected in those eyes—suddenly wrong-footed on a well-trodden staircase. A sister both familiar and unknown all at once.

"Oh," Izaveta said. She cleared her throat, folding her hands in front of her as she regained composure. "I will ensure that's noted. I have also assigned you each a guard to guarantee your protection within the palace." She waved a hand—so easily imperious—and two guards stepped forward in perfect unison. "Strashe Onishin will remain with you, Tarya, and Strashe Vilanovich with you, sister."

With those last words, Izaveta flicked her eyes to Asya. Something like a challenge glinted there, as if her sister was wondering how Asya might react.

Asya held her gaze. She got the sudden and uncomfortable feeling that she didn't know the person in front of her at all. A stranger hiding in her sister's skin. "I don't need a guard," she said, choosing her words carefully. "I know the palace well, and Tarya has trained me herself."

Izaveta's expression remained frozen. "I'm afraid I must insist. It's for your safety and the safety of the queendom." She turned toward the palace, as if her mind were already moving on to other matters. "I look forward to seeing more of you in the coming days, sister." She had an odd intonation to the way she said *sister*, as if she were testing the word in her mouth and found it lacking.

"Izaveta, I'm sure—"

Before Asya could protest further, Izaveta had vanished back through the arching doors.

Asya stared after her, a hollow ache resonating in her chest. That was not the sister she remembered. The Izaveta she had known would not ignore her or condescend to her. That sister would never have left guards to trail her.

Izaveta had not greeted her as a sister—not even as the Firebird—but as a threat.

That thought left a bitter taste in Asya's mouth.

She considered the two guards with a mix of apprehension and interest. Strashe Vilanovich was young, probably not much older than Asya, with pale white skin and dark hair pulled back in a complicated plait that wound around her head. But her eyes were what caught Asya's attention. Vividly gray—not the lifeless gray of the palace, but roiling and vibrant like the clouds when they foretold a storm. They blazed into Asya now as if lightning really were about to strike.

The strashe held out a hand to indicate their direction. "Firebird," she said, with a hard edge to her words. It mirrored the keen distrust in those storm-gray eyes, sending a shiver of unease up Asya's spine. It was the formal way Asya should be addressed now, but she couldn't ignore the undercurrent to the guard's voice.

She shot one last glance back at the distant forest, trying to shake the foreboding that had settled over her. Perhaps Izaveta was as unused to her new role as Asya. Perhaps that had just been for show, and after a few days together things would go back to how they were.

Asya clutched on to that *perhaps*, even as reason warned her not to.

She ducked through the wooden doors into the great entrance hall. The stone here was polished to a bright sheen, the carved walls depicting scenes from Tóurin's history. Firebird Saveya, known for banishing ancient sorcerers, sat crouched like a bird on a perch, her wings accented in glinting gold. Her stone eyes seemed to follow Asya, alive and predatory. A little farther along, the first queen of the Karasova line reclined on a throne illuminated with threads of silver. She was the woman who had conquered the queendom almost five hundred years ago and ensured her daughters would rule it forevermore.

Her Firebird was enclosed in a golden cage, carved flames desperately stretching between the bars. That practice of caging the Firebird—of using that power, allowing the Firebird out only for her hunts—had long since died out, but the sight still sent a chill through Asya.

"Firebird," the strashe prompted.

Asya tore herself away from the image, following the guard down a winding passageway. She glanced over at her silent companion, who seemed to be gritting her teeth as she kept her gaze staunchly ahead.

"You can call me Asya, you know."

The guard did not reply.

"It's shorter than *Firebird*," Asya probed.

The strashe flashed her a storm-filled glance. "It has the same number of syllables, Firebird."

Asya looked away, trying to ignore the slight pang of disappointment. An ally would have been a comfort as she stepped into this new arena. She returned to taking in the winding corridors of the palace—some familiar, some jarringly different—to distract from the creeping sense of unease that she could not seem to shake. It wasn't just the odd mix of grief and nostalgia she felt being back within these walls.

It was suspicion. Icy as a winter night, seeping into her

CHAPTER SEVEN

Izaveta stared down at the zvess board, a solid lump hardening in her chest. The pieces still sat where they had the night
before, as if nothing had changed. As if her mother might
sweep in at any moment and comment on Izaveta's poor
choice of strategy.

But of course, everything had changed. Izaveta was not
even sitting in her mother's high-ceilinged chambers, but in
her own. The window here looked to the north, out on to
the miles of grassland that stretched toward the rivers.

And her sister had returned to the palace.

Izaveta's whole world had tilted, and she couldn't seem to
find balance on this new terrain.

She'd thought the zvess board might help. She'd moved it—
well, ordered it moved, as she had not yet dared to enter her
mother's chambers. She did not want to face whatever phantoms and memories might lurk there. But she needed to have
the zvess board near. It was a way of sharpening her mind,
slipping into the strategizing and scheming that she needed.

Though it was expected of her to move into the queen's chambers at some point, she didn't know how she ever would. Being in that room would make her feel like Adilena was still watching over her.

Still playing her games.

Izaveta tapped the soothsayer piece against the edge of the board. It was ridiculous. Her mother was dead. Izaveta should just reset the game. But she couldn't bring herself to. A part of her wanted to figure out what her mother's strategy had been, as if she could glean something from the stone pieces.

It wouldn't make a difference, though. Izaveta would still be the little girl pretending at being queen.

She gritted her teeth, tightening her grip on the piece, as she tried to banish those thoughts. She was still letting her mother get under her skin, even in death.

Then there was her sister and all the tangled emotions that seeing her had dredged up. A chilling reminder that while part of Asya was the sister Izaveta had known, part of her was now the Firebird. A dangerous power to be controlled. A threat.

And Izaveta could not yet discern which part won out.

After the ceremony that had separated them, when Izaveta had been left alone in this too-large and too-empty palace, she'd wanted to write to her sister. But every time she tried, the words came out bitter, tainted. She couldn't hide the jealousy that leaked out. A small part of her had hated Asya for being chosen, for being able to leave while Izaveta could not.

Then a letter from Asya had arrived. And even despite that resentment, it was a lifeline, a small flash of sunlight in the clouded gloom of the palace. Izaveta had shown it to their mother, hoping it proved they could still have a relationship even if Asya was gone. Even if she would become something else, while Izaveta remained mortal.

But the queen had just smiled sympathetically and tossed the paper into the fire. "You're too young to understand now, but this is not an offer of friendship. It's a move in the great game, probably orchestrated by your aunt. A way to leverage your sister against me—against us."

Izaveta wilted, her insides as crumpled as the letter. "Not everything can be a game. Asya might just miss us."

"Why would she miss you? She has the power of the world at her fingertips now."

That evening, the queen taught her the rules of zvess. The way the queen and the Firebird moved around the board, eternally separate. The way each piece could be manipulated for one's gain.

More letters came, but Izaveta didn't open them. As the years passed she learned how to harden her heart, how to push that pain away until it was a distant pinprick—not something that could be used against her.

Except now Asya was back. And Izaveta, for all her planning, had no idea what it meant.

But there were other things she could control, other strategies she could begin to move into place.

Izaveta had already drafted letters to various conze and important courtiers, encouraging them to return before the coronation. Loyalty she could not be certain of. Loyalty could be bargained for and bought as easily as any commodity. No, she had to count on them siding with whoever appeared more powerful, and Izaveta would make sure that was her.

Those letters she had sent by sparrowhawk, but there was

one that she needed to arrive as quickly as possible. Conze Vittaria had been a member of the cabinet since before Izaveta was born, longer even than the archbishop. Where she led, others would undoubtedly follow. If Izaveta could secure her support, no one would dare question the conze's wisdom.

A queen's cabinet was always made up of six members—some in appointed positions, some in hereditary ones. The most powerful people in Tóurin, not only due to their proximity to the Crown but also their own spheres of influence. Sanislav had an advantage already with the power of the Church behind him; Izaveta didn't like to think what he would do if he gained a majority in the cabinet.

A queen may be able to break a tie—could even remove certain members. But Izaveta did not yet have a crown.

She glanced over at her desk, where she had left a bowl of water to soak in moonlight. It should only be a little longer before it was ready. The burst of magic from that would ensure the letter appeared at Vittaria's side moments later.

A knock punctured her thoughts. The door creaked open, and Strashevsta Orlov peered in. "Master Alyeven is here to see you, my lady."

Izaveta waved a hand. "Send him in."

Master Fyodor Alyeven was the head of the Uchev Saravne, an elite society of scholars. He was integral to the Crown's research into the Fading, and her mother had given him boundless resources in the pursuit of any knowledge that might help. But more than that, he had also been Izaveta's tutor. Izaveta didn't have much experience with fathers—or mothers, for that matter—but Fyodor was how she imagined a father might act.

He walked in slowly, his bright blue eyes unfocused and his brow furrowed. He always looked like that, not entirely concentrating on the present, his mind still absorbed in his last book. His shock of white hair had grown wilder since Izaveta had last seen him, and the firm set of his mouth said this was not to be a pleasant visit.

He clucked his tongue at the sight of the zvess board, but he didn't comment on it. He made to sit in the chair opposite hers when he noticed Lyoza already occupied it. He settled on the arm instead, stroking the fluffy white cat absently as he surveyed Izaveta. "How are you?"

"I'm fine," she replied, though her voice was not as steady as she'd intended.

It was always harder to maintain the illusion of indifference in front of Fyodor. He knew her too well. He was the one who had found her crying behind a library shelf after her sister had left. Who had tried to comfort her when she had first begun to understand the games of the court, the way anyone would turn against her for their own gain. Who'd given her a shelter in books when it all felt like too much.

That knowledge—that trust—might have made him dangerous, were he not so absorbed in his work that he barely noticed the world around him.

The furrow in Fyodor's brow deepened. "Is that so?"

Izaveta squared her shoulders, holding herself together. It felt like gathering tangled threads, clutching them to herself in some semblance of a whole. "I am the queen. I have to be fine."

His blue eyes—pale as the color of mourning—were unwavering. "Even queens are human."

She let out a choking laugh that sounded dangerously close to a sob. She looked down, into the bright light of the fire, wishing the flames could sear away the painful knot inside her. "I'm not sure my mother was."

Fyodor paused in his stroking of the cat, tilting his head toward the animal as if suddenly fascinated by her. "Either way," he said eventually, "you are not queen yet."

A fact everyone seemed intent on reminding her of. "In twelve days' time I shall be."

Fyodor met her gaze again. "A lot can change in twelve days. Princess Estava was deposed during the mourning days, to be replaced with her more powerful cousin."

"That was six hundred years ago," Izaveta scoffed. Perhaps, once, the mourning days had been a time for different parties to contest the throne, but it had not been that way for centuries. "The Karasova line has ruled for half a millennium. The mourning days are no more than a formality now." But even as she said it, she knew it was not entirely true. Just because no one had taken action against a would-be queen during the mourning days in recent years, did not mean it was impossible. The Church had its rich history and supposed divine right to draw on if its members tried to claim Izaveta was unfit to rule, and they certainly had their allies in court.

Not to mention that Izaveta was young. If crowned, she would be the youngest queen in generations. That fact alone was enough to make her position precarious. Sanislav's words—his threat—echoed through her mind. *Queens who ignore the counsel of the Church rarely survive long.*

Fyodor glanced down at the zvess board, his finger tipping the carved queen on its side. "One queen has already fallen.

That changes things. Already there are those who question the claim her death was natural."

Izaveta pursed her lips. She knew what her tutor was implying, the very same fear that lurked in her. If one queen could be killed, what did that say for the next? "Rumors and hearsay. Rumors that we must not entertain, lest we risk giving them weight. The voye already made their ruling."

She spoke the words half to herself, as if she could convince herself of their truth. Because she couldn't allow her mind to examine other possibilities. All she could do was focus on what was in her control, on what she allowed people to discern. And a perceived act of the gods—tragic, but uncontrollable—was infinitely preferable to whispers of assassination.

Fyodor tilted his head. "You also have not yet held an audience," he added. "In only a matter of days all six of your mother's cabinet will be in court, many with their alliances already swaying to the Church. It's enough to make people talk. To make them doubt."

"I'm aware of that," Izaveta snapped, her irritation tingeing her words. "But my mother has barely been cold a full day and somehow people already expect me to be prepared to face the cabinet."

"The queendom must continue on."

Izaveta let out a low sigh, gesturing toward the letter on her desk. "I cannot be certain of anything until more of my allies have returned to court. If we convene now, the Church will have the advantage. And I refuse to give Sanislav a platform in front of the cabinet to air his ridiculous ideas."

She frowned down at the board, eyes fixed on the Firebird, the last piece her mother had touched.

She rose to her feet, as if the movement could brush away those misgivings, the doubts gnawing at her insides. "I just need a few more days to get my pieces in place."

She stepped toward the bowl of water. Dried rosemary rippled across the surface, as if blown by an invisible breeze. The liquid had changed. It was translucent as ever, darkened to indigo by the night sky, but *something* shimmered through it. That intangible element that had once coursed through the very air but now had to be dragged from the earth like water from a stone.

She felt Fyodor's eyes on her, his scholarly appraisal of her actions. He knew far more spells than she, having grown up in the earliest years of the Fading, when magic was still commonplace. But he had taught her this one himself, and she was sure she had the measurements right.

Placing the freshly penned scroll onto the surface, she raised the candle closer. With her other hand, she lifted a small pair of scissors and cut a lock of her hair.

The most important step. The price paid to the Firebird. To *Asya*. The thought left a bitter taste in Izaveta's mouth. A curling fear that had nothing to do with the cabinet or Sanislav's plans.

She threw the hair into the flame and murmured the invocation Fyodor had taught her.

The fire flared a brilliant gold, and the letter vanished from the water in a small burst of moonlight. A miniature constellation, briefly suspended before her.

Fyodor let out a low sigh. "Once, a simple spell such as that would have required no more than a breath." He spoke as if she were not there, a deep sadness resonating through his voice. A loss Izaveta could never quite comprehend. "And now people die in their beds, unable to muster the magic for a healing. Our borders stand unprotected against the Versch, and the Depthless Lake fades a little more with each passing day."

Izaveta watched him, the deepening crease in his forehead. He had spoken to her about magic before, of course. It was all part of her lessons, an invaluable facet of their history. But she could never truly understand what had been lost. The way that, once, magic had flowed through the land as readily as blood through a body. The very air steeped in it, as though the gods had laced it through the fabric of the realm.

She had only ever known it as it was now—a thing to be clawed from the dry earth, even if it destroyed the caster in the process.

Fyodor leaned toward the zvess board and lightly tapped the tip of the carved Firebird's wing. "The Firebird may be the key to it all."

Izaveta glanced up, not following his sudden change in topic.

He shrugged. "Tarya always stayed out of politics and away from court, but your sister is new and untested. There are those who would persuade her to their cause while she is in the palace. And with her at their side, they would make a formidable force."

A prickle of unease crept along Izaveta's spine. She couldn't let that happen.

There were precedents, Firebirds who had attempted to work against a queen or who had deemed them unsuitable to rule and sought to overthrow them. Even her mother had not been able to bend the Firebird to her will. Queen Adilena had manipulated everyone in court like their elaborate puppet master, but Tarya had been a different story.

Izaveta still remembered when she was thirteen and war had threatened with the neighboring empire of Versbühl. Her mother had tried to call Tarya to her side, to show a powerful front to their enemies. Tarya had refused, claiming the Firebird's power was not a weapon in the queen's arsenal. A peace had been agreed, but it was a slight that had gnawed at her mother ever since. The Firebird was the one being she had never been able to control.

But Tarya was not Adilena's twin. She had always been a senior figure. Distant and immutable.

What would Asya be like? Would she be content to stay out of the machinations of court, or would she want to be at their heart?

If anyone could tip the balance of power away from the future queen, it was the Firebird.

Izaveta raised her chin, smoothing the fears from her face like wrinkles in her dress. "The strashe are watching my sister, and I have my own allies too. I shall ensure I do not allow her to sway under someone else's influence."

Fyodor rose to leave, giving the cat one last scratch behind its ears. His gaze was unusually focused when he spoke. "You must remember, Izaveta, the Firebird is not the sister you knew."

Izaveta looked away. She did not want to see the concern—the fear—on his face. "I know," she murmured.

The heavy door swung shut behind him with a snap.

Izaveta remained frozen. She couldn't get the image of Asya swinging down from that bear out of her mind. It was branded there, indelible as the mark of the Firebird. She could still see the sister she remembered in that face, in the soft brown of her eyes and the line of her mouth. She still *wanted* to see the sister she remembered.

But Izaveta couldn't let that deceive her, let that draw her in.

Like Fyodor said, Asya was not her sister anymore. She was the Firebird. The most powerful piece on the board, with no allegiance or loyalty to Izaveta left.

Asya might not have been in court, but that did not make her immune to its influences. Its temptations of power. It didn't make her any different from all the other people Izaveta had made the mistake of trusting over the years.

Vasha, who had pretended to be a friend during Izaveta's sadness after her sister's departure, only to report her movements back to the queen in an attempt to gain favor. Her first music teacher, who had seemed to give her a respite from the manipulations of court, only for Izaveta to discover that he had enchanted her flute to listen in on conversations with her mother.

And then there was Kyriil.

Izaveta took a slow breath. That one still hurt more than she cared to admit. But not as much as it once had.

She had learned from those lapses in judgment, and she wouldn't repeat her mistakes with Asya just because of who she'd once been. It was not a matter of trust or loyalty—it was merely a question of which sister would betray the other first.

CHAPTER EIGHT

Asya had half expected to be led to the chambers she remembered from childhood, her memories guiding her instinctively, so when Strashe Vilanovich drew to a halt two floors sooner than she'd anticipated, Asya almost walked straight into her. That earned her another frosty glance.

Tarya stopped too, accompanied by her far more cheerful-looking strashe. "I must speak to my niece in private. The two of you may wait outside."

For a moment, Vilanovich looked like she might argue. But even if Tarya was no longer the Firebird, she still commanded an air of authority. Without waiting for a response, Tarya pushed open the door and slid through.

Asya paused, shooting a sheepish smile at Vilanovich. "I'm sure there's nothing you need to protect me from in there."

The strashe's expression remained stony. Asya just shrugged, following her aunt into the chamber.

It was as pale as the rest of the palace. Soft gray stone fading to cream-white silk accented with gleaming silver. Asya was so used to the cramped warmth of the Roost that this room felt too big, too exposed.

Tarya sank into one of the delicate silk-covered chairs that sat opposite the fireplace. The polished stone was carved into intricate swirling feathers, giving it the illusion of tongues of flame leaping free.

Cautiously, Asya took the other chair. She scooted it a little farther from the flames, hoping her aunt didn't notice. But the memory of them devouring her—*re-forming* her—was still too fresh.

Tarya's piercing gaze sliced through her. "You need to take the firestone off."

Asya's fingers leaped instinctively to the stone, wrapping around it like a shield. "Why?"

Tarya pressed her lips together, a sign of displeasure that Asya was all too familiar with. "I wanted to give you time to get used to this, but you cannot hide from it forever, Asya."

Asya knew, of course, that she couldn't wear the stone forever. The burden of the Firebird was hers now, too heavy a weight to shift even if she tried.

But she wasn't sure she could face it tonight. Not when she still felt so raw. Not with the palace walls closing over her head like bars.

"You must get used to taking it off," her aunt continued. "You need to understand—to control—this power." She sat back in the chair as Asya fidgeted, twisting her fingers together.

"Only for a short time, at first," her aunt added. Tarya's face softened slightly, from immovable marble to weathered sandstone. "Let the Firebird settle into your bones, and then it will hurt less. It will become familiar."

Asya took a deep breath. *A short time.* She could do that. And even if she couldn't, she had to. Izaveta had clearly fallen into her role with ease, had become the perfect image of the future queen. So Asya could take on her responsibilities too.

Slowly, she unhooked the leather cord. The firestone swung like a pendulum as she held it out to Tarya. Asya's traitorous fingers tightened, unwilling to let it go. As soon as the stone left her grip, a spark ignited in her chest. The flames were still kept at bay by the firestone's presence, but embers began to shift just beneath her skin.

Tarya glanced up at her. "Don't fight it. Remember, you have prepared for this, even if you do not believe it." She held up the lead-lined box that was the firestone's home and nestled the stone safely in its casing.

With the snap of the lid, Asya's body contorted.

Her muscles pulled against her bones as that pain carved through her again—somehow worse for its familiarity.

But beneath that, something else flickered. An awareness drawn deep from the earth and into her mind. And then, Asya was no longer in the chamber. She was outside, beneath a great statue of Saint Meshnik. Their sword was raised, their face contorted in a battle cry. In the corner of her eye, the shadow of her mother and the silhouette of a man. Magic sliced through the air, so sharp it seared against Asya's skin, painful as the fire crackling through her veins.

A terrible wrongness hung over the scene. A sense of something off-kilter, something that should not be.

Faintly, she heard chanting. The low rhythm of a spell.

Before she could decipher the words or find their source, the vision disintegrated. The edges curled in, crumbling away like a painting aflame.

Asya's eyesight blurred as the flames finally burst through her skin. She couldn't see it—couldn't see anything—but she could feel it. The fire danced eagerly at her fingertips, a bear finally allowed to run.

With an anguished hiss, they suddenly sputtered out as if doused in water.

Her heart punched against her ribs, her breath coming in ragged gasps. She blinked. The world slid back into focus around her. She was on all fours on the cold floor. Tarya crouched next to her, one hand looping the firestone around Asya's neck.

Asya sank back on her heels, steadying herself against the spindle-legged chair. That was when she saw the scorch marks. One leg of the chair had been warped, charcoal black now edging the shining silver. The wooden floor too was marred with deep gouges. Several still glowed with dying embers, winking out with each heartbeat. Ash settled around them, the last remnants of the monster.

Asya turned away from it, her stomach twisting. But that sight was no better. The two guards stood frozen as they watched her, the door half-open behind them. Fear creased Onishin's face. He couldn't even look at Asya, his gaze darting around nervously like a trapped bird.

But Vilanovich stared straight at her. Her eyes had darkened to a roiling storm, threaded through with disgust.

Asya couldn't imagine she looked much like the all-powerful Firebird now. More like a scared child lost in the woods.

And yet it was still enough to draw that reaction from the strashe.

Asya turned back to her aunt, glancing down at her hands. Flames had burst from them only moments before, but now they were clean and unmarked. "That was a Calling, wasn't it?" she whispered. "I saw—"

Tarya cut her off, jerking her head to the guards. "Leave us."

This time both of the strashe melted away without hesitation, eager to be away from the blazing monster in their midst.

"You have to be careful with words here," Tarya murmured. "Like any blade, they can just as easily be turned against you."

Her aunt lifted herself back into the chair. From the expression on her face, one would think they were having a casual chat over tea. Not that her niece had just set the room on fire. "What did you see?"

Asya coughed—her throat still felt coated in ash—before answering, "I'm not sure. I was outside. Near a statue. My—my mother was there, I think." Her voice caught on that word. *Mother.* That was the closest she'd ever come to seeing her again. And she'd looked like a stranger. A distant portrait to line the walls of the palace.

Asya blinked, willing the fresh burn of tears away. "And I could smell magic. *Strong* magic."

Tarya looked down into the rippling light of the fire as though conversing with it. "When Adilena died so suddenly, I was afraid this might happen. That a powerful Calling would come too quickly. I should have prepared you better."

"Do—" Asya broke off, the meaning of Tarya's words billowing inside her, coalescing into a dark realization. *When Adilena died so suddenly.* Asya almost couldn't examine it, as blazing and uncertain as the Firebird's flames. A fever had killed the queen, unfortunate but not suspicious. That's what the letter had said.

She blinked, fragments of the vision fluttering behind her lids. The overwhelming magic, the wrongness. Her mother.

"This Calling…" Asya pushed the words out even as she wanted to hide from them. To not face the possibility that they might be true. "You think it's to do with my mother's death?"

Tarya's shadowed expression, the way the colors of her eyes shifted, was answer enough.

"Then I have to follow it," Asya said, hating how small—how pathetic—her voice sounded. Her hand found the firestone again. Her fingers were drawn to it like it was the last rope tethering her to safe harbor. "So I should take this off, shouldn't I?"

Tarya turned back to Asya, her gaze cutting as a blade. "No, I do not believe so."

Relief bubbled through Asya's veins, quickly quelled by guilt. She shouldn't feel relieved at not fulfilling her duty.

Her aunt's eyebrows creased slightly—the closest she ever came to a frown. "That was a powerful Calling. One that speaks of dark, forbidden magic. You are not ready for that yet."

Despite her measured tone, the words pounded through

Asya like a blow. "But what about the balance? The risk of tipping the scales?"

Tarya considered the blackened burns on the floor. "I believe we have time still." She spoke slowly, a detached analysis of the situation, with none of the turbulent emotions that still fogged Asya's head. "Raslava had to travel a great distance for one of her Callings, and it took some time for the effects of the imbalance to become destructive."

Asya swallowed. Raslava was the Firebird before Tarya. Her aunt rarely spoke of her own mentor, but judging from Tarya's methods, Asya imagined Raslava to be formidable and unwavering.

But that wasn't what caught in her mind, needling as stray thorns. No matter how many times Asya asked, Tarya had never told her precisely what happened if magic remained unbalanced. If the price was never paid. Even the previous Firebirds never went into detail in their writings. They spoke of power ravaging through the lands, unchecked. Of the sky burning and the very earth cracking. Firebird Saveya had called it the gods wreaking their price on the land—demanding what they were owed.

But none of that told Asya what to expect. Just an unknowable certainty that it would destroy.

And it would be her fault for not ensuring the price was paid.

"For now," Tarya went on, "the risk of following the Calling would be too great. It could overwhelm you to even try to disentangle those threads. It would be excessive to ask that of a newborn Firebird. We should continue your basic training, your exercises."

Burning shame crept up Asya's throat. She looked down at her hands, tears prickling behind her eyes. Not prepared enough. Not strong enough. Not *enough*.

"But," Asya said, an idea suddenly striking her. "A Calling isn't the only way to find the one who owes a price."

Tarya frowned. "Perhaps, though the scent of magic has likely already been lost in a place as populated as this."

"But couldn't there be other signs?" Asya pressed. Surely a spell that powerful would leave traces Asya could follow. "Perhaps physical remnants of the ritual?"

Tarya nodded slowly, an odd expression on her face—something Asya couldn't quite unravel. "I suppose so, yes," her aunt conceded. "And I imagine the person is close. For the Calling to consume you like that, they must be within the palace walls."

"But who could have done that?" Asya whispered.

Tarya tilted her head. "That is the question."

Asya pulled herself back onto the now-precarious chair. Her head was whirling. Thoughts rattled through her, half-formed and uncertain. That odd grief reignited for the mother she had not known, mingled with fear. Dark magic like that had no place within the palace. If someone had used a spell powerful enough to kill a queen, what else might they do?

A new determination solidified inside Asya. She had to do this. Not just for the balance of power, but for the dead queen. For her sister, who could be endangered by this too. For herself and the mother she had lost.

For the dark magic that could tear the queendom apart.

Asya would find a way to get used to these powers, to control them. And until then, there were other methods she could use. She would find the perpetrator and ensure the price was paid. Ensure justice was done.

She would be enough.

This time, she would not hesitate.

CHAPTER NINE

By the time the sun crept over the distant mountains and the people of the court began to rise, Asya was already on the prowl. She'd hardly slept the previous night as it was, so she was eager to get moving. To feel like she was doing *something*. The firestone still hung heavy around her neck. After the scorching blaze of the Calling she'd hoped to keep her head clearer.

But even without the Firebird simmering inside her, she'd found nothing. There were plenty of statues of Saint Meshnik around the palace, from the towering figures that guarded the great hall to the statuettes that lined garden paths, but none matched the one in her vision, frozen in a battle cry.

As light began to filter through the ornate windows, more people filled the passages. Courtiers in their sweeping robes—all still edged in pale blue—mingled with attendants and stern-faced strashe. Their eyes flickered to her, prying but hesitant. Taking her measure.

She didn't like the idea of having an audience to this Calling. If she could even consider it a Calling. There were hundreds of saint statues in and around the palace, and she had nothing more to go on than a flash of a vision.

But even Tarya didn't think Asya was ready for more. The burn of that disappointment was smothered by the truth of it. Because that Calling had been too much, an overwhelming song of tangled, scalding notes.

She paused at a fork in the passage, wavering. She found she remembered the layout of the palace better than she'd expected. A crumpled map she'd long abandoned in the corners of her mind. Left would bring her back to the entrance hall and its growing stream of people. Right would take her to the covered walkway that led down to the great cathedral.

Her mother was in there—or what was left of her. Her spirit waited in the In-Between now, ready to return to Dveda's embrace in the earth on the thirteenth mourning day.

The idea of the cathedral tightened around her, ribs squeezing her heart. The place Asya had not seen since her fate had been decided. There was a tug in her gut, a small pull that said she should go and pay her respects. Find some way to mourn the mother she'd never really had.

She blinked, pulling herself away from that thought. That wasn't her task this morning. Her responsibility was to ensure justice was done—to ensure whoever did this to the queen paid the price.

The firestone pulsed against her chest. With it suppressing the Firebird, Asya had no idea where to go. Where to even begin. That realization resonated through her like a blow. She'd so hoped that she could manage this. That she could find a way to be enough, even if she'd failed to follow the Calling.

But it was useless. She was nothing without the creature inside her.

"Which way, Firebird?" Vilanovich prompted.

Asya glanced back at the guard. Her constant shadow since she'd left her chambers.

"You know," Vilanovich added, watching her with a shrewd expression, "if you told me what you were searching for, this would go far more quickly."

Asya shot her a look. Maybe the court was making her paranoid already, seeing enemies all around, but she didn't want to share that information. Not with anyone.

Part of her had wanted to go straight to Izaveta when she'd felt the Calling, to warn her that someone dangerous was still out there, close to them. But this shadow was what had held her back.

Izaveta was the queen, and she was acting like it. Keeping her eyes on any potential threats or unknowns. So Asya had to be the Firebird, and the Firebird would not run to her sister at the first sign of danger.

"Just exploring," she said, with an unconvincing grin that the guard did not return. Forcibly not looking to the right, to the passage that would lead to her mother's body, Asya turned left—and straight into the path of more inquisitive courtiers.

She swallowed, trying to school her expression into one of indifference. Tarya would not care about these people watching her like some venomous creature. The Firebird would not care.

Asya tried to draw that strength—that ancient power—around her, but it felt frail as a cobweb. A pretense that anyone could see through.

More eyes skittered her way as they continued down the passage.

"Do they all have to stare?" Asya muttered, loud enough for just Vilanovich to hear.

The strashe glanced at her, the only indication that she'd even heard what Asya said.

Asya pushed on, frustration suddenly bubbling up inside her as scalding and desperate to escape as the Firebird's flames. "I'm not some prize to be dressed up and paraded around. A bird in a cage for everyone to gawk at."

She tugged at the cuff of her shirt. "Just because *it* lives inside me, doesn't make it me," she finished, her voice dropping to no more than a murmur. She hadn't meant to say that all out loud. But the stifling stares of the courtiers—the coldness in her sister, Asya's own failings—were making her emotions swirl up like silt from a riverbed.

And in this palace no one would let her forget who she'd become. *What* she'd become.

"It does."

Those words, the icy bitterness to them, stopped Asya in her tracks.

Strashe Vilanovich's stormy eyes bored into hers, the anger in them as unmistakable as thunder. "I have seen a price exacted, Firebird," Vilanovich spat. "I have seen what you do. So you can stand there and pretend to be a saint all you like— pretend to not care about power, to be *separate* from that creature, but I know what hides beneath."

For a moment, Vilanovich held her gaze. The anger in that look—undercut with something else, something more desperate—almost made Asya step back. Then the strashe looked away, slipping back into formality as if suddenly re-membering her duty.

Asya stood a breath longer. She tugged at her sleeve again, worrying free a thread that she wrapped around her fingers. A painful lump rose in her throat, but she swallowed it down. She wouldn't let them get to her. Tarya hadn't.

Besides, what did it matter what one guard thought?

But that didn't stop the feeling of ice solidifying in her lungs as she walked on. Because the worst thing about what the strashe had said was not the venom in her words, it was the truth that burned in their core. It burrowed down into Asya and took root like a parasite.

Because much as she wanted to be separate from the Fire-bird, it was a part of her now. And if she wanted to succeed in her task, as she'd vowed to herself she would, then she would have to accept that.

Which meant she could not follow this Calling as only a mortal.

Back in the cloying emptiness of her chamber, Asya wrapped her fingers around the leather cord that held the firestone. She thought back to those days when her aunt was hunting and she'd been left alone, surrounded by the collected tomes of all the past Firebirds. She'd read every one, even if only to keep the boredom at bay. She knew their techniques, how each of them saw magic and followed a Calling.

She could do this. She could let the creature out.

Tarya might not think Asya was ready for such a strong Calling, but how else could she follow it?

With a deep breath, she lifted the firestone from her neck.

Forcing her hands to remain steady, she nestled it back in its protective box. She tried not to think of the last time she'd taken it off. The way the flames had dug into her bones, burrowing down to her core before bursting free. Keeping her fingers on the cool metal—ready to reopen it if the power became too much—she closed the lid.

With the snap of the clasp, the Firebird reared inside her.

Not as burning, as fevered, as before. But like a creature awaking from sleep, comfortably stretching its wings as it settled into her bones.

Before Asya could so much as try to listen to the enchanting Calling lingering at the edge of her vision, there was a knock on the door. It swung open and the ever-glowering Vilanovich stepped through, followed by an unfamiliar strashe.

"Your sister requests to see you, Firebird," the new guard said.

Asya blinked, caught between the world in front of her and the fire bursting in her veins. Not waiting for a response, Izaveta swept into the room. She was already dressed in full royal regalia, not a hair out of place.

"Iza?" Asya's voice caught, ashes rising up her throat. She felt flames leaping toward her fingers, eager to run free. She clenched her fists, forcing them back. The firestone's box called to her, urging her to just open the lid and put it back on. But Asya couldn't give up that easily.

If Izaveta was able to uphold her duty so effortlessly, Asya had to as well. She wouldn't be the one to break. To let her sister down and ruin everything.

Besides, the firestone was a secret for only the Firebird. She couldn't reveal it in front of all these people.

Vilanovich's gaze pierced into her, as if she could see the monster rising inside her. Asya looked away, trying to focus on her sister even as the Firebird's song tugged at her. Desperate to draw her in. "Is everything all right?"

Izaveta smiled, an infectious kind of smile that made Asya want to smile too. "Yes, of course. Why wouldn't it be?"

Asya wanted to say *because yesterday you showed no interest in me*, but the words stuck in her throat. Their mother had just died, and Izaveta had known her much better. She had every reason to seem a little distant.

Izaveta waved a hand, and several attendants in brilliant silver hurried in, carrying a heavy trunk between them. "I wanted to give you something to welcome you back to the palace, so I had some new clothes made for you. We may need to make some sizing adjustments, but these will be more fit for your position."

Another stark reminder that the Firebird was out of place here, amidst the glittering beauty of the court. Heat flared in Asya's cheeks, a prickling embarrassment as red as her hair.

She grasped for the appropriate response, but all she managed was "You work quickly."

Izaveta's smile widened. "Only the best for my sister." The words should have sounded affectionate, but they rang oddly hollow. A rehearsed sentiment that had long since lost true meaning.

The first attendants were followed by another, holding a tray laden with airy golden-brown flat cakes glazed in sweet Araïse honey blossom. The smell wafted over Asya, a flash of memory from that life so long ago.

Izaveta inclined her head to the tray. "I thought you might

also like some syrnyki. Perhaps more suited for your tastes now."

Asya bit the inside of her cheek, trying not to remember the awkward moment from the day before. The many ways she'd changed that Izaveta could never understand.

"Uh—thank you," Asya said, when she realized her sister was waiting for her to speak. She grabbed a syrnyki, partly to give her hands something to do. The taste burst on her tongue, another stab of memory. Sneaking into the kitchens when their mother was in one of her endless meetings, stealing trays of the golden fried battercakes. Eating them in the hidden alcove behind a statue of Saint Lyoza in the east courtyard.

The syrnyki crumbled like ash in her mouth. She swallowed hard. Like everything else, it was as if she were reading a story. Feeling the memories of a different girl. One who used to understand her sister. Who used to be mortal.

Izaveta's expression softened into something more sympathetic. "I thought you could join me this morning as I greet courtiers and emissaries arriving to pay their respects."

Asya stared at her. The thought of emissaries and condolences had not even crossed her mind.

"I would—" Izaveta paused as if collecting herself. "I would very much like you to be there. It helps to have family close in a time like this."

Those words tugged at something in Asya. There was such a familiarity in her sister, a warm comfort she'd almost forgotten she'd longed for. She'd spent so much time alone, or in Tarya's near-silent company, that she hadn't realized how much she'd missed this. Missed having someone.

Asya looked away, picking at the end of her sleeve. Those flames still gnawed at the edge of her vision, luring her in. Reminding her of her responsibility.

But the other part of Asya, the part the Firebird was supposed to devour, still ached for the sister she had lost. Perhaps this would be a small step toward regaining that relationship.

If Izaveta wanted Asya there for comfort, surely that meant some of the sister she remembered remained? The Firebird might not cling to that connection, but it was the last thing Asya had. She wasn't ready to give up on Izaveta yet.

Brushing away her misgivings like cinders from a hearth, Asya nodded. "I would love to be there with you."

Izaveta turned to wave the attendants forward, when her gaze snagged on the small wooden icon around Asya's throat. "You still have that."

Asya's hand jumped to the carved figure of Dveda, twining the chain through her fingers. "Of course I do."

Her mother had given it to Asya on her eighth birthday as a mark of protection. She and Izaveta used to pretend it was a sign from Dveda, calling them to a quest like in the old fairy tales. They'd spent hours running around the palace gardens pretending to be warriors and witches and heroes.

Anything other than what they were.

"I wonder what Mother would think of that," Izaveta said, and coldness bled into her features again like the first creeping frost of winter. "She was not exactly *devout*," she added, at Asya's look of bewilderment.

Before Asya could respond, the attendants brought the trunk forward. They placed it in front of her and opened it with an elaborate flourish.

Asya drew in a sharp breath. It was full to the brim with garments, everything from day wear to swooping ball gowns. Likely more clothes than she could possibly need. But that wasn't what had made her gasp. It was the color. Every single one of them was red.

They spilled from the trunk like blood in glaring hues of scarlet and crimson. Some were accented with other shades, glinting with gold beading or edged with silver like gleaming fangs. Feathers and flames were woven into the designs, curling together until they were inextricable from one another.

Each was a glaring marker of who Asya was. Of *what* Asya was.

"What do you think?" Izaveta asked, her face hopeful.

Asya glanced from the flame-red garments to her sister. She couldn't bring herself to fracture this tenuous thing between them, the small seed of friendship that might grow into what they'd once had.

She forced herself to smile. "I love them."

CHAPTER TEN

Izaveta wrapped her fingers around the back of the carved throne, her heart pounding. She had never sat in it before, not even as a child when she had sneaked into the hall after dark. It was a forbidden entity. The throne was for the queen, for her *mother*. Not for her.

Comprised of twisting whorls of pale gold and silver, it swirled up to the sky like captured flames. That was the theme to all the royal architecture, as if the previous queens had been determined to show the Firebird was not the only one who could claim to control fire.

A starbird fluttered between the beams of the arched ceiling, drawing her eye. They were brought into the hall on occasions such as these, their faint glow a sign of power that illuminated the queen.

They were a sign of her power now.

Slowly, as if it might be hot to touch, Izaveta lowered herself onto the throne. Nothing changed, no great flash of light or crack of thunder. But something shifted in her. The fact that she was sitting here meant that her mother was not. It sent an uncomfortable echo of loss through Izaveta, tangled with the creeping sensation that she was still trying to impress—to live up to—the mother who was gone.

She would have preferred to avoid it a little longer, but it wouldn't be appropriate for Izaveta to receive guests anywhere else. And this morning, already, dukes and conze were flooding in from the far reaches of Tóurin, likely followed by emissaries from the neighboring lands. And soon all six of her mother's cabinet members would be present, every one of them eager to pay their respects to the late queen.

And to test the mettle of the new one.

Izaveta gritted her teeth at the thought. She was no fool. She knew they would all be searching for any weakness, any gap in her armor.

But she would show them none.

The small door to her right swung open, and her sister walked in, flanked by Strashe Vilanovich.

Asya was dressed in one of the outfits Izaveta had sent to her chambers. A bloodred coat with thin gold chains decorating the shoulders and dripping down her arms to end in heavy crimson gems. A short cloak hung down her back, trailing feathers like furled wings. Her boots were a brilliant gold, the fabric twisting together to form talons.

Izaveta allowed herself a small smile of satisfaction. It was perfect. She needed to appear strong, unbreakable, and having the Firebird so clearly at her side would accomplish that.

The guard melted away, joining the silver-clad strashe that lined the great hall. Asya tugged at her sleeve as she ascended the dais to join Izaveta, eyes flicking around the vast room.

Izaveta inclined her head in greeting. "Red suits you."

"You don't think it's a bit...much?" Asya asked, shifting in her boots.

Izaveta's gaze swept over her sister. Even with the somewhat anxious facade Asya put on, she would look impressive. "Certainly not."

Izaveta sat back in the throne, keeping her chin raised and her face a cultivated calm. This was her first true test, and everyone would be watching. The vibishop and his followers had already slunk into the room, standing by the great elm doors with several courtiers. Izaveta could feel Vibishop Sanislav's pale eyes on her, could almost sense his anticipation as he willed her to misstep.

Conze Bazin stood nearby, probably hoping to imbibe some of Sanislav's supposed holiness by proximity. He was one cabinet member Izaveta was not sure she could persuade, even if Vittaria offered her support. He had always been a devout man, ostentatiously so, and prying him from Sanislav's grip would be a challenge. A satisfying one, though, if she could succeed.

At least the sight of her sister at her side should dampen their hopes that the Firebird could be swayed.

Though Asya continued to fidget. The constant movement gnawed at the edge of Izaveta's vision, adding to her already contorted nerves. Some of that old resentment welled up in her, bitter and burning in her throat. Asya had all this power within her grasp and she shrank from it, while Izaveta had to claw for every scrap.

"Who're we waiting for?" Asya asked, leaning in a little.

As if on cue, the high doors at the other end of the hall

swung open. Izaveta sat up straighter, tugging her silk gloves to ensure they weren't wrinkled.

A procession entered, a large sea of black and red. The guards moved in smooth unison, each heavily armed and hulking. They parted for a short woman in crisp military dress, the saber at her side gleaming and clearly ornamental. A manifestation of her authority, more than anything else.

Commander Iveshkin had sat in her mother's cabinet as long as Izaveta could remember, overseeing the contentious western border with Versbühl. A stubborn and uncompromising woman, she had risen quickly in the ranks thanks to her strategic mind and ability to cut straight to the heart of a problem. But off the battlefield, she had no true artistry, no subtle skill, to her political maneuvers. Everything was black-and-white, dividing people into those who had power and those who did not.

More worryingly, she had no clear alliance to either the Church or the Crown—her only loyalty was to whichever she believed was the winning side, whichever would ensure Tóurin remained strong. With Sanislav circling, Izaveta needed to prove that she was the better choice. The more powerful piece to back.

She smiled in greeting as the woman approached, along with her interpreter. "Commander Iveshkin, it is an honor to have you return to the palace." Izaveta had some knowledge of the Signed Language from her study of languages with Fyodor, but in front of the court, Iveshkin's interpreter relayed her words.

Iveshkin bent in a stiff impersonation of a bow, the barest hint of respect. "Princess Izaveta, my deepest condolences," she signed, her interpreter speaking aloud as Iveshkin's fingers weaved with a fluidity at odds with her brash exterior. "Your mother will be greatly missed. She was a formidable woman."

She let the sentence trail off, her hands lowering slowly, the unsaid thought clear: *formidable, unlike you.*

Izaveta's fingers tightened on the arms of her throne, the tension hidden by her pale gloves. "Indeed, she shall be missed."

An irritating smile creased the commander's features, one that made Izaveta think she was laughing at her. "We were intrigued to see the Depthless Lake on our journey in," Iveshkin continued. "Its light is not what it was when I last visited."

Izaveta bit the inside of her cheek to hold back the icy retort that rose in her throat. "But still radiant, nonetheless."

Iveshkin tilted her head a little, sizing Izaveta up. "Perhaps," the commander signed. "And I am sure it is not related to the change in queenship." The slight curl of her lips implied otherwise.

But Izaveta just kept smiling. If the commander didn't see her as powerful yet, then Izaveta could play another strategy. Let them think she was weak and vulnerable for now. Let them underestimate her. It would make them all the easier to manipulate.

Iveshkin's gaze flicked over to Asya, and Izaveta did not miss the flash of surprise on the commander's face. "And the Firebird, how fascinating. It's an honor to meet you."

Asya nodded, her mouth pressed shut. Izaveta wasn't sure if she was silent to spite her or because she had nothing to say, but either way it was sufficient. The silence added to her mythical aura. Standing there, surrounded by the high, vaulted ceiling and dressed in shimmering gold, her hair fanning behind her like a bloodstain, she did look mythical. Like a creature of legend, just as Izaveta had intended.

Iveshkin's eyes returned to Izaveta, and she could see the calculations whirring in their depths. The military strategy falling into place. She read the question before the commander formed it, so clearly was it written in the gruff lines of her face. "The Firebird would be a worthy addition to our protections. The Versch would not question our magic if the Firebird joined my ranks."

Izaveta tilted her chin. The commander wasn't wrong that Versbühl had been eyeing their fading magic, testing their defenses, for years now. The Versch had always relied on their military prowess, while Tóurin had the magic that flowed through the land—a perfect stalemate that kept them uneasy allies. But the balance was shifting more clearly in Versbühl's favor with every day the Depthless Lake faded.

No one else would dare state it so directly, but Iveshkin was always like that, a blunt instrument in the delicacies of the court. At least it made it easier to get her measure. To use her to Izaveta's own advantage.

Asya's mouth opened, and she shot Izaveta a sidelong glance.

But Izaveta spoke before her sister could, with the smooth ease her mother taught her. "I'm sure we can come to some arrangement."

Chapter Eleven

Asya picked at the edge of the uncomfortably stiff coat for what must have been the thousandth time as she eyed the commander. She didn't like the way the woman was looking at her, as if she were a prize to be won.

When she had agreed to join her sister this morning, she had expected to be here in a familial role. Not dressed up and paraded in front of the court.

She leaned toward her sister, still keeping her gaze on the commander. "Izaveta, I can't do that. I—"

Izaveta brushed her off, voice barely more than a murmur. "We can discuss it another time."

Asya blinked, hurt prickling behind her eyes at the dismissal. It echoed of their mother, how she'd spin words and play people against each other. While Asya had been taught the ways of daggers and sabers, her sister had been trained in a different kind of weapon. One that Asya did not understand at all.

Izaveta wielded it with ease, twisting words and smiles into whatever she wanted. And there was still a coldness to her face. Like someone had taken the sister Asya remembered and warped her into something else.

Though Asya was something else too. Whether she liked it or not.

And that was hard to forget with the Firebird coursing through her. She'd left the firestone off, hoping to let the power sink in. To get used to its burning presence and then follow her Calling. But every moment she had to stand still and pretend to smile grated against her. The Firebird's song echoed in the back of her mind, begging her to give in to it. To succumb to its scorching strands even if they would overpower her.

Asya tugged at her sleeve again, trying to dispel some of that restless energy. "The Firebird's duty is to magic, to the price," she pressed. "She's not a weapon."

Izaveta's jaw tightened. She wouldn't look directly at Asya, still putting on a performance to the assembled court. "The people of Tóurin need to see us working together in these troubled times. It gives them comfort—hope—when we stand united."

Irritation flared in Asya, as bright as the Firebird's flames— bright enough to sear away the hurt. "That's what this was all about, wasn't it?"

Izaveta finally looked at her. "What do you mean?"

Asya took a step back, all the fears she'd tried to push away bubbling up inside her. The Firebird wasn't devouring them. It was fueling them. "This wasn't about us being sisters again. This was about appearing powerful."

"Asya," Izaveta said, with the tone of someone dealing with an irrational child. "I only—"

But Asya didn't wait for her to go on. The fire in her veins—the faint Calling nagging at her—spurred her words on as her voice rose. "I'm the Firebird, not another jewel for your crown."

Asya's words carried, bursting out of her like the Firebird's flames. A rustle whispered through the room, soft as wind through leaves—though far less comforting. This had a hardened edge to it. More like a snake slithering through dry grass.

The weight of their gazes hung heavily on her. The mingled fear and distrust was cut through with a tingling excitement, as if they were enjoying the show.

She swallowed, her eyes smarting. She didn't care. Let them stare. She could feel Izaveta's gaze on her most of all, unrelenting. But Asya didn't want to look at her. Didn't want to see the hurt or fear on her face.

Or worse, that same cold detachment.

Without glancing back, Asya swept from the room, banishing all thoughts of commanders and mourning and her lost sister. She had something more important to do. She had her Calling to follow.

Asya's heart was racing. She hardly knew where she was going, just that she needed to keep moving. The Firebird was a distant thrum in the back of her mind. A nagging itch she couldn't shake.

Anger still bubbled beneath her skin, as scalding as the Firebird's flames. She tugged on the ridiculous feathers that adorned her shoulders, cursing the seamstress's flawless work when they wouldn't budge. Asya settled for yanking the coat off and balling it in her arms.

The farther she walked from the claustrophobic throne room, the more her anger ebbed. It tempered to something less bitter, a hard knot of hurt that curled around her heart.

What had she expected?

Not this. She'd hoped that she and Izaveta could go back to the way it had been. And after this morning, when Iza had really seemed like she wanted that too—

Asya squeezed her eyes shut against the threatening tears. She couldn't muddle through anything with the Firebird pounding inside her so constantly. Especially not with eyes following her wherever she went. At least she'd lost the constant shadow of Vilanovich with her hasty departure from the throne room. Asya shook her head, trying to dislodge those thoughts. She didn't need to worry about the court and all its confusing manipulations, or desperately try to find the sister she'd once known. All she *needed* to do now was be the Firebird. And the Firebird didn't have to feel any of that.

She paused at a bend in the passage. Taking a deep breath, she let the Firebird seep into her senses. Not fighting against it but instead allowing it to burn everything away.

The statue was all that mattered. Finding who had cast that spell and righting the balance.

Asya'd hoped that, after spending a little more time with the power, she would be able to reach for the threads of magic, those curling vines Tarya had always used to hunt her prey.

But they were still too tangled. Every time Asya tried to grasp them, it was like she was seeing too much. She could feel that tug of magic, the pull of the stratsviye that would mark the culprit, but the fire inside her obscured the details, as if she were looking at a forest from a great distance. She could see the mass of green leaves, could even smell them on the wind. But she needed to find *one* tree.

With each stuttering beat of her heart, she felt the Firebird eating away at her. Eroding her bones and replacing them with fire. And with each breath the temptation to put the firestone on grew stronger.

Her feet moved almost of their own volition, her mind too preoccupied with the flames to realize where she was heading until she stood in front of the vast stone archway. The spires of the Cathedral of Silvered Saints towered above her, still dwarfed by the shadow of the palace at her back.

The burning fire in her chest sputtered out at the sight. But something drew her in. Not like the blinding flash of the Calling, something much quieter.

The distant cry of a little girl who still wished her mother could comfort her.

Stepping into the cathedral again was like stepping into a dream. A memory she'd replayed in her head so many times over the past seven years. The day of the ceremony. The day that had forever divided her life into jagged parts, before and after.

The cathedral hadn't changed. There was an immovable quality about the place, a sense that the gods would ensure it stood, even as the world crashed down around it. The eyes of the saints watched her as she walked down the aisle—Saint Meshnik's face serene and starkly different from the one she'd seen in her vision. There was a kind of peace here, even with the Firebird roiling beneath her skin. A quiet separation from everything else that soothed Asya's frantic heartbeat.

It was empty, morning prayer long finished and most of the court busy with the goings-on in the throne room. Asya stopped in front of the altar, staring up at the soaring dome painted with depictions of the gods. She couldn't bring herself to tear her eyes away. To look down at what she knew was laid out on that altar.

The pale blue shroud that covered what had once been her mother.

She took a breath, the air too hot in her lungs, and looked down.

The shroud was beautiful. Ornate and fit for a queen. She could almost imagine her mother's face beneath it, perfectly preserved and empty.

Something squeezed inside her, an unfamiliar feeling. A coldness that felt like it might fracture her from the inside out.

It wasn't love. Not like the love she had for her sister— as bright and dangerous as the Firebird's flames. But it was loss. An undeniable piece of herself that she could never get back. In many ways she'd lost her mother all those years ago, but this was permanent. Irreversible.

The tears burst out of her, unbidden and burning. Her mother would have told her not to cry. Not to make a ridiculous scene in public. But her mother wasn't here to tell her anything. She never would be again. And these tears were Asya's alone.

They spilled from her writhing center, from all these losses she could never truly understand. A mother she'd never known, who had likely never loved her. A sister who had been carved in the queen's image.

And perhaps they fell for Asya too. For what this death had cost her—for the humanity that could never truly be hers again.

She stiffened, suddenly aware of a presence behind her.

Asya turned, very conscious of the tears staining her face. But there was no point in hiding them, the person would have already heard.

Strashe Vilanovich stood framed by the glittering facade that decorated the entryway. The light glinted gold in her hair, making her resplendent as the saints that lined the walls. Her eyes were fixed on Asya, intense and storming as ever. But for a brief instant, Asya thought she saw something else in those eyes. Not hatred or disgust. Not the harsh whisper of *monster.*

It was a shiver of the same hollow loss Asya felt—an echoing emptiness that couldn't quite be filled. A reflection, and, perhaps, an understanding.

But then Vilanovich took a step forward, and it was gone, so quickly Asya wasn't sure it had ever really been there.

Asya looked away, wiping at her reddening cheeks. Monsters were not supposed to weep. "You didn't need to follow me."

The guard didn't so much as falter. "I'm not to leave your side, Firebird."

Asya paused, turning back to face Vilanovich as she searched for the right words in the unique language of the palace that would get what she needed. She didn't want a shadow now, didn't want someone to see her like this. "You're, uh, dismissed." It came out with a slight uptick at the end, far more a question than Asya had intended.

"My orders are very clear," Vilanovich replied, the gray of her eyes hardening to match the resolution in her voice.

Asya let out a sigh. The peace of the cathedral had been shattered, the rest of the world creeping in. And with it, the Firebird's flames stoked her annoyance again. "Your orders are to follow me *everywhere*?"

"My orders are to protect."

Asya's fingers twitched, reaching to worry at the too-stiff cuff of her shirt. The guard's *orders* brought all of those things Asya didn't want to think about bubbling up again. The nagging fear at the back of her mind, the poisonous doubts about her sister.

She closed her fist, forcing them away. "As you are clearly aware, I am the Firebird. I don't need protection."

The strashe's jaw clenched. Something flashed across her face, too quick for Asya to read. "Did you ever consider, Firebird, that I'm not following you for your protection, but for others'?"

Asya blinked, her mouth working to formulate a response as those words knotted in her mind. Tarya had always taught her that the Firebird was a force for good. It was not a pleasant duty, not one others would covet, but it was necessary. It kept balance and allowed the mortal world to live on.

But she couldn't ignore the disgust in the sharp lines of Vilanovich's expression. Or the truth in her words. The face of that little girl, desperate to do anything to protect her brother, shone in Asya's mind again.

Before Asya could speak, something shifted inside her. A tumbling coal that sent sparks flying.

It wasn't like before. Not a blazing flame that overwhelmed her, searing her senses. But it was unmistakable.

Another Calling.

CHAPTER TWELVE

Izaveta had half risen out of the throne before she caught herself. Even after so many years and so many hard-learned lessons of where trusting people left her, her first instinct was still to follow Asya. To *comfort* her even after that slight.

But her sister wasn't wrong. This was a political move, and Asya had seen straight through it. Izaveta still couldn't decide if the twisting sensation in her stomach was due to the Firebird outmaneuvering her in front of the court, or genuine guilt.

Her mother's voice echoed again, as clear now as it had been the day she died. *We both know you have no concern for anyone else. You are interested in your own power and position, no more.*

Izaveta shook her head, dispelling her mother's phantom. She shot a glare out at the assembled faces. Every one of them was turned to her. Their silent anticipation was enough to know they'd heard what her sister had said.

Izaveta could practically feel the triumph radiating from Sanislav, the satisfied set to his mouth as he stared up at her. Bazin had paled, clutching on to his small wooden icon as if asking Zmenya for protection. Iveshkin's frown deepened, eyes darting between Izaveta and the door Asya had vanished through.

Not the best start to bringing the cabinet to her side.

It doesn't matter, she told herself. Her mother would have found a way to spin it somehow to her advantage, and Izaveta would too. She had to.

She sank back down into the throne, trying to play off the movement as natural. Rolling her shoulders, she tugged on the end of her silk gloves, sliding them back into place like armor.

Forcing her expression to remain serene, she turned to the commander. "My sister has important matters to attend to. We shall have to discuss this further another time. For now, the strashe can show you to your rooms."

The commander held her gaze, a suspicious crease to her forehead. "I look forward to it."

Even as the commander and her interpreter left and the room settled, Izaveta couldn't shake her sister's words. Asya didn't understand. She had the luxury of staying out of these games. She didn't have to find ways to manipulate and scheme, didn't have to constantly wonder what a person was truly thinking.

In her distraction, Izaveta didn't realize who had approached her throne until the individual stood directly below her.

"Master Azarov," an attendant prompted.

Izaveta's stomach lurched. The rest of the room slid away. For a heartbeat, she was fourteen again, floundering in a game she still didn't understand. Finding what she thought was a lifeline only for it to ensnare her like a noose.

"Kyriil?" she breathed.

She hadn't seen him in almost three years, but he looked just the same. Perhaps a bit more filled out in his shoulders, his golden hair a little longer. But his green eyes glinted with that familiar hint of mischief, the flicker of laughter that had first drawn her in. Even now, she couldn't help the treacherous heat that prickled up her neck.

She slipped for barely a heartbeat, but she was sure he'd noticed. He always noticed.

She raised her chin, expression cool as winter air. "Master Azarov, we were not expecting you."

He smiled, a careful balance between polite and commiserating. "I apologize for not writing ahead, but my father wanted me to bring our condolences in person as soon as possible."

Izaveta narrowed her eyes at him. His father was not so old or fragile that he could not have made the journey himself. No, this was a calculated move. Using someone Izaveta knew against her.

The Azarovs had held a seat in the queen's cabinet until half a century ago when they'd been involved in an attempted coup. Despite that, they still maintained prestige in Tóurin. They controlled much of the eastern mining lands—anyone with that much gold at their command couldn't remain downtrodden for long, even with a treasonous history.

They'd petitioned Izaveta's mother more than once to get their seat restored, but she had always rebuffed them. It wasn't hard to guess the true purpose of Kyriil's visit.

Izaveta forced herself to match his easy calm, even as her mind whirled. "I appreciate it, Master Azarov."

His lips twitched, as if he could see straight through her

cordiality. But he couldn't—not anymore. She wasn't the same foolish girl she'd been when they last met. Trust was no longer something she gave away, no matter what her heart said.

"My father knows these are turbulent times, and he pledges to offer his support in any way he can." Kyriil's mouth spread into a smile, one meant for Izaveta alone. "As do I."

That was the last thing Izaveta wanted. To spend even a breath longer with this person who reminded her of her failings, of all the ways she should have been better.

But what else could she say? She was trapped by the customs of the court, by the need for smiles that hid her claws. Though that didn't mean they weren't there—didn't mean that she couldn't use Kyriil to her own advantage. "Thank you. Your support is invaluable to the Crown."

In the welcome quiet of the spymaster's rooms, Izaveta tightened her fingers around the letter, clutching it to her like a precious jewel. Conze Vittaria's crest stood stark against the paper, a promise and a possibility. Where, before, a restless uncertainty had churned in her stomach, it had been replaced with cool satisfaction.

The slip with Asya was unfortunate, as was Kyriil's arrival, but she couldn't let either of those things throw her. Izaveta could still salvage this. She might not have flames at her command, but she had other weapons.

She glanced up at the spymaster, standing still as the stone behind her. Zvezda's dark skin gleamed in the lamplight, hair pulled back in spiraling plaits to mark her dedication to Vetviya. Her clothes blended easily into the shadows, the only accent a pale silver clasp on her left shoulder. The curled silhouette of a mosovna, the bird that could not cry—the mark of a spy.

That symbol was what made Zvezda one of the few people within the palace walls Izaveta could truly trust. When a spy joined the prestigious ranks of the pakviye, they took an oath on the three moons, bound in blood. A pledge that their loyalty to the Crown was ensured, broken only by one who would risk damnation by the gods.

Izaveta put the letter down, smoothing its creases. "You will ensure the conze's journey is untroubled?"

The spymaster stepped forward, her every movement as polished and smooth as a musician playing an aria. "Certainly. I have already sent one of my top pakviye to oversee it."

Izaveta nodded, taking a slow breath. "And any word from our friends in Versbühl?"

"They are sending an ambassador," Zvezda replied.

Izaveta raised an eyebrow. She hadn't expected the kaizer himself to make the journey, but the fact that they were not even sending any of the imperial family was a clear statement. One that said they did not believe Izaveta was worth the effort.

They'd learn soon enough that they were wrong.

"Ensure the ambassador is brought to me as soon as they arrive," Izaveta added. She wanted to control the newest piece the moment it was on the board.

Izaveta turned away, some of the tension in her muscles releasing. It was all coming together. Vittaria's letter had as good as guaranteed her support, and with the conze at her side, it almost wouldn't matter that the Firebird had so publicly spurned her.

She gritted her teeth, ignoring the slight twinge of hurt that thought sent through her. She didn't need Asya, not as her sister and not as the Firebird. Izaveta's pieces were falling into place. It was all under her control.

But no matter how many times she repeated that in her head, she couldn't quiet the whispering doubts that crept through the back of her mind.

Zvezda stepped forward. "There was another matter."

Izaveta stilled, her shoulders tensing. Before Zvezda could reply, the door swung open. Tarya walked in, the shadows slipping around her like water. Zvezda stiffened, the barest hint of surprise flashing across her face.

Tarya paused, her gaze settling on Izaveta. "Apologies, my lady."

Izaveta's eyes flicked between her aunt and the spymaster, reading the unspoken things that shimmered between them. What business would the former Firebird have with Zvezda? Though, Izaveta supposed, they might have known each other before. Tarya had not aged as a mortal, and it was quite possible the two women had been at court together in their youth.

Izaveta forced her lips into a smile, slipping the letter into her pocket. "Conze Tarya, I had been hoping to speak with you."

"Indeed?"

Izaveta clasped her hands in front of her. "As you may know, the Fading is of utmost importance to the Crown. Your...unique expertise makes you highly qualified in the subject. I was hoping to offer you a position as advisor on the matter."

Tarya was not like the queen, who could craft an expression as easily as an artist sketched an outline. Tarya was stone, each movement slowly chiseled by an intent hand.

She cocked her head, examining. "I see so much of your mother in you."

The comment burned through the air, acrid as smoke. Izaveta had spent so long chasing that, so long trying to mold herself into the queen's image. So why did those words twist through her gut like a blade?

"And that is why my answer is no."

Izaveta froze, caught off guard for the third time that day. Three times too many. Every mistake—every misstep—was an opportunity for someone to strike. She swallowed hard, Tarya's remark worming its way down like splintered glass.

"Well," Izaveta said, voice hard as a frozen lake. "If that is all, I have other business to attend to."

She turned to leave when Zvezda raised a hand to call her back. "The other matter."

Izaveta lifted her chin, determinedly not looking at her aunt. "Yes?"

Zvezda moved closer, lowering her voice. "A scholar has arrived from the Amarinth."

Izaveta waved a dismissive hand. "I'll greet them tomorrow."

But Zvezda blocked Izaveta's path, her expression still grim. "It may be more pressing. Vibishop Sanislav escorted the scholar to Vetviya's turret. *Personally.*"

CHAPTER THIRTEEN

The familiar arched doors of the library, carved with whirling branches and misted skies to represent Vetviya, were usually a respite for Izaveta. But today, even that had been breached.

She had hoped to arrive before Sanislav's scholar, to cut off that problem before it began. But the sight of an unfamiliar figure, standing with an ease that implied he had every right to be there, showed she had failed.

He didn't look much older than her, with messy dark brown hair that fell into his eyes as he pored over an ancient text. One of the many books and scrolls that had been so carefully curated over the last century.

Nearly seventy years ago, when the Depthless Lake had begun to fade and it was clear the lifeblood of magic was draining from this land, Izaveta's great-grandmother had dedicated herself to finding a solution. She'd turned the northern turret, with its great spire that curled into tangled horns in honor of Vetviya, into a library committed exclusively to the study of magic. She had collected tomes and texts from the farthest reaches of the continent, as well as gathering scholars, philosophers, even soothsayers—anyone who might have knowledge that could further her work.

No one had found a solution, of course, but when her great-grandmother died, her daughter had continued the work until it had passed on to Izaveta's mother. Queen Adilena was more scrupulous in who she trusted to work in the turret, always careful not to let any powerful information fall into the wrong hands. Only three scholars remained, overseen by Fyodor, and each rigorously tested by Adilena for both their skill and their loyalty.

Yet, knowing that, the vibishop had chosen to bring the scholar here.

That was a careful choice, moving a piece to a new square. But the question was why—what did he want from this research? Just the possibility to steal information away so the Church could claim to have found the solution to the Fading first? Or something more sinister?

"Diye meshok," Izaveta swore under her breath.

The intruder didn't look up from the tome. "Don't let the vibishop hear you say that. The shock might kill him."

And that would be such a pity, Izaveta thought.

She raised her chin, deciding to gloss over her somewhat inappropriate language, saying, with an iciness she had perfected, "And what are you doing here?"

He finally met her gaze, his eyes the same rich brown as his hair, and sparkling with a smugness that made Izaveta bristle. "My name is Nikov Toyevski. I am the envoy from the Amarinth, here to pay my respects to the late queen."

Izaveta pressed her lips together. The Amarinth was a

vast archive of knowledge that stood on the border between Tóurin and Versbühl, not truly under the control of either country. But the timing could not be a coincidence.

"And what," Izaveta repeated, not bothering to keep the irritation from her voice, "are you doing *here*?" She waved a hand at the curving shelves, coiling all the way to the point of the tower some hundred feet above their heads, to make her meaning clear.

Nikov's casual demeanor didn't so much as flicker at her tone. "Vibishop Sanislav requested our assistance," he said. "He believes the Amarinth's expertise may be of use with the Fading."

Izaveta took a moment to study him before responding. She couldn't deny that the Amarinth might well have information that could help. But it was an unknown entity, one that swore loyalty to no crown, and as such could not be trusted. They guarded their knowledge carefully, and there was no guarantee that they would not just take anything they found as another treasure for their vault.

And then there was the question of Sanislav's involvement.

On the surface, Nikov Toyevski certainly had the appearance of a scholar. He wore the traditional sweeping half cape of the Amarinth, emblazoned with its twisting crest, the deep blue picking up the bronze tones in his brown skin. A jeweled pin glittered on his chest, a blindfolded woman rayed in sunlight—the Kharuri pictograph for wisdom.

But he didn't stand like a scholar. He held himself with an air that implied he was used to being obeyed, and his glinting eyes spoke of something other than a life in the Amarinth's dark archives.

"And *you* are an expert scholar?" she asked.

Nikov inclined his head, his lips twitching upward. "Master Oravin sends his regrets, but the journey would have been too difficult for him." He tapped a finger on the book he had been examining. "This is interesting. Were you looking at how the Firebird's magic has remained powerful despite the Fading?"

She wanted to march over and snatch the book away. The question alone cut far too close to what her mother and Sanislav had been discussing. But Izaveta had already let her irritation get the better of her too many times in this interaction. She had to remember that, just like everything else in court, this was an elaborate game of zvess. To win, Izaveta could not be crude and obvious. She had to use all the cunning her mother had taught her.

"That is one of the avenues of research we have been exploring," she said carefully. She smoothed the annoyance from her voice, switching easily to the winning smile she had spent years perfecting. She knew it was a mere shadow of her mother's, but it was usually sufficient, nonetheless.

She glanced at the curling staircase that wound its way up the tower, allowing access to even the highest shelves. Her eyes caught on a flash of motion, the slight flick of silver robes.

"Valerii," she called, keeping her tone as sweet as Araïse honey. "Would you please come down here and help our guest?"

Valerii's anxious face appeared from behind a bookshelf several stories above them, his brass monocle glinting. He glanced around, as if hoping Izaveta might be addressing someone else, before hurrying down to them.

He hopped from the ladder, a sheen of sweat glistening on his dark skin. He twisted the chain of his monocle through his fingers as he spoke. "I—I'm sorry. He said he was meant to be here…and he has the Amarinth crest…and the vibishop—"

"It's not a problem," Izaveta said with a smile. As soon as she stepped into this role, it was easy to maintain. "But I would like to ensure that Master Toyevski gets a full overview of our work." She turned to Nikov, iciness tugging at the edge of her words. "*All* of our work. Starting at the beginning."

Valerii's eyes twitched to the dust-covered uppermost shelves. "But some of that—"

"We would not want Master Toyevski to miss anything," she cut in. "Would we?"

Perhaps Izaveta couldn't outright refuse to accommodate the scholar without seeming petty—or giving Sanislav the ammunition to accuse her of putting politics over the good of the queendom. But she could certainly control what information he got.

Nikov smiled back, a smile that said he knew exactly what Izaveta was doing. "I am most grateful, my lady."

Valerii nodded, his curls twitching as he gestured for Nikov to follow. Izaveta watched the pair ascend the tight staircase, up toward the oldest section of research. Any of the useful tomes from that era had been moved or transcribed to ensure they were well preserved. The rest was largely fairy tales or speculation. Perfect for keeping the scholar occupied until the coronation.

But, despite that, Izaveta could not shake the unnerving feeling Nikov Toyevski was going to prove to be a more difficult piece to manipulate.

CHAPTER FOURTEEN

This Calling wasn't like the other. It didn't blaze like a dying sun, threatening to sear through Asya's senses. But it also wasn't the twirling vines and threads her aunt had described. It was more like a song, a distant but beautiful tune that tugged on some deep part of her. And when Asya let it course through her, it wasn't scalding or terrifying.

It was *right*.

Asya hardly noticed as she stepped out of the cathedral and its soaring roof was replaced by the cool canopy of clouds. All she felt was the Firebird's song, urging her on with every note. The flames pounded inside her, matching the rhythm of her racing heart. It wasn't fear, though, that sped its beats. It was excitement.

Vilanovich's voice shattered the spell, an edge of uncertainty to her usual disdain. "Where are we going?"

Asya pulled up short, momentarily thrust back into the harsh light of the real world. Trees rose up around her as if out of a winter mist. She'd gone farther than she realized, already to the edge of the wood that rimmed the palace grounds.

She glanced back at Vilanovich. "Like I said, you don't have to accompany me everywhere."

Asya couldn't quite bring herself to say she was following a Calling. The beauty of the Firebird's song still hummed through her, and she didn't want Vilanovich's disgust to taint it.

Vilanovich closed the distance between them, her frost-gray eyes meeting Asya's. Asya saw her own sparks reflected in them. Skittering around her irises like fireflies. The Firebird rearing up inside her.

The strashe stilled, the mark of a soldier preparing for battle. "You're going to exact a price, aren't you?"

Asya turned away, trying to ignore the storm brewing in Vilanovich's eyes. The look that said exactly what she thought of the Firebird's—of *Asya's*—actions. "It's of no importance to you."

The strashe put a hand on Asya's shoulder, forcing her around to face her. Asya's breath hitched as heat spread from Vilanovich's touch, feeding the Firebird's flames.

"You can't do that," Vilanovich pressed. "You—"

Asya stepped back, letting the strashe's grip fall away. "It is not my place to decide." For the first time in her life, she felt some of the certainty her aunt had always carried so easily. The understanding of this dark duty.

Vilanovich's hand jumped to her saber, knuckles white. "I won't allow you to hurt someone in front of me."

"It's not about hurting anyone," Asya said slowly, the words drawn from all those times her aunt had told her the same thing. Though she'd never believed them before—not like she did now with this burning song coursing through her veins. "It's about balance."

Vilanovich's jaw tightened, no cracks in her determination. "I'll raise my blade against you before I let you exact a price."

"You can try." A hint of the flames in Asya's core threaded through her voice. It was not a threat—it was not even anger. It was that terrible truth again. The Firebird wasn't a creature any mortal could face.

She shoved that thought away. Thinking like that would not help now. This was her chance, her first chance to prove that she could do this. Refusing to let those misgivings creep in, she stepped forward and fell into the melody again. Its smooth notes calmed her nerves, burning away her doubts like kindling. Pushing Vilanovich and her righteous anger from her mind.

Without so much as a glance back at the strashe, Asya let the song draw her on. Distantly, she heard the *shrik* of metal that meant Vilanovich had drawn her saber, but Asya didn't care. Not with this Calling inside her, the ancient rite that had to be fulfilled.

The notes of the song carried her into the welcoming branches of the trees. She could smell the magic now. She didn't know if that was because of the Firebird, or just because the scent was strong enough here. Not burning—not as overpowering even as it had been at the cottage those few long days ago.

But still unmistakable: overturned earth mingled with a sharp tang of metal.

She took another step, the trees momentarily parting above

her head, when the song died. Like the string of a viila snapping midnote, leaving only a pitiful echo of its beauty behind.

Asya staggered, clutching at her chest. The sounds of the forest crashed into her, suddenly too loud and too harsh. The rustle of the wind, their feet scraping over fallen leaves and twigs. The distant cry of a starbird.

She steadied herself against a tree, staring around. "What happened?" she muttered, ash choking her voice.

Vilanovich caught up behind her, the curved blade of her saber still raised, her expression wary. "What are you doing, Firebird?"

Asya ignored her. She had to find that song again, had to reach for the Calling—for that place where everything was right. But even as the Firebird seared through her, sparks dancing around her fingers, she couldn't find it.

It was just… Gone.

She squinted out through the tangled branches. She could still smell that hint of magic; perhaps she just had to follow that for the last part.

"Firebird," Vilanovich said again, a warning in her voice even as fear flashed in her eyes.

Asya didn't reply, holding on to this last strand as she picked her way forward through the mess of tree roots. The scent of magic grew, swirling around her thick as falling snow. The trees parted again, allowing the waning light to spill through.

It illuminated a woman in a flowing pale blue dress, leaning against the thick trunk of an ash tree. Not leaning, Asya realized, bile rising in her throat, but *propped*.

"Diye," Vilanovich murmured, her sword arm momentarily lowering as her attention diverted from Asya.

The markings of a ritual lay scattered around the woman, spilled and broken. Crimson painted the earth, staining it a dark, poisonous color. The sigils were haphazard, as if the caster had drawn them hastily. Desperately. Asya recognized some of them, but she couldn't work out what spell it might have been.

The dark lines of the stratsviye stood stark on the woman's wrist. The mark that magic left, calling to the Firebird. There was no doubt. This was the caster, the person who owed a debt.

But the Firebird did not rear up. It didn't leap out of Asya, intent on ensuring the price was paid. It just fluttered its wings, content within her skin.

She moved toward the figure, waiting for the flames to spring forth, for the Firebird to rise out of her just as she had seen it do with Tarya. But still, nothing happened.

Vilanovich shadowed Asya's steps, her gaze darting to the woman. The strashe froze. "That's Conze Vittaria's crest."

Asya took another step forward, even though she already knew. There was too much blood, the body at too awkward an angle. And she could feel it. In the hollow emptiness where the Firebird's song should have been, in the soft pulse of its flames. It was undeniable.

The woman was already dead.

Chapter Fifteen

"How did this happen?"

Izaveta paced, her footfalls ringing out against the cold marble. She hated to let her emotions seep out like this, but she needed an outlet before they suffocated her. Her plans had been falling into place, and now this. Now Conze Vittaria was dead and her sister had found the body.

All the pieces were tumbling away from her, the board tilting out of her grasp. Out of her control.

Strashevsta Orlov stood to attention in front of her, no hint of smugness on his face tonight, with his cohort of strashe spread out behind him. Zvezda stood in the corner, watching everything with her gleaming eyes and impassive face.

And Asya waited silently by the window, staring out at the Depthless Lake. In the stark light of the moons she looked ethereal, glowing with the magic that was draining from the land, eyes shadowed and inhuman.

Izaveta forced herself to stop pacing, pressing her palms into the silver birch of the heavy desk. She did not want to think about that. About what her sister had become—and what role she might have played in all of this.

"Well?" Izaveta prompted, ice sharpening her words. "How did this happen?"

Strashevsta Orlov glanced around, as though hoping someone else might answer for him. When no one did, he said, "We're still not sure, my lady."

She straightened, fixing him with a glare. It was so much easier to focus her frustration—her anger—on him. So much easier than looking at Asya or thinking about what this death meant. "Well, what do you know? As strashevsta, I imagine you must know *something*."

Orlov swallowed, a muscle in his jaw twitching. It was fascinating how his pompous self-satisfaction melted away when he had truly made a mistake. It proved how much of it was a fragile facade. "The strashe sent to meet Conze Vittaria followed the wrong route. We believe the conze changed her carriage path at the last moment, diverting it from its usual course. We don't know what happened between then and her death. We found her carriage upon further search of the woods. Both her personal guard and the driver were killed."

Zvezda shifted, her voice soft as the low notes of a flute. "The pakviye sent to ensure her passage has also not been found."

Izaveta nostrils flared. That was all they had. A changed route, several dead bodies, and a missing spy, with no explanation as to why the conze would have been casting a protection spell or who might have killed her. Or *why*.

Though Izaveta feared she knew the answer to that. It

could be no coincidence that the conze was murdered just after pledging her support to Izaveta.

"And," Izaveta went on, "we have no further information on the perpetrator." It was not a question, more a statement of the strashevsta's shortcomings. That was a method Izaveta had learned from her mother—forcing someone to restate their faults. Twisting the knife when they knew they had failed.

The strashevsta nodded. From the muscle twitching in his jaw, he would have liked to argue back. But Izaveta was carefully keeping her anger cordial, and he could not be the one to break decorum first. "That is correct."

Izaveta took a deep breath, trying to calm her jumbled thoughts enough to work through this. To find some strategy or solution in this mess.

But no matter how she looked at it, she couldn't deny that a well-respected and powerful conze had been murdered in sight of the palace.

Much as Izaveta wanted to admonish Orlov, she knew she was the one who would shoulder the blame in court. She would be the queen who had failed one of her own cabinet members—before she was even crowned.

"We do also know," Orlov added, as if eager to find a different target for Izaveta's disapproval, "that the Firebird was there, though we have no knowledge of her intentions."

The focus of the room shifted, eyes flicking to Asya's silhouette against the window, forcing Izaveta to look too. To examine her sister the way she would any powerful opponent. Asya hadn't said a word since returning from the forest, blood staining her hands. She had merely stood in silence as the strashe flitted around, the one point of stillness in this turbulent storm.

Izaveta couldn't decide if it was an act, if Asya was being purposefully evasive, or something else.

Orlov pressed on. "The Firebird claims she did not exact a price—"

"I didn't," Asya said, speaking for the first time. She stepped away from the window, and the image of the powerful Firebird fractured, the cracks wide enough to show Izaveta the sister she remembered beneath.

Izaveta looked away, biting the inside of her cheek. She hated how Asya could do that, could switch between Firebird and sister as quickly as she blinked, wrong-footing Izaveta every time.

"Or so she claims," Orlov said, with a knowing smile in Izaveta's direction. She did not return it. If the fool thought it was that simple to get into her good graces, he was sorely mistaken.

But Izaveta did share his misgiving. Even without obvious signs on the conze's body, could she really be sure that Asya had not played a part in the woman's death? That thought left an acrid burning in its wake, as if by considering it she was betraying her sister.

The sister you knew is gone, she reminded herself, gouging those words into her mind as though she could force herself not to lose sight of them.

"It's true," one of the strashe interjected in a low voice. "I mean—I think she would have. But she didn't."

Izaveta fixed her eyes on the girl, examining. Vilanovich, the one who'd been assigned to watch over Asya. The strashe's hair was falling out of its plait, slipping down to her shoulders, and tiredness lined her features. But her mouth was set, determined.

She seemed honest. Before all this, Izaveta would have trusted her own instinct on that. Trusted that her sister wouldn't lie, and neither would one of Izaveta's own strashe. But it was clear someone was working against her—against the Crown. And if she fell into the complacency of trusting, it would only make it worse.

But why would they lie? The price was an ancient Calling, one that not even Izaveta could overturn. If it had truly been about the price of magic, why would Asya hide it?

Izaveta rolled her shoulders, fixing Orlov with a condescending glare. "The Firebird is not the one I'm questioning."

Orlov stiffened. "You'll forgive me, my lady, if I do not allow personal connections to mar my judgment."

Izaveta narrowed her eyes at him, her tongue moving ahead of her mind. Frustration getting the better of her. "Then what is your excuse for your lapses in judgment?"

Orlov stepped forward, anger finally cracking through his words, unguarded. "I am not the one unable to find a traitor in her own court."

"My lady."

Izaveta whirled, drawn by the unfamiliar voice. A man stood in the doorway, flanked by an anxious attendant. He wore dark green robes, stark against his milk-white skin, and his black hair fell to his shoulders in the traditional Versch style. Everything about him was polished edges and a glittering facade.

He stepped into the room, too-shrewd eyes flicking over

the scene. "My name is Ambassador Täusch. I was told you wanted to see me at once."

Svedye.

The feeling drained from Izaveta's limbs, a damning cold that froze her in place. How much had the ambassador heard? He couldn't have missed Orlov's last words—her own captain of the guard speaking against her. Accusing her of turmoil within her own court.

Izaveta swallowed, counting three heartbeats to get herself back under control.

She smiled, the movement requiring more effort than it usually would. "Ambassador, we were not expecting you to arrive so soon."

He bowed his head, thin lips matching her hollow smile. "Kaizer Leonhar was deeply saddened to hear of Queen Adilena's death, and so insisted I leave at once." The ambassador's eyes were oddly colorless, and there was a glint that said he had gleaned precisely what was happening here. "But I do hope I am not interrupting."

"Certainly not," Izaveta replied, trying to keep her voice light despite the tension fracturing through the air.

Those eyes skimmed over to Asya, recognition flashing in them.

"And the Firebird herself," the ambassador said. "It is an honor."

Izaveta didn't like his expression—didn't like the way he looked at her sister as if she were a glittering jewel. One he was eager to possess.

Asya straightened, glancing back at Izaveta as if unsure how to respond.

Again she felt that tug, the old habit that would not die. The need to go to her sister. To find some way to protect her. Except now Izaveta wasn't sure if she was truly worried about Asya or about the Firebird. If she wanted to protect her sister or keep a powerful player from Versbühl's grasp.

Izaveta swallowed that bitter thought, though she could not scrub the taste from her mouth or dispel the fluttering guilt it left inside her.

Izaveta swiftly stepped in before Asya could reply, placing herself and the Firebird clearly on the same side. "My sister and I are happy to welcome you to Tóurin."

"It is certainly a beautiful country," Täusch replied. "With such a rich history. It's really been too long since I last visited."

His words were simple, the expected formalities, but there was something threaded through them, a threat Izaveta couldn't quite decipher.

Well, two of them could play at that. She softened her smile, the picture of the gracious ruler. "I look forward to showing you more of this country over the coming days. I'm sure you will find it quite remarkable." She gestured to one of the nearby strashe before Täusch could respond. "Please show the ambassador to his chambers."

The ambassador's gaze stayed on her as he turned to follow the strashe, a knowing gleam in its depths that set Izaveta's already frayed nerves on edge. She hadn't planned on the ambassador making the journey from the Versch capital so quickly. She'd wanted him to arrive once her control of the cabinet was secure, not as her allies crumbled around her.

The ambassador left a heavy silence in his wake. Izaveta felt all the eyes in the room on her, sharp as needles.

She glared at Orlov, abandoning all pretense at cordiality. If he wouldn't respect her position, she would have to force him to respect her power. "Strashevsta, I expect you and your strashe to find the culprit. Do not return to me until you have more than just excuses." The dismissal was clear in her tone, and he was sensible enough to heed it.

Izaveta folded her hands behind her back as the strashe filed out, twisting her fingers tight together where the tension couldn't be seen. Her mind couldn't settle on a solution, couldn't move away from the mistakes she'd made and into a cool detachment.

Her mother wouldn't have let this happen. Izaveta could hear the whispers already—not just from within her own court, but slipping back to Versbühl too. That she was weak. Unprepared. Too emotional.

Each word dug into her, another weapon for her opponents' arsenals.

The last strashe slipped through the door, and Asya went to follow.

"Stay."

Izaveta's voice sounded so small. As much as she tried to project the image of the commanding queen, it splintered away in front of her sister.

Asya paused. The moonlight filtering through the window limned her hair, soft silver threading through the red. Silence unspooled between them, laden with so many things unsaid. Izaveta wasn't even sure what she *wanted* to say.

Why had she asked Asya to stay? All that did was confuse everything even more. Tangle up the games with her emotions. Just what Izaveta was never supposed to do. That was her mother's first rule, the one she'd told Izaveta the night she hadn't quite managed to hide her tears. *No one can hurt you if you guard your emotions, if you keep them separate from the game.*

"Do you remember how we used to watch the sunset?"

Izaveta started, her sister's voice loud in the echoing quiet. Hesitantly—her mother's words pulling her back—Izaveta joined Asya at the window. The night had spilled ink black across the sky, swallowing the landscape. "We had that old book on soothsayers," Izaveta murmured. "We'd try to guess our fortunes based on which birds we saw."

A slight smile tugged at Asya's lips. "I'm pretty sure I pretended to see starbirds every time."

Izaveta gripped the windowsill. She didn't know how to do this anymore. How to have a conversation with someone without searching for double meanings, for the blade their words concealed. She felt her sister's eyes on her, but resolutely stared out at the faint glow of moonlight. The dark spread of the forest was much easier to watch than Asya.

Asya shifted, leaning against the glass. "You're good at this."

Izaveta shot her a sidelong glance, suspicion instinctively rearing its head. "At what?"

Asya waved a hand to the room. "Being queen. Dealing with all these people."

Izaveta bit back a hollow laugh. Everything she could do was hard-won, clawed for after years of being the one on the losing side. Perhaps she was good at this now, after all that time shaping herself in her mother's image.

But not good enough.

"I wrote letters, you know." Asya looked up at her, brown

eyes shining. "I didn't know if you'd ever get them. But I was lonely in the Roost. It was nice pretending to talk to you."

A lump rose in Izaveta's throat, jagged as broken glass. She knew that feeling. The constant ache of having her twin torn away. She'd just let herself believe that Asya was fine. That she would be too busy enjoying the luxury of freedom to care that Izaveta wasn't there.

Her mother's voice echoed through the years, so close she almost flinched. *This is not an offer of friendship. It's a move in the great game.*

A part of her had always hoped her mother was wrong, had held on to that tenuous belief in her sister. But that didn't change what Izaveta had done. It didn't change that it was too late. "I did get them."

Asya drew in a sharp breath. "Oh."

Words clawed up Izaveta's throat. She should just tell Asya she was sorry. That she got too caught up in their mother's games and made a mistake.

But she couldn't quite bring herself to. Not with the conze dead and Sanislav circling and Kyriil back in court. Each one a biting reminder of the price of trusting the wrong person.

Izaveta turned away, adjusting her gloves. "It's late. You should really get back to your chambers. And I must prepare for tomorrow."

Asya frowned. "What's happening tomorrow?"

Izaveta raised her eyebrows. Even though she was back in the contorted web of the court, Asya was keeping herself separate from its goings-on. And Izaveta still couldn't decide what that meant.

"The Hunte Rastyshenik," Izaveta replied. She fixed Asya

with a sardonic smile—forcing herself not to show any hint of weakness. Of uncertainty. "Did Tarya teach you nothing of the ways of the court?"

Asya shifted, looking down at the floor. "I didn't realize that was tomorrow. I remember Mother talking about it." She glanced up at Izaveta. "It always seemed cruel."

Izaveta waved a hand. "It's tradition."

Asya lifted a shoulder. "Just because it's been done before doesn't make it less cruel."

Izaveta stared at her sister. The sister who had been chosen to exact prices in blood, but cringed at the idea of a hunt. Asya, who had all that power at her fingertips, but didn't want it. A hard edge of bitterness cut through Izaveta, a buried resentment that wouldn't quite die.

She straightened her shoulders. "Then I suppose it's a good thing you were not chosen to be queen."

She didn't wait for Asya to reply. She needed to get her sister out of her head. And the farther she was from her, the better.

Chapter Sixteen

Asya's veins were humming. Her blood fizzling as the flames gnawing at her pushed it to boiling.

She couldn't stop seeing the woman's body. The hollow set to her eyes, the way the colors had all drained to make the scarlet of her blood shine bright. Izaveta's voice in her ears, cold and detached.

It was too much. Too burning, too overwhelming, this strange place where she couldn't tell friend from foe.

Movement helped a little, stalking the corridors like a restless bear. But even as Asya fought to keep herself in control, she could feel the Firebird's flames threatening to consume her. This was the longest she'd gone without the firestone.

It was like holding her breath underwater. No matter how much her mind wanted to fight it, wanted to stay submerged, her body screamed out for air.

And if it wasn't the dead woman's face looming up in front of her, then it was Izaveta's. The clear contempt there, the distrust. Though Asya could hardly blame her.

She had abandoned her sister in the throne room, allowed the flames to overpower her.

And she would have hurt the conze—perhaps killed her, depending on what the price was.

That is not the same as murder. But without the soothing notes of the Firebird's song, she no longer held that clarity.

Though there was still the other Calling. The first one that burned bright as a sun, too scalding to touch, even after allowing the Firebird to stretch free all these hours.

Asya hadn't managed to set the balance right with the conze, and she still couldn't face this other Calling. No matter how hard she tried, no matter the moments of understanding she found, she was still failing her purpose.

It didn't help that everywhere she turned in the claustrophobic confines of the palace there were more people. Servants and attendants, courtiers and dignitaries, all watching her with a nervous awe—or careful calculation. She wasn't sure if she was imagining it or not, but it seemed like the stares had grown heavier in the wake of the afternoon's events. As if these people also thought Asya might have murdered the conze.

She passed another group of courtiers and a whisper reached her ears, too loud to have been unintentional: "I heard she tore out her heart and devoured it while it was still beating."

Asya forced herself to breathe, to not let those words worm their way in. She remembered what Tarya had said in the forest. *To them, you will never be more than a monster that lurks in the night.*

There had been little comfort in that truth then, and there was even less now.

Almost without conscious thought, her feet turned back toward her chamber. She wanted the firestone. A respite from this thing inside her. From the heat devouring her and the smoke and memories muddling her mind.

Perhaps when she had that—when her mind was clear—she could go speak to Tarya. See if her aunt could help her navigate this strange landscape that stretched beyond the Firebird's obligations and into the labyrinth of the court.

Asya pushed through the door to her chambers, her eyes stinging. Everything felt too hot, all the details of the room in razor-sharp focus.

Hurrying for the dresser, she wrenched open the drawer and grasped for the small iron box. She flipped up the lid, and her stomach dropped, as if she had stepped out of one of the arched palace windows. Blood rushed in her ears, adrenaline warring with the flames inside her.

The box was empty.

CHAPTER SEVENTEEN

It couldn't be gone.

Asya tossed the box aside, scrambling through the drawer. She whirled, staring around the room as if the firestone might suddenly present itself. But there was nowhere else it would be. Deep down she knew that, even as she desperately searched every crevice. She remembered leaving the pulsing stone in its nest of silk and closing the drawer tight.

And she knew there was only one reason the stone would not be there: someone had taken it.

Fear clamored up her throat, smothering the flames. She had to tell Tarya. Surely her aunt would know what to do. But something held Asya back, a small inkling in the corner of her mind. Tarya would be furious—or, at least, detachedly disappointed—when she found out Asya had lost something this valuable. This *dangerous*. Especially after Asya had failed in her duty that afternoon. She wasn't eager to tell her aunt she'd managed to fail again.

But there was also a part of her that wondered if Tarya

might have been the one to take it. It was the kind of thing she might do, forcing Asya to have no option but to accept her power.

Asya sank to her knees, crouching in the middle of the too-big space. She could almost feel the Firebird smiling inside her, a crooning satisfaction as it clutched on to its freedom. She squeezed her eyes shut, digging her fingers into her scalp.

She just wanted to be away from this. From this court, from this world with its rules that she didn't understand. From who her sister had become.

And she wanted a little time without this monster clawing at her insides—contorting her, re-forming her to its will. She needed air. *Real* air, not the stifling air of the palace.

She bit the inside of her mouth, tasting blood as she tried to push down the Firebird. She needed to be outside, where she could feel at least partly herself. Where the earth and the trees could stretch around her, in the comfort of Dveda's domain.

She pushed back out the door, almost careening into Vilanovich. Asya took a gulping breath, trying to form coherent words.

The strashe frowned. "Where are you going?"

"Outside," Asya said, already moving past her. "And don't follow me this time." She didn't need Vilanovich's hostile presence plaguing her too. Especially not after that afternoon.

The unwanted companion inside Asya was more than enough for one night.

But Vilanovich persisted. "I'm not supposed to let you out of my sight."

Asya drew to a halt, spinning to face the strashe. With the

fire coursing through her, her emotions swirled tighter and tighter with each breath. She clenched her fists.

"Well then, I order you to remain here." There was an imperious note to Asya's voice. It almost made her sound like her sister—or this new version of her sister. The comparison sent a twisting discomfort through Asya's stomach.

But the Firebird was banging against the inside of her skull. Not content with burning her, its flames wanted to leap free. To burst through her skin.

Vilanovich wavered. Probably torn between her orders and her desire to be as far from the Firebird as possible. "My commands do not come from you," she said finally, voice still firm.

Sparks danced in Asya's vision. She saw them reflected in Vilanovich's storm-gray eyes like flickers of lightning. Asya didn't care. The guard already saw her as no more than the monster that lived inside her, so what did it matter if she acted like it?

"No need for you to worry," Asya bit out, an almost wild edge to her voice. "I've hunted enough for one day. There'll be no one out there for you to *protect*."

She turned on her heel and marched down the passage.

This time, no other footsteps followed.

Asya was relieved to find that she still remembered the way to the back staircase that led to a less-used door to the grounds. Stepping out into the cool night air, she felt a little more herself. More human than flame. Perhaps more able to sort through all that had happened.

The sky was clouded, muting the landscape to a cascade of grays. It hid the moons as if the gods had drawn their curtains, disinterested in the evening's proceedings. The palace loomed up behind her, its three turrets stretching toward the sky. As desperate to escape as Asya.

Several paths spiraled out in front of her, each paved with glistening marble that glinted like liquid moonlight. Whoever had designed them had probably wanted to give the impression of power, of magic spilling from every orifice.

Asya chose one at random. She needed to move, to use up the Firebird's burning energy. Neat hedges lined the walkway, enclosing her in the comforting scent of mountain laurel. A biting breeze rustled through them—a reminder that winter would soon close in. The sound calmed Asya. It was almost like being back in the forest, back where things made sense and people meant what they said. Where her sister was still a happy memory.

The well-tended hedges opened out into a series of courtyards filled with trickling fountains. There was something familiar about them, though Asya couldn't quite put her finger on what it was. Perhaps it was one of the places she and Izaveta had explored as children. They'd done a lot of that, in the hours when their nursemaid-cum-governess had not had her watchful eye on them.

Two different girls in a different life.

Asya shook her head, dislodging the memories. The Firebird ruffled its flaming feathers in satisfaction. That was just what the creature wanted: to burn away any connections Asya had to the mortal world.

Not that there were many left for it to destroy.

Asya forced her feet to keep moving, as if she could outrun

those thoughts. She ducked through to the next courtyard, and a long shadow fell over her. She whirled, heart skittering.

But it was just a statue. Saint Restov, knife plunged into his chest, stone threaded through with sparkling marble to reflect the moonlight in his veins. Asya's eyes trailed along the glittering strands. She wondered if moonlight burned like the fire in her own blood. She doubted it. Though even being moon-touched had been enough for some people to condemn Saint Restov as a demonya.

She turned and realized this was not the only statue. All nine saints stood around her in a protective circle, gazes upturned to the sky. There was something familiar about their formation, a long-lost memory she couldn't quite catch hold of. To her left, Saint Korona stood with her tearstained face and crown of branches. Then, Saint Lyoza with her clawed fingers and serene expression. And, a little farther along, the point of Saint Meshnik's sword.

Asya's breath caught. The flames inside her sparked. *That* was why this place felt familiar.

She hadn't seen it in a memory, she'd seen it in her vision. Had the Firebird led her here without Asya realizing it?

She crossed the courtyard, the Firebird's excitement thrumming with her own. The angle was nearly the same. If she closed her eyes, she could hear the distant chanting. She tried to grasp the Calling, to catch hold of its melody as she had that afternoon. But as soon as she reached out, it flared too bright, swallowing the faint words.

She opened her eyes, scanning the damp grass. If she couldn't hone the power yet, she would find another way to ensure the price was paid. She couldn't let this caster walk free, not when they might have played a role in her mother's death, and undoubtedly the conze's as well.

Someone—*something*—was stalking the palace. Asya couldn't let them strike again.

It had been at least two nights since the spell was cast, but she still clung to the hope that there might be some remnant of it. The scent of magic was long gone, washed away by morning dew and cleansing wind. But there had to be something.

Her hands scrambled through the grass, digging into the earth and singeing where they touched. Then her fingers caught on something smooth. Too smooth to be a stone, and hot as the flames inside her. A small white shard, broken off in a jagged line, nestled amongst the green, as if Dveda had kept it safe for her, waiting for just this moment.

Asya turned it over in her hand, holding it up to the muted moonlight. It was the pale white of fresh fallen snow, smoothed like a river stone. She couldn't be sure if it was just the flames pulsating under her skin, but she thought the shard hummed with its own power. She rubbed a finger over it, considering.

Something about this too was familiar.

When they were nine, Izaveta had found a book of spells. The two of them had been searching everywhere for a way to avoid being separated. Asya had been too young to really understand what the ceremony meant, the weight and importance of the responsibility. All she knew was that it would mean losing her sister. Either she would have to leave or Izaveta would.

Back then, that possibility had seemed worse than anything else.

Izaveta had managed to sneak the book out into the grounds, and they tried to perform a ritual to change their fates. They formed a makeshift ceremonial circle, laying out the ingredients as the book said, sanctifying the ground and vessels. But they had barely started chanting when the strashe found them. They dragged her and Izaveta away from the circle, destroying all their carefully drawn sigils and arranged ingredients.

It was the only time Asya had seen her mother angry. Not just regal, controlled disapproval, but truly angry.

Asya had always felt small in front of her mother, but that night she'd felt like a cornered animal.

"*What* were the two of you thinking?"

"We didn't want to be separated," Izaveta said, chin raised in defiance. Izaveta was never one to cower. She stood by whatever she believed no matter what, unlike Asya, who shrank from her mother. Who was still scared of fulfilling her own duty.

Asya blinked, and the memory vanished. Flames burned behind her eyes like unshed tears. It was strange to think that, once, staying with her sister was all she'd cared about. It sent a curling sadness through Asya's gut. Another thing she had lost.

She took a shuddering breath. None of that mattered now. Not the mother she hadn't known. Not who her sister had been.

Tarya would tell her the Firebird didn't have the luxury of grief or sadness. The Firebird had no mortal connections to mourn. All Asya could do now was ensure justice was done and the price was paid.

She tightened her fingers around the shard. It was smaller

than the one she and Izaveta had used in their failed ritual, but Asya was sure it was the same thing.

The bone of a saint.

A sound—jarringly out of place in the soft melody of the night—made Asya freeze. Her fist snapped shut around the bone. Turning slowly, she scanned the mingled greens of the hedges.

For one frantic heartbeat she didn't see anything.

Then a shadow slipped from behind Saint Restov's statue, a little to her right. It coalesced into a figure clad in black. Two more melted from the darkness.

Asya shifted her weight back. Her hand jumped to her waist—when she realized she'd left her shashka in her chambers. She glanced between the three figures, silent and prowling. "I don't suppose you're out here enjoying the gardens?" she asked weakly.

In response, the leading figure drew a gleaming blade.

"That would be a no then." Her eyes flicked around the clearing. There had to be something here she could use as a weapon.

But she couldn't focus through the flames gnawing at her insides. Her mind was still struggling to catch up to what was happening. Today had been as overwhelming as the first moment the Firebird had awakened. She was trapped in the claustrophobic walls of the palace where no one said what they meant. She hardly recognized her own twin. She had failed in her duty again, and a woman had died. Not to mention her firestone was gone.

Now, after all of that, three people were prowling toward her.

And all Asya had was a shard of bone and this creature inside her.

"I'm the Firebird," she said, trying to project the strength of that statement. Even if she felt nothing like that powerful creature. She grasped for that certainty she had felt earlier, the fearlessness even when Vilanovich had drawn her weapon.

But it was gone, as distant and untouchable as her Calling.

The lead figure stepped forward, uncaring. "A young Firebird who is afraid of her own power."

The truth of that dug into Asya's burning insides like a blade.

Before she could form anything resembling a plan, the figures attacked.

Chapter Eighteen

Asya ducked instinctively, the arc of the first blade sweeping over her head. She landed in the crouched stance Tarya had drilled into her. Another blade flashed toward her, and she threw herself to one side. She hit the ground hard, the air rushing from her lungs.

She rolled, aiming for the cover of Saint Korona's vine-tangled cloak. But another sword clanged against the stone in front of her, forcing her back again. She scrambled to her feet, jabbing out with her elbow. It caught the attacker on the side—not where she'd been aiming—and sent him stumbling back.

She dragged in a breath. The other two attackers surged forward, not allowing her any respite. One sword swung at her left. She ducked only to nearly send herself into another blade. The attackers moved in a blur of flickering silver and swirling ink. Too fast for Asya's already jagged thoughts.

She had never fought anyone like this. These were not desperate people lashing out. These were well-trained fighters. That realization shuddered through her, leaving cold panic in its wake. Even with Tarya's years of training—the endless days of practicing in the clearing—Asya couldn't keep up. Especially not when she already felt pulled taut and ready to fracture.

"I am the Firebird," she said again, her voice as frayed as her insides. "You can't hope to kill me."

But the attackers did not relent. Asya sidestepped, kicking out. Her foot hit only air. A fist careened into her. The momentum sent her staggering into a statue. Her head cracked against the stone, her vision distorting into a quivering whirl.

Pain sliced through her side as a blade scraped across her rib cage. Crimson flashed in her vision, bright as blood. She clutched at it, steadying herself on the statue.

"Perhaps we don't want to kill you, Firebird." The lead figure advanced slowly, leveling his dagger at Asya. "Not yet."

Asya's head reeled, distorting his words like ripples on the lake. They didn't make sense. None of this made sense.

The clouds parted above them. A glimmer of moonlight broke through, as though the gods had suddenly regained interest. The light glinted off the dagger's hilt, illuminating a symbol etched into the gold. A curling flame overlaid with three horizontal lines.

Asya ground her teeth together. Her grip was slipping, the edges of her vision swallowed by battling shadows and flames. "Then what do you want?" she bit out, putting as much force behind the words as she could muster.

The glint of teeth was only just visible beneath his dark hood. "You."

Then the figure lunged forward. He pushed her back against Meshnik's immovable shield, the point of his blade digging into her throat.

He jerked his head to his companions, and they advanced. One pulled out a length of chain while the other raised a sword, moving with caution as though approaching a dangerous creature.

Little did they know how far Asya felt from that. She tried to push back on the hands pressing against her, but her movements were too slow. *Weak*.

Without the Calling to center her, her old fears had crept back in. And keeping the Firebird in check was draining the last dregs of her energy.

But why was she bothering to hold it back?

Because you're terrified of letting it consume you. The answer ricocheted through her. Even with a dagger to her throat, she was still most scared of the thing that lurked inside her.

Izaveta wouldn't be afraid. Wouldn't shrink away from her responsibility. But Asya was failing before she'd even started, all because she was too scared.

No. Asya wasn't going to die here tonight, at the hands of attackers who could not even show their faces. The Firebird was not going to die.

All Asya had to do was let go.

She glanced up at Saint Meshnik's carved face, their unwavering determination. She sent them a prayer—brief and desperate. *May I draw from your strength of will.*

The other two attackers closed in on her, chains clinking in the still air. The dagger dug into her throat as she breathed out and let go.

Flames burst from her fingertips. A new energy seared through her. It flushed away her doubts. It remade her into something new, something without fear. Without emotion. She raised one burning hand to the blade at her throat. The heat tore through the metal, shining like molten sunlight. The attacker swore and dropped it with a distant shriek of steel on stone.

Asya closed her fists and more flames splayed from them, stretching like elongated fingers. They leaped for the closest figure, coiling around him. The attacker fell to his knees with a gurgling moan.

She turned to face the other two. The scorching tendrils surged forward, knocking one to the ground and sending the other scurrying backward. The fire clawed up Asya's throat, through her veins, eager to devour.

She whirled to face the fallen figure. She felt the moment the Firebird broke through her skin, flames pushing through bone and flesh to finally run loose. In the edge of her vision, its head loomed up above her. The image of Tarya in that cottage rose in Asya's mind, the Firebird's cruel features mirroring her own.

What did Asya look like to these people now?

This was her first true taste of her power. It filled the air with an almost exhilarating energy. Because justice had to be done. This man had tried to kill her—had tried to kill the Firebird—and for that he would pay.

Bright whirls of flame danced forward. Luminous gold twisting together with bleeding scarlet. They reached toward the crumpled figure and—

With a trembling gasp that shuddered down to Asya's bones, she called the fire back. It protested, dragged back inside and leaving smoldering pain in its wake.

Killing him would not have been justice.

The man stared up at her. Fear had swallowed his glinting

grin. Now he just looked fragile. Helpless. Soot and sweat and blood mingling on his face.

Asya's eyes were streaming, her head pounding from the blow and the still-blistering anger of the Firebird. When she didn't move, the man scrambled to his feet. He staggered away after his already scattered companions.

Distantly, she knew she should not let them go. They should have been taken in to the strashe and questioned. But what else could she do? She had no energy left to give chase, and she could hardly detain all three of them herself.

You could have killed them. The words floated into her mind, unwelcome. She shoved them away. Even if everyone thought she was a monster, she refused to become one.

Forcing herself upright, she swayed as the ground tilted beneath her. A jagged burst of pain cleaved through her side. She put a hand to it, her fingers coming away sticky with blood.

The Firebird would ensure she healed more quickly than a mortal. She'd seen Tarya recover from wounds in hours that would have taken Asya weeks to heal. But she didn't know the extent of that power. And she was pretty sure that if she bled out before it had time to mend, she would still die, Firebird or not.

She was about to turn back toward the palace when she remembered the shard of bone. It had been clutched tight in her fist, but she must have dropped it in the fight. Whirling around, she scanned the ground for a flicker of white.

But it was nowhere to be seen.

PART THREE:

WHEN THE FALCONS GATHER

When we watch the skies, we glimpse the realm of
Zmenya and the futures held there. A dove against a pale
morning foretells tranquility. A shimmer of starbirds portends a
new power on the horizon. A great murmuration of
sparrows tells of clashing storms ahead. And a single falcon's
dark wing warns of downfall and calamity.

—Extract from
THE HISTORY OF SOOTHSAYING
by Parakov Evanova

CHAPTER NINETEEN

Her only lead on who had killed her mother was gone. Asya stared into the deepening shadows, the darkness the three attackers had vanished into. Surely she would have seen one of them take the bone. But in the commotion and whirling blades, she couldn't be as certain as she would like.

She wanted to stay and search longer. To scour the ground and dig through the dirt until she found the only thing that would help her complete her duty. But her head was still whirling. The muted colors of the night blurred around her. She steadied herself against Meshnik's plinth. She needed to get out of the open. Bleeding and exhausted, she was too exposed here.

As she made her slow progress back to the oppressive weight of the palace—digging the fabric of her shirt into the cut to staunch the blood—one thought nagged at the edge of her mind. A thorn snagging on the hem of her cloak that she could not quite shake loose. Why had the first attacker not tried to kill her?

His response echoed in her head like distant thunder. *Perhaps we don't want to kill you, Firebird.*

Not yet.

The words sent a chilling whisper of dread up her spine that followed her into the tight passages of the palace. Because if they didn't want to kill her, then what did they want? And why would they risk attacking the Firebird?

Because they know you are unprepared. Weak. That voice—the burning shame that came with it—echoed through Asya.

But how could the attackers have known that?

Asya thought back to the shard of bone, to the searing Calling of that dark magic. The attackers' certainty. The dead conze. The missing firestone. Someone in this palace was working against her, someone who knew enough to be sure that she would be vulnerable.

Blood trickled between her fingers where she clutched her side, oddly cool against the fire burning beneath her skin. She wasn't sure if it was blood loss or the draining adrenaline of the fight, but her thoughts were dancing away from her like smoke.

She hesitated before rounding the corner to her chambers, steadying herself against the wall. She didn't want Vilanovich to know what had happened. Asya didn't want this getting back to Izaveta. Not yet. Not until she understood what in all the gods' names was happening.

Asya took a choking breath. She rolled her shoulders, crossing her arms to cover the bleeding wound, and turned down the passageway.

Vilanovich stood sentinel exactly where Asya had left her,

her mouth set in a hard line. Her gray eyes snapped to Asya as soon as she stepped into view.

"Firebird," the strashe said—Asya supposed that passed for a greeting in Vilanovich's book.

Asya nodded to her, swallowing down the flames that still clawed at her throat. Was she imagining the odd look on the guard's face? The one that suggested she knew what had just happened?

She pushed that thought away. The events of the day had put her on edge, not helped by the Firebird tearing her nerves ragged. She needed to rest. To bandage her wound and let the Firebird heal it. This would all make more sense after that.

Asya made to move past the strashe into her chamber, but the guard held out a hand to stop her.

"Did something—" Vilanovich's gaze fell on the blood staining Asya's shirt, and she backed away, mouth curling in disgust. "What did you do?"

Asya let out a disbelieving laugh. After everything that had happened that evening, it seemed like such a ridiculous question. "What makes you assume *I* did something?"

"Even after the conze, you still—" Vilanovich broke off, horror rising in her eyes. "You said you weren't hunting again."

"I don't owe you an explanation," Asya said, with far less force than she'd intended. She pushed past the strashe into the room, pulling off her jacket and hardly caring if the door had swung closed yet. Vilanovich had already decided what Asya was—nothing would change that now.

Asya spun, searching for something she could use to staunch the too-cold blood still trickling down her side. She threw open the leather pack she'd brought from the Roost, but all it held was a few more spare shirts. She pulled one out and grabbed the shashka from where she'd left it. She began tearing the shirt into strips and almost jumped when she saw the strashe still standing in the doorway.

A flash of understanding crossed Vilanovich's face, fracturing her glower like cracks in ice. "It's your blood?"

"Yes," Asya said shortly, digging the tip of the blade into the shirt. "The Firebird does bleed too, you know." She winced as the words left her mouth. She shouldn't have said that, not after three people had tried to exploit that weakness already tonight. Certainly not after Vilanovich had drawn a weapon on her.

Asya looked away quickly, turning her attention back to tearing the shirt into strips. It was more difficult than she'd expected, leaving her with somewhat misshapen pieces of bandage, but it'd have to do. The only other options were to go to the voye medics or Tarya, neither of which appealed to her greatly. If she went to the voye, the news would surely make its way back to Izaveta. And telling her aunt would mean admitting Asya had made a near-fatal mistake. Again.

Asya twisted, trying to examine the wound. It was deeper than she'd thought, the initial pain dulled by adrenaline and the coursing power of the Firebird. It would heal more quickly than it would for a mortal, but it would still take a few days.

She tried to wind the makeshift bandage around her torso, but the movement sent another jagged stab of pain through her. She let out a low hiss, digging her nails into her skin.

Frustrated tears burned at the backs of her eyes, swallowed by the flames before they could be shed. What kind of Firebird was she? Her first two Callings had been failures. One person had died before the price could be exacted. She couldn't even follow the other without being overwhelmed. All she'd got from trying to find the culprit on her own was a shard of bone—that she'd lost—and a wound from a fight that never should have happened. Those three people should never have thought they could take on the powerful Firebird.

They knew she was weak. Not the formidable figure of Tarya but a young and inexperienced Firebird who could be targeted.

She couldn't even manage to dress her own wound properly.

Asya threw the bandage to the floor. Not the most helpful course of action perhaps, but it did make her feel a little better. She wanted to drop her head in her hands. To curl up and escape this all.

Vilanovich sighed irritably and took a step forward. "Let me."

Asya drew back instinctively, narrowing her eyes. "Why?"

The strashe shrugged. "You're going to get blood all over the floor."

Asya let out a sound somewhere between a disgruntled laugh and a sob. "Oh, yes," she said. "Wouldn't want to ruin the decor, would we?"

For a moment she didn't move. She shouldn't be showing this weakness to a guard. She shouldn't need help—Tarya certainly never had. But Asya was not Tarya. She wasn't ready to do any of this yet, certainly not on her own. Not in this court, with its twisting words and the sister who'd outgrown her.

And besides, she really was going to get blood all over the floor.

She swallowed, not quite meeting the strashe's eyes as she held out the torn shirt. "Thank you."

Vilanovich gave her an odd look, but took the bandage without comment.

I have seen what you do. So you can stand there and pretend to be a saint all you like—pretend to not care about power, to be separate *from that creature, but I know what hides beneath.* Those words stretched between them, drawn sharply into focus by the day's events. By the scrape of metal as the strashe had drawn her saber.

If Vilanovich had thought Asya was a monster then, what did she think of her now? The Firebird's pulse burned beneath Asya's skin with each breath. Every beat a reminder of what was inside her.

But the guard had also spoken out in front of Izaveta. To call it defending Asya would be a stretch, but she'd backed up her story. That was more than could be said for anyone else.

Asya didn't miss Vilanovich's hesitancy as she moved forward or the shifting in the gray of the strashe's eyes that betrayed her distrust. But her fingers were surprisingly gentle, an odd contrast to the hard, unforgiving lines of her face. They were a welcome balm against the blistering fire in Asya's veins.

Vilanovich moved quickly, as if this were something she was used to doing, winding the fabric around Asya's torso in an even spiral. Asya gritted her teeth, trying not to wince as Vilanovich tied off a knot before smoothing the bandage into place.

Asya glanced up at her, anticipating the usually harsh set

of the guard's face—as foreboding as the storm that brewed in her eyes. But for that brief instant, Vilanovich's expression was clear. She wasn't looking at Asya like she was the Firebird, a creature to be feared, but as someone she could almost understand. It sent an odd fluttering through Asya's chest, something far more delicate and vulnerable than the flames that now lived there.

The strashe stepped back abruptly, and the moment shattered. "That should hold for now."

"It'll heal quickly," Asya murmured, sinking down onto the edge of the bed.

Vilanovich's jaw tensed, as if suddenly remembering who Asya was. *What* Asya was. The guard made to stride out, pausing in the doorway to add, "My orders are to be with you wherever you go, Firebird. Remember that next time."

Asya opened her mouth to reply, but the door snapped shut. She let out a long breath, allowing her shoulders to sag under the weight of her exhaustion at last.

She had failed tonight. Because she'd let the human part of her dominate, tried to fight against the power inside her, rather than embrace it. She'd promised herself she would no longer hesitate, and yet she had.

She couldn't allow this caster to run free. They might have killed her mother. They could, even now, be planning to move against Izaveta. The last person Asya had left, no matter how they'd both changed.

That thought solidified inside Asya, more comforting than her doubts. Above all, the Firebird's purpose was protection. Her second Calling had shown her that much, had taught her that in its comforting melody. And Asya would fulfill that

Chapter Twenty

The tradition of Hunte Rastyshenik stemmed from an old folktale that said that if one could take a feather from the Firebird's plumage, the Firebird would grant them a wish. The story had little bearing in truth, likely arising from fear of the creature's power and a desire to control a magic beyond their understanding. It wasn't even possible, given that the Firebird did not have feathers like a mortal bird.

But despite its clear inaccuracy, the tradition persisted. On the day that honored the fallen warrior Saint Meshnik, a swan adorned with an ornamental red feather would be released into the forest, and a hunting party would attempt to chase it down. If the feather was captured before nightfall, it was said to be a great blessing on the future queen's reign.

If not…

Izaveta didn't like to think of that possibility. Which was why, regardless of the biting chill and lingering mist, Izaveta found herself astride her great white bear, Olyeta, waiting at the edge of the forest.

At her back, more bears were assembled, their riders bundled up in warmest furs. She couldn't miss Kyriil, golden hair peeking from beneath his fur hat, astride his chestnut-brown bear. Ignoring the slight tremor the sight sent through her, she forced her expression to remain as cool as the air around her as her eyes flicked past him. The Versch ambassador sat a little behind him, on a dark horse that shifted uneasily amongst the towering bears. Izaveta had offered him a bear from the keep, but the ambassador had insisted his horse was sufficient, even if the animal was not as well suited to the snowy climate and difficult terrain.

It was a statement, undoubtedly. A firm stance that Versbühl needed no aid, that their horses and war-wolves were a certain match for the Tóurensi bears. She could feel his needling eyes sweeping over the proceedings, intent to catch any slip. Any hint of weakness.

But today, Izaveta wouldn't let him see her falter.

Four cabinet members rode in the party as well, and they were as much her targets this morning as the swan.

The hunt was more than just a tradition—it was an opportunity. A political arena.

There were those who chose not to participate in the chase itself but instead waited at the forest's edge to hear the judgment of their future queen. Sanislav had pulled up in a troika drawn by three small black bears and set out to watch. To see if she would succeed. Izaveta could almost hear his silent prayer willing her to fail.

And there was no denying the painful absence. Where Conze Vittaria's presence should have overshadowed the proceedings, her stoic calm soothing frayed nerves, instead her phantom lurked at every corner. The whispered rumors about her death hung in the air heavier than mist.

Some had even called for the hunt to be canceled, especially since it took place in the very forest where the conze had died. But Izaveta couldn't concede to that. The hunt was a tradition so deeply entrenched in the mourning days that calling it off would be far worse than causing a few disgruntled courtiers offense.

If anything, Vittaria's death gave the hunt even greater importance. Izaveta had lost her one certain ally on the cabinet, and she intended to rectify that today.

The swan had been released some time before, and any moment now the horn would sound out the beginning of the chase. Izaveta's heart pummeled against her ribs with every passing moment. She had spent much of the night reading up on the hunts of former queens, examining the likely patterns and paths of the swan.

But no matter how many times she reminded herself she had plans in place, that she could use this to her advantage, she couldn't escape the clawing fear. The forest was not like the court. It would not bend to her whims, and she could not predict its will.

No amount of manipulation would make this certain.

Her eyes swept over the party again, taking its measure. Preparing her strategies. She stiffened as she spotted another unwelcome face in the group—an, as of yet, uncontrolled variable. Nikov Toyevski. He must have arrived later than the rest, almost hidden near the back. He sat atop his bear with the strict posture and practiced ease of a nobleman. Another mark against his facade of scholar.

The harsh note of the horn shattered her thoughts. It jolted through Izaveta's chest, and she nearly sent Olyeta flying forward. But she held the bear back, not wanting to let her desperation bleed through in her movements.

She counted to five, each beat a slow metronome in her mind, before urging Olyeta into the trees. The rest of the party followed as the branches closed over her head like iron bars, each step trapping her farther in the labyrinth of the forest.

Some of the melancholy that hung over the party evaporated as they moved forward, pushed out by the excitement. They headed west first, following the direction of the wind—though several knots of riders split off to pursue the chase alone. Izaveta concentrated on the rhythmic pounding of the bears' paws, pretending each beat was the note of a song. Soft and comforting as her flute, not the brutal timbre of the forest.

But she couldn't lose herself in it for long. She had moves to make before she could even think of the swan.

Commander Iveshkin's black bear made easy work of the forest floor, trained for far worse conditions than these. After all, Iveshkin's reputation as a force to be reckoned with came in part from the long months she spent in the northern reaches of Tóurin, training her soldiers and bears in the harsh winters of the Skyless Hallows.

Izaveta drew level with the commander and her interpreter—pleased to see that Olyeta stood at least half a hand taller than Iveshkin's bear. She would take any advantage she could get.

Iveshkin glanced over, slowing to her pace. That was another trick of her mother's. Always be the one to set the terms, whether it be where one meets or how fast one walks around the gardens.

The commander inclined her head in greeting. "My lady," she signed. Her bear had been well trained to respond to commands from Iveshkin's legs, meaning her hands were free to sign.

Izaveta let her own reins loose, trusting Olyeta not to sway from their path at this slow pace, and replied in the Signed Language. "Commander Iveshkin, I'm so glad you could join us this morning."

"Glad, are you?" The commander let out a low huff of disapproval. "None of us should be traipsing through the forest. A cabinet member is dead. We ought to be making preparations."

Always straight to the point. There was no artistry to the way Iveshkin wielded her power—it made her a rather dull opponent. Izaveta forced a smile. "Tradition cannot be ignored so easily."

Iveshkin's gestures sharpened. "We should be searching for Conze Vittaria's murderer."

Izaveta raised an eyebrow, careful to keep her movements smooth, unbothered. "I assure you, Commander, that is our top priority. But I doubt you would want me personally performing the search, as it is rather outside of my expertise, which is why the pakviye are seeing to it."

Iveshkin's lips thinned, but she couldn't deny the truth in that statement. She tilted her head, reassessing her strategy. "Did you think more on my proposition?"

Izaveta's throat tightened. She didn't want to talk about Asya. Not after she'd returned from the forest yesterday with that haunted look in her eye. Not after she'd reminded Izaveta too painfully of what they used to have. "That is a matter for—"

Iveshkin waved a hand, letting out an irritated grunt. "An extravagant way of saying no. The conze's death could be a sign of the Versch on our very doorstep." She gestured behind them. "Look at the arrival of their ambassador. It cannot be a coincidence. In times like these, we must make use of every resource we have."

Izaveta followed her gaze to where Täusch rode, a little away from the rest of the group. If anything, the ambassador's arrival was proof that the Versch were not yet ready to act, instead sending someone ahead to get her measure. To test how far they could push this new queen. No, far more likely was an enemy within their midst. And uncovering a traitor took a delicate hand, not Iveshkin's blunt sword work.

She was about to turn back to Iveshkin when something caught her eye. It was the smallest shift, so slight Izaveta might've thought she'd imagined it if she weren't so practiced at looking for precisely that. The unspoken things that flitted between secret allies.

Nikov rode to Täusch's left, ensconced in conversation with one of Fyodor's scholars. But when Nikov's gaze snagged on the ambassador, there was a slight flicker across his features. A fractional tilt away.

Tiny on its own, but Izaveta had watched enough people to recognize it. Though that didn't help her to understand it. Because why would a scholar from the Amarinth, one she had been certain was under Sanislav's thumb, have any connection to the ambassador of Versbühl?

For now, she tucked the observation away. A new piece of information to hold in her arsenal.

She forced her concentration back to her current target. She didn't bother with the subtleties of the situation, none of which would persuade the commander. Iveshkin judged things by the number of weapons she could deploy against them.

"I am certain we can find ways to work together," Izaveta signed. "After all, I'm sure you do not want the vibishop's new decree to pass." She felt the change in the commander's attention, interest veering toward her.

"The one he was working on with my mother," Izaveta lied easily, keeping her movements light. "He plans to reroute funds toward the restoration of old church properties. And there aren't many places he could find that much coin…" She let her sentence trail off with a knowing look.

Her claims were not so far from the truth—the Church had been demanding money to restore crumbled buildings for years now. And Sanislav *could* have been working on a decree for all she knew, and if he was, then, in peacetime, the military was the only reasonable place to take the money from.

Iveshkin shot a glance over her shoulder, brow furrowed, as though she could see through the trees to where Sanislav waited. "And you would be more invested in the military?" she asked, with obvious disdain.

Izaveta considered her response for a moment. This was vital in persuading the commander, but pretty words would not be enough. In her peripheral vision, she caught sight of Kyriil. The pale light glinted off the crest on his right lapel. It ignited a memory in her mind, a bearded man with the same green eyes as Kyriil, and that same crest gleaming on a crisp uniform.

She might not like Kyriil's presence here, but that didn't make him any less a piece in her game. One she would not hesitate to use.

Her lips curled into a smile. "I do already have the support of the Azarovs."

Iveshkin lifted her finger to her chin, brows raised in disbelief. "General Azarov has pledged to you?"

Izaveta inclined her head in Kyriil's direction. "Why else would his son be here but to pledge his support?"

She could see the possibilities whirring in Iveshkin's mind, as carefully assessed as one of the commander's military strategies. She gave a curt nod. "Perhaps we may find common ground, after all."

"I am certain we shall," Izaveta replied, turning her bear away to mark the end of their conversation. A small bubble of relief expanded in her chest, loosening the tight fingers of tension wrapped around her heart. It was far from a strong alliance, but it was progress.

If there was one thing she'd learned from her games of zvess with her mother, it was that patience was the key to victory.

"You're winning over Commander Iveshkin, I see."

The voice sent a momentary prickle of apprehension up her spine—an old habit that wouldn't quite die. A reminder of the price of trust. But she was prepared this time, her mask remaining in place as Kyriil's bear fell into pace with Olyeta. "Master Azarov, good morning."

He gave a short bow—more mocking than reverent. "My lady."

She kept her eyes on the dark canopy of leaves, as if searching for a flash of white feathers. That left the impetus of the conversation on him, forcing him to reveal his hand.

He ducked his chin, a display of hesitation. "It's good to see you again. I know things ended...uncomfortably between us."

Izaveta bit back her derisive laugh. *Uncomfortably* was one way of putting it. *Disastrously* was perhaps more accurate.

She remembered all too well the night she'd walked in on the conversation between him and his father. The words echoed still, the sharp edge of the blade blunted by the armor she'd built up. *It takes a subtle hand to tame a princess.*

She schooled her lips into a smile. She was no longer that foolish girl, but he didn't need to know that. Not yet. "Think nothing of it. It's in the past."

He adjusted his grip on the reins, looking over at her. "I'm so glad to hear that. I think you'll find that I'm a powerful ally, especially in these turbulent times. I want to see you succeed, my lady."

She cocked her head, studying. Every word he said was so carefully calculated, chosen to play on what he knew of her. He hadn't considered how she might have changed, and that would be to her advantage. It was easy to manipulate someone when they were so set on their false preconceptions.

"That is both a relief and a comfort. This all..." She broke off, allowing a thread of emotion into her voice. "It's all been so much, so quickly."

He moved his bear closer, so their knees almost knocked together. The expression of sympathy was drawn across his features like paint on a canvas, every detail considered. "May she go well into the earth," he intoned. "I'm sure she would be proud of all you're doing."

She couldn't quite keep her face straight for that. It would be laughable, if it didn't churn up guilt like bile in her stomach.

Hiding her expression, she lifted her gaze to the snarled mass of leaves. A frisson of uncertainty drew her attention from the conversation. They should reach the swan soon, if her theory was right. Out in the cool, unforgiving light of the forest, that *if* grew with every step. Variables swarmed around her, all the possible ways this could go wrong. With an audience at her back just waiting to pounce.

She swallowed, forcing herself to the matter at hand. "Your presence is helping me already, both as a comfort and an ally. I believe, with the Azarov support, I shall be able to guide my cabinet into this change."

There was a distinct shift in the air with those words. A slight thrum of energy as Kyriil replied, "A cabinet with a vacant seat is hardly counsel at all." He paused, his eyes on her. "I know my family lost favor with your grandmother, but perhaps now is the time to rectify that."

There it was, the thing he really wanted. He couldn't hide the hunger in his eyes as he spoke it, even as he tried to shroud it behind the veil of false concern. It was as she'd expected, but it was satisfying to have drawn it out. To force him to show her his true aim.

She pressed her lips together, forcing her features into sadness rather than triumph. "That is not a decision that can be made in haste, especially in light of recent events."

For the first time, Kyriil's smile hitched. A slight crack

that gave away the serpent beneath. But then it was back in place, as well crafted as a statue. "I shall be here for the duration of the mourning days, my lady. I have a feeling I can persuade you."

There was a threat in those words. A dark undercurrent that made her stomach swoop. She adjusted her gloves, using the movement to center herself.

But even that could not quiet her other misgivings.

They should have caught up with the swan by now. Izaveta had followed the direction of the wind, moving through the less dense part of the forest toward the small lake that sat at its center. From what she'd read, that was the same route the swan should follow, eager to return to water.

But there was no hint of white among the unforgiving green.

She turned back to her current prey. "I appreciate your support, Master Azarov. Not all of the court has been so agreeable."

She let the words hang in the air, bait to a trap. In matters of subtlety it was always better to be asked for information than to provide it willingly.

Kyriil arched his eyebrows. "Who would stand against the rightful heir?"

She lowered her voice, shooting him a conspiratorial smile. "I cannot be certain. Some of the cabinet members are difficult to read. Conze Bazin is one whose votes I can never be certain of."

Something sparked in Kyriil's eyes—that hunger again. Bazin's family had replaced the Azarovs in the cabinet, and the animosity between them had never died. It was an emotion Izaveta could use.

A trickle of water punctured the soft sounds of the forest and footfalls of the bears. It drew her focus from the conversation again, the noise ricocheting through her like a horn blast. They were nearly at the lake, and still no hint of the swan. If she was wrong—if they didn't find it here, there was no telling where it could have gone.

Her mother had succeeded in the hunt. Every Karasova queen for the past five hundred years had succeded in it. In fact, the last person to fail was Princess Estava. Looking at it now, many saw that early misstep as the first in the path to her downfall.

Izaveta would not follow her. People thought her young and inexperienced as it was. She needed this blessing.

Her fingers tightened on the reins, the leather digging into her fur-lined gloves. But she kept her voice even, hiding the gnawing fear, as she went on. "He's a devout man, loyal to the Church." She glanced over at Kyriil. "Superstitious, though. I doubt it would take much to persuade him that he's chosen the wrong person to back, if we provide him with the right evidence."

Kyriil's smile widened, a wolf baring its teeth. "I'm sure we can find that *evidence* somehow."

She didn't doubt that he could. He had resources, and plenty of creativity when it came to subterfuge. He would find the right way to orchestrate a sign from the gods or a prediction in the stars. Perhaps a soothsayer with a well-placed omen.

If she could dangle that cabinet seat over him long enough,

he could prove a useful weapon—provided he didn't betray her first. Regardless, this would be a small way to test how far she could make him go.

She had just turned to seek out her next target when she spotted it. As the dark surface of the lake rose in front of them, a flicker of white against the dark green leaves. She moved closer and it coalesced into the form of a bird with an elegant arched neck, wings spread wide as it landed next to the shimmering surface.

A hush fell over the hunting party. Gone were the muffled conversations and shouts of laughter, replaced with a steely anticipation. The weight of their gazes pressed on Izaveta, suffocating and merciless.

Kyriil urged his bear forward. "Allow me—"

"No," she said firmly. "I'll do it." She wouldn't let someone else finish the task for her. She had to prove her aptitude alone.

She had a bow strapped to the saddle, more ornamental than anything else, as she did not have to kill the bird in order to win. Asya's words echoed back to her, unbidden. *Just because it's been done before doesn't make it less cruel.*

Izaveta shook her head. This decision had nothing to do with her sister. It was a matter of practicality. It would be a portent of her reign—that she was a queen who could succeed on her own without cruelty.

She slid off Olyeta's back, landing in the soft mud of the bank. The bear lumbered forward, eager to reach the water, but Izaveta held up a hand. She didn't want to spook the bird. Moving forward slowly, she crouched down to the swan's level, her coat trailing in the mud.

The water of the lake was perfectly still, as if it too had paused to watch.

She was close enough to reach out and touch the swan as its dark eyes locked on hers. She could pick out every color in its delicate feathers, the drops of water glistening along its back. But there was no flash of scarlet amongst its plumage.

Svedye. Was it the wrong bird? But no—light glinted off something around its neck as it turned its head. The silver links of the fine chain the feather had been tied to. Izaveta reached for it eagerly, her fingers feeling along the cool metal.

But there was nothing there. The chain was empty.

CHAPTER TWENTY-ONE

Asya welcomed the bite to the air that promised winter. It chased out the lingering flames of the Firebird beating relentlessly beneath her skin without the respite of the firestone.

But nothing could erase the burn of shame—of failure—that hung over her. She'd found the statue from her vision, but it brought her no closer to the culprit. The shard of bone might have helped, but that was long gone too.

And, worse than that, she'd been attacked. *Injured.*

The wound had mostly healed, leaving just a dull ache in her side and a layer of dried blood. But still, if Tarya found out, she would be horrified. Asya had let her fear get in the way, and it had almost cost her.

That same fear was what had driven Asya from her chambers that morning and out to the cold landscape of the palace training grounds. The fear that she'd already failed before she'd truly begun.

But the training grounds offered a possible answer. The attackers from the previous night had clearly been experienced, their style efficient and ruthless. If they were from within the palace, as she suspected, then there was a chance they'd be here. They'd been hooded, but she would recognize their movements—and certainly that dagger. The strange symbol, the flame and three lines.

Besides, she had not trained since she'd arrived at the palace. After last night, the need to maintain her skills had suddenly become all the more pressing.

The grounds sat in the western corner of the palace, beneath the shadow of Dveda's Tower. From its base, the spire seemed to brush the bottom of the clouds. The bear god's bronzed shield shimmered like captured sunlight, the only bright spot in the landscape of grays. The grounds themselves were sparse. Enclosed with a sweeping white brick wall, they consisted largely of frost-covered earth, broken only by a raked sparring ring and small archery range.

Statues of Meshnik and Ilyova, both known for their prowess as warriors, lined the courtyard. It made it feel as though there was a constant audience, a disapproving presence judging the bouts and exercises.

Despite the hunt, the courtyard was full. Several strashe—identifiable by the royal crest on their swords—sparred in the far corner. A young boy was trying his luck at the archery range, his arrows flying wide and erratic. A group of green-clad Versch stood to one side, sticking out like new blades of grass against the damp earth. Three people sparred in the ring, the clash of their blades echoing against the stone walls.

Asya's eyes darted around as she made her way to an empty patch, looking for any hint of that gleaming gold symbol or the practiced edges of the attackers' movements. But though one young woman held a blade with a handle fashioned to look like flames, there was no sign of the attackers or their weapons.

She swallowed down the bitter edge of disappointment. She'd known it was a long shot, but she'd let herself hope that she might be able to find a way to remedy her failure.

Exhaustion tugged at her, sudden and heavy. She hadn't managed to sleep much, the Calling seeping into her dreams. Distorted images of her mother's lifeless face, her half-forgotten voice shouting a warning. Hooded figures, relentless in their onslaught. And this time the Firebird wouldn't come to her aid. It remained trapped, scalding beneath her skin. Devouring her from the inside out.

She felt Vilanovich's eyes on her, sharp as nettles. She had followed Asya all morning without a word, no crack in her frosty manner. As if nothing had happened last night at all.

Asya gritted her teeth, drawing her shashka. She needed to move, to push out the rustling whispers already snaking around her. To find some semblance of the routine she'd created at the Roost, before everything had shifted again. She began to work through some of Tarya's training exercises. Her aching side protested, but as she pushed on, the pain faded away, lost in the peaceful familiarity of this exercise.

She could almost forget she was in the middle of the palace. That the Firebird nestled inside her. Doing this, she could pretend she was back under the canopy of the trees. Away from conspiracies and politics and—

She froze, blade half-raised. *Sisters* was the word that had caught in her mind, snagged like a stray thread on a thorn. To be away from the stranger her sister had become.

Except, Asya wasn't sure she wanted that anymore. She remembered Iza's face the night before, the vulnerability that had fractured across it. Her voice as they stared out at the trees. There was *some* of her sister in there; Asya was sure.

She shook her head, thoughts tangling themselves in her mind. The two possibilities had always felt so separate: having her sister or being the Firebird. A fragile hope, delicate as a cobweb, ignited in her chest: What if she could have both?

Her fingers tightened on the blade. She shouldn't think like that. She knew exactly what Tarya would say.

Asya tried to move back into the formation, but it was no longer enough to keep her thoughts from intruding.

Behind her, the clang of blades in the sparring ring died away. She spun round to face it. *That* was what she needed. A moment of forgetting.

Sheathing her blade, she approached the ring. The three fighters had been talking, laughing among themselves, but their voices died when they saw her.

Her fingers twitched, suddenly aware of all the eyes on her again. "Can I try a round?" she asked, her voice coming out a little more halfhearted than she'd intended, deflated by their abruptly serious expressions.

The woman standing nearest shot her companions a glance, as if searching for a way out. "Of course, Firebird." With a strained smile, she gestured to the ring.

Asya stepped forward. The flurries of movement and shriek of blades were replaced with a heavy silence. She suddenly wished she hadn't suggested this at all, wished she'd just stayed in her claustrophobic room.

But it was too late now.

A statue of Saint Meshnik towered above them, eerily reminiscent of the scene from the night before.

She drew her shashka, the familiar feel of the blade in her hand grounding her. She focused on her opponent, trying to push away the people staring. To ignore the distractions, just as Tarya would tell her.

Asya moved first, spurred by that restless energy. The woman leaped back, raising her own blade to counter with a screech of steel. The woman's eyes widened, fear twisting through them as visceral as a cornered animal.

It was over in three breaths. The woman's sword fell to the ground with a dull thud, Asya's blade pointed at her throat.

Asya lowered her shashka. She'd seen the woman fight, if only briefly, against two opponents. She'd held her own.

But not against the Firebird. Not because of Asya's superior ability, but because the woman held back. Because she didn't want to risk angering the Firebird.

Because she was scared of Asya. They all were.

That realization burned through her stomach like bile. Tarya's words ricocheted through her again. *To them, you will never be more than a monster that lurks in the night.*

Asya gritted her jaw. Maybe she wouldn't, but they could at least spar with her properly to keep her mind off that truth.

Her eyes traveled along the assembled onlookers. None of them met her gaze, afraid she might pick them next. Except for one. Strashe Vilanovich stared, unflinching. A hint of defiance flashed in the set of her jaw, as if she refused to cower just because the others did.

Asya took a step toward her, the restless energy that grated against her nerves spurring her on. "Spar with me?"

Vilanovich raised her eyebrows. "I'm your guard," she said, as if that answered the question.

Asya moved closer, lowering her voice enough that the on-lookers wouldn't be able to pick out every word. "Yes, but you don't like me, so I know you won't hold back."

Vilanovich let out a low, derisive sound—the closest Asya had heard to a laugh from the strashe. "Isn't that all the more reason for us to *not* spar?"

Asya's fingers worried at a loose thread on her sleeve, though her lips twitched toward a smile. "Spar with me," she said again. "And if you win, you don't have to say an-other word to me."

Something shifted on the strashe's face. The glint of a chal-lenge in those gray eyes. Not sharp, like the edge of a sword. But almost mischievous. It was a piece of the strashe Asya had never expected to see. "I'll hold you to that, Firebird."

Asya took a step back, gripping her shashka. "But if I win," she added, "you have to call me Asya."

The strashe held her gaze, a slight curve to her lips. She nodded.

Chapter Twenty-Two

Izaveta stared at the empty chain, her heart trying to claw its way out of her rib cage.

There were any number of explanations. It could have snagged on a tree branch or slipped off as the swan dived. Except there were no tattered remains on the chain—no ribbons of crimson or broken links. The feather had been removed carefully. *Purposefully.*

Another move against her. Another thing taken from her.

But Izaveta understood this game. The years of lessons at her mother's side had taught her she couldn't win when the rules were stacked against her, when the queen wasn't the only one who truly controlled the board. And until she had the crown, she would never truly be in control.

She blinked hard, staring at the space where the feather should be. She didn't believe the stories, the tradition, not really. But that did not ease the sting of failure. The scalding shame that rose inside her like a gathering fire. Or the quiet voice in the back of her mind that whispered, *your mother was right—you're not ready.*

Perhaps there had been no sabotage at all. Maybe Izaveta was just not worthy of being queen, not after all she'd done.

Or, perhaps, the only way to win was to cheat the game.

She rose to her feet, painting a smile across her face and swallowing down her doubts. Slipping her hand into a hidden pocket of her coat, she drew out a brilliant crimson feather. She turned to face the party and held it aloft as though she'd just pulled it from the swan's neck.

"It seems the gods have blessed our hunt," she said, her voice echoing through the thick trees. "We may return victorious."

The cheer that erupted from the crowd should have felt jubilant, a triumphant shout to usher in her reign. But it rolled over Izaveta like gathering thunder, a devouring storm on the horizon. She caught Kyriil's eye among the assembled. Was she imagining the slight curve to his lips, the glimmer that said he'd seen what she'd done?

She doubted she was the first queen to have cheated the hunt—she certainly would not have put it past her mother. But more than anything else, this felt like a lie. All her deceits laid out for the world to see.

Returning to Olyeta, Izaveta tucked the bright feather behind the bear's ear. A clear sign to all those waiting on the edge of the forest that they were victorious.

She turned the bear, opening her mouth to give the order, when another cry tore through the air. This one was not of jubilation—it was not even human. An echoing screech that rattled down to Izaveta's bones.

She looked up just in time to see the creature silhouetted against the sky above her, its wings oil black against the pale clouds.

A falcon.

Then it dived. She raised her hands instinctively, ducking her head. Its talons dug into the soft material of her gloves, shredding them and the skin beneath. Izaveta let out a cry of pain. She tried to pull away, but its talons dug in harder.

A low thump, and the falcon juddered away. A strashe had hit it with the flat of their blade, sending it spiraling back up to the trees.

Izaveta clutched her wrists. Slick blood ran down her arm, unpleasantly warm against the cold air.

But she didn't have a moment to examine them—for her mind to process what was happening. The falcon dived again, as sure and deadly as an arrow. But it didn't fly at Izaveta this time. Instead, its talons sank into the neck of the strashe that had defended her. Blood sprayed out in a great arc as the strashe's grip on her saber faltered.

Her eyes widened in shock, luminescent against the darkness of the forest. Then she toppled from the back of her bear. The thud of her body hitting the mud resonated through Izaveta's core. An arrow flashed, and the falcon let out a low cry before falling to the ground, as lifeless as the strashe. A fizzle of magic rose from its body, the scent piercing the air.

Silence engulfed the clearing, heavy and unsettling as a sudden fog.

Izaveta's whole body was shaking. Blood still dripped down her arm, but she barely felt it. She couldn't draw her gaze from the strashe's crumpled body. The mangled corpse of the falcon.

She knew she should say something—she could feel eyes on her, the expectation that she would reassure them. That she might somehow have answers. But she couldn't force words up her throat.

Kyriil moved toward her, reaching for her bloodied wrists. But she drew back sharply, clutching them close. She didn't want him near her. Didn't want *anyone* near her.

She turned Olyeta to face the rest of the party. Commander Iveshkin's expression had turned stormy, saber still drawn as though expecting a threat. Conze Bazin had paled. He clutched a wooden icon at his throat, staring at Izaveta in horror. And the ambassador just looked on, impassive and calculating.

Any progress she might have made was in tatters. No display of strength, no blessing from the gods. Just a scared girl cowering from a bird that foretold doom.

"We must return," she said finally, relieved that her voice did not tremble.

She pulled her gaze from the strashe, instead latching on to the scarlet flash of the feather. It gleamed against the soft white of Olyeta's fur, a bloodstain on snow.

A false victory, just like everything else.

CHAPTER TWENTY-THREE

It was easy for Asya to block out her surroundings—the gawking onlookers—this time. Vilanovich filled her vision, gray eyes locked on hers. This was the strashe who had called her a monster, had drawn her saber to keep Asya from the Calling. But in this moment Asya didn't see that. She felt like she was getting a glimpse of something else. A part of the guard that she didn't usually share.

Vilanovich nodded to the shashka. "You're going to fight me with that?"

Asya tightened her grip on it, protective. "Yes," she replied, somewhat indignantly. "It's lighter than any other saber and better in close combat."

Vilanovich shrugged. "If you say so." She drew her own weapon, the curved saber all strashe carried known as a znaya. It was longer than Asya's shashka, with a deeper curve to the blade and a delicate silver hand guard.

Asya had trained with a znaya too—Tarya had insisted she learn at least the basics in all weaponry—but she'd never liked the balance. She raised her own blade, beginning to circle. "You think yours is better?"

Vilanovich leaned back on her left foot, mirroring Asya's steps. "The znaya has farther reach, and its deeper hollow makes it better for slashing."

Shifting her weight, Asya flexed her fingers around her grip. The low hum of the Firebird still pulsed through her veins, urging her to move, but this time she waited. "Good thing we won't be drawing blood then."

Vilanovich smiled, feline and sure.

Asya had less than a heartbeat to consider that offering to fight someone who so openly disliked her might not have been the best idea, before Vilanovich lunged. She swiped forward, aiming low. Asya leaped aside easily, whirling back to face the strashe. Vilanovich was testing her, feeling out her reactions.

Asya didn't give her a moment to breathe. She darted forward, feinting right before slashing down. But Vilanovich saw it coming, shifting back so the blade just skimmed the fabric of her shirt. Using her momentum, she spun around. The blunted side of her znaya caught Asya's shoulder. She stumbled back, bringing her own blade up to counter before Vilanovich could press her advantage.

The hit added a sudden intensity to their movements. They fell into a rhythm, dancing around each other like two moons in orbit. It almost felt like they were working together, moving to the ringing music of their blades. For an instant, it was as certain as the Calling had felt. A symphony only Asya could hear, thrumming in her veins with just as much intensity.

Vilanovich's arm hooked around Asya's, pulling her back

and forcing the point of her shashka down. Their eyes locked. Asya was very conscious of how close they were, how aware she was of every line of the strashe's body.

Before Vilanovich could raise her saber and finish it, Asya reached with her free hand to catch the fine netting of the znaya's hand guard. The blade fell to the ground, and Asya twisted out of the strashe's grip.

"Hand guard," she said, managing a slight grin through her labored breaths.

But Vilanovich didn't hesitate. Weaponless, she kicked out, forcing Asya away from the fallen saber. The strashe lunged for her znaya, snatching it up and ducking Asya's swipe in a single swift movement.

Asya was beginning to see why the strashe had not backed down the day before. This was her element, as much a part of her very essence as Asya's fire.

The strashe pressed forward, forcing Asya onto her back foot. Vilanovich whirled, arcing her saber right before twisting her wrist at the last second and flicking it left.

This time Asya was ready for the feint. She ducked the blade and hooked her foot behind the strashe's knee, pulling her weight from under her. But Vilanovich's hand flashed out. It fastened on Asya's wrist, sending both of them toppling onto the frozen earth.

The impact jolted through Asya's bones, tinged with surprise. The strashe was good, as good as Tarya even—if not better. Though, of course, Tarya always had another weapon she could use. As Asya did now. It built under her skin, awoken again by the adrenaline. But she pressed it back, tightening her control.

The moment of distraction cost her. The strashe rolled on top of her, sharp side of the znaya to her throat, her knees trapping Asya's arms.

Vilanovich's gray eyes sparked, lightning cutting through the storm clouds. A triumphant smile curved her lips—so close to Asya's own that she could feel her breath. "Yield."

But Asya smiled too. "I don't think so." She nodded to her shashka, switched to her left hand in the fall and poised against the strashe's thigh—at the perfect point to sever the femoral artery.

The strashe's lips parted slightly in surprise. But no anger flashed across her features. More a grudging respect—mingled with something else, something Asya couldn't quite name. It sent another flush of heat prickling through her. She was suddenly aware of Vilanovich's fingers pressed against her, her legs against Asya's hips.

It happened without a conscious thought. An instinct that had already burrowed into her bones. A tongue of flame burst out, searing against the strashe's arm.

Vilanovich fell back as Asya scrambled away, desperately reining the Firebird in. "I'm sorry—I didn't mean—"

But the damage was already done.

She went to move forward—to try to help, but the strashe grunted, "Don't." The one word jolted through Asya.

Vilanovich rolled against the earth, dampening the flames until all that was left was the faint smolder of smoke.

Where the rest of the world had faded away during the fight, it now returned in harsh focus. The gasps and uttered cries scraped against Asya's skin. The scent of burning filled her nose, cloying and inescapable.

She took a hesitant step forward, hands tightly pressed behind her. "Are you all right? Do you need a voye—"

Vilanovich shook her head, still not quite looking at Asya. "I'm fine."

Asya's heart pounded, the crackle of flames echoing in her ears. How had she let that happen? She'd been so careful to hold her control until the very moment where it mattered most.

"I'm—" She swallowed the word. *Sorry* didn't feel like enough.

But as the strashe pulled herself to her feet, there was no hint of the disgust Asya had expected to see. The *fear*.

Vilanovich brushed a hand over her now-ruined shirt, sending ash swirling around her like snow. Her hair was beginning to fall out of its neat plait, dark wisps flying around her face. The scorched fabric exposed the pale skin of the strashe's arm, not freshly burned but lined with a lattice of ridged scars.

"I'll be fine," she said, covering her arm. "Asya."

Asya cocked her head in an unspoken question, certain she must have misheard.

The strashe shrugged. "I suppose you did win, even if you cheated."

Asya felt a smile blooming across her face, despite the Firebird still burning beneath her skin. Despite the onlookers, their eyes wide and afraid.

She glanced down at her feet, trying to fashion her expression into something more appropriate for the situation.

"You fight well," Asya said, reaching for something normal to say. "You didn't learn that from the strashe."

Vilanovich's head tilted, appraising. "No," she replied. "My brother taught me." She gestured to her ruined shirt. "I should change."

"Yes," Asya said hurriedly, not looking up. "Of course, Strashe."

Vilanovich started to head back toward the palace, but she hesitated. She looked back over her shoulder, face set as if steeling herself. "And, you can call me Yuliana. If you want."

Without waiting for a response, the guard pushed back through the crowd. Asya watched as her dark head vanished, a strange lightness flowing through her.

Yuliana.

The name was like a carefully kept secret, something precious for Asya to tuck away and only bring out to examine when she was alone. It left a fluttering ember in her chest, like the Firebird's burning wings beating against her rib cage.

It extinguished with a sputtering hiss as she turned around. Tarya stood at the edge of the courtyard, face half-shadowed by the towering statue of Saint Meshnik. But Asya could still make out her expression. The severe disapproval in the lines of her face.

Asya picked up her discarded shashka, sheathing it slowly as if she could postpone the inevitable.

Her aunt didn't speak as they walked from the frozen quiet of the training grounds back into the palace. She stopped only when they reached a deserted passageway, silent except for the sound of a trickling gold fountain that stood in an alcove, topped with a carved Firebird and flames so realistic they almost seemed to glow.

"What were you thinking?"

Asya kept her eyes on the water, the shimmering lights

bouncing across its surface. "I just wanted to get some training in," she replied, barely louder than the fountain.

"You let your power loose." Tarya's voice was low—not a soft whisper but a distant rumble of thunder. "In a crowded courtyard."

Asya swallowed. "I didn't mean to—"

"I know," Tarya snapped. "That's what makes it all the worse."

Asya's fingers twisted through the loose thread at her sleeve, pulling it tight against her skin. She didn't have anything to say to that. There was no defense, not when her aunt was right.

Tarya's lips thinned. "You still have no control over your power, no grasp of what it truly means to be the Firebird."

Asya opened her mouth, but the words died in her throat. *I'm trying.*

What use was trying? The gods didn't care if she *tried* to keep the balance, they cared whether she succeeded. It did not matter to magic if the Firebird was trying, only whether or not the price was paid. Tears prickled behind her eyes, but she blinked them away. They wouldn't help either.

"If you cannot control yourself within the court, you must wear the firestone again." Tarya's eyes swept over her, all seeing. "Where is it?"

"I—" Asya broke off. She couldn't quite force the lie out. She looked down at her now-mud-caked boots. "It's gone."

Tarya drew in a sharp breath, her dark eyes widening—the most animated Asya had ever seen her. *"Gone?"*

Asya just nodded. The respite of the training grounds—the

brief flash of calm it had given her—evaporated. Now her failings pressed in on her again, suffocating and inescapable.

Tarya was doing her impression of a statue. Not ethereal this time. Now she was a vengeful, furious god wrought from stone. "Do you understand what this could mean?"

Asya wrapped her arms around herself, digging her fingers in. She did understand what it could mean, but she didn't want to consider it. Not when she felt so helpless to do anything about it.

"A strashe was killed on the hunt," Tarya said. "By a falcon."

Asya's head snapped up. "What?"

"I had hoped we had more time," Tarya went on, some of the anger melting from her face. "But already we are seeing signs of the imbalance. Of the debt that is owed."

"But Izaveta—" Asya's voice caught, a hard weight rising in her throat. "Izaveta is safe, isn't she?"

Tarya gave her an odd, appraising look. "Yes, I believe the princess is safe."

Asya forced her fists to unclench. Izaveta was safe. But the flash of relief was eclipsed by Tarya's words.

"Was it because of the conze? Because she died before I—before paying the price?"

Tarya shook her head, her movements rigid. "No," she replied. "I do not believe so. It is not a situation many Firebirds have encountered, but I believe her death would have returned what was owed to the earth."

The other Calling then. The one that burned too bright for Asya to touch—the one that she could not blame on anyone else. And now a strashe had been killed. Someone was dead because she wasn't strong enough. That thought left a burning ache in her stomach.

"What do I do?" The question was so small, so insignificant against the enormity of the problem.

"You have to find who cast the spell and ensure the price is paid."

It sounded simple like that. Asya had hoped it would be simple, even when she wasn't able to follow the Calling. All she'd have to do was figure it out another way, a mortal way. But that hadn't worked either.

"Nothing else will stop it," Asya murmured. The words had formed in her head as a question but fell heavy from her lips. A certain truth.

"No," Tarya answered anyway. "Until the true price is paid, magic cannot be balanced, no matter what carnage it wreaks.

"We can practice control today," she added, her voice softening a little. "Trying to sit with the Calling, to hold it as long as you can before it is too much. It will come, and balance will be restored. It always is."

Asya stared down at her hands, at where the flames had burst through. The training grounds—whatever she'd thought she felt—seemed very far away now. A small inconsequence in the landscape of the world.

Tarya's eyes were still on her, and from her expression, she'd guessed what Asya was thinking. "You have to remember this duty is not only about you, Asya. There is a reason the Firebird must put her responsibility above all else. Above *everyone* else."

CHAPTER TWENTY-FOUR

Izaveta did not like things she didn't understand, and the past few days had provided far too many of them. Too many spiraling possibilities that no amount of thinking or scheming would resolve.

But the hunt had given her one path to follow, even if all the others were still obscured. Nikov Toyevski was a question she needed answers to.

It wasn't until the soft blues of twilight seeped into the palace that Izaveta was finally able to extricate herself from distressed courtiers and strashe to follow her inkling. To forget about the fiasco of the hunt and sink into the calm certainty of strategy—of manipulation.

The library was bathed in warm lantern light, the landscape beyond the windows fading to darkness. Nikov stood over an open tome with a piece of parchment in each hand, a quill balanced in his mouth, and an expression of deep concentration on his face. His shirtsleeves were rolled up, and his hair was significantly less neatly styled than it had been that morning.

It was a distinct change from the ordered young man she'd met the day before, as if time in the library had allowed him to relax back into his role as a scholar.

Zvezda had given Izaveta her report on him that morning, and it had shown nothing of suspicion. He was an Amarinth scholar, as he claimed, and it did appear that Sanislav had sent for him. And besides, he'd already been in the palace when Vittaria was killed.

Her eyes lingered on his half-silhouetted form for a brief moment. Dark umber curls spilled over his eyes, limned by the last strands of daylight. Perhaps she could not stop the vibishop's spy from sifting through her books—or undo the damage of the hunt—but she could at least find out exactly what Sanislav was looking for. How this scholar factored into their elaborate game.

"Master Toyevski," she said, her words smooth as the silk of her dress. "I was under the impression that Master Valerii was showing you our collection."

Nikov looked up, an easy smile spreading across his face that nearly dislodged the quill. He dropped the parchment to the desk, the quill following soon after. "My lady," he said, inclining his head in a bow. "I told Master Valerii he needn't worry. I'm perfectly capable of finding the texts myself."

She raised her eyebrows, stepping forward to examine the books spread out on the table. These were not the ancient, unnecessary volumes Izaveta had wanted Nikov to waste his time on. These were the books she spent her time studying, many with her own notes alongside them. Books that she and Fyodor had painstakingly tracked down. Ones that were meant for them alone, not for some scholar in the Church's pocket.

She clenched her jaw, but she forced her tone to remain even, casual. "Many of those books were merely for me to practice my translations. They will be of no use in understanding the Fading."

His lips quirked into a half smile, brown eyes glinting. "Is that so?" He tapped the parchment he'd been examining. "Because this one contains a detailed explanation of how the Firebird extracts a price, and the author's theory on how that influences the balance of magic. That certainly seems relevant to me."

She gave a noncommittal shrug, turning to examine the nearest shelf as though he were of little interest.

"I'm surprised to see you here this evening," he added, his eyes dropping to her bandaged wrists. "I do hope your injury was not severe."

Her hand froze on the shelf, her muscles tensing as she searched for the hidden meaning in those words. It took her a beat longer than it usually would to form the correct response. Even if she refused to admit it, the events of the day had shaken her.

The memory of the falcon lurked at the back of her mind, a dark blot of ink against a beautiful sky. The spray of blood from the strashe's throat. The bite of the falcon's talons, gleaming in the light. Was it the Fading that had caused the falcon to become rabid?

Or was it something else?

She clamped her fingers around the wound, using the clarity of the pain to eclipse everything else. "I'm perfectly well," she replied, hating the slight hitch in her voice.

His face broke into a smile, soft as the candlelight. "I'm glad to hear it."

The response itself was to be expected, but she felt there was something she was missing. She forced her hands to her side, letting the tension drop from her shoulders. Becoming the image of a queen.

Whatever game he and the vibishop were playing didn't matter. Izaveta had been using this library for six years, and the queen's scholars had plumbed its depths for even longer. Nikov would find nothing that they had not seen already. And soon enough, she would figure out what they were looking for. Each tome he had chosen had a meaning, and it would be easy enough to glean the truth from them.

She moved back toward the table, passing a cursory glance over the books he'd gathered. Her breath caught as she saw which one Nikov was currently studying. *Tales of the Flame*, an antiquated volume written in Old Versch and illuminated in gold leaf. It was a book Fyodor had only just acquired, the most recent text Izaveta had been translating. Could Nikov have known that? Or was it just a coincidence that he'd picked up the very book she was working on?

She shot him a sidelong glance, calculating. She expected to see the glimmer of a schemer in his brown eyes—or perhaps apprehension at being found out.

But she saw neither. Just a flicker of something else, like a ripple on a lake's surface. She could usually catch people's expressions, the slightest nuances, but his still evaded her. It was an unsettling feeling.

Though there were other ways to dig out a person's secrets.

Izaveta was thirteen when she had first understood the power of a kiss, how it could be just as effective a weapon as any blade. More so, even, as with a kiss the victim often did not even realize they'd been hit.

It was on the day of the Eternal Ball, the celebration of the anniversary of a Karasova first ascending the throne. The Liljendaän ambassador had died suddenly, leaving his young son in power, right when the queen was in the middle of negotiating imports across the Skyless Hallows. The son was a plain blond-haired boy, the same age as Izaveta. He was clearly unused to the attention of his position and overwhelmed by the Tóurensi court. Her mother had told her to keep close to the boy, to help him navigate the court. At first Izaveta had thought, naively, that her mother might have hoped she'd find a friend.

But when the queen had drawn her aside under the pretense of adjusting her hair, her true motives became clear.

Izaveta danced with the boy all evening, eager to please her mother—and enjoying the way she could draw the boy's attention with her every movement, how he craved her smile as if it was the sun itself. And when she led him out to one of the balconies, she let him kiss her, confident that was all she needed to convince him to her side.

And she was right. By the next morning, the queen had brokered a deal—one that favored Tóurin's interests.

That was the power of a kiss.

Izaveta placed a palm on the table, leaning forward as if in vague interest. Her eyes drifted to the parchment covered with Nikov's slanting script. His hand moved just as she got close enough to read it. The movement could have been casual—she wouldn't have noticed it had her eyes not been trained on the page—but there was something deliberate about the placement.

Everything about him was like that. Not unreadable, like her mother. He somehow balanced a thin line between genuine and act. It threw her off-kilter. A book she thought she knew, but when opened the ink was smudged and illegible.

He glanced up at her, his lips twitching into an inquisitive smile. He smiled so easily, giving away the expression as if it cost him nothing. "Joining me for some light reading?"

She ignored the question. "Since you made such a long journey to be here," she said, careful to offset the sweetness with a hint of annoyance—too sudden a change would give away any subtlety. "I could use your opinion."

She pointed to *Tales of the Flame*, her arm brushing across his. "I'm having a little trouble with the translation." She paused, meeting his all-too-knowing gaze. "You do know Old Versch, don't you?"

"What sort of heathen wouldn't be versed in Old Versch?"

Izaveta held back a withering retort. This would require a much shrewder hand—even if the effect would be less satisfying. Instead, she settled into the chair next to him, shifting the book so it sat neatly between them.

Her eyes caught on his hand, illuminated by the nearest candle. Sharp white scars cut across the brown of his knuckles, deliberate and repeated. Hard ridges that would likely never fade.

He noticed her glance and hastily moved his hand away, folding it in his lap. The first hint of a fracture in his careful movements. "'Vas Kennissen solte verdienne,'" he said with a tight smile.

The words of the Amarinth, inscribed around the dome of the great library. *Knowledge must be earned.*

Izaveta swallowed, tugging her gaze back to the book in front of her. That small crack—the hint of something that he wanted to remain hidden—should have given her some satisfaction. Another piece of information for her arsenal.

But instead she felt, for the first time, like she'd intruded on something personal. Because there was something all too familiar in that brief show of weakness. A strange reflection of the way her mother always made her feel.

She cleared her throat, dispelling those ridiculous thoughts. She tapped the offending line, the one she'd been stuck on the day before her mother's death. Before the board had tilted and the game had changed. *Vas eschen comt Valke das hivern, vasl jervoren Malocht.*

Nikov's brow wrinkled, running his finger along the sprawled letters. "'The falcons arise in the east by…conjuring of moonlight'?"

She put her hand on top of his, pointing to one word. "Except *Valke*—falcons—is written in the nominative, and it has the ending of a proper noun. So it could be read 'The moonlight arises in the east, by conjuring of the falcon,' which would have an entirely different—albeit nonsensical—meaning."

"I think you may be reading too much into ancient ramblings," he murmured, but his eyes were no longer on the words. Izaveta could feel them on her, trailing the lines of her face. "It's lyrical. Must you take it so literally?"

She looked up at him, not moving her hand from his. "Must *you* give the author so much poetic license?"

For a heartbeat, all she saw were his eyes. The spark that danced in them, so believable, so *real*, that it tugged on something in her chest. As she leaned in—as he mirrored her movement— she wasn't thinking about what she needed from him. About the information she was leveraging. For that instant, she wanted to just get lost in the feeling, in the glint of his eyes, the lingering warmth where their fingers touched.

But he stopped short, so close his breath mingled with hers. His lips pulled into a small smile. "You know," he murmured, "if you wanted information that much, you could have just asked."

Whatever tenderness Izaveta had imagined froze like the surface of the Depthless Lake in winter. She pulled back, her face hardening to match the heavy stone inside her. To not let slip how she had allowed herself—ever so briefly—to get lost in that moment.

She raised her chin, studying the lines of his face as she considered her response. He had a smudge of ink on his cheek, highlighting the slight blush beneath his bronze skin. That strange earnestness still lurked in his eyes, at odds with the mischievous curve of his lips—as if this were all some marvelous joke.

"I'm not your enemy," he said carefully. "I don't side with Church or Crown—my loyalty is only to knowledge."

She sat back, trailing a finger along the edge of the worn parchment. "That's a very pretty proclamation. How long have you been rehearsing it?"

"That is what we're taught at the Amarinth," he replied, without missing a beat.

She leaned forward, meeting his gaze. "You know, I've visited the Amarinth before. I met all of their scholars, but the funny thing is, I don't remember you."

His lips twitched into that smile again—a flash of sunlight cracking through a curtain. "Perhaps I'm not very memorable."

She almost snapped that he was most certainly memorable, but she caught herself. That was a concession she didn't want to give. Yet, there was something disarming about this envoy, something that made her usual facade that much more difficult to hold.

She gestured to the books spread in front of them, opting to follow his lead. "What is it you're looking for here?"

His smile widened. "Knowledge, of course. That is the life's work of all scholars of the Amarinth."

Every answer was quick—ready to combat her questions. A little too rehearsed to set Izaveta at ease. She sat back in her chair. "And what drove you to pursue that noble cause?"

He shrugged, resting his forearms on the tabletop. "My mother inspired me to join. She apprenticed at the Great Library of Kharur. I was born there, in fact. She was always fascinated by history, the power of the stories we tell ourselves, and she passed that passion on to me."

That did match the basic details Zvezda had uncovered, but Izaveta couldn't shake the seed of suspicion. It was likely the truth, but certainly not *all* of the truth. "Yet you chose to travel all the way to the Amarinth for your own studies."

"I was raised on the border with Stravínžk, with my father." He hesitated, his hands reaching for the quill as if to give himself some kind of outlet. His voice was forcibly light as he went on, unable to hide a thread of tension. The same kind of tension she'd noticed when he saw the ambassador. "Though it did take time for me to adjust to all of the Amarinth's ways. My mentor has always had a more rigorous approach to my training. Unforgiving to any mistakes." He looked up, his dark eyes piercing into hers. "I'm sure you understand that."

Her jaw tightened. She didn't like how much he saw with that gaze. As if he could cut down to her center and tell just how hard it was for her to hold herself together. How easily she could spiral away into nothing.

"Well, enjoyable as this was," she said coldly, rising to her feet, "we're done here. You can report back to the vibishop whatever you like. There are other ways I can stand against him."

Something flashed across his features, so quick Izaveta was sure she'd read it wrong. Because it looked almost like hurt.

"I don't answer to Sanislav," he replied, all lightness gone from his voice.

"Or anyone else, I'm sure," she said, with poisonous sarcasm.

He watched her, a sudden seriousness to the lines of his face that, again, made Izaveta feel oddly vulnerable—exposed. "Do you always assume everyone is lying?"

She let out a humorless laugh. "Don't you know?" she said, bitterness lancing through her words like an out-of-tune note. "Everyone *is* lying. That's how you win this game." She hadn't meant to say it quite so bluntly—to let a fragment of truth splinter through. She turned, adjusting her gloves so that she didn't have to see his reaction.

"Good night, Master Toyevski." She didn't give him a moment to respond, marching out of the tower without looking back. She suddenly needed distance from him. From those eyes that somehow saw too much.

She shook her head, forcing away the odd feeling cracking through her ribs. The ridiculous tinge of sadness at leaving his company. After all, she had more important things to deal with than a single scholar.

She had cabinet members to convince, people to manipulate to her side. And that was so much easier than thinking about the boy in the library and one oddly tender moment.

Chapter Twenty-Five

Asya stared at the door in front of her, at the carved lines of the wood. She couldn't quite bring herself to raise her hand to knock.

She'd spent the remainder of the day with Tarya in her chambers, attempting to take hold of the Calling. She tried all the exercises her aunt taught her, all the methods she'd read from different Firebirds' journals. But no matter what she did, no matter how she practiced her breathing or allowed the Firebird to burst free—she hoped no one noticed the singed silk at the bottom of her curtains—she couldn't hold on to the Calling.

Firebird Lirina wrote that Callings felt like the sun. Too bright to look at directly, but when she found a way to shadow her mind, it was easy. Asya still didn't understand what that meant, but this Calling certainly felt as unreachable as the sun. Except she had no idea how to *shadow her mind* enough to reach its core, to reach the perfect symphony that her second Calling had been.

Asya wanted to believe that her difficulties were because this Calling had come at the same moment as her powers and they were so intertwined that it was impossible to separate it from the flames. But she couldn't help the nudging feeling that it was not about her power, or the Calling. It was about *her*.

Tarya's words pulsed through her, biting in their truth. *This duty is not only about you.*

But how was Asya supposed to hold the weight of that responsibility? The strashe, killed by a falcon all because Asya had not managed to fulfill her purpose. The thought was suffocating, as cold and unforgiving as water closing over her head.

How had Tarya managed it? How had *any* of the Firebirds managed to go on when their every action could hold such terrible consequences?

And the more she'd thought about it, the more she realized there was only one person she wanted to talk to. One person who might understand the weight of a duty thrust upon them too soon, more than anyone else.

But now that she stood in front of the door to Izaveta's chambers, she couldn't bring herself to knock. Strashe waited on either side of the doorway, grim and foreboding, though one glance at Asya was all it had taken for them to step aside. Her own constant shadow had still not returned from the voye. She hadn't expected to feel the strashe's absence quite so acutely, but it was like standing out in the open after days under the protection of the trees. A sudden awareness that she was alone.

Yuliana, she reminded herself. The name tugged on her

chest, something entirely hers—not the Firebird's. Not the court's. *Hers.*

She shook her head, dispelling those thoughts. She shouldn't be thinking of the strashe at all, not after Tarya's warning. Taking a deep breath, Asya knocked. The sound thudded dully in the passageway.

There was no reply. After a moment's hesitation, Asya pushed the door a little, peering inside. Music spilled out, low and melancholy. Unlike the Calling, this music was soft and imperfect and wonderfully mortal.

She took a tentative step in. Her sister stood by the window, silhouetted by the faint light of the moons. Her eyes were closed, fingers dancing along the gleaming silver flute. She looked so much younger. None of the hard lines and forced smiles that she wore around the court. This was Izaveta as Asya remembered her.

She took another step forward, and the door fell shut behind her with a snap. The music broke off as Izaveta whirled around. Her eyes widened, face thrown in shadow by the faint candlelight, before she quickly regained her composure. "Sister. What can I do for you?"

Now that Asya was here, she couldn't find a way to voice the fears churning in her stomach. Speaking them somehow felt like she would give them life. She swallowed, her fingers knotting together to match her insides. "You haven't moved to Mother's rooms yet."

Izaveta turned away, disassembling the flute and wiping it clean with a small cloth. "No."

The hollowness in that one word resonated in Asya's stomach. A piercing reminder of their shared loss. Both grief and the absence of grief, tangled together with the memory of a mother who'd never truly been a mother.

She wished she could voice that to Izaveta. Find a way to put those feelings into words, to not be quite so alone in them. But they were too jagged, cutting at the inside of her throat even as she tried to force them together.

Izaveta slipped on her gloves, as if arming herself, before looking back. She sank into one of the embroidered chairs, gesturing for Asya to join her with a stiff formality.

She went to sit, before realizing the chair was already oc-cupied. A white cat lifted its head, regarding her lazily. Asya reached out a hand, letting the animal sniff her fingers.

"Meet Lyoza," Izaveta said, with a wave of her hand.

Asya paused, glancing up at Izaveta with a low sound some-where between amusement and indignation.

"I'm sure the bishops would think it blasphemous," her sister added, in a tone that showed just how little she thought of their opinions. "But she does have claws."

"Are you all right?" Asya asked suddenly, remembering that Izaveta's day had been shadowed by the strashe's death as well.

Izaveta's shoulders stiffened. "Why would I not be?"

Not a real answer, an evasion again. And not even a very good one. But Asya couldn't make her sister talk about it if she didn't want to.

She gripped the back of the chair, staring at a point a little to her sister's right, out into the darkened sky and the distant glow of the Depthless Lake. "How do you do it?" Her voice was taut, frayed threads that might wear away to nothing.

Izaveta folded her hands in her lap. "Do what?"

"How do you manage not to break under all of this?" Asya

could hear the low desperation in her words, reaching for answers she wasn't sure existed.

Her sister surveyed her with an unreadable expression. In this light, dressed in all her regal finery, she looked so like their mother. A ghost caught in these pale hallways.

"You know," Izaveta said, her voice so quiet Asya had to strain to catch it, "the night before the ceremony, I prayed that I would be chosen as the Firebird."

Asya shifted her weight back, breath catching. The night before the ceremony *she'd* prayed that the two of them could stay together. Held her small wooden icon and begged Dveda to find another answer. And all the while her sister had wanted to leave. The thought sent a ragged pain through her gut, an old wound torn open afresh.

Izaveta looked up, catching Asya's expression. "Not because I wanted us to be separate. Because I wanted to leave here. This palace and the people and the weight of the crown. I wanted to be free."

Asya let out a low laugh. "You think I'm free?"

"You weren't trapped here." There was no anger in Izaveta's voice, but it held an edge. A bitter resentment that cut deeper. "You weren't under constant scrutiny, friends and enemies alike eager to see you fail. You weren't left with Mother and her schemes. You weren't *alone*." The last word came out almost like a curse, a low noise drawn from Izaveta against her will.

Asya stared at her sister's bowed head, at the tight curl of her fists. Izaveta was wrong, of course, because Asya had been alone. Lost without her other half. She'd just never realized her sister felt the same way. She'd always imagined Iza was stronger than her—*better* than her—because she never faltered. Never broke.

But perhaps it was just that her sister was better at hiding it.

"You could have answered my letters," Asya whispered. Those letters had been her refuge—her one way of pretending Izaveta wasn't gone. A refuge it looked like her sister had needed too.

"I know. I should have. But they made it all…" Izaveta paused, as if she couldn't force the word out. "Difficult." She clasped her hands together, looking down at them. "Being here with Mother—being in this world—I had to question everyone." She glanced up, the resentment melting into something else. A look that made Asya's stomach clench. "Even you."

Asya blinked. She'd never imagined that. Never thought of Izaveta here with their mother, slowly steeping in her poison.

Maybe that realization was what made the words come spilling out. "You're right to question me. *I* question me. I'm…" she started, pushing past the lump rising in her throat. "I'm not strong enough for this. For any of it." Unsaid words bubbled up in her mind, too painful to voice. *The strashe's death is my fault. Our mother's killer may be running free, and I can't stop them.*

She blinked, tears burning behind her eyes again. "I've failed already—or I am failing. There's a price that hasn't been paid, a debt owed to magic. And I can't find the caster."

Izaveta's chin lifted, her dark eyes boring into Asya's. "Don't you just follow the Calling?"

Asya shook her head. She couldn't stop the tears now, dripping down her cheeks like raindrops falling from leaves. "It's too…" She searched for the right words, but there were none that truly described the scalding brightness of that Calling. "It's too much for me. I'm not strong enough. I suppose the gods chose wrong." Admitting that out loud cost her something. Took the deepest part of herself that she tried not to look at and made it real.

Silence unspooled between them, dense as dawn fog.

Izaveta opened her mouth, then closed it again. An unusual hesitancy creased her features as she spoke, her voice low as crackling flames. "What happens if you don't follow a Calling? If the price is not paid?"

Asya looked down at her fingers. That hard knot of guilt twisted around her heart as she imagined the empty eyes of the dead strashe from the hunt. "I don't know," she lied. She didn't want to tell Izaveta, to see the reaction on her face. The look of accusation that Asya deserved.

Izaveta shifted, leaning forward in her chair. Her hand twitched, almost as if she were about to reach out but then thought better of it. "You are strong enough."

Asya met her sister's gaze, blinking away the last of the tears. There was a fierceness in Izaveta's eyes. It reminded Asya of the days before the ceremony, of the night of their failed ritual. A flash of the sister she knew.

"And perhaps," Izaveta went on, rising to her feet, "there are other ways we can deal with this Calling. If we work together."

Asya wiped her eyes. "You truly think that's possible?"

Izaveta's lips set into a grim line, the expression that said

Chapter Twenty-Six

The nightmares chased Asya in her sleep again that night. Snatched memories mingling with the Firebird's Calling.

This time, instead of staying trapped in her bones, the fire rampaged unchecked. The wrath of the Firebird seared through every part of Asya, bursting free. It burned through her memories—her mother's ghostly face, her sister's unrelenting determination. Scorching it all away until Asya was left alone with nothing but the scream clawing at her throat.

And a voice.

Ancient and rusted with disuse, drawn from the depths of the earth itself and steeped in that same old magic. *The price must be paid.*

"Asya."

That voice rumbled around her, coiling tight as a noose. *I did not choose you to be weak.* It gouged at her mind, pulling on her fears. On those memories she'd clung to. The mortal pieces of herself she so desperately hoarded.

I chose you to remake this world, not to fail it.

"Asya." A hand gripped her, like someone reaching beneath the waves to pull her from drowning.

She opened her eyes and the dream melted away. Terror remained clutched in her chest, that terrible emptiness as the Firebird had devoured her mortality. Vestiges of imagined flames still seemed to flutter behind her eyelids.

She blinked. No, not imagined—*real* flames.

They licked up the curtains, grabbed at the sheets and bedposts. The flaming forest of her dream come to life. She shrank back, suddenly that scared child again. Trapped and powerless to do anything.

A voice—real and familiar, not the terrifying hiss of her dreams—cut through the flames. "Asya, you have to make it stop."

Stop it? With these ravenous flames licking around her, Asya couldn't imagine ever being able to control them. Doing anything more than huddling in their midst, smothered by her own failures.

Fingers grabbed hers, fervent and burning. "Squeeze my hand. You're here."

Asya reached for those words, but the sparks consumed everything. Her voice, her mind. It was true. She was weak— too weak to face this. Too weak to escape it.

Each thought drew the flames higher. They burrowed down into Asya's lungs, all consuming. She couldn't even do this. She wasn't strong enough for the Firebird, and now it would destroy her.

A hand cupped her face, forcing her to steady. "Say it."

Asya took a breath, choking on ash. "I'm—I'm here." There

was no conviction to the words, more a desperate plea. Willing it to be true.

"Again."

She raised her hand to meet the one on her face and gripped it. Her point of contact for the real world. The one thing keeping her from being consumed. "I'm here."

Slowly—like a long-tensed muscle releasing—the flames abated. They didn't snuff out, but instead slithered back to her. Snakes returning to their master. She hadn't known she could do that.

It was only then that the world seeped into focus around her, only then that she realized who was holding her. Anchoring her.

The strashe's hand was still on Asya's face, gentle as it had been the night she'd bandaged her wound. Her gray eyes were so close Asya could pick out the shape of the storm clouds—not lightning filled but oddly soft.

Yuliana was no longer in her uniform, but in a loose shirt and trousers. Her hair hung unbound to her shoulders, framing her face in dark waves. It made her look younger. Not the harsh strashe who'd drawn her saber when Asya hunted, instead another glimpse of the girl beneath.

Yuliana pulled away. "I didn't want you to burn the palace down." Her words were guarded, as if Asya had accused her of something.

With a start, she realized the remnants of the flames' destruction still smoldered around them. Tendrils of smoke curling up from the sheets. But they hadn't reached Yuliana—a ring of protection for the strashe alone.

Asya blinked, her thoughts still moving too slowly, tangled in sleep. "How did you know to do that?"

"I—" Yuliana looked down, the shadowed light hiding her eyes. "I used to have nightmares. That was how my brother helped me."

Asya's lips parted, a question rising up her throat. She wanted to ask what those nightmares were. How they'd stopped. But that would be pushing too far. The strashe was acting out of obligation. She didn't owe Asya anything.

Even if there was a part of her that wanted to know. That was drawn to the things Yuliana kept close. That needed to understand every cloud that put together this quiet storm of a girl.

She looked away, heat creeping up her cheeks as she realized she'd been staring. "You—" Asya swallowed. "How's your arm?"

Yuliana tugged her sleeve down. "It's fine."

Asya reached out, a strange reflection of the strashe bandaging her. Except Asya was the one who'd caused this. Her fingers brushed over Yuliana's bandage, settling on her hand. A different kind of heat jittered across her skin, oddly soothing against the burn of the Firebird.

Yuliana pulled her arm away. "The voye only just let me go. And I thought I should check on you. After…everything."

Those words blossomed in Asya's chest. A tiny flicker against the Firebird's flames, but enough.

The day before, she might've read them as a threat. As the strashe ensuring the monster wasn't roaming free. But there was a softness to her voice now. Something that had shifted between them after what happened in the training grounds.

Despite the fact she'd burned her, despite Tarya's warnings about duty.

"Thank you," Asya murmured, some of that emotion threading through her voice. Too much for the Firebird. But for a brief moment, it didn't feel like it mattered.

Yuliana held her gaze, something unreadable snapping across her eyes. Straggling embers. Asya was suddenly very aware that she was only wearing a thin nightgown.

Yuliana stood abruptly. "I should go."

Asya watched the strashe's retreating steps. She curled her legs in, wrapping her arms around her knees. The tense knot of fear that had been crushing her ribs loosened, just a little. The pressing weight of all her failings suddenly lighter.

"Perhaps," Asya said, the words skittering out of her before she could catch them, "we could spar again?"

Yuliana turned in the doorway, her hair curtaining her face. The stuttered heartbeat it took for her to respond thrummed through Asya. A burning fear that she'd stepped too far.

But Yuliana raised her chin, the glint of a challenge. "We don't have anything else to wager."

Asya raised an eyebrow. "I suppose we could just debate the virtues of different sabers."

A slight smile curved Yuliana's lips—another flash of who she'd been in the training grounds. "You had to resort to magic in order to win. I believe that proves the znaya is superior."

With that, she vanished around the corner. The flames of Asya's nightmares still lurked in the corners of her vision, but they stood a little farther away, as if she were now shielded by a soft canopy of branches.

Chapter Twenty-Seven

"How did I never see this before?"

Izaveta suppressed a smile at the look of wonder on Asya's face as she stared at the coiling rows of books that wound their way up to the spire of Vetviya's Tower. There was a low hum of activity to the space this morning, from Valerii fetching texts to Nikov at his table by the window, half-hidden behind his own tower of tomes.

Izaveta shrugged. "Mother was hardly forthcoming about it."

Two full days had passed since Izaveta had told Asya they might find another way to deal with the Calling. Her sister's trust, the crack in her voice as she spoke about her failures, still felt surreal—fragile. Something Izaveta had to approach with caution lest she shatter it against the cold stone inside her. It was so much more than she could have dared hope for.

A dangerous hope.

Izaveta had always known that lies were the currency of the court, and growing up with her mother, she thought she'd learned how to protect herself from them. How to dissect them, to spin them to her advantage. She'd become used to deception, to expecting the worst from anyone who tried to get near her.

Yet, here she was now, allowing someone to get close to her again. But Asya wasn't like Kyriil. She wasn't a scheming courtier—she was her sister. That mattered.

Even with those warnings resounding in her head, it truly felt like she had her sister back. She was the one person who made all of this a fraction easier—even if Izaveta couldn't yet offer her the same honesty in return.

She'd tried. The words had risen to her lips a dozen times over the past few days. But she couldn't voice them, couldn't run from her lies quite yet.

Asya moved to the nearest bookshelf, her fingers twitching toward the tomes. "Surely there must be something in here. Something that explains—" she waved a hand as if trying to catch the right words "—all of this."

Izaveta recognized the longing in her sister's words. It was the same dazzling hope she'd had upon first seeing the library. Before the years of disappointment had begun to eat away at it.

A creaking voice answered, descending from the stairs. "If there is, I assure you I will find it. I know this library better than I know myself."

Izaveta turned to see Fyodor, his wild white hair bobbing as he moved over to them. "Good morning." She inclined her head to her sister. "Asya, meet my tutor, Master Alyeven."

He waved a hand, twinkling eyes fixing on Asya. "Please, you may call me Fyodor."

Asya shifted back, nervousness shivering around her again.

In moments like that, Izaveta could so clearly see the differences between them. The distinct skills they had been schooled in. "Nice to meet you," Asya murmured.

Izaveta stepped closer to Fyodor, lowering her voice—more out of habit than anything else. "Did you have any progress with Commander Iveshkin?"

Fyodor shook his head. "She continues to refuse a meeting. She claims the mourning days are a time for introspection, not politics."

Izaveta swore under her breath. That was the same response Iveshkin had given all her requests since the fiasco of the hunt. She'd hoped the commander might be more receptive to a note from Fyodor, who had known her longer and served under the former queen with her, but apparently even that route was compromised.

And Izaveta highly doubted it had anything to do with *introspection*, far more likely the commander had decided Izaveta could not offer her what she wanted.

She glanced over at Asya, the bargaining chip that could change everything.

Izaveta forced her eyes back to Fyodor, a bitter taste rising in her throat. That wasn't what the regained truce with her sister was about. Even if there was a part of her that couldn't help calculating the advantage it gave her.

Just like their mother would have.

Fyodor shifted. "But the commander will be in attendance this evening. That could provide you with an opportunity."

Izaveta nodded, folding her hands behind her as she realigned her strategy. That night, the sixth night of mourning, the palace was to play host to a ballet—organized at the express request of the envoys from Versbühl to honor the late queen. Everyone who mattered would be in attendance, from rich courtiers to foreign dignitaries to wavering cabinet members.

The mechanisms of a plan were beginning to spin into place in Izaveta's mind. And the performance tonight was the perfect time to put it into action.

"Your next steps will be crucial," Fyodor added, his eyes trailing to Asya. His warning from the day of her sister's arrival resounded in Izaveta's ears, the risk that this newfound trust brought. "And the alliances you choose will define your queenship."

But she didn't rise to his unspoken question. "My alliances shall show that Tóurin is unshakable."

Fyodor nodded, though there was still a slight crease between his brows. Something in that look unsettled Izaveta, needling at her own doubts. She had always heeded his advice before. But she didn't need him to question her—not when it came to her sister.

He raised his voice, glancing over to Asya. "If you have any questions, do not hesitate to ask. I always enjoy showing a newcomer around the library."

Asya looked up from the shelf. "Thank you, but I think—" She broke off, something stirring in her eyes. "Does the library have information on other things too?"

Fyodor cocked his head, as if confused by the question. "We study many subjects here."

Asya chewed her lip, deciding. "I saw, uh, a symbol that I had a question about."

Izaveta stared at her sister. "A symbol? What sort of symbol?"

Asya glanced around, reaching for a scrap of parchment and quill on a nearby desk. She bent over, hair falling across her face, as she scratched out a quick drawing. A flame—or perhaps a feather—with three thick lines running over it.

Fyodor took the parchment, squinting down at the mark. "I'm afraid it's not familiar to me, though I can certainly look into it."

"I've seen it before."

Izaveta almost jumped at the sound of Nikov's voice. She hadn't heard him approach.

She narrowed her eyes at him, examining. For someone who wanted to convince her he wasn't a spy, he certainly sneaked around like one. "Thank you, Master Toyevski, but—"

"You know what it is?" Asya interrupted, ignoring Izaveta's warning look.

Nikov turned, brow furrowing as he scanned the shelves. "Aha!" he said, with the flourish of a showman performing a trick. He pulled an ancient tome from the shelf, sending a shower of dust into the air. He set it down on the desk, and Izaveta couldn't stop herself from moving forward, drawn into the intrigue of it.

He flicked through the thick pages before he landed on one filled with crests. The ink was faded, several of the drawings reduced to no more than smudges. He pointed to one in the bottom corner, barely discernible.

But as Izaveta leaned in, she could make out the faint outline, the same as her sister's sketch. Faded letters beneath it spelled out *Order of the Captured Flame.*

"What is it?" Izaveta asked, curiosity getting the better of her.

"It's an old records book of the Church," Nikov said, far too pleased with himself for Izaveta's liking. "It denotes sects and orders that tithed money to them."

She reached forward to turn the page, hoping for more information—and was rewarded with a stinging pain in her wrist. The bandages were still wound tight around it, and the ache from the falcon's claws lingered. A constant reminder.

But the next page just showed more crests, no clearer than the previous ones.

"So that's all you can tell us?" Izaveta asked, scorn lacing through her words. "How helpful."

Fyodor squinted down at the page. "Those old books are not all accurate, I'm afraid, and rarely contain much of any use."

Nikov grinned, unperturbed. "Never tempt a scholar with information. I'm sure I can find more with time."

Izaveta's lips pursed. She didn't like the idea of Nikov looking into this—whatever it was. And his words strayed far too close to her mother's. To understanding what valuable currency information could be.

But she could no longer deny he would be a useful resource. And she was still in control here—still able to regulate what he knew. Then she could wait and see who that information trickled back to. Sanislav, or the ambassador. Or someone else entirely.

Either way, she'd work out where Nikov's loyalties lay.

Izaveta pulled her sister aside, lowering her voice. "Where did you see this?"

Asya glanced up at her with an apologetic grimace. "I didn't want to worry you."

"But?" Izaveta prompted, ice leaching through her veins.

Her sister looked down at her boots, fingers tangling together. "But someone tried to attack me. One night when I was walking in the grounds."

Izaveta's stomach turned over. Possibilities burst in her mind like kindling flames. Who would dare attack the Firebird? And within the grounds of the palace? She thought of Vittaria and the missing spy. Too many variables—too many unknowns—piling on top of her.

She took a slow, steadying breath. One problem at a time. She gestured to the book. "The person who attacked you was wearing this symbol?"

Asya nodded.

Izaveta turned back to the symbol, glaring down at it as if it might give her answers. But the drawing was resolutely unhelpful.

Would the vibishop be so bold as to attack the Firebird outright? Despite all his theories and posturing, Izaveta wasn't sure he would go that far. Not yet.

But there were so many pieces to all of this. Fragments of someone's plan that hovered just out of reach. If only she could see the whole picture, then it would make sense.

She put a hand on Asya's arm, the movement unfamiliar in its tenderness. "I shall inform my spymaster at once. We'll find out who's doing this."

And we will destroy them.

CHAPTER TWENTY-EIGHT

Queen Adilena had always told Izaveta that the ballet was the best political arena. It created a closed space, a limited time before the performance started, and the advantage of choosing who would be in attendance. It was a perfect opportunity not only to ensure that she mingled with the right people but also to see who everyone else spoke to. Who stole a whispered exchange as the candles were extinguished, who attempted to divert from the seating arrangement. And who was obviously trying to avoid someone else.

The Hall of Lost Moonlight had been transformed for the occasion. Not often used, Izaveta had chosen it specifically to suit her needs. At the base of Zmenya's Tower, the hall was a location that acknowledged the queendom's shared grief, while still allowing enough grandeur for the guests to remember Izaveta's position, her power. It was circular and low ceilinged, both of which lent to an intimate atmosphere, undercut by the bright orbs that hung in the air. Enchanted by the voye, they looked like captured sunlight, illuminating the proceedings in a warm golden light. It gave the event an ethereal glamor, a sense of magic that made people feel anything could happen.

Beyond the arched windows, the moons were rising. Zmenya's was fullest tonight, the pale reflection of their collected grief. The hole inside Izaveta where she *should* mourn.

She smoothed the slight crinkle to her skirts as she surveyed the room. The dress was a wonderful creation of pale blue silk, embroidered leaves spilling to the ground—the same shining silver of queenstrees. A delicate cape fell from her shoulders, a thin dusting of snow.

On her head she wore a kokoshnik of whirling silver, falling down to a sparkling gemstone in the center of her forehead. It was beautiful.

But it wasn't a crown, and tonight that could be all that mattered.

Izaveta moved through the assembled courtiers with an expression of detached warmth. Offering them welcome without yielding power, showing strength without appearing too severe. It was a look she'd practiced, modeled after the one her mother had perfected.

Her cabinet members were easy to spot. They were each like moons themselves, drawing the other guests to them like stars. Holding court in their own small spheres of power.

There was no sign of Asya yet, but that was hardly surprising. Even as a child, Asya had spent events like this hiding in the passages, climbing ornate columns when no one was looking.

For now, Izaveta would have to do without the Firebird.

Her eyes narrowed on a woman in the far corner. Commander Iveshkin and her retinue stood to the side of the hall, under the glow of one of the floating orbs. She wore military dress, as ever, the long kessek coat held in place by a gold embroidered belt, an ornate saber hung at her waist. It was as pristine as her dark hair, every facet of her appearance perfectly in place. She was deep in discussion with Conze Bazin, his bushy eyebrows furrowed in interest, as well as a third figure Izaveta could not quite make out.

The sight sent a flare of anticipation through her stomach. It wasn't unusual for the two cabinet members to talk, but something in their postures, in their keen expressions made her pause. If Bazin was trying to draw the commander to the Church's side, Izaveta had to ensure he failed.

She cut through the crowd easily, pausing occasionally to greet other guests and dignitaries. It wouldn't do for her to make it too obvious who she wished to speak to.

Izaveta fashioned her expression into a welcoming smile as she reached her targets. "Good evening, Commander Iveshkin. Conze Bazin."

Her smile slipped a fraction as she took in their companion. Kyriil's hair was threaded with golden light from above, like an old painting of a saint. Though the saintlike image was fractured by the caustic gleam in his eyes.

"My lady," he said, in a tone of conspiratorial familiarity that set Izaveta's teeth on edge, "we were just discussing a matter of great interest to you."

"Indeed?"

"Yes," the commander interjected, brusque as ever. At her side, her interpreter relayed her words aloud. "The matter of Conze Vittaria's murder."

Izaveta kept her expression blank, even as her stomach swooped. She still had no answers to that, no idea as to who would go to such an extreme. Although Zvezda's spies were looking into it, digging out any information they could, Izaveta knew they were getting further from the truth with each passing day. There were no leads to follow, no theories to pursue.

But she didn't say any of that, schooling her features into a look of deepest sympathy. "Her loss will certainly leave a wound at the heart of the queendom."

Iveshkin straightened as if on military display. "A wound that cannot heal without justice."

Izaveta nodded along, even as she fumed internally. They'd had this same conversation before. Short of producing a culprit out of thin air and blaming them, what more did the commander want her to do?

"We need to move past the tragedy, I believe, Commander," Bazin interjected, his thin voice wobbling like a missed music note. "We must persevere." He glanced over at Izaveta, weaving his fingers together. "My soothsayer has assured me that the stars bode well for you, my lady, despite recent tragedies."

Izaveta forced her eyes not to slide to Kyriil. He'd sent her a letter just that morning ensuring that he had a *friend* in Bazin's inner circle. That must be this soothsayer, threading support for her through their predictions. She had to give it to Kyriil—that was a good plan, one he'd pulled off successfully. Leveraging this cabinet seat against him might prove fruitful after all, even if it meant enduring his company.

She clasped her hands in front of her, mimicking Bazin's

movements. Another trick of her mother's to put one's opponent at ease. "I am so glad to hear that, Conze Bazin. I promise we shall not rest until we understand the source of the strange attack by that falcon and, of course, until we have found those responsible for what happened to Conze Vittaria."

Bazin touched a finger to the hollow of his throat, warding off the memory of that evil. "My advisors believe that may have been a reaction to the queen's sudden departure, spurred by her connection to the lands. Or, perhaps even—" he glanced around, lowering his voice before continuing "—discontent and ill faith within the Church."

Izaveta bit the inside of her cheek to suppress a smile. "Did they now? What an interesting theory."

That was a clever bit of misdirection, one that could serve her well. She hadn't thought Bazin would be possible to sway to her side, but here he was speaking against the Church.

Iveshkin raised her chin. "Theories are all well and good, but we must not let grief overshadow our duty." She kept her fingers held in the interlocked sign of duty a beat longer, emphasizing her disapproval. "We are missing a vital cabinet member. Mourning days or not, we cannot rest on our laurels."

"Certainly not, Commander," Izaveta replied, pouncing on the opportunity. "In fact, I have been thinking a great deal on the matter. The conze had no heirs to speak of, and, as such, we are left with one fewer familial seat." She could feel Kyriil's eyes on her, their fervent expectation. "You have served the cabinet well in your time, Commander. I am sure my mother would have wanted to reward your family for that, as I do."

Kyriil shifted back, unable to hide the disappointment that

flashed across his features. It sent a cool satisfaction through Izaveta, watching him squirm for once.

But the commander's expression didn't change. "That's a very lovely promise, my lady. But it is mere words."

Izaveta pressed her lips together. Out of the corner of her eye, she watched Bazin's brow furrow, his head tilt. All that progress she'd just made could be snatched back if she let the commander gain an edge here.

"Do you question the value of my word, Commander?" A hardness crept into Izaveta's smile, a reminder of who Iveshkin was speaking to.

But Iveshkin did not flinch away, her gestures crisp as ever. "Certainly not, my lady. But I do question whether you will have the power to fulfill it."

Izaveta stilled, trepidation freezing in her veins. That was more than mere words. A statement like that questioned the very foundation of her position. Of her crown. "And why would that be?"

"Tóurin must now, more than ever, stand strong against those who would do her harm," the commander signed. "And to ensure that, we must have the best leadership in place."

Izaveta straightened her shoulders, taking her time to respond. Showing the commander—and Bazin—that such comments did not worry her. Even if, underneath, her heart was pressing painfully against her ribs. "Tóurin is strong as ever," she said. "With the Firebird and the queen standing together, no one would be foolish enough to question that."

It was as much a truth as a threat. A threat that she would happily make good on if the commander truly did decide to stand against her.

Iveshkin raised her eyebrows, a slight twitch to her lips. "Is she?" she asked. "Is the Firebird standing with you?"

"Of course," Kyriil interjected. "They're sisters, are they not?"

Izaveta shot him a look. A perfectly crafted statement to come across as supportive, while it could still undermine her. Just the kind of double meanings Kyriil excelled at.

Bazin shifted his feet, worrying at his lower lip. "She didn't appear to be in agreement with you when she stormed out of the throne room."

Izaveta suppressed a hollow laugh. Appearances were everything here. It didn't matter that, this time, Asya had truly expressed her support. All that mattered was how it *appeared*. "A misunderstanding, now resolved. I assure you."

"Then why is it," Iveshkin pressed, "that I see her with the vibishop far more than I see her with you?"

She inclined her head to a spot somewhere over Izaveta's left shoulder. She followed the commander's gaze, careful to keep her movements languid. Uncaring. Indeed, not far from where they stood, the vibishop had his arm wound through Asya's, talking earnestly.

Svedye. Izaveta had been so engrossed in the conversation that she hadn't even noticed her sister enter.

She forced a smile, dragging her eyes away from her sister and Sanislav. "You shall see the Firebird's support is unwavering at my coronation."

Much as she wanted to, Izaveta did not run to her sister's side and pull her away from the vibishop. Instead, she kept smiling as if it was of no concern to her. Another trick she'd perfected from her mother.

She opened her mouth to redirect the conversation, but something else snagged in the corner of her vision. A figure dressed in indigo, his umber hair bathed in pale silver from the soft light. Nikov Toyevski appeared to be examining the paneled ceiling, his brow furrowed in apparent scholarly interest.

But that wasn't what had drawn her attention.

Izaveta had spent enough time at her mother's heels to be able to catch shifts in a room, changes in power that rippled out like a stone dropped in water. And something in Nikov had shifted.

Izaveta blinked and turned back to smile at Iveshkin and Bazin, trying to cover her sudden distraction. "Do enjoy the rest of your evening."

She didn't make directly for Nikov, instead meandering through the assembled guests with cursory greetings. But she kept one eye on his dark hair as it bobbed through the crowd, so she didn't miss when he moved away from the knot of scholars and out one of the side doors.

Nodding to the various courtiers she passed—and likely causing minor offense by not pausing to speak—she followed his steps. It was a break in decorum, one her mother would have scolded her for, but there was something in the set of Nikov's shoulders, in the intangible threads that trailed from him, that Izaveta needed to untangle.

She didn't take the same door as him, but instead one a little farther along, planning to come upon him as if by accident. It opened out to a narrow marble-lined passageway filled with statues of the former Karasova queens. The burbling voices of the guests were reduced to a quiet trickle out here, a distant stream rather than a bellowing river.

She was about to step out of the shadow of the alcove when a voice made her freeze. Not Nikov's soft tones, but a voice she recognized, speaking in crisp Versch.

Ambassador Täusch.

CHAPTER TWENTY-NINE

Asya almost wished more mysterious figures would leap out of the shadows. An onslaught of masked assailants would be preferable to the oppressive weight of the courtiers' accusing, fearful eyes.

Certainly better than this conversation, and the hundred missteps she was undoubtedly making. But the vibishop wouldn't leave her side, his arm fixed through hers from the moment she'd stepped into the room.

"I'm surprised your sister has not brokered more formal introductions for you," the vibishop went on, his voice soft as spun silk. "The cabinet has been eager to speak with you."

Asya swallowed. Izaveta had warned her of the potential pitfalls this evening would provide, of the way members of the court might try to use her. And Asya felt the trap in those words—one she wasn't adept enough to evade. "I—uh, she's had a lot to do."

She looked around for any way out, but there was no sign of her sister's gleaming kokoshnik. And with the whispers rustling around her, hungry wolves all eager for a piece, Asya couldn't remember her sister's advice. The people she'd told her to stay near, the ones she should avoid.

She shot a glance at the doorway, as if she might ask it to swallow her back up.

Then she felt a light touch on her elbow, the barest brush of fingers. Not more than the flutter of a cobweb, but it sparked across Asya's skin. She looked back to meet Yuliana's steely gaze. The strashe's expression was set, and she gave Asya a small nod. A tiny movement that said she wasn't entirely alone.

Something had changed between them, a shift in the balance, after the night Yuliana had helped stop her nightmares.

The nightmares still hovered, as constant as the Calling. But Yuliana's words helped, her soft intonation. Her calming presence. They'd been sparring too, spending mornings in the training grounds—luckily, without the Firebird making an appearance. Asya felt like she saw a little more of the strashe in those precious snatched moments. And, perhaps, that Yuliana was seeing a little more of her.

Seeing her as more than the flames.

The vibishop inclined his head, simpering. "Of course, especially with the events of today."

Asya picked at one of the glittering beads sewn onto her gown, staring down at the flowing flame-red fabric, dripping in embroidered feathers, to avoid the vibishop's piercing gaze. "What events are those?"

Out of the corner of her eye, she saw his lips twitch toward a smile. "I'm sure she didn't want to bother you with strange tales."

Asya gritted her teeth. Couldn't he just say outright what he meant?

He steered her through another knot of courtiers, drawing their attention. "An odd story from a small village near Vas Tiraviya." Sanislav leaned in, conspiratorial. "A trader claims the occupants have vanished, humans and animals alike."

She stopped short. "What?"

"Indeed," Sanislav went on, with an air of vague interest. "A most puzzling situation. The trader claims all that was left was a whispering fog. Perhaps a new symptom of the Fading."

An icy dread crept up Asya's spine. That was not a symptom of the Fading. That was something else entirely.

The bead she'd been toying with popped off her dress, skittering across the floor.

With every breath, the dress seemed to squeeze tighter around her. A painful joke—a testament to her failures. To give off the illusion of the powerful Firebird when she was nowhere near that. She should have spent the evening trying to feel the Calling—doing more of Tarya's exercises. Or at least trying to look into that shard of bone.

But instead she'd let herself get distracted by her mortal ties.

And an entire village had paid the price.

Tarya's warning loomed over her. It pulled into a tight knot in Asya's chest, that constant tug between girl and monster.

But when her failures meant a village had blown away like leaves on the wind, could the girl who shirked her duty be seen as better than the monster?

Perhaps it truly was inescapable. Whether she embraced the Firebird or fled from it, it always came back to the same thing.

"Are you all right, Firebird?"

Asya blinked. She'd almost forgotten where she was. She swallowed, each of her failures grating along her throat like shattered glass. "Yes," she managed, her voice a little hoarse. "Quite all right."

The ingratiating smile painted across his face made her skin crawl. "I'm sure it's been difficult to adjust," he pressed on. "It's understandable that the reunion with your sister could be fraught. But know that there are those here who keep your best interests at heart."

Asya wasn't listening. Something else had suddenly flared in her mind, a shining possibility. She'd thought that without the shard of bone, without being able to reach the Calling, all hope at finding the caster was lost. But there was still another path she hadn't tried.

"Vibishop," she interrupted, "are there any saints' relics kept within the palace?"

His smile slipped. "Saints' relics?"

"Yes." A new excitement thrummed through her veins, drowning out the small voice that told her she was most definitely breaking some unspoken protocol.

"Well," he said slowly, clearly disconcerted by her sudden shift. "The archbishop certainly keeps several in the cathedral. Saint Korona's cape of woven branches, Saint Restov's knife—"

"Any bones?" The question flew too quickly from her lips, coming out far more bluntly than she'd intended. But this was important, this was a chance at a reprieve, and she couldn't bring herself to worry about the strange rules of the court.

The vibishop's forehead creased as he surveyed her. "Why the sudden interest in the bones of a saint?"

Asya hesitated for a heartbeat before drawing herself up to her full—if somewhat unimpressive—height. She hardened her features, matching Tarya's unwavering ferocity. The unquestionable power of the creature inside her. "The Firebird's business is between her and the gods, Vibishop. No one else."

He blinked, all traces of the fawning smile falling from his face. It was replaced with a shrewd appraisal that nearly made Asya's certainty crumble. The vibishop might act the part of a simpering fool, but that look betrayed there was something far more dangerous beneath.

She wished she could snatch the question back. Retreat to the comforting embrace of the forest, where it didn't feel like every word she said was a weapon that could be turned against her.

"There are some who might say the Firebird stands between us and the gods." His voice was soft, yet there was a dangerous thread to it. The slither of a snake before it struck. "That she takes the magic Dveda gifted us for herself."

Asya stiffened. She'd heard the accusations before—wondered herself at the role the Firebird played in magic, in the Fading. But no one had ever said it so openly. Her mind darted to the echoing voice of her nightmares. The creeping hiss that shuddered across her skin.

I did not choose you to be weak. Which left the question: What had she been chosen for?

"Not me, of course," he went on, with an acquiescing smile. "As for saints' bones, I'm afraid there are none in the palace."

Asya's stomach fell. She'd given away something with that question, and she hadn't even found answers in return.

"Though," the vibishop added, "there are some kept within the grounds. Heavily protected by enchantments, of course." His eyes met hers, something unreadable glimmering in their depths. "In the Grove of the Fallen Queens."

CHAPTER THIRTY

"All queens are the same." The ambassador's voice floated down the passage to Izaveta. He spoke in Versch, hard consonants resonating against the marble floor. "Hiding behind their smiles and lies, believing they can bend the land to their will."

Izaveta trod carefully, moving farther into the shadowed alcove of Queen Teriya's statue. Teriya's unseeing eyes overlooked the proceedings with disdain, as though admonishing Izaveta for acting like a spy when she should be queen.

But Izaveta didn't have a crown yet, and this information could be worth the breach in decorum. Besides, she was not planning on letting anyone see her.

Nikov replied in Versch too. His accent was polished, but Izaveta thought she could pick out the slight errors, the smoothness of Tóurensi slipping in. "And I suppose the kaizer you answer to is benevolent."

"He does not hide behind smiles," the ambassador replied,

his inflection pointed. He went on, in a soft murmur that was too low for Izaveta to catch.

She leaned forward, her hair falling precariously close to the edge of the alcove, but all she could hear was the faint mutter of the ballet guests. She risked a glance around, trying to glean something from their posture if not their words. The ambassador's back was to her, all but obscuring Nikov. Täusch's stance was relaxed, head turned to the carved statue beside him as if this conversation were of little interest to him. That spoke of power—not power someone had clawed for and scrabbled to keep cupped in their hands, but power that someone held comfortably.

"If you merely want to admire the statuary," Nikov said, his voice louder and forcibly casual, "perhaps I should return to the hall. I was quite enjoying contemplating the historiography of the ceiling decor."

He went to walk away, but the ambassador blocked his path with the slightest shift in his weight. Nikov flinched back, and Izaveta caught the edge of his expression. A tight set to his jaw, eyes guarded. The look of someone who knew the balance of power had been snatched away from them.

The ambassador leaned in, and though Izaveta couldn't see his face, she thought she could hear the smile in his voice. "You have been rather hard to find, Nikov."

There was a familiarity in that use of his given name. It sent a prickling unease across Izaveta's skin—she'd been right about the connection between them. About those unspoken things she'd sensed.

She should've felt victorious in that, a weapon she'd kept sharpened. But that didn't hold off the sting of betrayal.

A foolish part of her had thought perhaps there was something to Nikov that wasn't an act, that wasn't another part of a twisted game. But she'd been wrong about that too.

Nikov's voice was tight when he spoke, all pretense at lightness gone. "I didn't know you were looking for me."

"Always an answer for everything." The ambassador let out a low noise of contempt, a hollow echo of a laugh. "But you are forgetting yourself. You can't stay locked in that tower forever."

"I'm a scholar first," Nikov replied, and there was a careful edge to his words. One that Izaveta recognized—it was the same way she'd spoken to her mother as she stepped around carefully laid traps. "You can't change that."

The ambassador took a step forward, though Nikov didn't back away this time. Täusch's voice was a low thrum, threaded with something Izaveta couldn't quite catch. She pressed closer, cursing the echoing acoustics of the passageway that snatched away their words.

"Well, we both know the answer to that," the ambassador finished, voice rising. The words hung in the air, a threat that Izaveta couldn't quite decipher. Fractured pieces of something that were still too disparate for her to put back together. The frustration of that burned through her, her mind failing her at this crucial point. Her mother would be able to work this out, would be able to see the strategies and anticipate moves before they happened.

But Izaveta was still just muddling through. For all her plans and information, she was still on the defensive.

A bell chimed from inside the hall, echoing into the passageway, and Izaveta quickly pulled back into the alcove. The flow of distant conversation faltered, leaving a sudden silence. The ballet was about to start.

"We should find our seats," the ambassador said. "I do hope you appreciate the performance." There was an odd shift in his tone—as if he wasn't speaking only to Nikov anymore. Izaveta shook that thought off like an unwelcome cobweb. He couldn't possibly know she was there.

The ambassador's harsh footsteps retreated first, followed by Nikov's. Izaveta let herself fall back against the wall, a lack of dignity she so rarely allowed, even if she was alone. All the variables spun through her mind, the connections just out of her reach.

But she couldn't think on them now. She had to go back in there and show that nothing shook her. Besides, the Versch and whatever scheme some Amarinth scholar were hatching were not her priority. She had to focus on the internal problems first, face each obstacle as it came, just as her mother taught her. All moves in the larger game.

Even if the thought of that Amarinth scholar made her throat constrict.

Izaveta counted five heartbeats—too fast and stammering—before forcing herself to straighten.

She strode back into the hall with her chin raised high, not looking at anyone as she made her way to her seat in the front row. Asya joined her a moment later, Sanislav still holding her arm. Despite that, Asya was smiling. The sight sent a quiver of unease up Izaveta's spine.

Sanislav's eyes glinted as they alighted on Izaveta, the hidden fangs of a beast caught in the light. "I am told this performance is dedicated to you, my lady." He sat down, his gaze never leaving her.

Izaveta sank into her own seat, pulling her sister with her. "You shouldn't speak with him," she hissed, leaning in close. "Anything he says he will use for his own gain."

Asya waved a hand, her excitement not dampened. "I know, he's awful. But I found a lead, Iza. A place where the caster may have found the bone of a saint."

Izaveta stared at her sister, horror cresting in her chest. "You told him about that?"

"Of course not," Asya replied. "I just asked a vague question."

Izaveta's fingers curled, crushing the soft silk of her skirt. "Any question you ask is something he could use against you." *Against us*, she added inside her head. She wasn't quite ready to say that out loud yet—to believe that they'd gone back to being an inseparable pair.

Asya reached over and squeezed her hand. "Don't worry, Iza. This is a good thing. It's a chance to fix all of this."

The orbs above their heads extinguished, and the first notes of music floated through the air, ending their conversation.

When Izaveta was younger, she'd loved the ballet. The way the music transported her to another place, a story told with nothing more than whirling movements. But tonight she couldn't leave the hall. Couldn't forget the commander's pointed remarks, Sanislav's gleaming eyes, or the ambassador's veiled threats. The cabinet that was poised to tip away from her.

And there were still so many things her sister did not understand.

The ballet started in a swirl of color, dancers twirling around each other in a suspended harmony. As soon as the principal dancer produced the matryoshka doll, Izaveta recognized the story. Understanding washed over her slowly, a creeping fog that one didn't realize they'd stumbled into until they were submerged. *The Trials of Vasilisa the Beautiful*, an old folktale. Helped by her enchanted doll, Vasilisa tried to save her father from a witch hidden deep in the forest. But the witch demanded Vasilisa complete a task: bring her the pelt of a sacred banewolf. In hunting something holy, she fell out of favor with the gods. Determined to escape her fate, she turned to magic.

Vasilisa succeeded in her task and freed her father, but she had not paid the price of her spell.

The Firebird appeared onstage in a burst of flames and golden light, eliciting gasps from the audience. Izaveta couldn't help but wonder what price someone had paid for that spectacle. The dancer was beautiful—graceful and unforgiving in her movements. She felt Asya shift at her side, muscles coiling. But Izaveta didn't look over at her sister. All she could see was the fear on Vasilisa's face. And the clear certainty in the Firebird's movements as she took the girl's heart.

The price was paid, and the gods' vengeance fulfilled.

Sanislav's words echoed in Izaveta's head, drowning out the final crescendo. *I am told this performance is dedicated to you.* A pointed choice by the Versch kaizer. The story of a girl brought down by the gods—and the Firebird. A reminder of the power they had, how Sanislav could leverage the Church against her. The poison he'd already begun to spread.

PART FOUR:

VENGEANCE OF THE GODS

A mere breath to conjure a spark of flame,
A tongue to twist another to your game,
A tooth to cure a simple malady,
An eye if you want the future to see,
A year of life for true loves to never part,
And for the darkest of deeds: a heart for a heart,
But be warned now, do not evade the price,
For the greatest power demands sacrifice.

—"The Caster's Rhyme,"
an old Tóurensi folk song

CHAPTER THIRTY-ONE

A thin dusting of snow had settled underfoot, crunching beneath Asya's fur-lined boots as she made her way through the grounds. She hadn't wanted to wait for the next morning, but she had to admit she wouldn't make much progress searching the queenstrees in the dark. The first glow of dawn shone above the distant tree line, spilling cool gray light across the landscape.

Yuliana, as ever, shadowed her steps. There was a comfort to her presence now, a familiarity that had begun to take root in Asya's heart, fragile as a new seedling in winter. Because despite their time training together, despite falling into this new rhythm with each other, she was still waiting. Waiting for Yuliana to see the monster.

Asya felt like she was teetering on a precipice. And once she stepped over the edge, there would be no way back.

She blinked, banishing the tangled images from her mind. Touching a finger to her wooden icon, she sent down a prayer. She needed Dveda to look kindly on her today.

The wide expanse of the bearkeep spread out in front of them. To one side stood the tall wooden enclosures the bears were kept in at night, to the other the frost-tinted ground of the exercise yard. The stench of bear was overwhelming, mingled with the salty tang of fish.

Guilt twinged through Asya's gut. She hadn't been to see Mishka since she'd arrived at the palace. At the Roost he was used to having free roam of the forest. He wouldn't like the forced enclosure here.

"We're taking a bear?"

Asya paused. She glanced over her shoulder to see Yuliana hanging back by the path. "Yes," Asya said. "It'd take all day to get to the queenstrees on foot."

Yuliana still didn't move. She had an odd expression on her face. A slight crease to her forehead, a tightening to her lips. It took Asya a moment to recognize the emotion because it was so out of place on the strashe. Apprehension—almost fear.

Asya tilted her head. "Have you not ridden a bear before?"

Yuliana's throat bobbed. "No."

Asya couldn't suppress a smile—which elicited an irritated sigh from the strashe. "Come on," Asya said. "I'll introduce you to Mishka."

The bears' stalls were warm as summer, the smell intensifying. At this hour the building was devoid of humans. The only sounds were the shuffling of paws and the soft snores of the large creatures. Asya hurried along the stalls, searching for that familiar hazelnut-brown fur. She paused only at the sight of Olyeta, Izaveta's snow-white bear, whose eyes glinted over the top of the wooden door. An odd flash of another life.

Mishka was two doors along, his snout resting on the stall

door. He let out an irritated snuffle as Asya approached and retreated into the stall, turning his back on her.

"Don't be like that." She grabbed a salmon from the nearest bucket. Pushing the door open, she held it out to him. A peace offering.

Mishka's nose perked up. After a few more angry snorts, he shuffled forward and took the fish with a look that said Asya hadn't been forgiven yet. But he still consented to her scratching his muzzle as he ate. The soft warmth of his fur eased some of the coiled tension inside her.

Yuliana lurked in the doorway, eyeing Mishka with a deep suspicion.

It was oddly comforting to see someone usually so certain afraid of Mishka, who could barely manage to hunt for his own food.

Asya offered Yuliana a small smile. "The worst he'd do is sit on you by accident."

The strashe did not look reassured.

Asya rubbed Mishka's side, shooting Yuliana a furtive glance. "How did you come to the palace if not by bear?"

The question hung tentative in the air. They might have spent more and more time together, but they had never divulged anything too personal, apart from a few hints. Certainly nothing this direct.

Yuliana shifted, not quite meeting Asya's gaze as she replied, "In a troika from Kirava. Where I could stay in the sleigh and be nowhere near the bears' fangs." She studied Mishka warily, his snout still busy with the salmon. "My father always called them unholy beasts, a false image of Dveda."

Asya snorted, then tried to pass the noise off as a cough—but judging from Yuliana's expression, did not succeed.

"Sorry," Asya murmured, trying to keep her face straight. "But Mishka is far from that. Besides," she added, "how can they be unholy when they were created by a saint?"

Yuliana leaned against the doorpost, with raised eyebrows that said she was humoring Asya for now.

Asya curled her fingers in Mishka's fur, half talking to him. "Saint Ilyova journeyed to the Skyless Hallows to find the weapon that would ensure her victory against the demonye. She succeeded but, exhausted from the fight, couldn't summon enough magic to travel through the stars, as she usually did. So she called on Dveda for help, and he created a creature to aid her. Sculpted from snow and ice in his own image. That's why Ilyova is the protector of travelers, watching over all bear riders."

Yuliana's eyes narrowed, but the slight quirk of her lips gave her away. "You made that up."

Not quite. Elaborated, maybe, but it had always been Asya's favorite of their rambling tutor's obscure folktales. She and Izaveta had acted it out with their bears on the banks of the Depthless Lake, imagining lives that were separate from their own. Thinking of it now didn't give Asya the same spiraling sadness it would have a few days ago. Even with the mess of problems she was caught in, she did have her sister. She wasn't alone in this anymore.

Her breath hitched as she glanced up at Yuliana, at her ghost of a smile. That fragile flame glowed again, tiny against the Firebird's might. Maybe she had someone else too.

"Perhaps a little," Asya replied, her grin creeping back. "But would you want to risk offending Saint Ilyova herself?"

Yuliana's jaw tightened. A steely glint flashed in her eyes as she took a step forward. She wasn't one to back down from a challenge.

Her fingers reached tentatively for Mishka. But she stopped just short, hesitating before she touched his fur. Asya's hand moved of its own volition. Her fingers entwined with Yuliana's, drawing their hands into the warmth of the bear's fur.

Yuliana's lips parted slightly, staring at Mishka with an almost childlike wonder. It tugged on something in Asya's chest—kindling to a spark. Another piece of the strashe she hadn't seen before.

Yuliana pulled away suddenly, her left hand jerking to cover her right.

Asya looked down at her feet, heat creeping up her neck. The image from the first day in the sparring ring rose in her mind. That lattice of scars. She wanted to ask—but couldn't quite force the words out. She didn't want Yuliana to pull further away.

Asya turned back to the bear. "We should get going."

Between the two of them, they made quick work of saddling Mishka and looping the loose harness around his neck. Before the sun had crested the distant treetops, they were ready. Yuliana didn't wait for help, scrambling up into the saddle with a look of stoic determination, as if to make up for her earlier uncertainty. Asya hesitated a moment before following. The saddle wasn't big, and she still felt too aware of the limited space between her and the strashe. Of the fluttering moments when that space disappeared.

But that didn't matter now—it couldn't matter. Asya had more important things to think about.

As soon as she settled into the saddle, her tangled nerves unraveled a little. This was something that made sense to her. A constant through every tumultuous change.

A grin spread across her face. She shot a half glance back at Yuliana, her dark hair stark against the winter backdrop. "Hold on."

Mishka didn't give Yuliana a breath to respond. As eager to run as Asya, he jolted forward. The air whipped the world away. In only a few hammering heartbeats the imposing form of the palace became nothing more than a blur behind them. All Asya could feel was the biting cold, snapping at her exposed skin. The pounding rhythm of the bear. And the warmth of Yuliana's arms, wrapped tight around her waist.

In that moment, Asya couldn't think about anything else. Couldn't see her failures imprinted behind her eyelids.

It was over too soon. Mishka came careening around the southern bank of the Depthless Lake—its glow fainter than the hazy dawn light—and the queenstrees rose up around them. Silent sentinels stepping out of the mist like warriors of legend.

Asya slowed Mishka to a walk. The quiet of the silver-white trees was sudden and oppressive, spreading from their spidery roots. No distant starbirds calling, no rustle of wind through branches. Just silence as heavy as a fresh blanket of snow.

It was said that the veil between the earth and the In-Between rippled here. One misstep, and you might fall into Vetviya's realm, trapped neither here nor there.

Asya suppressed a shudder. Mishka seemed to feel it too.

His ears twitched, muzzle swinging from side to side. She drew him to a halt and jumped off his back, boots crunching against the untouched dusting of snow on the ground.

Yuliana slid down after her, the movement lacking her usual grace. In her eagerness to be away from the bear, her foot tangled in a root, and she stumbled. Asya caught her, hands tight on Yuliana's shoulders. The sudden proximity made Asya's breath catch. They'd been close on Mishka, but not facing each other. Not near enough that Asya could see the frost clinging to Yuliana's eyelashes, sending glimmering light across her irises.

"Diye," Yuliana murmured, lips pressed firmly together as she straightened. "Now I know why I've never done that before."

Asya's laugh died in her throat, smothered by the weight of the queenstrees. She swallowed her unease, focusing instead on picking her way through the roots. The white trunks opened out into a clearing. The pale stone of the grove mingled with the snow, the markers of where the queens had been returned to the earth—to Dveda's embrace—breaking through the ground. A statue of Zmenya stood at the very center, her serene face overlooking them all.

Everything inside Asya stilled, her lungs solidifying like ice. Not because of the unnatural quiet or the dead queens. Because of the starbirds.

Their pale bodies, leached of the usual warm glow of magic, lay strewn across the grove like fallen leaves. Their eyes had been burned out. Nothing but scorched sockets of blackened flesh remained, as if they'd been consumed from the inside out by flames.

No, not by flames. By *magic.*

Asya gagged, bile rising in her throat. The scent of burned flesh, cut through with the sharp tang of magic, was suddenly too much.

"What in all the realms—" Yuliana breathed, touching the hollow of her throat as if to ward off the sight.

Asya didn't reply. This was because of *her.* Because of the imbalance. Innocent creatures reduced to burned-out husks. The Firebird prickled beneath her skin, drawn out by the magic. It was the reminder she needed. This might be because of her, but she also had the power to do something about it.

She didn't look at Yuliana, though she could feel the strashe's horror like a wave at her back. Instead, Asya dragged her eyes away from the birds, sending a small prayer to Saint Ilyova for their peaceful passing, and strode across the clearing.

Above each of the queens' grave markers was a small egg, sculpted of marble so thin it almost looked like silk. Magic buzzed around them, protecting the saints' relics contained within. Moss and grass had crept across their surfaces as if claiming them too for Dveda. If any had been opened recently, she should be able to tell. And if the person had used magic— even if the price had been paid—there might be traces left. Something she could use to track the culprit.

Her eyes caught on a grave marker so close to the edge of the clearing that the silver roots of a queenstree clutched to its sides. Dark green crept across the egg's surface, but there was a patch of sparkling marble. As if a finger had smudged the ancient moss.

Asya hurried over to it, squinting down at the grave. Queen Katvesha, the queen who had pushed the Versch back to beyond the Gilded River. Asya ran her fingers over the small egg. Magic prickled against her fingertips like nettle leaves. Her heart leaped. The tiny silver clasp was gleaming, freshly cleaned of moss.

She closed her eyes, focusing on the scent of the magic. The feel of it against her skin, just as Tarya had taught her before she'd got her power. It had been at least nine days since the spell was cast, but the queenstrees had a way of clinging to magic. Preserving it within their realm.

Beneath the soft smell of sap and frost—and the cutting scent of the dead starbirds—was something else. A small residue, separate from the old magic of the grove. It was oddly familiar, but Asya couldn't quite place why.

"Asya?"

Her eyes flew open, concentration shattered by Yuliana's voice.

The strashe stood several paces back, watching. A realization seemed to have fallen over her, a heavy shroud covering her eyes. "This is for a price, isn't it?"

Asya's hands clenched. There was an echo in Yuliana's voice, a terrible reflection. *I know what hides beneath.*

"Yes," Asya said. The word was oddly hushed in the clearing, like a whispered confession.

The blade that she had been waiting to fall slammed down between them.

Everything about the strashe tightened. The innocent wonder, the easy camaraderie that had spread between them vanished. As if Yuliana had allowed herself to forget that she was accompanying a wolf, until she realized it was hunting.

For a long moment, she held Asya's gaze. "Why?" Yuliana

said finally. Such a simple word, but the slight shake to her voice betrayed its significance. The weight that came with it. "Why do this when it hurts people?"

The question ricocheted through Asya. The same one she'd asked herself for so many years. "Because of this," she whispered, unable to keep the desperation from her voice. The sudden need for Yuliana to understand. She gestured to the starbirds—and her mind traveled beyond just them, to the dead strashe and the strangely empty village. "Because if I don't, then *this* happens."

Something inside her settled with that admission. The scorching guilt, the suffocating pressure of her duty morphing into something else—a new understanding that was somehow both terrifying and comforting. "It's not a cruelty. If the price isn't paid, then so many more will be hurt. All because of me. Because of what I failed to do. I don't relish it, but I couldn't live with myself if I let it go unanswered. If I stood back while people were killed, while magic ran wild. You can see the Firebird as a monster, but the truly monstrous thing would be to do nothing."

The words abruptly ran out, leaving Asya breathless. She felt as if she'd carved out a piece of her core and pulled it into the light. All her misgivings and uncertainties, the true weight of this.

And there was no going back now.

No more pretending.

Yuliana would either accept that or she wouldn't. Asya tried to narrow it down to that simple statement, even if she knew how much Yuliana's choice could hurt.

Asya couldn't read anything in the strashe's eyes, as inscrutable as the swirling surface of the Depthless Lake. Asya took a tentative step forward, closing the distance between them.

She knew the burden of the Firebird, to be seen as the terrible monster of legend. But in these snatched moments with Yuliana, she'd let herself hope. A fragile pretense that someone might see her as more than that.

Yuliana's lips moved, her mouth opening to reply, when a sound from behind them cut her off. A low whooshing, like a bird swooping through the trees. In the contorted confusion of the moment, it took Asya a heartbeat too long to realize what it was.

It skimmed against her side, then slammed into the earth with a hollow *thunk*.

An arrow.

CHAPTER THIRTY-TWO

The clouded morning light pressed against the palace windows, making Izaveta feel like she was caught inside an immense spider's web, glistening silk strands pulling tighter and tighter around her. Even the warm glow of the library, which had always been Izaveta's haven, wasn't enough to stave off the growing sensation that she was trapped. Entangled in the remnants of her mother's schemes, and unable to pull herself free.

But that didn't mean she was powerless. Or that she would let herself be played for a fool.

Which was why her smile was unwavering as she sat down opposite Nikov and his teetering tower of books. "I trust you had a pleasant time last night?"

Nikov looked different in the soft light of the library, tousled hair falling into his eyes, a dark smudge of ink on his jaw. Back into the role of scholar, wrapped in the comfort of ancient tomes.

His lips hitched into a grin. "I'm flattered you noticed I was there."

His conversation with the ambassador resonated in her ears, each word a frustrating question she still couldn't answer. But despite her suspicions, there was a part of her—the part she'd thought her mother had destroyed—that was drawn to him. His presence brought a strange calm, a point of certainty among the half-truths and schemes.

Even if she'd now faced clear evidence that he was tied up in those too.

She raised an eyebrow, keeping her expression serene. "I'm to be queen. It's in my best interest to notice everything." She caught herself, stomach clenching. That had always been such a certainty, ever since that fateful day. And now it was slipping away from her, all because she'd let a fool like Sanislav get the best of her.

She felt like she was staring down at a zvess board, her opponent's pieces closing in on her queen. Everything out of her control.

No, not *everything* out of control. She just needed a new strategy. A new way to bring the commander over to her side. To sway Bazin away from Sanislav. To unravel the ambassador's plans.

Then there was the more pressing question—who had dared attack the Firebird? Zvezda and her pakviye had heard no whispers of a scheme, no hints of anyone trying to breach the palace walls. Which simply produced more questions.

But there had to be a way out. There was always a way out.

Nikov sat back in his chair, warm eyes on her. She couldn't help but feel he'd noticed the slight crack, the hint at the weaknesses she hid.

Izaveta pressed on before he could pounce on it. "Did you enjoy the ballet?"

"It was remarkable," he replied. "Although *The Trials of Vasilisa the Beautiful* was an unusual choice to honor the queen."

She considered a moment before choosing her response. Conversations with him were not like conversations with other members of the court. Those were battles, each party dealing in blows and deflections. But talking to Nikov was like a dance, carefully prepared steps and fleeting touches. Two people whirling around a center point that neither could quite reach. And Izaveta still didn't know what secrets that center held.

She leaned back in her chair, mirroring his posture. Part of her wanted to push further, to toss aside the game and just ask. But there was danger in revealing one's hand too soon, so instead she said, "It was at the request of Ambassador Täusch, so I'm sure he had his reasons."

Izaveta watched for his reaction, for those threads that connected Nikov to the ambassador to flutter into place. Perhaps some of that unease she'd sensed in him last night.

But Nikov's voice remained light, no hint of tension to his shoulders, as he replied, "I imagine so."

The door creaked open behind her, the sound splintering the careful steps of their dance. Kyriil entered, his blond hair gleaming even in the shadows cast by a nearby candle. He stopped short as his eyes swept across the room, catching on Nikov.

"My lady," Kyriil said in greeting, though his gaze lingered on Nikov.

Izaveta rose to her feet, slipping into stiff formality. The sight of him in this library sent a barb of annoyance through her. He only knew about it because she'd been foolish enough to show him, one of those nights when she'd believed he understood. That he was on her side.

Now he was taking her refuge and using it against her. "Master Azarov. It certainly is a surprise to see you in a library," she said, unable to withhold the gibe.

Kyriil ignored it, his eyes sliding back to hers. "I had wanted to speak in private."

Izaveta watched him for a heartbeat, calculating. Permitting him to interrupt her—and to set the terms—was a concession. But in front of Nikov, with his loyalties so uncertain, she couldn't allow Kyriil to speak freely.

And, besides, Kyriil had proved useful with Bazin last night.

She settled on a compromise. "Come," she said to Kyriil, gesturing for him to follow her toward the arched window. It was far enough from Nikov that he wouldn't hear their whispers, but not such a change as to inconvenience her.

She faced outward, surveying the landscape as if it was of great interest. Frost crept around the edges of the glass, thick white clouds rolling out from the palace and down to the distant queenstrees. From here she couldn't see the Depthless Lake, but it hovered in the edge of her vision. A constant reminder.

Kyriil joined her, standing too close for propriety. But Izaveta didn't rebuke him or step away. She didn't want to appear to back down in any sense.

His face was grim, though there was a spark of something else in his eyes. A prickle of unease crept up her spine. "My spy was expelled from Bazin's household."

Izaveta's stomach hardened. She thought back to the ballet, to Bazin's remarks against the Church. What could have drawn him back into their clutches? Perhaps the ballet itself, the thinly veiled threat of a girl who stood against the gods. Or perhaps seeing the Firebird with Sanislav had been enough.

She looked back at Kyriil. "How?"

He shook his head. "I don't know. After the hunt, I paid off a soothsayer to work their way into his circle. As you heard last night, it seemed to be working. Then I received this letter."

He pulled a piece of parchment from his jacket pocket, holding it out to her.

She took it slowly, a poisoned offering. Written in neat, curling script was a single line.

Bazin suspects. I have been forced out.

Izaveta turned back to the window, crumpling the parchment in her fist. "That fool has gone crawling back to the vibishop."

"I met with the soothsayer just now. He heard one more thing before he was sent away." Kyriil's eyes bored into hers. "Sanislav is going to move against you at Noteya Svedsta."

Izaveta's fingers gripped the windowsill—her one concession to the fear spiraling through her. Noteya Svedsta, Saints' Night, was a ball held on the final night of mourning. It honored the saints and asked them to speed the late queen's passage into the earth.

The day before what was meant to be Izaveta's coronation.

She kept her tone cool—measured—even as her blood raced. "And who is to be their replacement?"

"A niece of Conze Bazin's."

Svedye. No wonder Bazin had gone crawling back to Sanislav.

Izaveta dug her nails into her palms, the pain bringing clarity. She glanced up at Kyriil. Could he be lying? She examined the stark planes of his face, the carefully crafted concern in his eyes. How would fabricating this story benefit him? Her mind whirred through possibilities but kept returning to the same point: Sanislav moving against her was not surprising—it was nothing she had not suspected, especially after the fiasco with Commander Iveshkin at the ballet.

Perhaps it had been enough to make the commander pledge her support to Sanislav. The vibishop could easily have claimed that he now held the Firebird's confidence, that he could persuade her to help the commander. After all, that was what Commander Iveshkin wanted. Magic and power.

She glanced up at Kyriil. "How can you be sure?"

His lips twitched, and she could see just how much he loved having information she didn't. "I told you before, I'm a useful ally. I have ways of hearing things."

She dug her nails into the edge of the windowsill. That answer relied too heavily on accepting Kyriil's word as fact, and if there was anyone who spun lies with every word, it was Kyriil.

But she'd long since learned the most powerful weapon was the truth. Triumph wouldn't be glittering in his eyes for a lie.

He leaned forward, voice eager. "There is still a way for us to salvage this."

Izaveta almost rolled her eyes. Kyriil was not nearly so adept at the art of subtlety as he liked to think.

"If you reinstate the Azarov seat," he pressed on, "we could tip the cabinet back in your favor. Sanislav wouldn't risk a stand unless he was sure he held the balance."

Her eyes flicked across the distant forest, a pretense at disinterest as her mind worked. "You have certainly thought this through."

"Our interests are the same, Izaveta." Her teeth gritted at the omission of her title. No amount of feigning familiarity would get him what he desired. "I want you on the throne."

That invisible zvess board rose in her mind's eye again. All her possibilities narrowing down. Was she allowing her emotion to cloud her judgment? Her personal dislike of Kyriil was no reason to ignore a good political move, especially not with Sanislav so emboldened.

But the idea of accepting Kyriil's help, of giving him what he wanted, sent apprehension crawling over her skin. It strayed too close to placing trust in him, a mistake she refused to repeat.

The semblance of a plan fluttered into her mind, half-formed and liable to fall apart at her touch. There was still another way to persuade the commander: by giving Iveshkin the thing she wanted. Though that option sent guilt pooling in Izaveta's stomach.

Which choice was worse?

She took a slow breath, selecting her words carefully. "I am deeply appreciative of all your support, Master Azarov, but as I told you before, now is not the time for drastic change. The matter of the vacant seat will be addressed after the coronation, and I assure you that your claim will be considered among the others."

A muscle in Kyriil's jaw twitched, his features hardening like stone. "If you are relying on your sister, I'm afraid you will be sorely disappointed."

Izaveta raised her chin, not bothering to hide the ice in her voice now. "I think I am capable of judging that for myself."

He leaned in, each syllable clipped. "Mark my words: before the mourning days are up, you'll come running to me."

She held his gaze, refusing to show the slightest flicker of fear. Her fingers flexed at her side. If she were the Firebird, she could burn him alive for daring to question her sister. But she wasn't. She had to settle for cordiality. "We shall see, Master Azarov."

For another heartbeat, he didn't move, as if hoping to get in a last word. But then he turned on his heel and marched away, tossing an irritated glance in Nikov's direction.

Izaveta looked back out the window, clasping her hands in front of her to hide their slight tremble. The pale landscape beyond blurred into nothing more than gray smudges. Five days. Five days to keep herself from the gallows. But all her certainty—her plans and schemes and allies—was unspooling at her feet like a ruined tapestry.

She rolled her shoulders back. She couldn't think like that now. She still had one more move to make, a last desperate attempt to bring the commander to her side. To prove she was the more powerful wager.

And if she had Iveshkin, then at least some of the cabinet would follow. Enough to keep Sanislav at bay.

Spinning around, Izaveta snatched a piece of parchment and a quill from the nearest desk. She penned the letter quickly—

there was no need for embellishments or subterfuge here. She was simply agreeing to what the commander wanted.

When it was finished, she sat back to examine the swirling lines, reading them over once more. She should have felt victorious. This would work, she was certain. It would keep Sanislav from the crown—from the *Firebird*—for at least a little longer, and perhaps even deter Versbühl.

But the letter left a bitter aftertaste burning on her tongue like poison. Asya would forgive her. She had to.

"The Firebird agreed to be sent to the western border?"

Izaveta started. She'd forgotten Nikov was even in the room and hadn't felt his presence at her shoulder.

Ink now dry, she rolled up the parchment, sealing the letter from view. It might not be a perfect solution, but it was better than the alternative. Better to parade Asya at the border than let Sanislav test his *theory* and drain her magic, reclaiming the power he believed the Church was owed.

Izaveta clutched on to that reasoning, the rationalization. The last shreds of decency she could pretend to have.

She stood, feeling Nikov's eyes on her, even as she determinedly ignored them. "I don't see what concern that is of yours."

"It seems like it would be your sister's."

"This isn't about what any of us *wants*. Asya doesn't understand that yet." She glanced down at the scroll held tight in her fingers, and added, half to herself, "But she will."

There was no gleam in his eyes now, no mischievous twitch to his lips. "I imagine if you spoke to her instead of using her like a zvess piece, that might help."

Izaveta's nostrils flared. She didn't want to let him see how deep those words cut. This was who she had to be, as versed in the art of manipulation as her mother. And that didn't change just because she cared about someone. The queen's phantom shimmered at the edge of her vision, mouth twisted into a cruel smile. *So now you care about your sister?*

Izaveta blinked, trying to push that memory away. Her sister didn't understand—none of them did. And they couldn't, not when she couldn't tell any of them the whole truth. Least of all Asya.

Izaveta straightened, reaching for venom rather than let those fractured pieces show. "And what about you, Master Toyevski? Whose piece are you?"

"As I told you before," he replied, his tone carefully measured, "the Amarinth answers to no one."

"Yes, you've said your pretty words," she snapped. She could hear her voice getting away from her, the sting of his words—so close to her mother's—splintering through her control. But she couldn't stop it. "And I'm sure your interest in the Firebird's movements has nothing to do with your intimate conversation with Ambassador Täusch last night." She hadn't meant to say it so bluntly, but the swirl of emotions burning in her chest got the better of her. *He* got the better of her.

Where none of the others could, somehow this scholar managed to see through her in a way that set her on edge. That made her careless.

Nikov's jaw tensed—perhaps the first real reaction she'd garnered from him. "I talked to a lot of people at the ballet last night. Many of those discussions could be considered intimate."

Izaveta raised her eyebrows in a practiced look of scorn.

"Always an answer to everything," she shot back, echoing the ambassador's words. "Though you weren't quite so sure of yourself—of your supposed loyalty to the Amarinth—last night."

He rocked back on his heels, as if the reminder of Täusch's words were a blow. When he spoke, his voice was low, threaded through with an anger she'd not heard there before. "Did you ever consider that you're not owed the details of every person's life? That not everything is about you and your supposed game?" His dark eyes met hers, so close she could pick out every glimmer of contempt. "Since you have decided you must know, the ambassador is my father. He rather disapproves of my life choices—as I imagine you surmised, if you were listening to our conversation."

Izaveta stiffened, the pieces falling into place in her mind. That was not what she had expected. Because he was right. She was so used to calculating everything based on power and politics that she hadn't stopped to consider there could be something more personal at play. And she could hear the raw truth of those words—the way they cost Nikov something to utter aloud.

Without conscious thought, her eyes slipped down to his clenched knuckles, the scars standing out white. The slight movement from the night before played in her mind again, the shift of power between Nikov and Täusch. That flash of understanding he'd shown about her mother.

Something like shame twisted in her stomach—unfamiliar and gnarled as ancient tree roots, worming their way down to her core. She looked away, trying to ignore the hurt that stirred in Nikov's brown eyes, the determined set of his jaw.

"I hope that helps you and your games," he said, his voice still flat. "I'm honored to be another piece in your collection."

The biting scorn in his words grated against her, a warped mirror of his usual humor. But she met his gaze unflinchingly, retreating into the safety of her armor. "In fact, it does help," she replied coolly. "You can say whatever you want, Master Toyevski, but everything I do is to protect this queendom."

She turned to leave before he could see the cracks in her mask. The fissures that ran right down to her frozen heart. Because she couldn't be sure anymore. Couldn't tell if her actions were really for the good of the queendom—for her sister—or if she'd become so embroiled in schemes and manipulations that there was no escaping them.

Just as her mother had taught her, Izaveta had turned everyone into playing pieces in her own game. For better or worse, there was no turning back now. Even if she was no longer certain she knew the difference between fighting for the right reasons and fighting for power.

Chapter Thirty-Three

Another arrow whirred over Asya's head as she rolled for the cover of a tree. The trunks of the queenstrees were too thin to hide her properly, but they gave her some protection as she searched for the source.

Her heart thundered against her ribs, her side stinging where the first arrow had grazed her. Through the pale branches, she spotted four figures, too far away to be distinguished beyond the silhouettes of their bows.

She couldn't tell if their weapons bore the same symbol as her previous attackers. The Order of the Captured Flame. But who else could it be?

She scanned her surroundings, all Tarya's lessons running through her mind. More archers were just visible on the far side of the clearing, partly hidden by trees. That made seven in total, spread out to form a loose ring around her. Cutting off any possible escape routes.

Yuliana had lunged the opposite way to Asya, crouched now behind the base of the statue of Zmenya. She'd drawn her saber, not that it would be much use against assailants at that distance. An arrow hit Zmenya's hand, sending a shower of stone over Yuliana's head.

A strange calm settled over Asya. Having Yuliana there made the choice easy—instinctual. This wasn't just about Asya, this was about keeping someone else safe. And, really, that was what the Firebird did. It protected.

She reached for her flames, prepared to let them roll through her. To let the fires consume any threat.

But they didn't come.

Where usually the creature thrummed beneath her skin, ready to surge free, it had retreated. A glittering veil had fallen between her and it, leaving its magic just out of reach.

She closed her eyes, trying not to think about the arrows sailing toward her, and took a deep breath. Tarya's lessons floated back to her. All she needed to do was control it.

A weak tongue of flame sputtered around her fingers and went out.

What was happening?

An arrow slammed into the trunk above her head. It jolted her out of her shock. But as she turned to move, her eyes snagged on the arrowhead. Usually forged of iron—this one was much darker, with threads of something else running through it. Deep bloodred veins that almost glowed.

Asya's heart lurched. There was only one substance that looked like that.

Firestone.

She pressed a hand to her side, where the arrow had skimmed her. It was barely more than a graze. But enough for a scraping of the mineral from the arrowhead to enter her bloodstream.

Dread skittered up her spine. The Firebird couldn't help her. All she had was the shashka strapped to her side. And if she was hit squarely with one of those arrows, there would be no quick healing. No magic to protect her.

Another arrow flew over her head. The archers were closing in slowly, tightening their circle like a rope around her neck. But she could sense their hesitation still. They couldn't be sure if her power had been subdued yet.

She scanned the trees, searching desperately for a way out. But the storm of arrows was unrelenting, a deadly haze she couldn't hope to pass. Except...

A chance—fleeting and risky, but still a chance—flashed into her mind. Just beyond the opposite side of the clearing, the queenstrees coiled together into a tightly growing thicket. The archers wouldn't be able to maneuver through the snarled trunks with their bows.

But Asya could.

The branches would provide some cover, and if she wove through them, she should be able to avoid the arrows. Her thoughts darted back to the night of the previous attack, to what they'd said. They weren't trying to kill her.

And the arrows so far seemed to fit with that—aiming to incapacitate, not kill. Maybe she could use that.

Her muscles tensed, readying themselves to move. She stared at the thicket, trying to calculate the distance. The points of cover between here and there. She didn't have any margin for error. Her gaze skimmed over Yuliana, still pinned down behind the statue by the volley of arrows. She wouldn't be able to reach the thicket. The angle was all wrong, and the arrows would cut her down in an instant.

The realization settled over Asya like a morning frost. She could escape—could get the Firebird to safety. But that would be the price.

She met Yuliana's storm-gray eyes across the clearing, and the strashe's military mind seemed to read the strategy in Asya's face. Yuliana shook her head, grip tightening on her saber. She made a shooing motion with her free hand. The message was clear. *Don't wait for me.*

Tarya's voice whispered in the back of Asya's head, a dark warning. But her own voice drowned it out. The words she'd said to the strashe only moments before. *I couldn't live with myself if I let it go unanswered. If I stood back while people were killed.*

She still didn't know if Yuliana could accept what Asya was, but she'd been telling the truth. And she knew she couldn't live with herself if she ran free and left someone else to die. Especially not Yuliana.

Helplessness tugged at Asya's heels, a lapping wave that threatened to overwhelm her. What use was she without the Firebird? If she could reach even a drop of magic—

Her heart lurched as the realization slammed into her. There were other kinds of magic here.

The nearest grave marker was only a few paces away, the egg concealing the saint's relic gleaming on top of it. She ducked low and ran for it, another arrow whipping over her head. A twinge of misgiving prickled through her stomach as her hand closed on the cool marble of the egg. This was undoubtedly sacrilege. It could destroy a holy relic.

But she couldn't think of any other way out.

Her fingers tightened. Asya didn't know exactly which protective enchantments had been placed on the eggs all those years ago, but she hoped it was something distracting.

She reached for the distant tremble of the Firebird, where it had retreated into her bones. She needed just a spark to dislodge the clasp that held the egg in place. She gritted her teeth, scraping the power from her very core. With a low splutter, a flame twisted around her fingers. It melted through the metal and the egg fell into her palm.

Asya spun—the egg thrumming in her hand like a living thing—and threw it.

It hit the ground with a sound like cracking ice. Like some great monster shifting beneath the surface of the earth. Light—the bright gold of dawn—spiraled from it. No, not light. *Mist*. Somewhere between solid and gas. It reminded her of the murmuration of birds at sunset, a distant creature whirling through the sky. Except that this wasn't distant.

It reeled toward Asya, as if it knew she had been the cause.

But it had the desired effect. She heard faint shouts of the archers, and the hail of arrows momentarily ceased. She used the distraction to sprint across the open space toward Yuliana— grabbing another of the precious eggs as she did. She skidded to a stop, almost crashing into the strashe.

"What were you thinking?" Yuliana hissed, eyes wide and storming.

Asya gripped the egg, peering through the haze the spell had left. "I wasn't going to leave you." She didn't give Yuliana a chance to respond—to say she didn't want her help, not after Asya had shown her that burning piece of herself. "Hold your breath."

Before the eerie not-quite-fog could dissipate, Asya dived into its midst, dragging Yuliana with her. It burned against Asya's skin, a searing cold that threatened to creep into her bones. But she didn't stop. They just had to get through the thicket—to reach Mishka. And once the cut was healed, the Firebird would come back. This wouldn't be another of her failures.

Her lungs were screaming out for air, but she didn't dare breathe in that writhing magic. It clung to her, trying desperately to hold her back. The grove wasn't large, but running through the mist it felt eternal, time moving strangely within the grip of this ancient magic.

Suddenly—as if the earth had sighed and blown it away—the mist vanished. The welcome trunks of the queenstrees were only a few paces ahead. The whirl of arrows had stopped, but now the archers could see, surely they would resume at any moment.

Gasping for air, Asya dived for the cover of the trees. The other egg pounded in her hand, an erratic rhythm to match her heart. In her peripheral vision, she could see the shadows of two archers, bows raised. But within the tangle of trees Asya would make a much more difficult target.

She wove between trunks at random, trying not to create any kind of pattern they could aim for. Yuliana was close on her heels, following Asya's footsteps with a practiced grace. They had to be almost where she'd left Mishka now. But with her head whirling and adrenaline spiking through her, it was impossible to tell one silver trunk from another.

An archer reared up in front of them—leaping from a hidden dip behind a clump of trees. Asya skidded to a halt, her boots sliding on the frost-covered ground. The archer was just far enough to be out of range for handheld weapons but too close for either of them to survive one of those arrows.

Without hesitation, she threw the second egg—another relic that might be damaged irreparably. It hit the trunk next to the archer, just as they loosed another arrow. Asya didn't have time to move. Her momentum from the throw was still sending her forward, right into the arrow's path.

Yuliana slammed into Asya's side, sending her flying out of the way. The strashe rolled, her head cracking against a tree trunk with a shuddering *thump.*

Asya didn't have a breath for her mind to process what had happened. What Yuliana had done—what it could mean. Asya's muscles moved instinctively, fueled by fear. Yuliana's eyes were dazed as Asya pulled her to her feet. She dragged the strashe out of the path of the curling magic that now enshrouded the archer and on through the twisting trees.

She had no weapons left now. No more magic, no flicker of flames from the Firebird. If the archers caught up with them again, they'd be trapped. Asya pushed that from her mind. She focused on their pounding feet, on leaping over the roiling roots.

But even so, she could hear the sounds of pursuit, drawing closer with every step.

Finally, through the spindled trunks, Asya spotted a patch of brown. Relief flooded through her. Mishka. She opened her mouth to call for him but couldn't draw in enough air to form the shout.

The bear's great head turned in their direction, amber eyes

glinting. He seemed to sense Asya's fear. He lumbered forward, hampered by the tightness of the trees.

Something whistled in her ears. She couldn't tell if it was the biting wind whipping around them, or another volley of arrows. But she could pick out the shape of Mishka's snout now. They were so close—

A sharp pain seared through Asya's back. The world tilted. She must have stopped, because she felt a hand on hers, dragging her forward. But everything around her was moving. A swirling haze of pale white and gray.

She looked down, and it took her mind a moment to catch up with her eyes. Because that couldn't possibly be right. She raised a shaking hand. It was solid—real.

The gleaming firestone head of an arrow, protruding from her chest.

Chapter Thirty-Four

It was what the Tóurensi called a burning sunset. The last of the sunlight spilled across the sky like flames, morphing the clouds into an expanse of embers. Soothsayers had argued for centuries over its meaning, the significance of the position of the sun or the birds that flew against the backdrop. But they agreed about one thing: it foretold great change.

Izaveta barely noticed, even as it limned the furniture of the Voya Wing in glowing crimson. All she saw was her sister. The blood seeping across the white bandages like a slow-blossoming flower.

Sitting in a chair next to the narrow bed, Izaveta was still as the statue of Saint Xishin the Unseeing that presided over the room. Izaveta's hands were clasped in her lap, fingers tightly entangled. There was an odd calm in the air now, but remnants of the chaos still shimmered in the edge of her vision. The rushing voye, the strashe darting between them. The ashen face of the one who'd brought Asya back. The cloying scent of fear, suffocating in its density.

Izaveta had ordered them all out once it was clear there was no more to be done for Asya except to wait. But the silence they left in their wake was like the hollow quiet of an empty cathedral. Izaveta suppressed a shudder. That thought strayed far too close to the memory of her mother, draped in her blue silk shroud.

She knotted her fingers tighter together. Asya wasn't dead. Not yet.

The door snapped open behind her, and Izaveta leaped to her feet. Her great-aunt stood in the doorway, mouth set in a grim line. Izaveta swallowed down the admonishment that rose to her lips, forcing her voice even. "We've been looking for you for hours."

Tarya's eyes narrowed. "I don't wait on the whims of a princess."

Izaveta's mouth worked, but she couldn't push the words past the lump in her throat. So she just stepped aside, revealing her sister.

Tarya's face paled. Without a word she strode forward, crouching down next to the bed. Her nimble fingers ran over the bandages, pulling them aside to reveal the gaping wound beneath. Scarlet darkening to a poisonous black.

"Why isn't it healing?" Izaveta hated the frayed edge to her voice, the desperation seeping through it. But she couldn't pretend, not staring down at her sister like that.

Tarya didn't look up. "Where is the weapon?"

Izaveta gestured to the table beneath the window, where the arrow—now broken in two—lay bathed in orange light. Tarya stared at it, something finally fracturing through her impassive calm. The look sent cold dread spiraling through Izaveta's veins.

Tarya moved toward the arrow pieces slowly, almost reverently. She picked them up, turning them over in her hands. When she spoke, her voice was barely louder than Asya's shallow breaths. "Where did this come from?"

Izaveta swallowed, taking a moment to compose herself. "We don't know."

Tarya's fingers tightened on the arrow. "This—" She cut herself off, eyes lifting to Izaveta. "No one should know about this."

The questioning, rational part of Izaveta's mind wanted to ask what Tarya meant. But fear submerged it, dragging Izaveta down with it. "What can we do to help her?"

There was a long pause, the only sound the low sputter of candles. "With this in her blood, the Firebird will be helpless." The words seemed dragged out of Tarya, as if she was unwilling to not have an answer. "She may heal, but if she does, it will be as a mortal."

The ground swayed beneath Izaveta's feet. It wasn't damnation yet, but it held only a scrap of hope. She didn't need to know much about healing to see that Asya's wound was likely fatal for a mortal.

"What would—" Izaveta swallowed, forcing the words out even as they burned with bitter shame in her throat. The dutiful question—not the quiet plea of a girl terrified of losing her sister. "What would happen to the Firebird?"

Tarya's eyes were bright in the moonlight. "I do not know. No Firebird has ever been killed. Many did not believe it possible." She straightened abruptly, hands still clenched on the arrow. "I'll see if I can find anything, any stories of other Firebirds."

She didn't wait for Izaveta to respond, instead striding out without so much as a glance back.

The sound of the door shutting was like the snip of scissors, cutting the last strings that held Izaveta up. She sank onto the edge of her sister's bed, a heavy weight settling onto her shoulders. A paralyzing fear that burrowed down to her very bones.

She couldn't lose Asya. Not now, not when she'd only just got her back.

But what could Izaveta do? Manipulating people, scheming. Neither of which would do anything to save her sister. Tears burned at the backs of her eyes, as futile as anything else she did. All those years Izaveta had spent crafting herself after her mother—everything she'd done—and none of it mattered when it really counted.

The door opened again, and Izaveta jumped. She blinked, hurriedly schooling her expression. Surely Tarya couldn't have returned so soon?

It wasn't her aunt in the shadowed doorway, but a dark-haired strashe.

Izaveta didn't get up, barely lifted her eyes from Asya. "I want no one in here."

But the strashe didn't balk at the cold edge to Izaveta's tone, instead moving farther into the room. The strashe's gaze strayed to Asya, to the blood that stained her front. Izaveta thought she saw a tremble of guilt cross the guard's face, but it was gone so quickly she couldn't be sure.

Izaveta straightened, suspicion rousing in her chest.

But as she studied the strashe closer, the pale glow of

candlelight illuminating her features, Izaveta recognized her. Vilanovich, the one who'd brought Asya back from the queens-trees, half clinging to her bear, dirt streaked, and stricken.

A cold lump solidified around Izaveta's heart. The strashe who *should* have protected her sister. Who had been assigned to her for that sole purpose—to prevent exactly what had happened.

Guilt was the least of what Vilanovich should be feeling.

"You," Izaveta spat, "have no right to be here." She rose to her feet, pulling the wave of anger with her. Letting it wash away the terror snaking its way to her core. "Your orders were to protect the Firebird, with your life if it came to it. Yet here she lies, while you stand there unscathed." Izaveta took a step forward, drawing herself up into that image of her mother. The unyielding queen who held no mercy. "I never want to see you in the palace again. A strashe so remiss in their duty is useless."

Izaveta knew, in some distant part, that she was being un-fair. Something strange had happened in the queenstrees, something not even Zvezda's spies had heard tell of. But Vilanovich was here, a waiting target for the restless frustra-tion that tore through Izaveta.

The strashe dropped her eyes, jaw tight. "You're right."

Izaveta's charging anger stuttered to a halt. She hadn't expected that.

She rolled her shoulders, composing herself again as she examined the curves of Vilanovich's expression. The way her gloved hands were clasped behind her. The determined set to her shoulders. The picture of a soldier.

But despite that, there were cracks in her appearance. The

hastily pressed uniform, undoubtedly replacing the one from the queenstrees. The small coils of hair falling out of the plait that wound around her head.

And her eyes were pink, the last tendrils of red receding.

Vilanovich lifted her chin to meet Izaveta's gaze. "I came here for just that reason, my lady. To recuse myself of my duties to your sister. I—" The strashe's voice hitched. "She needs someone more worthy to protect her."

The words evaporated the last of Izaveta's anger, leaving only sizzling pain behind. It wasn't this strashe's fault. In truth, if Izaveta had anyone to blame, it was herself. She should have been more careful, should have insisted Asya take more guards if she left the palace. Should have sent more people to patrol the forest after Conze Vittaria's death.

Izaveta had always been the protector. She might only be a few heartbeats older, but that had always been the role she'd fallen into. The one who stood between Asya and her mother, shielding her from that poison. The one who quickly took the blame when they were caught exploring or who distracted their tutor by throwing inkpots when Asya was late to their lessons.

Izaveta was the one who would do anything to keep her sister safe, no matter the cost.

Not because she was braver or stronger—certainly not because she was kinder—but because she was selfish. Because seeing Asya suffer hurt more than suffering herself.

Izaveta's eyes drifted to her sister now. After everything, how had she managed to fail so completely?

"Very well," she said eventually, a small concession. "I shall instruct the strashevsta to give you a new post."

For a moment, Vilanovich looked like she might speak. Her lips twitched, a decision darting across her eyes. A question formed there, one Izaveta could hear as easily as if it had been spoken. *Will Asya live?*

A question Izaveta didn't want to—*couldn't*—answer.

But then Vilanovich swallowed, the question dying as she tugged her gaze from the bed. She bowed her head to Izaveta before turning and marching from the room.

A terrible stillness was left in the strashe's wake, as stifling as a shroud. Because Izaveta couldn't help but think that Vilanovich hadn't voiced the question because she already feared the answer.

Izaveta sank back down into the chair, dropping her head in her hands and pressing her eyes shut. She had never felt this helpless. For the first time in years, Izaveta was moved to pray. A last, desperate cry in an empty night.

She froze. The spark of an idea fluttered at the back of her mind—a possibility. But it would mean going to the last person she ever wanted to ask for help. And there was no telling what price he would demand.

The burning sunset had faded to no more than dark trails of ash when a knock at the door heralded the arrival of the first of the two people Izaveta needed.

She rose to her feet, scrambling to regain some semblance of composure as she opened her mouth to greet Fyodor.

But it wasn't Fyodor who stepped through the door.

Nikov's face was drawn, his bronze skin glinting in the flickering candlelight.

Izaveta's rib cage tightened, constricting around her heart.

She couldn't stop their last conversation echoing in her mind. The words that cut down to her core, those shadowed pieces of herself that no one should see.

"What are you doing here?" She'd intended for her voice to be filled with the same rage she'd had addressing the strashe, the same imperious indignation. But instead it came out as a ragged whisper—the last dregs of what she had left.

"The strashe said you needed a scholar," he replied, not moving from the doorway. "I couldn't forsake someone in need of knowledge," he added, with the shadow of a grin.

Izaveta narrowed her eyes. "I asked for Master Alyeven."

Nikov shrugged. "He'd already left for the night."

"So you just decided to come in his place?" She managed to inject some venom into her words again, though she was merely a frail imitation of her normal self.

"It sounded important."

She sat back down, clasping her hands together. "This matter is of no concern to you."

He took a hesitant step forward, his eyes flicking across every surface as if the room were an unopened tome to explore. They landed on Asya, and realization crashed across his features.

"What happened?" he asked, a low note of fear thrumming through his voice.

Izaveta wished he would shout or make another irritating comment she could dismiss. That shadow of fear made her want to fall apart. She twisted her fingers in her lap, clenching tighter and tighter as if she might hold herself together.

She should order him away. This was a weakness, not something she should allow anyone to see. Certainly not someone who she still wasn't sure she could trust, who was somehow connected to Versbühl.

But she suddenly didn't want to face this alone.

"Asya—" Izaveta started, but her voice cracked. Her voice, usually her most reliable tool, was failing her tonight as well. Pieces of her slowly falling away. She swallowed hard, reaching for impassive formality. For the queen who didn't have to feel. "The Firebird has been attacked, using a mineral that suppresses her power. The wound will not heal."

"Diye," he breathed. For a moment he held her gaze, still hanging back by the doorway. Then he moved forward with sudden conviction, as if he'd finally made some decision. He put one hand on Izaveta's shoulder, oddly comforting. "We'll find a way. There has to be a way."

Izaveta felt herself unraveling with the gentleness of that touch. She bit the inside of her cheek, pushing down the sob that rose in her chest. Somehow, hearing his reaction, seeing him try to reassure her despite everything, threatened to fracture her mask more than anything else had.

But she couldn't break now, not while Asya lay bleeding.

Izaveta inhaled slowly. Her mind refused to sink back into unfeeling calculations, to the strategic place where she could logically decide how much to tell Nikov.

But, after all, he was an Amarinth scholar, he would have as much—if not more—knowledge on ritual magic as Fyodor did.

"I do have one theory, a possible way to save her," she said, not quite meeting his gaze. She didn't want him to see the uncertainty burning in her eyes. The terror.

As quickly and concisely as she could, she told him her plan. When she'd finished, Nikov let out a long breath.

"Well?" Izaveta prompted. "Could it work?"

"It's a myth," he said slowly—gently, as if breaking some terrible news.

"Plenty of myths are real, at least partially."

He pushed stray hairs from his face, thinking. "I have read of people attempting it, and by all accounts the story is true. But it would be lethal for any mortal. And you'd have to ask—"

"I know," she interrupted. She'd thought of all that herself, at least a hundred times since she'd sent for Fyodor.

"But you're going to try, aren't you?"

She raised her chin, finally meeting Nikov's eye. "Of course I am. It's for Asya."

Silence spread between them, laden with all the things unsaid. The remnants of the conversation in the library.

She swallowed hard, steeling herself. "I feel," she began, "I feel I ought to apologize for this morning. I should not have pressed you about your father."

His dark eyes were shadowed in the half-light, impossible to read. "Saying you *ought* to apologize is not quite the same as apologizing."

Izaveta's lips lifted toward an unfamiliar smile, not one sculpted by her careful hand, but drawn to the surface of its own accord. "A queen does not apologize."

Slowly, as if unsure how she would react, he sank down onto the edge of the bed next to her. His eyes darted to Asya. "Perhaps I also shouldn't have said what I did."

Izaveta raised her eyebrows, head tilted in an unspoken question.

He shrugged, a little of the tension leaching from his shoulders as his mouth quirked upward to match hers. "But a scholar cannot apologize either. We must stand by our work."

Izaveta almost rolled her eyes but caught herself. Decorum couldn't be completely thrown aside, even in the strangest of situations. She pressed her lips together, swallowing down the instinctive frosty retort that rose in her throat. The weapon she'd usually arm herself with to protect from any vulnerability. But sitting here, her sister lying pale as marble, she couldn't force it out. All this was too raw—too *real*—for any games.

"There was truth to what you said," she murmured, her eyes straying to Asya. "I hadn't seen my sister in more than seven years, and I wasted our reunion trying to manipulate her. Because that's all I know how to do. Because that's what I spent all those years making myself into." Izaveta caught herself. She shouldn't have said that, but her snarled emotions were tearing up her insides like thorns. She needed to get some of them out, or they'd destroy her.

She didn't look at Nikov, didn't want to see the reaction to that admission.

"I know what it is to try to make yourself into something else." Nikov's voice was soft, with none of the teasing lilt it usually held. A thin gossamer thread that could flutter away at the slightest touch.

As fragile and impermanent as Asya's shallow breaths, still loud in the empty room.

Izaveta glanced out at the darkening sky. How long had it been since she'd sent her messengers?

She didn't want to let that thought stretch into another question, the one wound tightly around her heart. But it whispered through her mind anyway, searing cold. *How long does Asya have?*

"Distract me," Izaveta said suddenly. Though it had the cadence of a command, she couldn't miss the faint tremor to her words. Her mother's phantom shimmered in the corner of her vision, her face etched with disapproval. She would have been furious to see Izaveta like this.

But Nikov didn't comment on the weakness. He sat back, his posture straightening like a master preparing to lecture. "Once, a boy was born in the Great Library of Kharur. But the library was no place to raise a child, and so his mother had to choose: she could remain as a scholar or leave to be with the boy. It was a test of sorts—which was more important: her child or knowledge?"

He looked over at her, the shadow of his lashes drawing tear tracks down his cheeks. "And she chose knowledge." He took a breath, pushing on. "So the boy was sent to Tóurin to live with his father, but he always understood the importance of his mother's choice. He tried to follow her same path to knowledge, wanting to learn everything he could. About Tóurin, about his Kharuri heritage—much to the annoyance of his father, who placed much more value in power and how to wield it. But the boy continued to study everything he could find. Maps, histories, folktales. He even tried—rather disastrously—to re-create the basbousa cakes he remembered from the library. All in the pursuit of knowledge."

Izaveta sat frozen, strangely suspended in this moment as if caught in the In-Between. Other than her sister, no one had ever confided in her before. Not truly—not in a way that did not somehow benefit them. She felt that if she moved, she might break it, this precious thing Nikov was holding out to her. The thing she wasn't sure she deserved.

He rubbed his thumb over the back of his knuckles, a nervous tic. "But even that was not enough to reunite him with his mother. So then the boy tried to model himself after his father, because that seemed easier. But that made the boy miserable, because even then, he was not enough."

He lapsed into silence, frowning down at his hands as if they were a difficult translation to be cracked.

"Is that the end of the story?" Izaveta asked, her voice hushed in the heavy quiet.

Nikov shifted, suddenly jolted back into the present. "The boy realized it didn't matter that his father never saw him as enough. That his mother chose knowledge over him. Because in the end, it would be his own choices that made him who he was. Not the people who raised him. Or the ones who tried to control him."

Izaveta swallowed, looking down at her tangled fingers. "Must every story have a moral?"

"Izaveta." She glanced up despite herself, surprised at the sound of her first name in his soft tone. "The point is that what you're doing now is what matters, not what your mother molded you into." His hand caught hers, warm fingers curling against the smooth silk of her gloves. "*This* is what counts."

Something in that pulled her back from the teetering edge. The despair that threatened to drag her down to its depths. Nikov had a way of saying things that made them feel so true—not in the way her mother had, where she twisted words until one believed them. But like a trusted friend, someone apart from all these games. For that brief instant, Izaveta almost believed it.

The door opened again, and the moment shattered, crumbling to nothing more than splinters at her feet.

A figure walked in, heavy crimson robes pooling behind him. His kokoshnik tapered to a point, gleaming like a blade.

Izaveta rose sharply, drawing her hand out of Nikov's. "Vibishop Sanislav, good evening."

His expression was carefully crafted into one of deepest concern, shadows carving harsh lines into his face. "My lady, I heard of the tragic events. May Dveda look kindly upon you."

Izaveta gritted her teeth. His false niceties were grating against her skin tonight. "No tragedy yet, Vibishop. My sister is still very much alive." *For now* echoed unbidden inside her head.

Sanislav gave a tight smile. "Of course."

"Though her situation is grave." Izaveta hesitated, almost choking on her next words. "I do believe the Church may be able to help."

Sanislav's expression didn't shift, but something flickered in his eyes. Something Izaveta did not like at all. "Is that so?"

Izaveta pushed on, trying to ignore the misgivings crawling up her spine. "Her blood needs to be cleansed, so I thought of the story of Saint Restov."

"I am well versed in the stories of the saints, my lady."

Izaveta bit back a frustrated sigh. The vibishop was not going to make this easy. "I thought, given that Asya is no mere mortal, perhaps we could perform the ritual on her. The moon-blessed knife is one of the relics kept in the cathedral, is it not?"

The vibishop's forehead furrowed, a careful display of uncertainty. "That is true, my lady. But that does not mean the ritual is possible."

"I have discussed this with the emissary from the Amarinth." She nodded to Nikov, who was watching Sanislav with an expression of unbridled dislike. "We believe the theory is sound enough to attempt."

Sanislav smoothed his robes, pretending to think. He knew he held the power here, that this negotiation tipped in his favor. And he was going to relish it. "I don't believe it is possible."

Izaveta kept her voice carefully measured, reasonable. "We cannot allow the Firebird to die. Surely it is your responsibility as a man of the Church to protect her. Her death could mean devastation for Tóurin."

Sanislav shrugged, as if the matter were of little importance. "You know my beliefs about the Firebird already, my lady. And you have made your position quite clear."

She took a steadying breath, forcing herself not to leap forward and wring the vibishop's neck, tempting though it was. From the look on Nikov's face, he wouldn't even protest. "That is not the matter at hand, Vibishop."

Sanislav studied her, eyes narrowed. It reminded Izaveta of how he had looked at her the night her mother died. A flash of the same helplessness she'd felt then cleaved through her. She'd returned to the same point again, watching a fool like Sanislav decide her sister's fate.

"I suppose not," he conceded. "And perhaps I *could* attempt the ritual. But I will not. From what I have heard of the events that transpired, the Firebird desecrated holy relics during the commotion. Perhaps this is the gods' vengeance, their price for her sacrilege."

The last of Izaveta's patience died, the facade of politeness slipping from her face. "Enough games, Vibishop. Name your price."

A calculating smile curled his lips, a cat satisfied that it had the mouse where it wanted. "I think you know it, my lady."

"I will not abdicate." She straightened her shoulders. Even with this concession, she refused to look weak. To crumble before him.

"I do not ask for so much," he replied. "I only ask that you tell the truth."

Izaveta stiffened, ice crystallizing in her veins. What could Sanislav know? "And which truth would that be?"

His thin lips curled, smug in his certainty. "The day of Hunte Rastyshenik, my prayers told me that you were not to be deemed worthy. That the feather you produced was a forgery."

Izaveta let out a low noise of disdain, a bitter echo of a laugh. She should have known the vibishop had orchestrated the feather's disappearance—it fell so neatly in line with his political actions. Tying a divine tradition to his bid for power.

She kept her face blank, forcing herself into that reflection of her mother. Even if with every faltering heartbeat, she felt more and more like a little girl playacting. "And I suppose you will use that to claim I am damned by the gods and present a new queen, with the cabinet's support?"

Sanislav pressed his lips together. "Perhaps. But none of that is of your concern." He cocked his head, making a great show of calculating what he could gain. "So what do you say, my lady? Will you admit to your lies?"

Nikov's words echoed in her mind. *In the end, it would be his own choices that made him who he was.* And ultimately, this was her choice. In that moment, she realized just how much she would concede to save her sister. She would lay the crown at Sanislav's feet if it gave her so much as a sliver of a chance. It sent cold fear ricocheting through her, silent and immovable.

She couldn't let Sanislav see it. Couldn't let him know how much leverage he truly had.

Finally, she nodded. "I will."

He couldn't keep the smug satisfaction from his voice as he spoke. "Swear it by the three moons. Swear that you will tell the court, on Noteya Svedsta, that you falsified the feather."

Her jaw twitched. Sanislav was a formidable opponent, almost as formidable as her mother. An oath sworn on the three moons could not be broken, not without earning the wrath of the three gods. "I swear by the three moons that I will tell the court the truth about the feather on Noteya Svedsta, on the condition that you perform the ritual to the full extent of your ability." The words were jagged in her mouth, each one a shard of broken glass. But she couldn't let Asya die for her pride.

"I will hold you to your word, my lady."

Izaveta forced a smile. Not a pleasant one, used to manipulate and pander, but a predatory one. The vibishop was not the only one who could play at intimidation. "Certainly. For what are we without our word, Vibishop?"

CHAPTER THIRTY-FIVE

Saint Restov the Moon-Touched was destined from birth never to see adulthood. Despite a terrible illness coursing through his blood, he prayed not for his own health, but the health of his village. Through various convoluted methods—Izaveta had never much enjoyed the story—Dveda gave Restov an enchanted knife to reward him for his selflessness. If he plunged the knife into his chest on the night of the full moons, it would distill moonlight into his blood and cure him.

Just like everything else, this cure still had a price. Restov could never remove the blade or the disease would return. Even though he had been blessed by a god, people saw the hilt of the knife in Restov's chest, the shimmering silver of his blood, and assumed he was a demonya. He was killed brutally for it, as saints so often were.

But none of that mattered. All that mattered was that it could work. There were accounts, writings of ancient voye, that claimed the knife was real. Though mortals might not survive it, Asya should. The moonlight would burn through the mineral, they could remove the blade, and then the Firebird would return and heal her.

Even Tarya agreed that it was possible—if not probable—when she returned empty-handed from her own search. There was a fear in her stoic aunt that Izaveta had never seen before. A tremble beneath the unshakable surface.

Izaveta hadn't moved since the vibishop left, sitting in the wooden chair at Asya's side. Watching the reassuring rise and fall of her sister's chest. Nikov sat on the other side, silent and steady amid the turmoil, while Tarya remained by the window as motionless as the glass.

When Sanislav finally returned, dawn was threatening on the horizon, pale gray threading through the dark. It was the first time Izaveta had ever been pleased to see him. There was no change in Asya. Her breathing was still a shallow flutter, blood seeping across each fresh bandage. And with daybreak looming, they were running out of moonlight.

Sanislav held a heavy tome in one hand and a velvet-draped knife in his other. He set the book on a small table and unwrapped the heavy crimson velvet to reveal a gleaming blade. The hilt was dusted with rust, creeping along to claim the heavy opal set into the metal. But the blade was sparkling and clean. A vein of crystal ran down its center, the channel that would conduct the moonlight.

Izaveta rose to her feet slowly. Seeing the knife, the razor glint of its point, made this real. An actual blade that would have to be plunged into her sister's heart.

Izaveta couldn't pull her eyes away from it. There was no guarantee that this would work—and no certainty that Asya could not heal on her own. The moon-blessed blade might make it worse. It could kill her.

Misgivings whispered in the back of her mind, growing louder with each pounding beat of her heart. A voice that sounded painfully like her mother's. Was Izaveta really taking this risk for her sister, or for the Firebird and its power? Had she become so entangled in all these games that she could no longer tell?

She thought of the letter she'd sent that very morning. How much her plans hinged on the Firebird.

"Shall we begin?" Sanislav's voice jolted through her. He held the knife far too casually in his thin fingers, with too much anticipation in his pale eyes.

Izaveta met Nikov's gaze. There was something steadying there. It gave her the final push she needed, the certainty that she had to do this. This was her choice, one that very well could define who she was.

"Yes." One word that held consequences she couldn't hope to control.

Her fingers tightened on Asya's, unwilling to let go. But Izaveta forced herself to step back. She couldn't risk interfering.

Nikov's eyes flitted between Asya and Sanislav. That uncertainty mingled with Izaveta's own, growing with each quivering beat of her heart. With every spidery twitch of Sanislav's fingers on the blade.

Even Tarya was unsure. She hid it well, but Izaveta could see it in the stiff set of her shoulders, the way she stood a little too still.

Izaveta took a shuddering breath. This was their only chance.

Sanislav gestured to Nikov, and the two of them turned Asya's bed so the last dying moonlight spilled across her face. She looked so pale lying there, so vulnerable.

The vibishop raised the knife to the window, reading from the faded tome in a low hiss. The sound made the hairs on the back of Izaveta's neck prickle. Rather than reflecting the moonlight, the blade seemed to drink it in. Drawing light from the surrounding air like scrambling roots searching for water.

Izaveta's fists clenched, digging her nails into the scar on her left palm. Much of the Church's workings might be posturing and grandeur, but the knife truly did have some kind of magic. That thought shuddered through her chest, a terrible mingling of hope and fear.

Sanislav's words coiled through the air, ritual and magic intertwining to form a living thing. It was nothing like the spells Izaveta had seen before—this was something ancient and godly. Something mortals shouldn't touch.

But Asya wasn't mortal.

Usually that thought would sting, the way it separated Asya from her. But now it was the very thing Izaveta was relying on.

When Sanislav turned to face Asya again, a soft light pulsed at the blade's core. Not glowing like a candle but contained, as if the knife were unwilling to share its luminescence.

Izaveta wasn't sure if she imagined the flicker of triumph on Sanislav's face as he raised the blade, a projection of the doubts crowding her own mind. His chanting didn't cease, the last prayers to the gods to allow this to work. Not truly a spell—it required no price, no new magic—more of an appeal. A plea to the gods.

The moment crystallized around Izaveta. A divine oil painting brought to life in slow brushstrokes. Moonlight spiraling through the window, far brighter than it should be at this hour. The three moons visible against the sky, watching. Nikov frozen at her side. Sanislav's shadowed face. The sharp edge of the knife, suspended like the waiting blade of an executioner.

Izaveta lurched forward. "Wait—"

But the dagger was already moving. It finished its shining arc and plunged into Asya's heart.

A hand dug into Izaveta's arm, holding her back. Asya's body arched, light raying out from it like the last gasp of a dying star. No blood spread from the wound, instead that strange, absorbent light danced across her skin.

It was over as quickly as it had started. The light faded, leaching into Asya's veins, and she fell back against the bed. The soft rise and fall of her chest was Izaveta's only comfort, her lifeline in this battering storm.

Sanislav stood several paces back, clutching the tome to himself like a shield. He straightened, trying to regain some dignity. But he didn't move toward Asya. None of them did.

Izaveta couldn't tear her eyes away from the hilt that protruded from Asya. How could they tell if it had worked, if the moonlight had truly cleansed that mineral from her blood? If it hadn't, and they tried to take out the blade, it would kill her.

Red still seeped across the bandage, like sand trickling

through an hourglass. A constant reminder of their dwindling time.

Tarya spoke first, voice hoarse. "We need to remove the knife."

Sanislav eyed the hilt, unease settling over him now he had to get his hands dirty.

Izaveta stepped forward. "I'll do it."

She swallowed, her throat constricting as she reached for the hilt. The metal was strangely cool to touch, pulsing as though blood ran through its veins. For a heartbeat, she hesitated. But she had to do this, or it was all for nothing. She would be letting her sister die.

Izaveta gritted her teeth and pulled. The knife came out with a low scrape of bone that sent chills up her spine. There was no blood on the blade. It was as spotless as when Sanislav had first presented it. Somehow, that was worse. It made the object into something unnatural—inhuman and unpredictable.

In the folktale, people had seen that magic—seen the hilt sticking out of Restov's chest—and decried it as demonyesha. What if they'd been right?

Izaveta bit down on that thought, clutching the knife. There was no going back now.

Blood seeped from the second wound, no longer protected by the knife's magic. Not the crimson red it should be, but a shimmering silver so light it was almost vapor. Izaveta held her breath, unable to pull her gaze from that steady stream. That meant something had certainly happened. But then shouldn't the Firebird's power be back by now? Shouldn't the wounds already be knitting together?

Flashes of scarlet threaded through the silver, heavy and

undeniable. They spread, expanding like a poisonous whisper until the red of Asya's own blood was overpowering. No moonlight left now. And still the gaping wound didn't heal.

An awful fear clamped around Izaveta's heart. She stumbled forward, Nikov's hand sliding from her arm as she pressed her fingers against the flow of blood. A childish, futile attempt.

"This shouldn't be happening," she murmured, her words reeling away from her. Pulled on the rising tide of fear.

Without warning—almost as if Asya had heard her—her sister's eyes flew open. Two burning coals, unseeing. Izaveta froze, desperate hope kindling with those fires. In an instant, the coals burst from sputtering embers to roaring flames.

Izaveta leaped back, colliding with Nikov. His hands steadied her as the fire slithered down Asya's body like a great serpent. It ate away at the woolen blanket, charring it to no more than ash. A low keening noise rent the air, like the distant hunting cry of a bird of prey. Still not satisfied, the fires curled outward. A skeletal hand of flame, clawing through the air.

It reached for Izaveta, so close its heat seared across her skin. But she didn't move—couldn't move. Her mind was so fixated on Asya that it barely registered the burning fingers. Then a hand pulled her back, and her thoughts snapped into place.

But the flames were already subsiding, drawing back into Asya. Her eyes fell shut, and suddenly the room was quiet again. All that was left of the destruction was the scorched remains of the sheets and clothes and the acrid burn of smoke in the air.

The two wounds were dark and smoldering, thick lines of ash spreading from them like veins. But they weren't bleeding anymore—neither the silvery threads of moonlight nor

CHAPTER THIRTY-SIX

All Asya remembered was a flutter of magic. The faint, familiar remnant of the spell that had been used to retrieve the bone. It lapped at the edge of her mind, an incessant gleam of light against a sea of black.

But when she opened her eyes, it was gone. Replaced with lingering smoke. It clouded her head, pressing against the inside of her skull. Everything around her was a swirl of color, a landscape viewed through a rain-drenched window. A quiver of worry in storm-gray eyes.

Blinking, the room swam into focus. Dark swirls of indigo night cast shadows across pale stone. An arched ceiling rose above her, unusually simple for the palace.

She pushed herself up onto her elbows, sending a dull thud of pain through her chest. She let out a muffled groan, and something moved in her peripheral vision. A shimmer of palest silver hair. "Iza?"

Her sister jolted upright, nearly toppling the ancient tome balanced in her lap. "You're awake," Izaveta breathed. Deep shadows were carved beneath her eyes like smudges of ash, and her usually immaculate hair hung loose and disheveled around her shoulders.

She leaned forward, tentative. "How do you feel?"

Asya heaved herself into a sitting position, eliciting another low hiss of pain. Memories were shuffling back into place. Towering trees, the delicate marble of the protected eggs, the whiz of arrows. She ran a hand down her right side, moving inward to where her lowest ribs curved to meet. "I was hit."

Izaveta nodded slowly, fingers tightening around her book.

Asya traced higher, toward the other spiraling ache. Through the thin wool of her shirt, she felt hard ridges like old scar tissue above her heart. "What happened?"

Izaveta's lips pressed together. She didn't quite meet Asya's eyes as she replied, "You—you wouldn't stop bleeding." Izaveta's voice was soft, thin as a frayed thread. "Because there was something on the arrowhead."

"Firestone," Asya murmured, remembering its biting sting. How the Firebird had retreated, how helpless she'd been. But even through the dull haze in her brain, she could feel its flames now. A faint prickle beneath her skin.

She was surprised at the relief accompanying that realization. The odd comfort that she was no longer powerless, not quite alone.

She looked up at Izaveta, at the brown eyes that reflected her own. They were shimmering in the candlelight. Almost like unshed tears. It had to be a trick of the light—of Asya's still-swirling head—because Izaveta didn't cry.

"But it's healed now," Asya said, the question shining through her words.

Izaveta swallowed. "Yes. I found a way to cleanse your blood." She finally met Asya's gaze. "Using the knife of Saint Restov."

Asya blinked. She must have misheard—must be more addled than she realized. The knife was a myth, an ancient magical relic. And even if it was real, it couldn't possibly work on her. Could it?

Her fingers crept to the wound over her heart again. She pulled down the collar of her shirt. Blackened ridges spiraled from a deep gash, sealed by the Firebird's flames.

Izaveta stared at it too, eyes still bright. "That happened when your powers came back."

Asya stared. She was moon-touched, even after what she'd done in the grove. The gods had somehow seen fit for her to live.

No, that wasn't quite right. They hadn't wanted Asya to live, they needed the *Firebird* to live. She was just the vessel— the sword wielded by an unseen hand.

She sank back against the pillows. The weight of it all was suddenly too much. Each fear, each mistake, was another stone pressing against her rib cage.

"I'm sorry." Izaveta's voice was so quiet, Asya almost missed it.

"Why are you sorry?"

Izaveta let out a hollow laugh. "Perhaps because I had someone drive a knife into your heart?"

Asya leaned forward, grasping her sister's hand. "Without you, I'd be dead. The Firebird would be dead." Saying it aloud, the true terror of the possibility clamped around her. Not only her own death, but the deaths of so many others it could have caused. The imbalance the Firebird would have left behind.

Izaveta closed her eyes, squeezing Asya's hand back. It was so strange to be comforting Iza. For Izaveta to look so fragile she might shatter at the slightest touch. The sight clenched around Asya's heart.

Such a mortal feeling. One the Firebird shouldn't have.

Even after what had happened, Asya couldn't bring herself to believe that. The fact that she cared for her sister, had that burning need to keep her safe, was what drove her.

A sudden thought occurred to her, and her eyes snapped back to her sister. "Where did you get Saint Restov's knife?"

Izaveta's lips pressed together, gaze firmly on their entangled fingers. "The vibishop."

Asya stared, trying to find the meaning through the haze in her mind. "Why did he agree to that?"

Izaveta glanced up, a humorless smile tugging at her lips. "I don't suppose you'd believe it was for the good of the queendom?"

Asya thought back to the vibishop's coiling smile, the way his words snared together like a trap. She might not understand the workings of the court yet, but she did understand when something would demand a price.

Izaveta read the answer on her face. Her jaw tightened, as if trying to stop the words from coming out. "He required that I swear on the three moons to tell the truth about what happened at Hunte Rastyshenik."

"What does that mean?" Asya asked, though she had a creeping feeling she knew.

Her sister waved a hand, a vain pretense at indifference. "It's a means to an end. He believes he can use it to garner support in the cabinet to depose me."

Asya jerked upright, ignoring the stab of pain that came with the movement. "You didn't agree to that."

"Of course I did." Izaveta looked away, as though embarrassed by the admission.

Asya swallowed, tears prickling behind her eyes. Her sister had done that for her, despite all the years they'd spent apart. Despite what Asya had become. "We can't let him do that."

A smile spread across Izaveta's face. In an instant she was transformed back into a queen, one who wasn't bothered by anything. But Asya could still see the sliver of fear beneath.

"Don't worry about that. I have a plan." Izaveta rose to her feet, tucking the book under her arm. "And you should rest."

Asya opened her mouth, but she couldn't quite find the words. Not with her head pounding and her chest aching and her veins burning.

"Where's Yuliana?" It wasn't what she'd meant to say, but it slipped out anyway. Formed from that deep part of herself she was supposed to ignore.

Izaveta paused. "Who?"

"Strashe Vilanovich," Asya amended quickly.

"Oh, she requested to be removed as your personal guard," Izaveta replied with a dismissive curl of her lips. "Which was the least she could do. She may have managed to bring you back to the palace, but she clearly failed to protect you."

Asya's throat constricted. A hollow throb of pain resonated through her, though it had nothing to do with her wounds.

When Asya awoke again, her head was clear. Soft winter light streaked through the window, illuminating the figure now occupying the chair next to Asya's narrow bed. The harsh lines and impassive features of her aunt.

Except today, her expression wasn't blank. A burning anger sparked in her eyes, as though the Firebird still lurked there.

Tarya leaned forward, interlacing her fingers in front of her as if in prayer. "Asya."

Asya sat up carefully, though all that remained of the aching pain was a faint twinge. "Izaveta told you what happened."

"Yes," Tarya replied. "But I'd like to hear it from you."

Asya swallowed, tugging at the edge of the wool blanket. As quickly as she could, she explained what had happened in the queenstrees. What she'd been searching for, the sudden appearance of the archers—how one had aimed to kill this time, how she'd used the sacred relics.

And how she'd stayed behind for Yuliana.

When Asya finished, Tarya didn't say anything for a long moment. Her aunt would never shout, but this quiet disappointment was worse. It cut down to the failure that had already burrowed into Asya's core, dragging it back out into the light.

"Your actions were reckless," Tarya said finally. "The secret of the firestone has been exposed, and already it's been used against you. You have still not followed this Calling and the scales are tipping out of balance." Her voice lowered, each word clipped. "Worse than all of that, you risked the life of the Firebird for a single mortal. I thought I taught you better."

Asya let her speak. Let her lay Asya's failings at her feet like a perverse offering, a reminder of what she'd done. Because she couldn't ignore the truth in the words.

That unknown strashe still lingered in her mind. Those

innocent starbirds, charred to ash. And only the gods knew what might come next.

But she hadn't forgotten her shift, her blinding realization that the Firebird *did* owe something to the mortal world.

After all, how could Asya protect the mortal realm if she had no love for it?

"I couldn't leave her behind," Asya murmured.

Tarya's lips thinned. "And that's why you are not ready. The mourning days are not an excuse for you to act like a child. It's high time you learned the discipline required, before we all suffer for it."

Asya's fingers clenched on top of the blanket, knuckles white. "What kind of person would I be if I left someone to die?"

Tarya's eyes pierced through her. "And if you let the Firebird die? What would that make you?"

Asya looked away. A hard lump rose in her throat, squeezing the air from her lungs. Tarya was right, as she always was. Painfully and indisputably right.

Her aunt stood up abruptly, staring down at Asya. "It is not usual for Callings to keep you in one place for this long. Your time in the palace—your attachments here—are impermanent, as all mortal things are." Tarya's voice sparked with a hidden fire, scalding into Asya as she turned to leave. "But your duty as the Firebird is undying, and you'd do well to remember that."

CHAPTER THIRTY-SEVEN

By Saints' Night, on the twelfth day of mourning, Asya felt herself again. The wound on her ribs was no more than a scar, though the one over her heart was still dark and jagged.

A heaviness had settled over her as she'd healed. This strange liminal period, where it made sense for Asya to be in the palace, would be over soon. Izaveta would be queen, and Asya would be called away. She could return, of course, though as Tarya said, there would never be any permanence to it.

But Asya owed Izaveta tonight. Her sister had almost sacrificed everything to save Asya with Saint Restov's knife. The least Asya could do was help her remove the threat of Sanislav. Assuming everything went according to the meticulous plan Izaveta had laid out.

It was a good plan—a great one even. It neatly skirted around Izaveta's vow, hopefully not so closely that it still managed to offend the gods. But there were still so many aspects of it that could go wrong, not least of which that Sanislav probably had a plan of his own. And Asya's part involved subtlety and manipulation, two things she had never been very good at.

Noteya Svedsta was traditionally held on the twelfth day of mourning, a night to honor all saints and ask them to carry the queen down into the earth. Knowing that, Asya hadn't been quite sure what to expect. But as soon as she stepped through the entrance to the Hall of Saints, she realized this would be far more a ball than a religious event.

The hall was as large as any cathedral, rising up to a high, vaulted ceiling. Stained glass windows ran the length of the room, each one depicting a different saint, leading up to a vast candelabra of spun iron that dominated the far wall. Golden chandeliers swung from above, illuminating the already teeming sea of people. They were all dressed in elaborate costumes of the various saints, giving the scene an otherworldly feel. As if Asya had stepped from the palace into some ancient painting of gods and monsters.

Though, tonight, Asya wasn't dressed as a monster. Izaveta had sent the outfit to her room that morning—Asya still had no idea how her sister had managed to get it ready that quickly. Her long white cloak was made of spun silk so thin it looked as if she'd draped a spiderweb over her shoulders. The gown was silver, threaded through with a pale red that darkened to crimson at the hem. A kokoshnik of embroidered silver, like captured moonlight, sparkled in her hair. And the costume was completed with glittering jewels surrounding a golden hilt over her heart, as if a dagger still protruded from her chest.

For one night, she had become Saint Restov.

Perhaps a little too close to the truth, but Iza had never shied away from the macabre.

In this mass of people, bodies all pressing too close, Asya felt strangely alone. Not just separate, as she always did. But truly alone.

An absence shadowed her every step. The space where, even after only eleven days, Asya had grown used to someone being.

When Asya left the Voya Wing, she'd almost gone to find Yuliana, despite Tarya's warning. But something held her back, snagging in her mind like a thorn. Asya had told Yuliana exactly who she was in the queenstrees, and this was her answer. The one Asya had been afraid to hear. The strashe had asked Izaveta to be recused. Again, those scars filtered into Asya's mind. Scars that could only have come from one thing. One creature.

She swallowed hard. She couldn't think about that now, couldn't ponder on the hollow space it carved in her chest. Tonight, she had to help her sister.

Asya cut a path through the assembled people, heads turning and rustling whispers mingling with the music. Long tables lined one wall, laden with food. Piles of knish dumplings heaped next to steaming blini topped with shining black beads of caviar. An elaborate korovai sat at the center, shaped to look like a Firebird. Sweet breads twined together with berries and currants to form its extended wings, glittering with orange honey glaze.

Normally that would have been Asya's first stop. Korovai was one of her favorite things, and she hadn't had it in the years she'd been away from the palace. Her aunt wasn't one for unnecessarily elaborate food.

But her stomach was too knotted, nervous energy thrumming through her veins. She really hoped this worked.

The first few couples took to the dance floor as the music switched to a soft waltz. Asya's eyes were scanning the twirling guests when someone stepped into her line of vision. Vibishop Sanislav.

"Good evening," he said, his voice smooth as the silk of her gown. "I trust you are better than when we last met."

Asya tugged on the bottom of her sleeve, trying to remember what her sister had said about not giving the game away. But her words still came out forced as she said, "Yes, thank you." She cleared her throat. "The Firebird certainly appreciates your efforts."

She bit back a sigh. Now she was talking about herself in the third person.

But Sanislav didn't seem to notice. "Of course. You know I have always been your truest supporter."

She bristled, clasping her hands behind her back. There was a biting undertone to the statement, an implication that if he was the truest supporter then there were other *false* supporters. And Asya was sure who Sanislav meant to discredit.

She opened her mouth to reply, but something caught in the corner of her vision, stealing her breath. A familiar dark head of hair and a crisp uniform.

"Sorry," she said hastily, not looking back at Sanislav. "I've just seen someone I need to speak to." She pushed past the somewhat bemused vibishop, knocking into his shoulder in her haste. She steadied him with a quick hand before hurrying away.

She moved through the crowd easily—her unwelcome presence useful for once—and followed that dark hair out into the passage beyond. Yuliana stopped in front of a curling stone pillar, standing to attention to match the strashe spread along the passageway. The gleaming silver of the formal uniform reflected the bright gray of her eyes. A distant storm, beautiful and unreachable.

Yuliana hadn't seen her yet, and for a moment Asya hovered in the doorway. If she just turned around and went back in the hall, then she'd never have to know why Yuliana had asked to be removed. Would never have to confirm the painful suspicions that bubbled in her stomach.

But perhaps not knowing, being stuck in this liminal space where she constantly wondered, was worse.

She bit her lip, steeling herself, and stepped into the passage. "Yu—" Asya cut herself off, swallowing the too-familiar word. "Strashe Vilanovich, good evening."

Yuliana stared straight ahead, her eyes not so much as flickering in Asya's direction. "I'm not supposed to speak while I'm on duty."

The words hit Asya like a blow, echoing through her chest as if the jewels on her dress really were a knife. She glanced around. The passage was almost deserted, out of the main thoroughfare so no more than a few fluttering courtiers were heading for the hall. The next strashe on guard was far enough to be out of earshot and likely too preoccupied with their own position to notice.

Asya twisted one of the glimmering beads that hung from

her sleeve. She managed a weak smile. "I could just stand here and muse on the qualities of the shashka compared to longer-bladed sabers and see what happens?"

She'd been trying for some levity, to somehow grasp the easiness they'd so fleetingly had, but the strashe's face remained cool as the stone pillar behind her.

Asya tugged the bead again, ducking her head as two courtiers dressed as matching Saint Meshniks hurried past. They disappeared into the hall, leaving the passage oddly quiet. The bubble of music and chatter of voices seemed so distant here. A separate realm that left this one quiet and frozen. A silence Asya couldn't find a way to break through.

The bead finally popped free, leaving its frayed thread wrapped around Asya's fingers. "I wanted…" She swallowed, trying to find the right words. Words that might fix this. "Just to say thank you. For bringing me back to the palace."

Yuliana stayed fixed in place. "That was my job."

The past tense stung Asya more than she'd expected. She took a step back, looking down at the shining marble floor. What had she even hoped to accomplish by coming out here? Yuliana had made her position clear. She'd walked away, and Asya didn't have any right to push for more.

The certainty of that clamped around her like strangling vines, squeezing her heart. She wanted to say something else—but what else was there? No words would change what Asya was.

Nothing would.

She went to turn away. To slink back into the hall and try to pretend none of this had happened, to focus on the thing she was meant to do tonight. But as she moved, something caught her eye. Almost hidden in shadow, but undeniable. A mottled bruise, tinged already with green, ran from Yuliana's left temple up into the line of her hair.

Asya moved forward without conscious thought. She closed the distance between them, her hands stretching toward Yuliana instinctively. The strashe flinched away, finally meeting Asya's gaze.

"How did that happen?" Asya asked quietly.

For an instant, it wasn't hatred that Asya saw burning in those gray eyes. It wasn't even the horror or disgust she'd expected. It was something else entirely. A brief flash of the girl she'd sparred with, the one who'd wrapped her arms around Asya's waist on the back of a bear.

But in the next blink it was gone, so fleeting she was sure she'd imagined it.

Yuliana shifted, tucking an invisible stray hair behind her ear. "From the grove."

Another swirl of guilt curled in Asya's gut. The image flashed into her mind. Yuliana slamming into her, pushing her out of the path of the arrow.

If Yuliana didn't care—if she hated what Asya was—then why had she saved her?

It was her job. The words echoed in Asya's mind, the answer she didn't want.

She teetered. She knew she should just turn away. She didn't need to dig the knife any deeper into her wound, to twist it further. But the question leaped from her lips anyway, too quick for her to take it back. "How did you get those scars?"

Yuliana's left hand twitched, reaching toward her right as

though to pull down her sleeve. "I don't know what you're talking about."

"I saw… I saw the—" Asya almost choked on the word, desperate not to let it out "—the burns."

Yuliana watched her for a moment, her face tight and unreadable. "I think you know."

Asya stumbled back, almost tripping over the sparkling bloodred train. Bile burned in her throat like flames. She did know, so why had she asked? Why had she bothered to ask when it was written so clearly in the hard lines of Yuliana's body, the stiff set of her shoulders?

Asya wanted to say something—anything. But words felt so hollow in the face of that. Nothing she said could change what had happened.

Inside the hall, the music shifted from a jubilant waltz to a slower melody. Its echoing notes twined through the passage.

Asya's heart jolted. *The music change.* That was her cue.

Chapter Thirty-Eight

Izaveta's dress had been carefully chosen for the occasion, both to project an image of power and to give herself the confidence she needed for this to work. Pale gray silk that fell to her feet in waves, the hem jagged as if torn. She wore a simple kokoshnik of dark gray, accented with silver that glinted like fangs.

The highlight was her gloves. Silk adorned with molded silver that tapered to a point at the end of each finger. For just one night, she could pretend that she really had grown claws.

Izaveta stood at the far end of the hall, directly beneath the stained glass window of her inspiration for the evening, Saint Lyoza. From this vantage point she could watch her plan unfold, making sure each piece played its part, as well as keeping an eye out for the vibishop. He was always easy to spot, holding court surrounded by a knot of sycophantic admirers.

Though she was pleased to see that Commander Iveshkin was not among their number.

Sanislav clearly did not have the support he'd been so sure

of when he made her take that oath. Her letter—her promise to the commander—had done its job. She swallowed down the guilt that came with that. It was her only option, the only way to keep the vibishop at bay.

But that didn't mean Sanislav might not try something. And it didn't mean she could let down her guard.

A figure clad in deep red detached from the crowd and moved toward Izaveta. His crimson cloak looked a little the worse for wear, and he'd slung what appeared to be kitchen scales across his shoulders, presumably to represent Saint Petrik's balance of knowledge. Even with the somewhat un-conventional costume, Nikov had certainly put more effort into his appearance than he did in the library. His hair was smoothed back—though several curls still stood resolutely out of place—and his clothes beneath the cloak were sleek and well crafted. This was Nikov as the Amarinth's emissary, the boy who did not stand like a scholar.

But the realization no longer sent suspicion coiling through Izaveta. These weren't masks that Nikov donned to further his aims, but two sides of the same person. Seeing him now, it was like knowing his secret. Something small shared be-tween them.

He smiled as he approached, and it sent a skitter up Izaveta's spine. In the past few days, she'd become too comfortable with his presence. It veered far too close to trust, a commodity that Izaveta didn't like to give away so freely. It didn't hurt when one expected a traitor and found themselves to be right. But when one trusted a person and was later betrayed, that could be their undoing.

But she couldn't ignore the way her treasonous body relaxed a little at his arrival. The tension seeping away at the sight of his ridiculous costume.

He swept her a bow. "Good evening, my lady."

She raised her eyebrows, unable to stop her lips from twitching toward a smile. "Saint Petrik, I take it? Not very original for a scholar."

He shrugged, eyes sparkling. "I wouldn't want to offend him."

Over his shoulder, Izaveta caught Ambassador Täusch's colorless gaze. There was calculation in his expression, though Izaveta couldn't quite be sure if it was directed at her or at his son.

Nikov grabbed a pelmeni from a passing tray, apparently oblivious to his father's stares, and took a relishing bite of the thin beef-filled dough. "Oh, I do miss these." He shot her a sidelong glance, gesturing with the dumpling. "The Amarinth kitchens leave much to be desired."

"I can imagine." That smile tugged at her lips again, a prickle of warmth creeping up her neck. "Have you seen the other offerings from our kitchens?"

He cocked his head questioningly, and Izaveta threaded her arm through his, drawing him over to the long table. Nestled among the traditional Tóurensi dishes was a plate of small, thin cakes topped with sliced almonds. Even through the cacophony of smells, she could pick out the sweetness of the rose syrup that soaked them.

"Basbousa," she said proudly, "made from a traditional Kharuri recipe."

Nikov's lips parted with a soft sound of surprise as he stared down at them.

Izaveta pulled her arm from his, suddenly far too aware of their closeness. "They are my true apology," she said, the words only a little stilted. She was not well practiced in apologies. Lies and manipulations came easily, but even brief sincerity felt like stepping into battle without her armor.

But after everything, she felt she did owe Nikov this.

He glanced up at her, eyes gleaming with an edge of mischief. "I thought queens did not apologize."

She smoothed her skirt, waving a hand as if it meant nothing. "Well, I am not quite queen yet."

He picked up one of the small cakes almost reverently and took a savoring bite. When he looked up at her again, the glinting humor was gone from his eyes, replaced with something else. An unguarded earnestness that sent a flutter through her stomach. "Thank you."

She turned her head to hide her smile. "And what of those?" She gestured to the scales, edged with rust, that lay across his shoulders. "Did they come from the kitchens too?"

"I beg your pardon, these are ancient relics. The pride of Saint Petrik." He shifted, readjusting the cast-iron plates with a low clang of metal. "Though I am humble enough to admit they may have been a mistake. Not the best choice for an event that requires dancing."

She straightened the ends of her gloves, admiring the way the claws glinted in the candlelight. "Well, if you're going to ask me to dance, I'm afraid I must disappoint you, Master Toyevski."

He half turned toward her, an odd look flashing across his face. "You can call me Nikov, you know."

She held his gaze, her mutinous heart fluttering against her rib cage. She should scoff at the impropriety of that statement. She was to be queen, and titles could not be shirked so easily in her presence. But in that instant she wished they could. Wished it could be that simple.

A grin broke across his face, lightening the moment. "I believe once two people have stabbed one's sister in the heart, first names are acceptable."

Before Izaveta could respond, a sudden hush fell across the hall. She turned, gaze fixing on Sanislav. He stood next to the musicians, using their raised dais to garner attention. He was at least a hundred paces away from her, but she could feel his eyes boring into her.

"Good evening," he said, his voice carrying across the room like a scurrying spider. "On this final night of mourning for the late Queen Adilena, we turn our minds to the saints, who will guide her into Dveda's embrace."

Izaveta's fingers curled, the silver claws scraping against her palms. A part of her wanted to run, to flee from these weighted gazes before this all went wrong. But she stood her ground, face blank as Sanislav pressed on. Tonight she was Saint Lyoza, and the clawed girl ran from nothing.

"We also turn, tonight, to our future. To Princess Izaveta, who shall tomorrow stand before our gods and the Crown." He gestured to the crowd, and two acolytes hurried forward, setting an aged wooden box at his feet.

Sanislav knelt down to open it with great reverence, lifting out an ancient bronzed goblet. Voda Svediye, the blessed water, used for all the Church's divine rituals. Izaveta was almost surprised she warranted such an offering, but then she supposed Sanislav wanted to be sure it at least *appeared* as if he did not despise her.

His argument was going to be that the gods had turned their backs on her, not that he had.

"We present her with this," he pressed on. "The Voda Svediye, used to cleanse past sins and move us all into a new era."

She gritted her teeth, almost flinching at *sins*. There was nothing that could cleanse her past sins.

But all eyes were on her now, a coiling anticipation threading through the hall. This was a sacred ritual to the Church, not one she could dismiss without severe repercussions within the court. And Sanislav knew that.

Raising her chin and tightening her claws at her sides, she moved through the sea of people. They parted before her like waves at the prow of a boat. Apprehension curled in the air, squeezing around her throat. With everyone hidden beneath layers of jewels and costumes, it was almost as if she walked before the saints themselves. Awaiting their judgment.

She spotted Asya in the crowd, her brown eyes worried. But just the sight of her sister was a flash of comfort, a small push to move Izaveta forward.

Stepping onto the dais snapped her away from that strange realm of saints and sharply back into her own. Sanislav's eyes glittered, his fingers tight around the goblet.

She turned away from him, looking out to face the glistening swarm of the court. "We stand on the precipice of great change. The turbulence of these past days has been difficult for us all. I hope that we may now begin to heal from the pain of my mother's death and continue to keep the queen-dom strong and united."

With the candles silhouetting the crowd, Izaveta couldn't see their reaction. Couldn't tell if they were nodding their heads with her or biting back disdain.

Sanislav held out the goblet, leaning in close. "'Svediye ya vidichik toroli,'" he said, so quietly Izaveta was the only one who could hear. A phrase from their holy book, written in Old Tóurensi.

May the saints judge you worthy.

The way Sanislav was looking at her, that glint in his eyes, it was almost as if he knew—

She cut that thought off. There was only one truth he'd demanded she reveal tonight. Her fingers fastened around the rough surface of the goblet, warmth seeping from it despite the chill in the air. The silver claws gleamed, but the bright light bleached their mysterious air, showing them to be no more than the playthings they were.

Showing Izaveta to be no more than what she was. Not the woman with claws who could defy anyone, but the girl scrambling against a rising tide.

As she raised the goblet to her lips, she didn't look at the vibishop but down into the mass of people. She couldn't pick Asya out now, but she could feel her sister's presence.

Izaveta tilted the goblet and drank.

The taste prickled in her mind, tingling down to the scar on her left palm. The only other time she'd drunk blessed water was on the day of the ceremony, when all she'd wanted was to turn and run from the cathedral. She'd almost choked on it then.

But tonight she was prepared.

The liquid was sharp against her tongue, scalding down her throat like flames. The hint of rosemary drowned by the alcohol—whatever spirit the bishops tossed in there and claimed to be holy.

It was only a moment later, once the burning subsided, that she noticed the bitter aftertaste. Poison.

CHAPTER THIRTY-NINE

As soon as the liquid passed Izaveta's lips, Asya knew something was wrong. She saw it in the way Izaveta's eyes widened, her lips parting. But it wasn't until the goblet tumbled to the ground—droplets spraying the air like rain—that Asya moved. Diving through the crowd, she scrambled onto the dais as Izaveta fell.

This wasn't supposed to happen. They had a plan. Iza was meant to be safe.

Izaveta's breaths were shallow, her face white as marble. Already her lips were paling, soft pink bleeding into a sickly white. Asya snatched up the goblet. A thin coating of white powder, like the first dusting of snow, mingled with the last trickle of blessed water.

Her heart lurched. She glared up at Sanislav. "Did you do this?"

Sanislav took a hasty step back, staring down at Izaveta with an expression of artful disbelief. But Asya had seen enough of that by now to know how easily he could fake a look.

No one else moved. The whole hall felt suspended, as if the floor had been wrenched from beneath them and they were all about to go crashing down a steep drop. Even the strashevsta in his burnished formal jacket just stared. The strashe were trained to protect against threats, but what could they do when the threat had already come to pass?

Asya's eyes danced around the room. Surely there had to be someone who could help? Something—*anything*—they could do.

A gargled choke pulled Asya's attention back to her sister. Izaveta's lips moved, forming words Asya couldn't quite catch. She grasped her sister's wrist, feeling for the flutter of her pulse. But Izaveta pulled away, trying to speak. "Voya," she choked out. "Xishin."

Asya looked around, eyes searching for the stained glass figure of Saint Xishin. But there was no one in front of it. No glimmer of black voya robes.

"Somebody fetch the voye!" She didn't direct the command at anyone, more a desperate plea to the room at large.

She looked back to Sanislav. Her throat tightened with each of her sister's labored breaths, every choking gasp, as if Asya were the one who'd been poisoned.

"What did you put in there?" Her voice rang out too loud, echoing off the high ceiling. She didn't care.

"I—" Sanislav stammered, hands clasping in front of him. "I— It should just be Voda Svediye. I don't under—"

Asya leaped to her feet. Her hand jumped instinctively for her shashka, but of course she wasn't wearing it. But that wasn't her only weapon. Flames licked along her fingers before she'd even consciously made the decision to set them free.

She moved closer to the vibishop. "I won't ask again."

Sanislav's eyes widened, the deep orange reflected in his dark irises. "Please—I don't know—"

She didn't wait for him to finish. She grabbed the fabric of his robes, searching through the folds as errant sparks burned holes in the thin wool.

But all she found was an empty vial.

Asya threw it to the ground with a low growl of frustration. He was useless. And she didn't have time to force the answer out of him. Not with Izaveta's lungs gasping for air, the pale blue of lost skies tingeing her lips.

Asya vaguely heard the strashe move behind her, the protests issuing from Sanislav as they surrounded him, all eyes on the small vial. Gasps burst from the courtiers. But they didn't dare surge forward. They were all trapped in this moment, powerless as their queen lay dying on the ground.

Asya looked around desperately. How long until the voye got here?

Too long, said a quiet voice in her head. Soft and final.

And even if they did, how would they know what to do? The voye would have no idea what kind of poison this was— and without that information, there was no hope of an antidote.

The scholar from the Amarinth appeared at her side, absurdly out of place in the gravity of the situation with his odd costume. But fear coated his voice as he spoke, biting as a blade in Asya's side. "Where's the poison?"

She gestured to the fallen goblet, and he snatched it up. He ran a finger through the powder, raising it to his nose.

"Do you know what it is?"

He shook his head, face ashen as he stared back at her. "He—I mean, I—I never learned much about poisons or antidotes."

Asya turned away, tears burning in her eyes. Flames still coiled around her hands. All this power and there was nothing she could do for her sister. Nothing—

A thought kindled at the back of her mind. One of the many lessons Tarya had hammered into her. The Firebird often spent weeks—months—wandering the wilderness when hunting, so she had to know how to live in the forest. How to forage; which plants were poisonous and which could be used to heal.

The picture bloomed in her mind. A small yellow flower. Karaznoi. The petaled sun. Inconspicuous to look at, it was said to cure almost any poison.

There would be none nearby. It only grew in the far reaches of the Skyless Hallows, taking root in the ancient magic of that forest.

But there was one way Asya could find a blossom.

In order to fully understand the Firebird, to understand what the price was, Asya also had to understand magic. She'd only cast a few spells, all under Tarya's strict supervision. But this wasn't asking the magic for much. She couldn't risk a magical healing—not only was she far too inexperienced, but the price for that would be too high for her to pay. Especially as Izaveta's heart slowed with every beat.

But all Asya needed was a few leaves. A simple conjuring. Her mind strained, trying to remember that day at the Roost when Tarya had shown her how to conjure a stone. The words, the markings. How to throw the price into the flames.

She spun around, her own heart beating double time, as though somehow that might stop Iza's from fading.

Asya turned to Nikov, gesturing to the food table. "Fetch the parsley from the knish and a knife. The sharpest you can find."

To her relief, Nikov obeyed without question. Grabbing the goblet again, Asya cleared a space next to her sister. Only a small trickle of the blessed water remained, but it should just be enough for it to work. She *prayed* it would be enough.

Izaveta's eyes were closed, her lips no longer trying to form words. Her erratic pulse—the last dying flutter of a butterfly's wings—shivered in her throat.

Nikov knelt down next to her, holding out the items. From the slight hesitation to his movements, he knew—or at least suspected—what she was going to do.

But Asya didn't say anything as she took the blade. There wasn't time to explain.

She tried to keep her hands from shaking as she gripped the knife, to not think about how it might already be too late. Even though that fear had already wrapped around her heart, taking hold like a thorned vine.

The blade dug into the polished wood floor easily, moving across it with a low scrape that prickled along Asya's spine. A few outraged gasps burst from the onlookers, but she didn't so much as glance around. She would happily deface the crown itself if it would save her sister. She drew three hasty circles, interlocking like links in a chain, to invoke the power of the three gods.

She placed the parsley at the center—slightly greasy from garnishing the knish, but she had to hope it would work all the same—and let the flames spread from her fingers. They caught hold of the small sprigs, devouring them quickly. But the fire didn't stop when the kindling was gone, it crackled on at the center of those circles. A burning heart that would bring life to the spell.

She took up the goblet, pouring the last drops of blessed water over those flames. "Stavoye verenish," she murmured. The only invocation she remembered from that day with Tarya, more plea than spell.

Now all that was left was the price. The crucial act that if a person forewent would send the Firebird after them. With a bubbling, almost hysterical laugh, she realized that skipping this step would mean sending her own power after herself.

Not that she was planning on evading the price. She ran the blade along her palm, an almost mirror image of the scar on her left. The scar from the day that had tried to separate them forever.

Fate had failed then, and Asya wouldn't let it succeed today.

For a small conjuring like this, the price shouldn't be more than a thimbleful of blood. Perhaps less, as her blood was not that of regular mortals. The thin trickle of red didn't hiss as it hit the flames. It didn't make any sound at all, devoured before it could even touch the ground.

For the first time, a fleeting question crossed her mind. Where did the price go? If not turned to ash, what happened to the things the flames devoured? But the next instant it was swallowed as she turned her attention back to the spell. She conjured the picture in her mind, focusing on that tiny yellow flower. No more than a flicker of sunlight on water.

She closed her eyes, sending her prayer up to Zmenya. *Please don't take her yet.*

For several sickening heartbeats, nothing happened. Asya felt like the whole world was holding its breath, the very wind pausing in its rushing path.

Then the fire sputtered out. It left behind no dark smudge of ash, no remnants of the herb. Instead, one small blossom sat in its place.

Asya scrambled forward, careful not to crush the precious flower. She put a hand behind Izaveta's head, forcing her up. Her lips were colorless as mourning skies. The color of a person ready to be reclaimed by the earth. That was what the Saints' Night was for, after all—to speed the queen into the earth.

But the saints were trying to take the wrong queen.

Asya lifted the blossom to her sister's mouth. "Iza, you need to eat this."

Izaveta let out a gasping choke in response. Her eyes were clouded, barely registering her surroundings. Asya forced her sister's mouth open, pushing the blossom in. "Come on, Iza," she murmured. "Come *on*."

Asya watched, her heart stuttering in her chest. The flower had to work. She was sure she'd remembered right. As long as it wasn't a poison that was somehow invulnerable to the flower's properties. That fear rose inside Asya like a towering wave. One that would crush her if it broke.

"Please," Asya whispered, a child's desperate prayer to the gods.

Izaveta blinked slowly. Some of the mist had receded from her eyes, returning them to their rich brown. She took a shaking breath. And then another.

Asya sank back on her heels, finally able to fill her own lungs again.

Diye, that had been much too close.

CHAPTER FORTY

Being poisoned was a far more unpleasant experience than Izaveta had expected. Not that she'd thought it would be enjoyable, but when she'd laid out the plan in her head, she hadn't anticipated what it really meant. The way the poison would steal away her breath, clamping down on her lungs like a vise. A drowning girl desperate for air. The cold that had come with it, icy fingers of death that scraped along her spine.

Sitting in her chambers, staring down at the zvess board, it had seemed simple. Zvezda had informed her Sanislav intended to present her with blessed water, the first step in his own plan to make her appear out of favor with the gods. From there, it seemed obvious. Izaveta had Fyodor procure the poison—powdered vineberry leaves found in many of the Church's rituals—while a loyal acolyte had placed it in the goblet, and Asya had slipped the empty vial into Sanislav's pocket.

Izaveta was to drink from the goblet and then collapse while Asya accused Sanislav of his involvement. One of the voye would be waiting underneath the stained glass depiction of Saint Xishin with the antidote, and then everyone would be certain of Sanislav's treachery.

Removing the would-be queen through political maneuverings or supposed divine revelations was one thing, but attempted assassination was something else entirely. Something that few would be willing to stand by, especially when the powerful figure of the Firebird so clearly opposed it.

Only the last phase hadn't worked. That nagged at the back of Izaveta's mind, souring what should have been a victory. She'd entrusted the antidote to Zvezda, counting on her oath to ensure she would follow through. The spymaster had overseen it herself, passing the vial to one of her pakviye who should have ensured the voya was waiting under the statue of Saint Xishin.

Where had that gone wrong? Could she have misjudged Zvezda? Would the woman risk angering the gods to work against her?

Izaveta shook her head, dispelling the question. It was not one to examine yet. What mattered now was that it had worked.

No one person, other than herself, had known the entire plan. Even Asya hadn't known everything.

But guilt twisted in Izaveta's stomach as she glanced over at her sister, sitting on the edge of the dais, shoulders hunched with her arms pulled tight around her. Still, it was better this way. Asya would never have agreed to it if she'd known the true risk.

But it had *worked*. Perhaps not quite as Izaveta had intended, but she was alive and Sanislav was in chains. Not to mention that the Firebird had saved her. That was almost better than her plan.

Through the voye flitting around her—eager to offer water, blankets, or any number of other useless things—Izaveta could see Commander Iveshkin out in the sea of onlookers. After tonight, she wouldn't dare question the Firebird's loyalty again.

Izaveta shrugged off several of the voye's anxious hands, forcing herself back to her feet. Her legs shook beneath her, the final traces of the poison still curling in her veins. She knew they wanted her to return to the Voya Wing for further examination, but she wasn't going to waste this opportunity to show her strength. The last step that truly made this plan her best work: a ruler who survived an assassination attempt could never have their fortitude questioned.

She glanced over at the knot of strashe surrounding Sanislav. She did not even have to accuse him herself—the entire court had seen his guilt with their own eyes.

She knew his imprisonment risked offending the Church, of course, but Izaveta would simply pardon him after the coronation. An act of mercy that might even garner her their favor. And by then, it would be too late for him to stand against her. He would already be ruined.

He caught her gaze. No anger burned in the lines of his face, more a considered interest as he examined the realigned pieces of the game. "You would dare forsake the gods so?" he asked, his words clear even over the murmurs of the court.

Izaveta did not answer. She knew what he meant—he believed she was breaking the oath she had sworn on the three moons, bringing the damnation of the gods upon herself. But Noteya Svedsta was not over yet.

Izaveta turned to the crowd, the spell of their costumes broken by the disturbance. She no longer looked out at the saints assembled, but instead at pretenders desperate to understand what had happened. And Izaveta was the only one with answers. It gave her no undue pleasure to know that. To watch them all turn to her as if she were already their queen.

"People of the court," she said, her voice coming out a little rough, still coated with poison. Not that it mattered—it would just be another sign of what she had overcome. "What we all witnessed here tonight was a terrible act of treachery from within our own ranks. An act that cannot go unanswered. I have suspected for some time that there may be a traitor in our midst, ever since Hunte Rastyshenik, when the feather was stolen from the swan's neck."

Gasps burst through the room like miniature explosions. She saw Conze Bazin drawing himself up, eyes wide and staring. Ambassador Täusch watched from his corner, impassive as ever. Hushed whispers rose to bitter mutterings and anguished glares.

Izaveta pressed on, spinning this truth to her advantage. "I showed the court a false feather in an attempt to draw the traitor into the light. Vibishop Sanislav wanted to manipulate the gods to his own ends, to use our beliefs against us, but now the truth has been revealed."

She caught Kyriil's sharp eyes, and he made no attempt to hide his annoyance. After this, Izaveta wouldn't need his help, and he knew it. There was a vindictive edge to her pleasure at that, a satisfying vengeance years in the making.

"I owe a great debt of gratitude not only to the strashe who continue to protect me," she went on, with a small nod to the strashevsta, who visibly swelled at the praise. She had to suppress an eye roll. Men like him were far too easy to manipulate. "But also to my sister, the Firebird. Without her quick thinking, I would not still be standing before you. I hope we can continue this unity in the face of any threat."

Asya didn't look up from the edge of the dais, and another spike of guilt shot through Izaveta. But all this was for Asya too. Now she would be safe. Izaveta held on to that—to the idea that she'd had some noble intentions. Because the truth gnawing at the back of her mind wouldn't go away. The truth her mother had seen in her. That Nikov had seen. In the dark recesses of her heart, the thing that mattered most to her was power. Was making sure she would never be without it again.

Izaveta blinked, turning back to the court. "We know there are those who wish to weaken the queendom, but tonight is proof that Tóurin is strong. Tóurin will not be broken."

It was at that very moment—as if on the whim of the gods' cruel sense of humor—that something massive crashed through the stained glass window behind her.

CHAPTER FORTY-ONE

Glass exploded over Asya's head, showering down on them like falling stars. The sound rang in her ears as sharp as the shards now scattered across the floor.

She jumped to her feet, adrenaline spiking through her veins. No one else moved. It was as if a sudden spell had fallen over the rest of the partygoers, freezing them in place. All transfixed by the enormous creature that had landed in the middle of the hall. It was at least twice as tall as a human and almost four times that in length, with glittering silver fur that flowed like water. Two pointed ears stood at the prow of its head, leading down to its huge jaws.

The beast turned its head, and Asya's blood ran cold. Paralyzing, primal fear gripped her. That same feeling she remembered from watching her aunt transform into the Firebird.

Volke otrava. A banewolf.

They weren't meant to be real—or if they were, they were never seen. And they certainly weren't vicious creatures. In all the folktales Asya had read of them, they offered help to the heroes. They sent them off on their journeys or provided the vital object at the last moment.

This creature didn't look like it wanted to offer help. Its great fangs were bared, each one longer than a sword and just as deadly. Its head hung low, hackles raised as it advanced.

But its eyes were what sent that suffocating fear through Asya's veins. In stories, a banewolf's eyes glittered like captured starlight, all the constellations visible in their depths. It was believed that a mortal could see their dreams in them, all their happy memories splayed before them.

There was no flash of happiness or glimmer of starlight in this beast's eyes. They were black as the night sky, but hollow. Empty. A once-vibrant land scorched to nothing. Staring into them felt like teetering on the edge of a void, a hopeless chasm that would swallow her whole.

It was then that Asya realized. Those starbirds flickered in her mind. Another peaceful creature had been corrupted by the imbalance of magic.

All around the room the low shriek of metal told her sabers were being drawn. But what good could they do against a creature like this?

The sound made the banewolf spin, jaws snapping. The image sent a twinge of uncertainty through Asya's gut. A cornered animal, more afraid than violent.

But then a strashe took a brave step forward, saber slicing through the air, and the banewolf's great claws swiped out.

They caught the woman's arm. A spray of blood burst from her, bright and burning as a flame.

Whatever spell had held the hall captive broke as suddenly as the shattering glass. Screams rent the air, and the assembled people scattered. Asya moved instinctively, diving in front of her sister.

The Firebird reared beneath her skin, as if drawn to the surface by the presence of another beast of legend.

Asya forced it back down. "Izaveta," she said. "Iza, you have to run."

Her sister stumbled, murmuring something too quiet to catch as she stared at the banewolf—still cornered and snarling but not attacking.

Izaveta was unsteady on her feet—the poison perhaps still clinging on—and Asya grabbed her arm. "Run!" she yelled, raising her voice over the panicked shouts. "You have to get out of here."

But Izaveta still didn't move. Asya grasped her shoulder, pushing her toward the doors, when she saw why. Bodies blocked the exits, all tumbling over each other as they clawed for safety. Her sister would never make it through that.

Asya whirled, heart hammering its way up her throat. As if in answer to her unspoken question, the Firebird's wings fluttered beneath her skin.

Strashe surrounded the banewolf, but they hung back, out of reach of its massive claws. Trying to corral it rather than subdue it. That wouldn't work for long. Asya could see it in the banewolf's eyes. The way its fur bristled with each gleam of a saber. It was cornered, and it knew there was only one way out.

Asya saw it a breath before it happened. She was already leaping off the dais, flames rising to her fingers, when the beast pounced. It seized the nearest strashe in its massive jaws, throwing him aside as if he weighed nothing.

A woman, still in the leaf-strewn dress of Saint Korona, rushed forward. Her blade winked in the candlelight as she raised it—and then she froze. Horror spread across her face like blood from a wound. For a heartbeat she was transfixed. Then the banewolf batted her aside too, turning to the onslaught of strashe.

But their blades were barely more than an irritation to the beast. They glanced off its fur with a spattering of sparks, leaving not so much as a scratch behind.

"Get back!" Asya yelled, her voice barely audible above the clanging cacophony of the fight.

Some of the strashe glanced over, scrambling away as they realized who it was. Most didn't move—either they hadn't heard or didn't care. But Asya couldn't wait for them to notice.

She drew in a deep breath and transformed. Not just flames bursting from her but the creature itself. It was easy, as if the Firebird had been waiting for just that. She felt its great head hovering above her own, the cresting point of its flaming beak rising over her kokoshnik.

It was almost like the Calling—a brief moment of pure clarity. A sudden crest of music that thrummed in her head. The Firebird moved with her, its power singing through her veins. The screams and clashes of blades faded away, replaced with that roaring song. Somehow everything was both heightened and farther away, sight sharper but focused on a single point. The very air hummed. She could feel the threads of magic, the way they twisted around the banewolf's mind, transforming it into something monstrous.

The beast raised its head to face her, the minor irritations of the strashe forgotten.

Asya didn't wait for it to pounce. She lunged forward, the Firebird moving with her in an ethereal dance. Burning flames and inhuman grace coalescing into something else entirely. The banewolf let out a howl, a piercing note that battered against the Firebird's wings. From the way the remaining strashe fell back, it must have been a devastating sound.

But it didn't affect the Firebird, didn't stop her devouring fire. Asya jumped, the Firebird lifting her far higher than should have been possible, and let loose a vine of flame. It snapped out, reaching for the banewolf's front legs.

The creature moved—faster than a mortal eye could follow—dodging her attack. It rounded on Asya, a new tension coursing through its massive body. As if it knew that, now, it had a true opponent.

It sprang, powerful back legs launching it into the air. It wasn't aiming for Asya herself, but the flaming bird that rose from her. Her body reacted instinctively, drawn out of the banewolf's path by a single beat of the burning wings.

Everything moved in perfect harmony, the Firebird her partner in this dance.

Another coil of flame burst from her as she rounded on the creature, a sudden staccato in the symphony.

Still trying to turn, the banewolf didn't have time to move as the flame cut through its fur, heat scorching the air. It reared back and let out a low cry of pain, pitiful and echoing in the vast hall. The sound dug into Asya's chest.

It was almost human.

It made her stumble, the bright harmony of the Firebird slipping away from her.

None of this was the creature's fault. This was because of her, because the price hadn't been paid. Maybe if she could just find a way to restrain it, then they'd be able to help it somehow. To cleanse whatever magic was driving it to this.

She moved forward more slowly now, drawing the flames back into herself. Trying to appear less of a threat. She could still feel that magic, its metallic tang burning in her nostrils.

The banewolf shifted its paws. It lowered its head, teeth bared as it stared at her. Its eyes—

Asya froze. She'd been wrong before. Its eyes weren't empty at all. But they weren't the hopeful beacons of legend. They were a nightmarish reflection, all Asya's darkest thoughts dragged painfully into the light.

Her sister as cold and heartless as Asya had feared when she returned. The distant glimmer of her mother, as far away in death as she'd been in life. Yuliana, blade drawn and eyes accusing. The little girl from the cottage, but this time the flames didn't stop at her arm. They blazed around her, devouring her heart without hesitation.

And then Asya herself. She stood alone—separate. Her expression as blank and emotionless as Tarya's.

Asya staggered back. She blinked hard—for a moment those images still flashed behind her eyelids, like the remnants of a bright light.

Something slammed into her, heavy as a stone, and she went flying. Stars popped in front of her. She scrambled to right herself, hand scraping along the wall to find purchase. The banewolf filled her vision, blurring at the edges as her head spun.

Flames sputtered from her fingers, glancing off the banewolf's fur. The ceiling swirled behind it, mingling with the glittering metal of the great candelabra on the far wall. She tried to focus on it, to get the world to stop whirling around her.

The banewolf prowled forward, black eyes lowering toward her. She lurched back, a hand flying up to shield her vision. She couldn't look into those eyes again. Couldn't get lost in their depths.

Her heart punched against her ribs, scorching fire pulsing in her veins. She needed something else—something that might hold it back. Her gaze danced around the room, everywhere except those consuming eyes. The candelabra behind the beast sharpened into focus, its twisting arms stretching out like tree branches. Or…

A fresh wave of adrenaline jolted through Asya. The Firebird rose out of her skin again, its wings spreading wide. That harmony surged in her veins, a beating rhythm to match her own heart.

The banewolf hesitated, flames reflecting in its eyes. The sparks flew from Asya like music notes made liquid. They coalesced into a bright fire that slithered around the candelabra, burning blue at its edges.

The creature lunged, and the flames soared inside Asya, the Firebird's song crashing in her head. Moving almost before she formed the thought, the wings curled around her, protective as she darted aside.

The banewolf followed, ducking out of the path of the candelabra's arms.

Asya backed away with a burst of brightest crimson to keep the creature at bay. The metal arms of the candelabra were curving slowly, heat radiating along them. It would collapse at any moment. She needed to get the creature back under it.

The Firebird spread its wings again, and she whirled, letting a few tendrils of flame flick out toward the banewolf. She took a step back, bringing herself beneath the teetering candelabra. The creature followed her, crouching low as it prepared to attack again.

She gritted her teeth, fighting against the Firebird's instincts, the burning need to run. But she had to hold her ground until the last possible moment. Another flicker of flame leaped out to join the dancing fire of the candelabra, pushing it closer to toppling.

Asya felt the moment before it pounced. Her muscles screamed at her to leap aside, to send out another flare of flame. But she didn't move. Even as the gleaming claws flew toward her.

The banewolf's eyes almost caught her again, giving her a flash of herself—a cruel smile twisting her lips—as she threw herself aside.

The claws scraped against her side in a blinding flash of pain. It broke through the Firebird's certainty, fire sputtering out. She hit the ground hard. Air burst from her lungs. But her last tendril of flame had already done its work. With a final creak, the candelabra crumpled.

The tangle of metal caught the banewolf's back and sent it collapsing to the floor. The metallic clang of the beast's fur against the marble resonated through Asya like a struck bell. She couldn't get her lungs to fill with air. Burning pain spiraled from her side. But she wasn't done yet.

Pulling herself up, she forced out another curl of flame. It spun around the edges of the collapsed candelabra, molding the points down into the ground to form a cage.

Even trapped, the banewolf didn't settle. Its eyes rolled, dark sprays of magic shattering across the pupils. Asya averted her gaze, moving around it tentatively as she headed for the now-cleared doorway. She didn't want to look into those depths again. That monstrous mirror.

The few people remaining—gathered strashe and a scattering of guests—were staring at her with a strange mix of awe and terror. They'd likely never seen the Firebird before. And even though she'd been protecting them, the fear was still there. That sent a wrenching pain through her chest. The image from the banewolf's eyes hovered in her mind. Standing alone—*abandoned*.

Izaveta stepped forward, a silent comfort in the sea of faces.

A low growl made Asya whirl around. The banewolf thrashed against the makeshift cage, its claws gouging deep trenches into the marble as it scrabbled. The metal broke with a wrenching heave. The banewolf let out a howl that carved through the room and turned its glinting eyes on Asya.

She didn't have time to move, to avert her gaze. Her mind had only just registered those eyes—the haunting depths that wanted to drag her down—when the beast was on top of her. One massive paw pinned her, its fangs lowering toward her.

"Asya!" The word cut through the air like a blade, and the beast turned its head, teeth grazing her cheek.

Izaveta pushed to the front of the strashe, still unsteady on her feet.

Asya tried to speak—to yell at her sister to not come any closer. But the banewolf's weight pressed into her chest, claws sinking a little deeper with each breath, stealing her voice. She couldn't even call for the Firebird, as if the claws clutched it too.

Izaveta grabbed the saber from the nearest strashe, brandishing it as she moved forward. "Get away from her!"

The banewolf's grip loosened, its attention drawn away from Asya. Slowly, it pulled back, turning to face this new threat.

Izaveta held her ground, so tiny in front of the massive creature.

Asya lurched forward, one hand clutching at her shredded chest. A strangled cry tore from her lips. "No—Iza!"

And the Firebird responded. A blaze of golden red leaped from her, a blinding shadow of the Firebird itself.

Even with its preternatural speed, the banewolf didn't move in time. The fire consumed it like a living storm. Burning ropes tore across its fur, leaving angry red welts.

The banewolf thrashed, swiping at the fire with a heart-wrenching desperation. But Asya wasn't sure she could stop it now, even if she wanted to. It had dragged a part of her with it, as if her own life were feeding its flames.

The banewolf's feet collapsed beneath it. The blaze of crimson was unrelenting, tearing through the shimmering fur to the bone beneath. In only a few more stuttering heartbeats, the beast was dead.

But the flames weren't finished yet. They reared up, turning toward the remaining people. Toward Izaveta. She stumbled back, sparkling gold reaching for her.

Asya scrambled to her feet, trying to rein the fire back under her control. But the pain was still cleaving through her side. Too bright, too sharp. She couldn't grasp the strength she needed. The image in the banewolf's eyes would come true. Asya left standing alone.

For a paralyzing instant, the fire reared in front of Izaveta.

Then Asya wrenched it back to her. The flames reluctantly sank into her bones.

All that was left was the banewolf's burned-out husk—a beautiful creature charred in ashes—and the scorched ground that stopped just short of her sister.

Chapter Forty-Two

A terrible silence settled over the room. The hush of new-fallen snow. The wretched scent of the burned banewolf was overpowering, and the last tendrils of smoke stung Asya's eyes.

She took a shaky step back, away from the smoldering corpse. From the scorched remnants of the fight. The remaining guests and strashe all stared at her. There was no relief on their faces. More a shadowed fear—a sudden understanding of the creature that walked in their midst.

She couldn't even look at her sister. Not when the blackened marks of Asya's power stretched toward Izaveta like scars.

Asya had done that. She'd wanted to try to help the beast, and this was the result. It was dead, and she'd nearly hurt more people in the process.

It was all too much. The smoke, the fading adrenaline, the slowly knitting wound on her side. Too much to have to see their expressions—each one digging into her like a knife. She turned on her heel, the tattered skirt of her gown flicking behind her, and ran for the door. The last stragglers recoiled as she passed. She distantly heard a voice calling after her, but she ignored it.

The colors blurred around her as she hurried down the passage. Pale whites and golds flashed through with the indigo of the night sky beyond. She turned a corner to see more courtiers, scattered and waiting. Their expressions—the flinching horror—were so like the images in the banewolf's eyes.

She doubled back, bile burning in her throat. She opened a door at random and threw herself inside, slamming it shut behind her. The room was near pitch-black. She could just make out the shadowed outlines of storage shelves, an empty candleholder balanced at their peak.

The darkness was comforting. It provided a hidden place she could sink into, where she could pretend none of this was happening. She felt her way to the far wall and turned her back to it, sliding down to meet the cold stone floor. She curled her arms around her legs, pressing her eyes into her knees.

She couldn't shake loose the last flash in the banewolf's eyes. Just before it died—before it was consumed. She couldn't be sure if it was another conjured illusion or a true reflection. The whirling fire, her hair flying out like a tongue of flame. The curved beak of the Firebird grim and unforgiving, a mirror image of her own face beneath.

Girl and monster, one and the same.

A painful knot tightened in her chest with each breath. A rope crushing her ribs together, squeezing them around her heart.

Tarya was right. Why had Asya even bothered to try? Why had she thought that because she'd come to understand how the Firebird's purpose was protection, she could make other people see that as well?

She dug the heels of her palms into her eyes, trying to press back the tears. Sitting here now, curled around herself in the dark, it felt like the pathetic hope of a child. A fragile dream so easily crushed in the harsh reality of day.

"Asya."

Her head jerked up as a sliver of light sliced through the room. It illuminated Yuliana's face, peering around the doorway. An unusual hesitance shadowed her gray eyes. It made her look younger suddenly. Less the formidable strashe, more an uncertain girl.

Asya hurried to push the hair out of her face, wiping her eyes on her scorched sleeve. Part of her knew she should stand up, but she couldn't make her legs respond. Couldn't bring herself to care if Yuliana saw this. It couldn't be any worse than what the strashe already thought of her. Asya lowered her eyes, waiting for the door to slide shut again now the strashe had confirmed the Firebird hadn't vanished into the night.

But a flicker of movement drew her gaze. Yuliana took a slow step forward. Tentative, as if approaching a cornered animal.

Asya didn't move. She dug her fingers into her knees, wishing suddenly that the Firebird really did have the power of flight. Then she could fly away from this moment, from having to see the person who made all of this so much harder.

But Yuliana didn't say anything. Didn't glare down at her or demand she come back to deal with the mess she'd left. Silently, the strashe lowered herself to the ground next to Asya, so close their knees knocked together.

Asya glanced up. She was so used to being looked down on at her height that it was disconcerting to suddenly be level with Yuliana's eyes—glimmering even in the darkness of the room.

Yuliana took a slow breath, looking down at her interlaced hands. "You asked where I got these burns."

Asya blinked. That wasn't at all what she'd expected. "You don't have to tell—"

"I was thirteen," Yuliana interrupted, eyes firmly on her lap. There was a frayed edge to her voice, as if she suddenly needed to say this as much as she wanted Asya to hear it. "It was a bad harvest that year. An early frost killed everything we had. My father didn't know what to do. How to get food for any of us." Her fingers tightened, knuckles shining white. "I don't know where he got the spell. I just saw him leave on the night of the half-moons, and he didn't come back until morning. I didn't understand what it meant then."

A bitter smile tugged at the corner of her mouth. "The next day—well, it was like magic. Fresh shoots sprouted from frozen ground, growing so quickly you could see the blades moving. I thought we'd been blessed by Dveda." Her jaw tightened, tension coiling through her, but she didn't stop. "My father didn't understand the price. And the next day the Firebird came."

The knot in Asya's chest pulled taut like a strangling noose. She didn't want to hear this. She didn't want to know what the Firebird—what *Tarya*—had done. But Asya's throat was dry, and she couldn't find a way to form words. Couldn't bring herself to interrupt Yuliana's fractured confession.

"I'd heard of the Firebird, of course." Yuliana's voice was

no more than a whisper now, as if the story were drawn from some deep part of herself. A part she didn't want to let out but couldn't quite stop. "That wasn't the same as seeing her. Watching her come to take the price." She let out a low sound, somewhere between a laugh and a groan. "My brother tried to stop her. He threw himself at her with a saber, and she brushed him aside like it was nothing."

Yuliana's hand jumped to her right side, tracing the ridged scars hidden beneath her shirt. "I didn't have a weapon, but I stood in front of my father all the same. And the Firebird pushed me aside too. I'm not sure she even noticed. Just a burst of flame to deal with the distraction. I didn't even matter. And then, she took his heart. All he wanted to do was protect us, and the price meant he never could again."

Asya dug her nails into her palms, a painful bubble expanding in her chest. "Why are you telling me this?" It came out pained, strain splintering through every syllable. Did Yuliana just want Asya to know what she truly thought of her?

"Because you asked," Yuliana said quietly. "And because I wanted you to understand."

Asya ran a hand through her knotted hair, digging her fingers into her scalp as if she could scrape the image from her mind. A much younger Yuliana, face set in that same grim determination. The Firebird rearing up, as unforgiving as winter. The blaze of flame.

It sent another painful twinge through Asya. A surge of affection tinged with a terrible sadness. Such a mortal feeling. And not one she could ever do anything about. Not when there was nothing she could do to change what had happened.

What she was.

She met Yuliana's gaze, unable to stop herself. Even if Asya knew it would hurt, she had to try to understand why the strashe had chosen to tell her, of all people.

Yuliana's gray eyes were bright as they bored into Asya's. But they held none of the anger Asya had braced herself for. None of the accusation she deserved.

Instead, there was a flutter of that young girl—the one who'd been so desperate to save her father and failed. A child lost in the woods, screaming for help even as she knew no one would come. It wasn't something she'd expected to see in Yuliana, who always seemed so sure, so unwavering.

It resonated through Asya, painfully familiar. The weight of a responsibility—a guilt—that was almost too much to bear. A lost child who knew, deep down, that they'd never be found.

"I didn't want to kill the banewolf." She hadn't meant to say it. But something in that look had drawn out a need to confess her own shame. "I—I wanted to help it. It was corrupted by magic, by an imbalance. Because of a price left unpaid." She almost choked on the words, as bitter and smoldering in her throat as the smoke.

"Asya." The sound of her name in Yuliana's voice, spoken with such uncharacteristic gentleness, made her breath catch. "That wasn't your fault. *You* saved everyone tonight."

Asya's head snapped up, and she stared at Yuliana as she tried to find some bitter edge to those words, a double meaning that would snake back around her like a snaring vine.

But there wasn't one. It was a last lifeline—one she wasn't sure she deserved. A ragged thread trying to keep her from teetering over the edge. That traitorous, mortal part of her wanted to take hold of it. Even if she knew that would only make it hurt more in the end.

"Did you ever hear the story of Petyr and the Banewolf?" Her voice was as frayed as that thread, threatening to spiral away into nothing.

A slight frown creased Yuliana's brow. "I think my brother used to read it to me. Petyr decides to hunt down the banewolf, but when he finds it, he realizes its eyes can show him the path to great riches."

Asya's lips pressed together, her arms squeezing around herself as if that could keep her from crumbling. "That's not what I saw. I don't know if it was the corrupting magic. Or maybe the story is just wrong." She swallowed, those images burning behind her eyes again. "But all I saw was me. How everyone sees me. The monstrous creature that lurks in their nightmares." She picked at her sleeve, the tattered edges fraying beneath her fingers. "That's all I am. No matter what I do—what I *try* to do—it's all I'll ever be."

Saying it out loud—admitting the fear that had shadowed her since that day seven years ago—crystallized the painful truth of it in a way that nothing else had.

Yuliana shifted, turning toward Asya. "I don't think you're monstrous."

Asya let out a low noise. She'd intended it to be a laugh, but it came out more like a sob. "I find that hard to believe."

"Maybe I did, once." Yuliana folded her hands in her lap, looking away. There was a softness to the movement, a grace she usually reserved for the arena. "When we first met, I thought I knew what to expect. I was ready to see that creature I remembered, the cruel Firebird." She glanced up, a new intensity burning in her eyes. Lightning crackling around storm clouds. "But you—you're something else entirely, Asya. You're caring and brave, and you fight for what you love no matter the odds. You saved my life more than once, even though I was—"

Asya's lips twitched despite herself. "Unwelcoming?"

"I was going to say something less polite, but yes." Yuliana's fingers wound through Asya's, sending sparks dancing along her spine. "But you have to see, you're so much more than just the Firebird."

They were so close that even in the darkness of the room, Asya could pick out every strand of hair that fell across Yuliana's face. She didn't know which of them moved first—but suddenly there was no more space between them.

Yuliana's lips were on hers, her hands tangling through Asya's hair. Heat prickled where their skin touched, though it had nothing to do with the Firebird. This wasn't about her duty or the creature inside her skin. It was like her Calling. A blinding moment where everything felt right. A distant symphony made clear as the two of them drew together. Where Asya mattered just for herself—not for the power that thrummed in her veins.

She pressed closer, losing herself in the feel of Yuliana's body against hers. The swirling colors of their kiss.

Then—just as abruptly—Yuliana pulled away. The brief elation, the flash of rightness, sputtered out like a doused candle.

Yuliana stood, straightening her jacket sleeve as if she'd suddenly been called to attention. "I—I shouldn't—" She cleared her throat, eyes jumping around the room to rest on anything but Asya. "I'm sure your sister is looking for you."

Asya pulled herself to her feet, her heart hitching. "I...yes, I'm sure she is." Her words came out breathless, her head still caught in that moment. That kiss.

Yuliana turned—the only indicator that anything had even happened the slight flush to her pale cheeks—and moved toward the door. "You should go find her. I'll check in with the strashevsta."

Asya watched the door fall closed again, hanging back as she tried to catch hold of her whirling thoughts. Her face was burning, her emotions curdling in her stomach as the cold absence of Yuliana settled over her. What had just happened?

The sudden dismissal, Yuliana drawing back into that formality, left Asya unsettled. Yuliana was right, of course. Asya should go and reassure her sister. She couldn't deny that— so why did it still sting like a glancing wound?

She bit the inside of her cheek, trying to ignore the painful twist in her gut. For an instant it had felt like Yuliana had seen her—not the Firebird, but Asya. That vanished with the strashe, leaving Asya with the feeling that, somehow, she'd done something wrong again.

But a shiver of suspicion cut through it. Something that had tugged at the back of her mind, even as she desperately tried to ignore it. *Because I want you to understand.* What did Yuliana want her to understand? Memories flashed in Asya's mind, each one bathed in a new light. The way Yuliana had covered her wrist outside the hall. The way the coiling flames of the Firebird had reacted to her touch. How she'd pulled away so suddenly, adjusting her sleeve.

Almost as if there was something there she didn't want Asya to see.

CHAPTER FORTY-THREE

Izaveta had never seen the Firebird before.

Of course, she had read accounts, seen paintings and re-enactments. But none of them quite captured the reality of it. The fear that took hold of her like a clawed fist around her heart. Deep and instinctual, as if her mortal body knew what she was facing, knew on the most basic level that a threat from this creature would be insurmountable.

It's to our advantage in the end. Not only did the future queen survive a poisoning—the Firebird also defeated a banewolf. It showed Tóurin's power beyond dispute, queen and Firebird united. Izaveta clung to that, to the cold certainty of it. It stopped the other thoughts from creeping in, the lingering guilt from smothering her.

The door behind her opened, and she jumped, whirling to face it. Her sister stepped through, hair falling around her face in dark red tangles. She still wore the gown Izaveta had given her, though it was torn and bloody now. Ribbons of fabric hung from her left side, stained with darkening scarlet—the remnants of the damage inflicted by the banewolf's claws.

"Asya," Izaveta said, unable to hide the relief in her voice. "I was afraid—well, I'm glad you're all right."

Asya hurried forward, stopping just short of Izaveta, suddenly hesitant. In that moment Izaveta knew they were both remembering the wall of flame. The blackened and blistered ground that ended just at her feet.

Izaveta could still feel the heat, nothing like the tame fires they kept in their hearths. No, that fire was a living being. A rage of crimson and gold, driven by an ancient magic she could never hope to understand. To stand against.

And to see her sister beneath the Firebird, the two of them moving together in an otherworldly dance—even the memory of it sent an icy chill through Izaveta's blood.

Asya's arms curled around her chest, as if holding herself back from Izaveta. "Are you?"

Izaveta waved her hand, forcing lightness into her voice. "I'm perfectly fine. My dress was barely even singed." Her eyes flicked over Asya, catching on the deep claw marks. They were beginning to heal already, but the skin was still an angry red. "I fared better than you, I think. Are you sure we shouldn't take you to see the voye?"

Asya shook her head. "The Firebird's wounds heal quickly."

Izaveta thought she caught a tinge of bitterness to those words, but the next moment it was gone as her sister looked up at her. Izaveta's own worry was reflected in Asya's dark eyes.

"It's not just that," Asya added. "The poison—"

A slow smile spread across Izaveta's face, despite the situation. That was their one success of the evening. The one thing that had gone right. "It went just as I had hoped."

She'd met with several of her cabinet members already, all

eager to assure her that they had always suspected Sanislav's treachery. Lies, of course, but lies that suited Izaveta. Zvezda had come to speak to her as well, to assure her that the spy should have been there with the antidote. That the person in question had still not reported back to her.

Izaveta didn't know what to make of that yet, not with so many other things clouding her mind.

Asya's forehead creased as she took a slight step back. "I thought you were just meant to pretend?"

Izaveta shrugged, as if it was nothing, as if she couldn't still remember the vivid feeling of clawing for air. Of bitter venom snaking through her veins. "That never would've worked. Besides, it made your reaction far more convincing."

Asya's mouth worked, searching for words. "You could have died, Iza."

"But I didn't," Izaveta replied, grasping her sister's hands. She had to get Asya to understand this was a *good* thing. That part of the evening had worked. "Because of you, Asya."

Asya stared at her, disbelief etched into the lines of her face. "Was that your plan? Just blindly hope that I would work something out?"

Izaveta pressed back against the cool glass of the window, trying not to let herself think about the true weight of Asya's words. How close she'd come to being overtaken by the poison. "Of course not. I had a plan in place that fell through. But no matter, at least now I know where I stand."

Asya pulled away, watching her with a wary expression that sent a cold anticipation trickling down Izaveta's spine. "That's why you didn't want to tell anyone all of the plan, isn't it? You wanted all the pieces separate so you could know who let you down. What was this, some kind of test? A way of finding out which of your allies is loyal to you?"

"Not entirely—"

Asya's jaw clenched. "And I suppose I passed, did I?"

Izaveta froze, caught off guard by the hard edge in her sister's voice. This wasn't about the two of them—this was about the rest of the court. "No—I trusted you. Of course I trusted you."

Silence stretched between them, Asya's shoulders still tense even after Izaveta's assurances. When Asya finally spoke, the hitch to her voice sent guilt curling through Izaveta again. "I thought we'd agreed to tell each other everything. To work together."

Izaveta stepped forward, putting one hand on her sister's un-injured arm. She wished she could explain, but how could she make Asya understand the ways the years apart had changed her? That no matter how hard Izaveta tried to be the sister Asya wanted—the sister she deserved—she couldn't shake those habits.

"I'm sorry," Izaveta whispered. Despite her teasing with Nikov, it truly wasn't something she said very often. "I know I should have told you. But then you wouldn't have agreed to it. And look, it worked, didn't it?" She gripped Asya tighter, trying to make her understand. "It *worked*. Sanislav is out of the way, and Commander Iveshkin wouldn't dare stand against me now. She knows how to sniff out the most power-ful person to back. We probably won't even have to send you to the border—"

Izaveta caught herself a moment too late.

Asya shrugged her shoulder out of Izaveta's grip. Her voice was low, each syllable clipped. "Send me *where?*"

"Nothing—nowhere," Izaveta said quickly, scrambling to regain control of the conversation. "I just meant that after tonight it's clear where the Firebird's allegiance lies. And Iveshkin knows supporting me is the better option."

Asya met her gaze, staring through her in the way only her twin could. Seeing straight through the lie. "You made that bargain with her, didn't you?"

Izaveta's mouth went dry. She could twist words so easily with most people, but not with Asya. Her sister made Izaveta want to be better than that. "I—I had to." The explanation hung in her throat, so desperate to burst free. Why she had to do anything to keep Sanislav from power. What she knew he'd planned with their mother. The whole truth. But she couldn't bring herself to say it. To destroy Asya's memories of their mother too.

When Izaveta didn't say anything else, Asya let out a low noise of disgust. "You *had* to? That's your only answer?"

Her sister spun away, as if unable to even look at Izaveta. Asya strode toward the next window, pushing her hair out of her face. "I shouldn't have been involved in any of this. The Firebird's duty is not to the court or the queen." Her lips pressed together, her face shadowed by the clouded light beyond the glass. "I only wanted to help because of you. Because of who I thought you were."

Izaveta didn't look up. Each word dug into her like a knife, as burning and corrupting as the poison in her veins. "This is who I am," she said—almost a whisper. A hushed confession. "I can't change that any more than you can change being the Firebird."

Asya's head snapped to her, eyes flashing. "Maybe I don't want to just be the Firebird. Did you consider that? Maybe people don't like being used like pieces in your games?"

Izaveta flinched. That cut through her armor like nothing else, too much a reflection of her mother's words, of Nikov's. Of what Izaveta was afraid she was becoming.

"You don't understand this world, Asya." She swallowed, hating that she was defending this even as the words poured out. "It has to be this way. This is the only way to survive here. The only way *I* survived here all these years."

How was it that her sister had been taken to live with a monster, but somehow Izaveta had become one? A creature molded by her mother's manipulations, by the constant betrayals of the court. Asya might have a monster beneath her skin, but Izaveta had one in her heart—in her very essence. So much a part of herself that she no longer knew how to separate one from the other.

For a long moment, Asya didn't reply. She stared out the window, at the darkened landscape of gloaming shadows. "I won't be staying much longer."

Izaveta stared at her sister. "What?"

Asya glanced back, the candlelight sending flickering embers across her shining eyes. "I can't be distracted by your politics and manipulations. The Firebird's place is not in the court—only this Calling is keeping me here. I have to fix this, to ensure the price is paid and restore the balance. And then I'll be gone."

The detached determination in Asya's voice rang hollow,

rattling against Izaveta. Those words registered in her mind too slowly, seeping like ink through parchment. Like poison through her veins. "Ensure the price is paid? How will that fix this?"

Asya paused, a darkness shadowing her face. Izaveta recognized that look—guilt.

The air rushed from Izaveta's lungs as the pieces fell into place around her. "The strange things that have been happening. The falcon, the village...the banewolf. Those are because a price hasn't been paid?"

Asya gave a stiff nod. "It's not just a metaphorical balance. When the balance of magic tips, we fall toward chaos. That's why I'll have to go, why I have to make sure I don't fail again." Her voice was frayed, threads unspooling to reveal the fear beneath.

Izaveta wanted to comfort her, to reach for her and tell her it would be all right. But even in her mind, the lie burned like ashes. All the things Izaveta should have told her sister weighed on her chest. They crushed her voice—too heavy to shift. Too much for them ever to be able to move past.

Asya turned toward the door, boots ringing against the marble.

Izaveta hurried forward. "Wait, Asya—no, don't go like this." She stretched out to grasp her sister's hand, but Asya stepped out of reach.

Izaveta let her arm fall back to her side. They stood facing each other, the queen and the Firebird. Eternally doomed to be at odds, pieces on the opposite side of the board.

How had Izaveta managed to destroy this too—to ruin the chance she'd had at getting her sister back?

"You'll at least stand with me at the coronation, won't you?" Izaveta could hear the plea in her voice—the desperation. But for once she didn't care.

Asya's eyes narrowed, a shadow of the Firebird flashing across her face. "Do you want me there as the Firebird or as your sister?"

Izaveta swallowed, her words catching. "Can't it be both?"

"That's what I thought." Asya's voice was hard as midwinter ice—so out of place for her. She was the lighthearted one, the one who saw the good in everything. Izaveta was supposed to be the cynic.

What did that make Izaveta now? If even her sister—the girl who would rescue venomous spiders from puddles—couldn't see the good in her?

Asya shook her head, as if even she couldn't believe the depths Izaveta would stoop to. "After all that happened tonight—all the manipulations and games, the *banewolf*—you're still standing here and calling it a political victory because it made you look powerful. People could have been killed—people *were* hurt." She stepped back, carving out space between the two of them. "How can you not care about any of that?"

The hurt twisted in Izaveta's chest, solidifying into something that was so much easier to feel—anger.

How dare Asya come here and try to pretend she understood? Try to pretend it was all that simple?

Izaveta let out a biting laugh, a plate of armor sliding across her heart. "Diye, how can you be so naive?" She threw up a hand, gesturing to the door. "This is *all* about power and manipulation. That's what politics is. That's how the queen-dom survives."

Asya held her gaze, her eyes sparking. "Perhaps I am naive. But I'd rather be naive than heartless."

A ringing silence fell between them, their words echoing through it. Izaveta could feel the blows pounding against her, searching for a chink in her armor. They would ache later. But she didn't want to feel that now.

Not tonight—not when she was to be crowned tomorrow. Not after the banewolf attack. After watching her sister trans-form. No, she had to be as cold and unyielding as the Fire-bird. As their mother had been.

This was not the moment for her to break.

"You know," Izaveta said, her voice taking on the dan-gerous quiet of a distant storm. "Queen Teriya used to keep her Firebird in a cage. She would send hunters out to find those who were marked and throw them in the cage with the Firebird during feasts. They'd sit and watch as the Firebird extracted the price. All to prove the power the queen had."

Hurt flashed in Asya's eyes, so sharp it almost broke through Izaveta's wall. But then it was gone, replaced with that grim determination. "Is that a threat?"

Izaveta's lips twisted into a smile. She felt like she was run-ning down a hill, feet slipping and stones scattering around her. She wanted to stop—knew that the fall would be too much for her to come back from. But it was too late, the mo-mentum was already dragging her down. "It's a story. Make of it what you will."

Asya raised her chin. In that moment, she didn't look like the little girl Izaveta remembered, the sister who had cried the night before the ceremony. Her hair wild around her face, clothes bloodstained and tattered, she looked like the powerful creature of legend. The unwavering Firebird.

She shot Izaveta one last glance, loaded with so much that Izaveta wanted to ignore. "The Firebird submits to no crown."

And with that, she left.

PART FIVE:

THE PRICE MUST BE PAID

The Firebird's flames burn scarlet,
The mourning skies shine blue,
If you don't pay the price,
She's coming for you.

—An old Tóurensi nursery rhyme

CHAPTER FORTY-FOUR

Asya pushed the door to her chambers shut, her hands still shaking. She wished she could bolt it, barricade the entry, and hide in the dark corners of the room. But even that wouldn't block out the conversation still resonating in her ears like a clanging bell.

After all they'd been through together, she'd thought Izaveta understood. Thought she knew what it was like to have this duty thrust upon her. But Asya was wrong. Izaveta had used her. She saw her as the Firebird first and Asya second. Just like everyone else did.

The anger sputtered out too quickly, leaving a gaping hole in her chest. An echoing void gouged out by everything that had happened. Everything she'd done. All she'd failed to do.

She sank down onto the bed, trying to push it all away. She squeezed her eyes shut, digging her fingers into the cool silk of the bedding. Everything was suddenly too hot, the Firebird bursting beneath her skin.

The door opened and her heart lurched, momentarily dousing that burning fire in her veins. A brief hope reared inside her—tempered only a little by her anger. But it wasn't her sister. It wasn't even Yuliana.

Tarya was still dressed as Saint Dyena, the starling. Dyena's fur cape draped from her shoulders, the bright clasp of entangled wings shining on her chest. The costume looked so out of place on her aunt. A splash of bright color in a painting of the night.

Asya didn't bother to hide her face. To swipe at the tears and pretend they weren't there, as she had all that time in the Roost. Tarya had already seen. And not even her disapproval could make Asya feel worse tonight.

Her aunt's gaze swept over her, a cursory assessment. It lingered on the tattered fabric around Asya's ribs, still stained with blood even as the wound healed.

Tarya's jaw tightened, the only hint at her displeasure. "You should clean your wound."

Asya sniffed, scrubbing a hand across her tearstained face. She didn't have the energy to move, let alone to clean the innocent creature's blood from her hands.

She should say that Tarya had been right all along, there was no place for Asya here. But she couldn't quite force the words up her throat. Even after everything that had happened that day—even after Izaveta had tried to use her—Asya still couldn't cut that thread. The intangible string that tied the two of them together.

And she still wasn't sure she wanted to.

"Why did you leave court?" She didn't know what had made her say it. She should have long ago given up on getting any kind of answer from her aunt, let alone any comfort. But Asya was teetering, and Tarya was the only rope she had left to grasp.

Her aunt watched her for a moment, something unreadable flittering across her dark eyes. "I didn't want to, not at first."

Asya looked up, her mouth opening in surprise. All through her training, through the years she'd lived with Tarya, her aunt had never spoken of her mortal life.

Tarya moved forward, setting herself down on the edge of the bed. "Mira and I were never close, even before the ceremony." She spoke in a low voice, eyes focused on the distant candle flame. "Two pieces of a whole that never quite fit together. But I had other ties here. Mortal ties."

It was almost impossible to imagine that the woman Asya knew—the reserved, duty-bound Firebird—could have wanted to stay in the palace.

She swallowed, her throat still clogged with the memory of ash. "Then why didn't you just stay?"

Tarya stiffened, as though suddenly remembering Asya was there. She looked older, Asya realized with a start. As if a heaviness had settled over her. The years of being frozen in time had been swept away, and now mortality had her in its grasp again.

Tarya folded her hands in her lap. "It was a turbulent time for the Firebird. The Fading had only just begun, and suspicion devoured the court as their magic slipped through their fingers. Tricks and manipulations, betrayals all in the name of power." Tarya glanced over, and for a brief instant Asya saw a shadow of something else on her face. A shadow of who Tarya had been before she allowed this duty to consume her. "I didn't want any part of it."

Asya certainly understood that. The same urge burned in her veins, the desire to be separate. To stay in the forest where things were simple and familiar. Well, never simple. Not with the Firebird.

But at least there Asya wouldn't have to worry about her sister.

It would be so much easier to not feel. No burning guilt over her actions. No questioning or doubts. No ache in her heart when she thought about her sister. About Yuliana.

Asya swallowed, her throat suddenly dry. "Did you ever regret it?"

For a long moment, her aunt didn't reply. So long Asya thought the unusually intimate conversation must have been over. But just when she was about to turn away, Tarya spoke. "Once." Her voice was soft, a hushed prayer in an echoing cathedral. "There was…one person I regretted leaving."

Asya's breath hitched. "And now?"

For an instant, Tarya's face softened. A flash of sympathy cracked through the marble features. "It fades. It gets harder and harder to remember now. That life was so long ago— it hardly belongs to me anymore."

Asya swallowed hard. Was that all she had to look forward to? The memory of her sister falling further and further away, dragging the pain along with it. Dragging everything with it.

No. She wouldn't let that be the end of their story. Wouldn't let politics and lies get between them. Not like Tarya had, not like their mother always had. Whatever happened be- tween them, Asya and Izaveta were irreparably bound. Asya could force that away, could push down her emotions until she ground them into dust, but that would never change.

Because it wasn't truly the Firebird that had made her aunt into who she was. It was simply Tarya choosing to take the easier path.

Asya got to her feet. "I have to go," she said quickly.

She didn't wait for her aunt's reply as she slipped back out the door. She hurried down the maze of passageways, not even caring that she was still in the blood-soaked costume.

The anger she'd felt for her sister—for the lies—had been eclipsed, reduced to a sputtering coal. This possibility was too important. A new realm unraveling before Asya's eyes, filled with a kaleidoscope of colors beyond what she'd ever imagined. An option she'd never thought possible before. Just because the Firebird and the queen had always been separate didn't mean it *had* to be that way.

Asya and Izaveta could change it, could make a new choice. They could find a way to make it work.

Something caught in the corner of her vision, drawing Asya to a halt. She whirled around, but only saw clawing shadows.

Her hand went to her waist, but her shashka was still hanging back in her chambers. She caught the flutter of movement again. Not in the passageway, she realized, but beyond the arched window. Blacker than the night around it, a flickering silhouette.

Asya moved forward and pressed her forehead against the cool glass, staring out into the dark. The night transformed the grounds into a landscape of smudged brushstrokes, dark indigos and purples obscuring the details. She squinted, trying to make out the shape. A person, their dark cloak flying behind them like wings.

The figure stepped into a pool of moonlight, momentarily

illuminated by the silvery glow of Vetviya's moon. Asya's breath caught. She recognized that dark hair, the sharp nose, and those flashing eyes. Yuliana.

What in Dveda's name was Yuliana doing sneaking through the grounds in the middle of the night? Hadn't she said she was going to report back to the strashevsta?

Yuliana glanced behind her, as if checking she wasn't being followed, before ducking around the edge of the turret and out of sight.

Asya stared at the spot where the strashe had vanished. A prickling dread was spreading through her veins. It likely had nothing to do with her. Some private matter she shouldn't intrude on.

But she couldn't shake her suspicion. The way Yuliana had covered her right wrist. The cloying fear of what that might mean.

Asya had to know.

Her feet moved toward the stairs before she'd consciously made the decision. Yuliana had been heading east, along the wall of the palace. From there she'd have to either cut right toward the woods or left toward the manicured gardens. There were a hundred places Asya could lose her in either, especially with the thick canopy of cloud.

She almost jumped down the last flight of stairs, pushing through the door and out into the night. The frosted air was biting. It cut through her thin dress, still hanging off her in tatters. Asya was tempted to call on her flames for warmth, but she held them back.

If she was right, she didn't want to have the Firebird near the surface when she found out.

Asya wrapped her arms around herself and pushed on. She followed the line of the palace wall, toward where the path split. The night was quiet, with only distant calls of owls and the faint flutter of wings breaking the silence. No sign of Yuliana. No hint as to which way she'd gone.

Then a low crunch, the crack of a twig underfoot—out of balance with the usual sounds of the night. Asya's head snapped to it. She followed the faint sound into the shadows of the trees, treading carefully over the frozen ground.

The branches closed overhead, covering the last of the moonlight. Asya could just make out the strashe ahead of her, cloak whipping behind her in the wind.

"Yuliana!" Asya's voice was too loud in the quiet night, cutting through the trees like a scream.

The strashe whirled, her hand jumping to her saber. Her eyes widened. "What are you doing here? You're not meant to be—"

Asya stepped forward. "What are *you* doing out here?"

Yuliana glanced over her shoulder. "Nothing. Out for a walk."

It was a poor attempt at a lie, and Asya could see Yuliana knew it. Asya took another step, closing the distance, palms out. "Whatever it is, you can tell me."

Something fractured across Yuliana's face, that look of someone lost. "I can't."

Asya stared at her, the shivering cold worming into her bones. "Yuliana—"

A sound made them both jump. Asya spun round, her eyes scanning the twining trees. But she couldn't see anything. Not so much as a flicker out of place.

Yuliana's hands gripped the shredded fabric at Asya's shoulders, pushing her away. "You have to go back inside, *now*."

Asya tried to shrug her off. "No, I just—" The question clawed its way up her throat, her eyes stinging. "I have to know. Is it you?"

Yuliana froze, her grip loosening. Asya used the distraction to her advantage, twisting around and grabbing Yuliana's right wrist. Asya pushed up Yuliana's sleeve, her skin flashing white in the moonlight.

Asya drew in a breath. Her fingers tightened as she stared down. No tangle of black marks pulling together to form a feather. "It's not you. Then why—"

She broke off. She'd been so focused on looking for the stratsviye that she hadn't noticed something else. Pale lines—more a brand than a mark. But Asya knew that symbol too.

A flame intersected with three horizontal lines.

She stared up at Yuliana, her grip on the strashe's wrist going slack. Yuliana's eyes were shadowed by the overhanging trees. But Asya caught the flash of guilt, as sharp as a blade in her chest.

Something cracked across her temple, sending her staggering back. Bile rose in her throat. The ground tilted beneath her feet for the second time that night. Shadows moved around her, coalescing into people. The same people who'd attacked her in the gardens. Who'd shot at them in the queenstrees.

Her thoughts crashed in her head like waves, beating against her skull. This didn't make sense. None of this made sense. She blinked, the world swimming into focus around her. The Firebird burned beneath her skin, eager to rise to her defense. She let the fire coil out as she tried to pinpoint her attackers.

Then something snapped shut around her wrist, and the flames sputtered out. A suffocating weight closed around her throat—one that she recognized at once. Firestone.

Hands fastened on her, pulling her arms behind her back. Another cuff snapped shut around her other wrist. The firestone seared cold as ice against her skin.

She kicked out, catching something solid and earning a satisfying groan of pain. But more hands closed in, ropes pulling tight around her. She thrashed against them, desperately reaching for the Firebird. Clawing into the hollow place in her core where it should be.

But there was nothing. No spark of power for her to grasp on to.

A hand fisted in her hair, a final rope slithering around her throat. She couldn't move without it pressing against her windpipe.

Her eyes landed on Yuliana. She stood a little back, still as the tree trunks behind her.

"Yuliana?" Asya choked out.

A damp cloth pressed over her mouth, cutting off any more words. She breathed in something sweet, gagging on the sedative.

But Yuliana just stepped back, eyes lowered.

That small movement dragged the fight out of Asya, the betrayal more suffocating than the cloth.

CHAPTER FORTY-FIVE

Izaveta sank down into the nearest chair. With no one around to see her, the mask splintered away. She dropped her head into her hands, digging her fingers into her scalp. Tears spilled down her cheeks, a deluge she'd held back for so long.

She wasn't just crying for the rift with her sister, but for everything. For the years she'd spent crafting this persona, hiding behind the cold mask. For the mother she'd never see again and who she hadn't even known.

For what she'd done.

The door swung open, and for one pathetic instant she thought it was her sister. Come to make amends even if Izaveta didn't deserve it. But instead of Asya, Nikov stepped through, no longer in his ridiculous costume, his hair falling back into messy curls.

Izaveta leaped to her feet. "You can't just walk in here unannounced," she snapped. "Get out."

But Nikov didn't move. He just stared at her with that look of his—the one that saw more than she wanted. "What happened?"

She gritted her teeth, words coming out as a low hiss. "Get out."

He still didn't move. "Are you all right?"

Izaveta threw up her hands, a choking laugh bursting from her. "I'm perfectly fine. Why wouldn't I be?"

Nikov took a step forward. "You don't have to be fine all the time."

She swiped at her eyes, the infuriating tears still leaking out. "What? Do you want me to tell you that I nearly died tonight—more than once—and it terrified me? To say that Asya left, and it feels like part of my heart has been torn away? To cry about how the guilt of all of this is trying to tear me apart from the inside?" She whirled, unable to stop even if she'd tried. "How everything that happened is my fault?"

Her breaths came in gasping pants, heart pounding as if she'd been running. She turned away from Nikov, sinking back down into the chair.

She felt him move closer, felt the warmth of his body as he sat next to her. "How is it your fault?"

A pressure grew in Izaveta's chest—a scream building, desperate to claw its way out. This secret had almost destroyed her. Had poisoned her from the inside out. Of all the lies, all the manipulations, this was the one that strangled her.

And suddenly she wanted it gone.

She met Nikov's gaze, her heart steadying. There was something calming in finally saying it—in admitting it out loud. "The imbalance is my fault. Because I didn't pay the price."

Asya's words resonated in her ears. The truth that Izaveta had so desperately tried to avoid. Her mind had conjured any other solution it could—any answer for the strange events.

But she couldn't ignore it now. Couldn't wash this blood from her hands.

She wrenched off her right glove, turning her wrist over to expose the angry mark. The swirls of black that twined together to form a burning feather. The mark of the Firebird.

"A stratsviye," Nikov murmured. "I've never seen one before. I'm not sure the drawings I've seen are fully accurate to its—"

She almost laughed at the absurdity of that statement. She'd just told him she was marked as the Firebird's prey—as her sister's prey—and his mind still fell to scholarly research. "Yes, it's a fascinating piece of evidence."

"I—" He swallowed, looking away. "Sorry. Force of habit. When I'm scared, I fall back on research. It makes things easier."

Izaveta pulled her arm into herself, fingers fastening around the mark. The one that had burned into her skin the day her mother died. She wished Nikov hadn't said he was scared by the mark. That made it so much more real.

"Does Asya know?"

"That's the best part." Izaveta's voice rose, and she knew she was teetering toward hysterical, but she couldn't stop. "Asya told me herself about the Calling she couldn't follow. I knew it was mine, and I didn't say anything. Didn't *do* anything."

Nikov laced his ink-stained fingers together, resting his elbows on his knees. "Are you sure it won't just be something small? What spell did you cast?"

The fragile hope in his voice, the naive belief that she hadn't done something truly terrible, squeezed around her heart like a vise. She took a shuddering breath. "The night my mother died, she had a meeting with the vibishop. They were planning to use the Firebird's blood to stop the Fading. He had a theory that sacrificing the Firebird might bring magic back."

Nikov let out a snort. "Interesting theory."

Izaveta didn't look up. "That's what I said. But it didn't make a difference. I was always helpless against my mother." Her fists closed, the memory of that night still so sharp in her mind. "So I found a way to change the game."

She stared down at the mark, the coiling lines blurring together. "I didn't mean for it to kill her. I just wanted to stop her plan—to stop what Sanislav had convinced her to do. The spell was supposed to divert the course of fate in my favor. I should have known that magic never works how one expects it to."

She blinked, the room around her shimmering to be replaced with that clearing. The statue of Saint Meshnik towering above her, that shard of bone tight in her fist. The brief flash of triumph at finding a way to best her mother at her own game, followed by the chilling sensation of the magic slithering away from her. That deep sense of wrongness in her bones.

And the terrible realization of what she'd done.

"I tried to pretend that everything was happening because of the Fading—" Her voice cracked, finally breaking beneath the weight of it all. "But it was me. That strashe died for me. That village…" She trailed off, the truth of her words suddenly too much. The guilt of her mother's death had coalesced into stone in her heart, a thing she could push aside and ignore. But this was all consuming. It battered against her skull like a storm, each rumble of thunder a reminder of what she'd done.

What she'd *caused*.

"Izaveta." Nikov's voice was soft, as low as a crackle of flames. "We'll find a way around this. There's always an answer."

Izaveta forced a smile, even as a sob clawed up her throat. "I'm not sure I deserve a way out. I *should* pay the price for what I did."

Chapter Forty-Six

Asya woke with a headache like a cleaver digging into her skull. Her mouth was dry, coated with remnants of the sedative. Memories floated around her, just out of reach. Vague flashes of a giant creature. The shadowed woods. *Yuliana.*

Slowly, like a pale dawn trying to break through darkest night, the world filtered into place around her. Asya was lying on something hard, cold seeping through her tattered dress. She tried to move, sending another spiraling pain through her head.

Her hands were still bound behind her, but no longer with the suffocating chill of firestone. Cool metal chains jangled as she shifted. They stretched above her, wrapped around something she couldn't quite see. But the stifling pressure was still there. She could feel the Firebird inside her, at a distance. Not a roaring fire in her veins but smoldering embers.

She blinked, trying to shake off the last tendrils of the sedative. The ceiling above her was broken up by thick bars. A cage. No, not just a cage—bars that pulsed like blood in her veins. A cage made of firestone. That realization closed around her tighter than the chains, a suffocating fear tightening around her neck.

The icy floor beneath her wasn't firestone, but she was surrounded by it. Trapped.

Asya shifted the chains, forcing herself into a sitting position. The headache was dissipating, the scene filling in around her as the Firebird healed her. That was her one spark of hope. The Firebird wasn't gone completely—without the firestone in contact with her, the power was still there.

A circle of candles scattered across the ground illuminated not more than five paces around her. High, vaulted columns rose above her to what should have been a soaring onion dome. But the brickwork had crumbled, leaving the space exposed to the elements. Not just in the ceiling, she realized. The whole place was a ruin. Weathered statues of the saints stood on ceremony, their eyes smoothed and unseeing. Vines snaked around the walls, burrowing through crevices and dragging them down. Reclaiming the place for the earth.

And the cage—her heart lurched. The cage sat atop a cracked stone altar.

"Ah," said a voice as cold as winter frost. "You're awake."

A man stepped out of the shadows of what would have been the pews, but instead was rubble overrun with grassy moss. He wore dark blue robes and a heavy gold chain around his neck—the kind usually worn by church members. But instead of a symbol of the gods, it was that same flame overlaid with three bars. It glittered against his chest, as if it really did burn.

The Order of the Captured Flame.

With her head still clouded, it took Asya a moment to place

him. And even then, her mind couldn't quite believe what her eyes saw. "Fyodor?"

He stepped farther into the light, his white hair gleaming. The kindness she thought she'd seen in his eyes before had evaporated, replaced with a stoic sadness. "I am sorry it had to come to this. I'd hoped we could do the ritual before the power passed on to you. But, alas."

Asya's heart stuttered, words clogging her throat. "But you—how—"

He pressed his lips together, the grim expression of someone delivering bad news. "I know this must come as a shock. But I have dedicated my life to this, to the Fading. You've seen my library. I have explored every avenue, every slight possibility. There is no other way." He met her gaze, blue eyes sincere. "I do wish I could separate you from that creature, but I cannot."

His words crowded through her mind. This was too much. All of it was too much. Her eyes darted around the ruins, searching for something that might help her. Anything that could somehow get her out of this. Help her make sense of this.

Izaveta would talk her way out of it, wield her words like weapons. Asya had never been any good at that. But she had to try. She rolled her shoulders back, reaching for that imperious air her sister carried, even if she was hunched in a cage. "Think about what you're doing. You know Izaveta. You know she will come looking for me. You do not want to make an enemy of her." She hesitated, trying to grasp on to her fracturing facade of confidence. "Or me."

Fyodor's face didn't so much as flicker. "Izaveta will understand. When magic no longer fades from this land, she will raise me above all others. That's what she wants, what she has worked for too." He raised his chin, unwavering. "She will understand the necessity of this sacrifice."

Asya saw it in his face then. The manic fervor—he truly believed what he was saying. She swallowed, trying to think of a way to buy time. Everything was slipping through her fingers. Running away from her like water.

"You can't keep me here." She'd meant to sound imposing, the legendary Firebird who couldn't be threatened, but it came out more like a child trying to stand against a storm.

His lips twitched. "I assure you, we could. Though we don't intend to."

Her stomach lurched. The unspoken threat hung in the air. And she was as helpless to do anything about it as a caged animal brought to the slaughter. Because that was all Asya was without the Firebird.

"The members of your order are the ones who attacked me in the courtyard." She spoke more to herself than to him— trying to put her thoughts in order. To understand what was happening. "They said they didn't want to kill me—not yet. But then in the queenstrees…"

Fyodor waved a hand, reading her question on her face. "That was a lapse in judgment." He glanced back into the shadows, and Asya realized with a start they were not alone. Figures stood assembled behind him, as quiet and unyielding as the statues. How many of them were there? "Dima was supposed to take more care, but he got a little carried away in the excitement. You know how it is when family is involved."

Asya stared at him. His words swam in the air around her, fogging her mind more than helping her find clarity.

"He didn't want to see his sister ensnared by you," Fyodor continued. "Especially not when she was the one who found your weakness. The Firebird's weakness." He turned toward the crumbling pews, to the shadows that Asya's eyes couldn't quite penetrate. "Isn't that right, Yuliana?"

A figure stepped into the pool of candlelight. She had changed into crisp black, blending into the darkness behind her. Her eyes were harsh and unyielding as they'd been on the day they first met.

No flash of the girl Asya had come to know.

Asya bit the inside of her cheek. Part of her wanted to shrink back—to close her eyes and pretend this wasn't happening. But even with the aching echo of betrayal in her chest, she wouldn't let Yuliana see it. Wouldn't flinch away from her.

Fyodor put a hand on Yuliana's shoulder. "Your personal guard. Perfectly placed to follow your every move. To find what made you vulnerable."

"My firestone," Asya breathed. Of course, Yuliana had taken it. Who else could have gotten into her chambers? Who else could have worked out it dampened her powers?

The realization crawled over Asya's skin. She'd been such a fool.

She kept her eyes on Fyodor, on the person who didn't make her heart twist. "This won't work—whatever it is you're trying to do. My sister will find me." That was her last hope, so much more fragile than she dared admit.

His face creased, genuine pity creeping into his eyes. "According to my source, your sister may not want to look for you."

That statement jolted through Asya, cutting far too close to the truth. To what Iza had said.

Fire burst from Asya's hands, snaking toward Fyodor. A desperate and futile attempt, wrenched from that deep, terrified part of her. The trapped animal lashing out. But the firestone bars absorbed the flames, drawing them in like water to a rag. Not so much as a spark fluttered free.

The brief flash of power—the failure—left a hollow ache in her stomach. Again, she wasn't enough. Never enough.

"Now, now," Fyodor said in the tone of a parent admonishing a child. He took another step forward, his hand closing around a length of chain that trailed from the top of the cage down to his feet. "None of that."

His fist clenched and he pulled. Asya's arms were yanked skyward, dragging her up until her toes scrabbled against the ground.

A hiss escaped through her teeth as her chest tipped forward, her shoulders wrenched back, straining against their sockets. "Whatever you're doing—if you want to use me or my power, it won't work."

Fyodor took a step toward the bars, his face changing. No longer speaking to Asya but to the creature within. "That's where you're wrong, Firebird. Tomorrow night your reign—your tyranny—will be over." His voice came out as a low growl, venomous and grating. "When we sacrifice you back to the earth, no more will you be able to extort a price for magic. It will no longer fade from this land. It'll be free once

again. As will you, Asya. No longer held hostage to the creature inside you."

Asya stared at him, his meaning slowly coiling around her.
They thought the *Firebird* was the one who chose the price,
the one who'd caused the Fading.

That wasn't possible—was it?

The voice from her nightmares whispered through her
mind again, a strange mirror of Fyodor's words. *I chose you to
remake this world, not to fail it.*

Surely this couldn't be what the gods meant? That she had
been chosen as sacrifice, to return magic from the Firebird?

Fyodor let the chain go slack, and she collapsed back to the
ground. The impact jolted through her teeth.

She pushed herself up, glaring at Fyodor. "If that's really
what you believe." Her eyes flicked to Yuliana. "If that's really what you *want*, then just do it."

She wanted Yuliana to look away—to at least show some
glimmer of guilt. But those gray eyes bored into her, unwavering. "Not yet, Firebird."

That word—the sharpness in it—dug into Asya. A final
twist of the knife.

Fyodor turned, robes skittering along the debris, as he
glanced back at her. His voice was almost comforting, as if
he were truly trying to help her. "It won't be long now, Asya.
Once the new queen is crowned, the Firebird will burn for
the last time."

Asya watched the sky above the collapsed dome turn from
deepest ebony to smoke gray, tendrils of light fracturing across
it as the next day dawned. She had her knees pulled tight

against her chest, trying to stave off the creeping chill. The heavy weight of firestone pressed over her like a hand on her mouth.

She couldn't stop her mind from replaying her every interaction with Yuliana, everything she thought she'd seen.

I don't think you're monstrous.

Tears prickled like nettles behind her eyes. She should have known it was all a game. An elaborate ruse to learn her vulnerabilities. And Asya had played straight into it. Naive and weak as ever. The secret of the firestone had been protected for centuries, and she'd let it out in fewer than thirteen days.

In the end what her aunt had said was true: Asya would never be more than the monster in her skin. And her mortal ties would be her downfall.

Crouched in this cage, she'd never felt more alone. Even those first nights at the Roost after she'd been dragged from her sister, with only the intimidating figure of Tarya for company, were not like this. Then there'd been a distant comfort. The certainty that her sister was thinking of her too.

Fyodor's words wormed back into her mind, unwelcome and painfully true. *Your sister may not want to look for you.*

That certainty—the desperate hope that Iza might find her—was crumbling to nothing. Because Izaveta had no reason to believe anything was amiss. Not when Asya had told her she was leaving. Even Tarya might not realize until the coronation itself. And by then it could be too late.

Now, in the cold light of the ruined church, their fight seemed so ridiculous. Stirred up by the pain and terror of the evening. Too many emotions tangled together that needed a way out.

And that would be the last thing Asya said to her sister. That she was heartless.

The brief flash of hope she had found—the fantasy that their choices could somehow make them different—had been snatched away from her. Stolen by a betrayal that still burned inside her like a wound.

Her nails dug into her palms, scraping against the ice-cold metal. *No. This can't be the end.* A small whisper of determination, an ember that wouldn't quite die—one that sounded very much like Izaveta.

After everything, Asya couldn't give up here.

She shifted, taking stock of her surroundings again. Fyodor had left a guard, who was standing near the now-burned-out candles. He watched her with a wary hesitancy, one hand clutching the hilt of his saber, embossed with that same burning crest.

The rest of the space was illuminated now, crumbling walls and vine-twisted statues rising out of the early-morning mist.

She didn't have a weapon or the Firebird's fury. But Asya wasn't nothing. She refused to be. Even without the Firebird, she was *someone*. Yuliana had helped her feel that, if only for an instant. Even if none of that was real, the feeling still was. The feeling that she could be more than the monster.

So what *did* she have?

A half-destroyed ball gown, a sliver of power, and chains around her wrists.

She had to start with those. If she could just get her hands free, she might be able to work something out. She gave an experimental tug on them. The slight clank of metal made the guard's eyes narrow.

She shot him what was meant to be an encouraging smile—but judging from the how the color drained from his cheeks, he didn't take it that way. "Don't worry, still chained up."

He turned away, toward the toppled statue of Zmenya. Asya supposed there were some situations where being thought a monster was useful.

Her wrists scraped against the cool metal of the chains, the smallest amount of give. She wouldn't be able to slip out of them. Unless…

Her stomach lurched at the thought. But what else could she do? Keeping her eyes on the back of the guard's head, she let a coil of fire slither around her fingers. With the heavy weight of the firestone she couldn't make it burn hot enough to melt the chains, but the heat would make her hands slick with sweat.

The flames licked against her skin, leaving no mark. They were as much a part of her as her bones. She held on to that spark, but it was so much more difficult than before. The magic was desperate to slip away, to collapse under the weight of the firestone.

But she was Asya Karasova. She could do this.

Gritting her teeth, she ducked her head to let her hair fall across her face. She hoped she was displaying the picture of the captured bird, forlorn and defeated. It was hardly a pretense. A bead of sweat trickled down her neck that had nothing to do with the heat of the Firebird. Fear still wanted to claw its way up her throat, to drag her back down.

She shook her head, trying to dispel it. The flames were sputtering, but it didn't matter. Her hands were slippery with sweat—enough to slide her left a little farther out of the chains.

But not enough to pull it free. She curled into a ball, pressing her forehead against her knees. Her breaths trembled against her rib cage, shallow and frantic. She didn't want to do this. *The Firebird will heal me.* Not as quickly as usual, but it would.

She bit down on the ragged fabric of her skirt to stifle the scream and wrenched her left wrist up. The snap resonated through her body, sharp as a breaking tree branch. A strangled cry of pain scrambled up her throat, barely muffled by the fabric.

The guard's eyes jolted up to her. He took a step forward, weapon partly lifted out of its sheath.

She rattled the chains as if in frustration, trying to play off the sound. "Just let me out," she hissed, the pain layering her voice to a growl. "Or I'll make *you* pay the price."

The guard let out a splutter, an attempt at a laugh, as he grasped his saber again. "You can't make anyone pay from inside a cage."

Asya let out a low moan—one she hoped he interpreted as a sound of defeat—as she clenched her right hand around her left wrist, forcing the bone back into place.

She was shaking. Her whole body trembling like a leaf in the wind. If there'd been anything left in her stomach, she would have thrown it up.

But it was done. At least she could move now.

Her wrist was buzzing, the Firebird's flames coalescing there as it worked to heal her. She kept her hands behind her back, holding on to the metal links to maintain the illusion.

Her eyes scanned the cramped space, desperate for something. A small forgotten stone or glimpse of metal.

A glimmer of light caught her eye. The gold hilt of Saint Restov's dagger, still clinging on to the tattered fabric of her costume. There was no blade attached to it, of course, but it was a possibility. And the fat jewels that surrounded it—glittering blue and silver—could be fashioned into something sharp.

But she had to make sure the guard didn't notice what she was doing.

Or perhaps just the opposite.

They thought she was a monster, a captured beast lashing out. So she would be.

Rising to her feet, Asya let sparks creep into her eyes. "Let me out."

Reaching for the Firebird—pushing through the suffocating pressure of the firestone—she let the flames leap out. They burst around her like a bonfire, bright orange and bloodred and burnished gold. A burning sun trapped inside this cage.

She couldn't sustain it. It flickered down to smoldering embers, but the smoke was enough. Enough for her to slip one hand forward and dig her nails into the loose threads of her gown. The golden hilt fell into her palm.

The guard moved toward her, squinting through the haze. "Stop that!"

The deep blue gem was more of a challenge. It was still stitched in tight, and she had to ensure she maintained the cloud of smoke and shimmering fire as she scrabbled at it. Just as the guard reached the bars, it came free with a satisfying pop. She clamped fingers shut around it. The cool edges dug into her palm, not sharp enough to draw blood.

Her heart pounded in her ears, her chest heaving under the strain of pushing against the firestone. She forced out another burst of flame. The guard blanched even as it dissipated against the barrier of the cage. Asya used the brief cover to step back—gritting her teeth against the icy firestone—and banged the jewel against the bars, letting the clang of the chains mask its clatter.

It wasn't going to work. Whatever substance the jewel was made of, it wouldn't break. And she couldn't keep up this distraction for much longer. Not without the exhaustion overtaking her—or the guard deciding to take a closer look.

The guard's voice cut through the fire, only wavering slightly. "I'm warning you—"

She gritted her teeth, drawing on her last scraps of strength. The Firebird seemed to understand, its faint flames pooling around her wrists. With a final clang of metal, a shard of gemstone broke free. It splintered away—clattering against the base of the crumbled altar—leaving a jagged edge.

In the same breath, the last tendrils of smoke cleared. She snapped her hands into place behind her back, praying that the guard didn't notice the gleam of blue that now lay among the cracked stone.

But the guard only had eyes for her. He gestured with his saber, the edge glinting. "Sit down."

Holding his gaze, she stepped back to the center of the cage. With a last push of energy, she sent a sliver of flame around the hilt. The gold softened easily, molding around the shard of gemstone. Not the best weapon, but it was something. She spun it into place in her palm.

The small movement jolted through her half-healed wrist.

The ache sharpened acutely, a momentary distraction. A heartbeat too late, she saw it. The guard's saber flashed out, jabbing between the bars. It caught her in the leg—a bright and piercingly familiar pain. She staggered back, almost ruining it all by putting her hand to the wound.

She stared at him, at the shining edge of the blade. It wasn't the bright silver of iron, but the dark gray of firestone. Pain radiated from the cut, stealing the last of her flames.

"That's right," he said, following her gaze. "We're ready for you and all your tricks."

"What do you think you're doing?"

The low growl of pain died in her throat. Yuliana.

Asya hated how even the sight of the strashe sent a wrenching ache through her gut—more painful than the firestone. A stinging reminder of all she'd thought to be true. What she'd let herself believe.

The guard jumped to attention. "I was just—the Firebird was trying to escape."

Yuliana's face was hard, eyes flicking over Asya with obvious contempt. "Well there's no need to antagonize it. Not yet. Now go get some sleep. It's my turn on watch."

The guard didn't need further prompting. With a fleeting glance back at Asya, he scurried away.

His echoing footfalls faded, leaving the two of them alone. Yuliana advanced, gaze lingering on Asya's fresh wound.

Then she paused. Yuliana's eyes lowered toward the altar—to that shard of blue. Asya's mouth went dry. She couldn't move, couldn't do anything without giving it away.

Yuliana moved forward, brow creasing as she reached toward the shard of stone. "What is—"

Asya didn't hesitate. As soon as the strashe was within reach, she leaped into action. She threw herself at the bars, bringing the loose chain with her. She grabbed Yuliana's hair. With a heave she banged the strashe's forehead against the firestone, looping the chain around the back of her neck with one hand to hold her in place.

Before Yuliana had a moment to try to fight back, Asya had the makeshift knife at her throat.

Chapter Forty-Seven

Izaveta was pacing. Her heeled boots clicked against the stone floor of the vestibule, the black train of her gown sweeping behind them. The color of certainty, of power, and authority.

The gown was designed to portray just that. With minimal ornamentation the black velvet fell to the ground in artful swirls. A half cape swept from her shoulders, embroidered with cascading pearls like falling tears. The high collar arched up behind her neck in a fan of finest Araïse lace, her hair pulled back in a simple knot. Her head was bare, waiting for a crown.

But as she glanced in the ornate looking glass, the outfit didn't feel powerful. It felt mocking. The child who played at being queen.

The muffled sounds of the cathedral echoed through the small room. Everyone preparing, waiting. Even at a distance, they felt too loud. Claustrophobic and suffocating.

Beyond the arched window, a storm brewed on the horizon. Izaveta wasn't sure if it was just her fractured nerves, but it didn't look like a normal storm. The clouds roiled across the faraway tree line like waves crashing across the ocean. Even from this distance she could see the sparking lightning, so bright it seared the sky.

She turned away, forcing her feet to stop. This was the final moment. The crown would be on her head soon. She couldn't let herself break now, not after holding herself together for so long.

But Asya's words rang in her head, biting and true. *I'd rather be naive than heartless.*

Izaveta's fingers clamped around her gloved wrist, around the hidden mark embedded in her skin. Because Asya was right. What kind of heartless person caused their own mother's death, and couldn't even grieve? What kind of person hid from the price even as it hurt others?

Izaveta gritted her teeth, scrambling for the reassurances she'd spent the past twelve days perfecting. That she'd intoned to herself over and over as she kept her heart hard. She'd done it for Asya. To ensure the queendom wouldn't be compromised by Sanislav's plan. And Izaveta would be a good queen. She'd find a way to solve the Fading, and then the price wouldn't matter.

But the words were hollow. Meaningless in the face of the reality. Because even if Izaveta hadn't anticipated the consequences, and as much as she wanted to deny it, she knew why she'd done that spell. The other reasons were a part of it, but at its heart she'd wanted to feel powerful. To finally find a way to outsmart her mother.

Now Asya had seen who Izaveta really was. She had every right to never come back.

And if Asya didn't return, then at least Izaveta didn't ever have to tell her the truth. The truth that Izaveta was so much worse than her sister could ever imagine.

A faint knock made her startle. She whirled, a traitorous flash of hope flaring in her heart again. Her sister returned—a chance for Izaveta to try to make this right. "Come in," she called.

For the second time in two days, she was disappointed.

Kyriil was gleaming in his gold-trimmed shzuba, lined with fur to keep out the chill of the cathedral. The Azarov crest glittered on his chest, unmissable. A reminder. "Hoping for someone else?"

Izaveta put her hands behind her back, fashioning her expression into something presentable. "Not at all."

He mirrored her calm, his small smile setting her teeth on edge. "I notice your sister is not yet in the cathedral."

Izaveta's jaw twitched, but she forced her face to remain neutral. To not show how Asya's absence felt like a missing limb. A piece of her that had been carved out. She knew she should use civility, manipulation, but the harsh words jumped from her lips anyway. "How observant of you, Master Azarov." She turned, fixing her eyes on that distant storm. "If there is nothing else?"

He took a step closer. "I wanted to speak with you before the coronation."

She pursed her lips. "If you're here to discuss the cabinet seat, I'm afraid I must disappoint you again."

His smile warped into something more predatory. It made Izaveta's stomach plummet. It was the look of someone who knew they had a winning hand. "Are you sure about that?"

She raised her eyebrows. "It's the day of my coronation. This is certainly not the time."

But Kyriil's smile didn't falter at her tone. "On the contrary, this could be the only time. You've angered the Church already. Bazin is lost. Commander Iveshkin is teetering. It'd take less than a push to sway her. And the Firebird is notably absent. You need a strong ally. With the Azarovs' history— and our gold—you could still salvage this."

Izaveta raised her chin. She kept her hands at her sides, even as they itched to reach out and slap him. To wipe that patronizing smile from his face. "What does it matter? The Firebird was called away on important business. It doesn't change her loyalty. She will return." That last sentence was spoken more to herself. A desperate hope. Because Asya would come back—wouldn't she? Even after all that was said, she had to come back.

Izaveta couldn't lose her too.

Kyriil took another step, too close. "And what if the Firebird doesn't return?"

Izaveta stilled. The question crystallized in the air, frigid as ice. "What would make you say that?"

"There are those out there who want to do harm to the Firebird." His dark eyes glistened, that smile lingering on his lips. "People who needed only a little guidance to take action."

Izaveta closed the space between them, her hands fisting. She almost couldn't form words through the rage that clawed up her throat. "If I find out you did *anything* to hurt my sister—"

"Not me. But the Order of the Captured Flame needed

only a small push to persuade them that Saints' Night was the perfect opportunity to act."

The name prickled at the back of her mind, a faded symbol in an old book. "A religious sect?" she said, a note of disdain hardening her voice. "Did the vibishop put you up to that?"

Kyriil raised his eyebrows. "You overestimate him. He would never have the scope to plan something like this. The Azarov gold has power. And firestone is expensive, not to mention hard to come by on short notice."

She recoiled, her heart hammering in her ears. How had she missed this? All her calculations and observations, and she hadn't put together the pieces of Kyriil's plan—hadn't realized he was still working against her. This was what he always did. He conspired and manipulated, all while wearing a smile.

Izaveta gritted her teeth, trying to pull back to her logical, scheming place. The one that could sort through a plan— outmaneuver the enemy—in an instant. But his words wormed through her. The gloating certainty. *And what if the Firebird doesn't return?*

Asya was gone—*taken*. He'd made sure of it. Izaveta's mind couldn't get past the paralyzing terror that she might not see her again. That their conversation the previous night could be their last.

She clenched her jaw. "You are going to regret that you ever returned to the palace." She strode toward the door, prepared to shout for every strashe within earshot to drag him down to the dungeons until he told them where Asya was.

But Kyriil's voice called her back. "I wouldn't do that."

She didn't want to listen—to let him manipulate her even

now. But that arrogance made her hesitate. The certainty in his voice that he'd already won. "And why is that?"

He gave a shrug, fastening his hands behind his back in a display of complete composure. "I told you before, I'm loyal to you, Izaveta. I'm doing this *for* you."

She shot him a glare, one that would make most people wither. "Having my sister kidnapped is an odd way to show loyalty."

"I suppose it depends on the situation, doesn't it?"

Izaveta narrowed her eyes. She didn't have to listen to this, to his useless riddles. She reached for the door again—and Kyriil's hand pressed over hers, holding her back.

"If you want me to," he said, "I can tell you where the Firebird is. To prove my loyalty, I won't even ask for anything in exchange."

She pulled her hand out of his, suspicion crawling up her spine. "Why would you do that?"

A moment too late, her mind caught on his odd phrasing. *If you want me to.*

His eyes flicked to her wrist. To the mark hidden beneath her silk gloves. "Are you so sure you want to save her?"

She took a sharp step back. Her other hand twitched, desperate to cover the mark. Even though he couldn't possibly see it. He couldn't know.

He seemed to read the question in her silence. "I'm good at finding things out. Especially things people want to stay hidden."

Izaveta didn't say anything. She refused to confirm anything for him, not when he hadn't even accused her yet.

He leaned forward, eyes fervent. "If Asya returns, it will

only be a matter of time. This is the only way for you to escape the price."

She scrambled to regain control, to grasp at the unfeeling queen who would spin this away. "These accusations are ridiculous and unfounded. I refuse to hear any more of them."

Kyriil's lips twisted, a mock shadow of sympathy. "Does she even know what you did? *Who* you killed?"

For all her practicing—for all her hours of maintaining the mask—that question managed to crack through. Her anger crumbled, unable to stand up to that truth. The thing she'd been asking herself over and over.

"You don't know what you're talking about," she snapped. But a memory flashed in her mind, unbidden. The day of the hunt, the falcon that tore her gloves to shreds. Kyriil reaching for her...

His smile widened. "She doesn't know, does she? And what do you think she'll do when she finds out? Just forgive and forget—as the Firebird and your sister?"

Izaveta wanted to be indignant, to scoff at the mere suggestion. Asya was the other half of her. But how could Izaveta ask her sister to forgive what she'd done? She didn't deserve a reprieve, least of all from Asya.

Izaveta stared at Kyriil, and suddenly she felt fourteen again. As helpless and out of her depth as she had when he'd walked away from her. "I can't let my sister die." The words came out a plea, a pathetic whimper.

"This is better for you." Kyriil put a hand on her arm, voice soft and enticing. "No one would suspect your involvement. It removes a powerful figure who could be used against you, and it protects you from the price. All you have to do is stand back and let the order do their work."

The words curled around her heart, immovable as the brand upon her wrist. What if he was right?

CHAPTER FORTY-EIGHT

Asya's knuckles shone white against the golden hilt as she stared into Yuliana's gray eyes. Storm eyes, ones that hid so much more than Asya had ever realized. Suddenly face-to-face, Asya didn't know what to say. Where to begin.

Yuliana glanced down at the gleaming blue that pressed into her throat. "Is that a gemstone?" Her lips twitched. If the situation were not so dire, Asya might've called the expression a smile. "You really are unbelievable. You made a weapon out of a ball gown."

There was a shadow of the Yuliana Asya had thought she'd known in those words. The one she'd ridden a bear with and challenged in the training grounds. It set Asya off-kilter, two conflicting images at war in her mind.

It wasn't real. None of that was real. She clung to that, an attempt at cold indifference. That was what she needed now. "Well, I didn't have many options."

Yuliana held her gaze, unflinching even with the blade digging into her skin. "What's your plan here? You can't keep me at knifepoint *and* get me to open the cage."

Asya swallowed. She hadn't quite thought it through that far. "Maybe I'll just kill you." The words leaped out, born of that dark anger. The wrenching pain of Yuliana's betrayal sharpened to a point by the Firebird's detachment. If everyone saw Asya as that monster, she might as well live up to it.

A shadow quivered across Yuliana's face. Not fear, but something else. "That's not you, Asya."

At the sound of her name, Asya's fingers tightened on the knife. "Not just *Firebird* anymore then?"

"Let me explain—" Yuliana started. Her voice frayed with every word, a desperation seeping through. "I had to be convincing. They couldn't suspect I was going to help you."

"That's easy to say with a knife at your throat."

"You have no reason to believe me, I know," Yuliana whispered. She had that lost look again, the one that tugged at Asya's heart. Too familiar.

She squeezed her eyes shut. She couldn't let Yuliana get in her head again. "Stop lying."

But despite herself, she felt her hand slacken, her grip on the makeshift blade slipping. The questions—the uncertainties—that had bubbled beneath the surface of her mind surged up. "Why did you save me in the queenstrees? If you're working *for* them, why did you help me escape?"

Yuliana looked down. "I wasn't supposed to."

Asya's throat constricted. Four words that were somehow both an admission and a reprieve. They meant Yuliana really had been working with the order. Even if she'd helped Asya in the queenstrees, it didn't change that. "Was everything you did because they told you to?"

"I—" Yuliana broke off, taking a shaky breath. "Let me

start at the beginning." She hesitated again. The silence of the vast, hollow space roared in Asya's ears. "After my father died, the order took my brother and me in. They're a subsect of the Church, claiming to help those orphaned or in need. They trained us. Nurtured that desire for revenge by giving it an outlet. The Firebird." Her eyes rose to Asya's. "You."

Yuliana squared her shoulders, as if forcing herself to continue. "They got me a job as a strashe and had someone paid off to ensure I was the best option for your personal guard. I was supposed to watch you. To see if you had any secrets, any weaknesses we could exploit."

Hearing it aloud, laid out in such detail, was like salt in the fresh wound. All the things Asya had missed. The lies that had been such a comfort. She almost told Yuliana to stop—to not make Asya examine all of this. But she couldn't speak. Yuliana's words clogged her throat, as suffocating as the firestone.

"And that day in the queenstrees was when I realized I couldn't do it. I couldn't be a part of this. That was why I asked to be removed as your guard. I thought then they couldn't use me anymore." She paused, a shadow crossing her gray eyes. "But it's not that easy to leave."

Asya's free hand lifted to Yuliana's temple, fingers skimming the fading bruise. The wrong side, she realized—not the side that had cracked against the tree.

Yuliana winced. "You know everything has a price."

Asya swallowed the lump rising in her throat. "What about last night? The trap?"

"You weren't meant to follow me. I didn't realize you were there until too late."

Asya stared at her, wishing she could tell if any of this was true. Or if it was just another convenient ruse, telling Asya what she wanted to hear.

"Was—" She paused, almost unable to force the question out. She wasn't sure she wanted the answer. Not after everything. "Was anything real?"

Yuliana's gray eyes met hers, so open and unguarded. So unlike the indifferent soldier she'd first seemed.

"Yes." The single word was hushed in the wide space. A confession for Asya alone. "I—I should have told you. After Saints' Night..." She trailed off, the unspoken thing hanging between them. After the kiss. The moment Asya had thought meant something.

"You could have told me." Asya meant the statement to come out angry, accusing, but it sounded more like a feeble whisper. In some ways that would be easier, if Yuliana had been pretending the entire time. Then Asya could close herself off, could let that anger heal her wound. But this gray in-between was harder to know what to do with. "Why didn't you?"

Yuliana's jaw twitched, her eyes bright against the shadowed ruins. "Because I was scared. You think you're the monster, Asya, but I'm the one who's done terrible things. Who lied and manipulated. And I didn't want you to look at me like that." She paused, lowering her gaze. "The way you're looking at me now."

Asya's heart wrenched, her mind fighting to make sense of all of this. Because she understood that feeling, understood that fear.

She just wished Yuliana had trusted her.

A sound from behind Asya jerked her back to the present situation. To the bars of the cage. The knife at Yuliana's throat.

The slap of feet on stone.

Yuliana's eyes strained to follow the noise. She spoke quickly, voice low and urgent. "It doesn't excuse it, I know. But you have to let me help you now."

Asya's grip tightened on the hilt again. Her heart skittered against her ribs. So much hung on this decision. So much more than just her and Yuliana. If Asya chose to trust her again and she was wrong, there wouldn't be another chance at escape.

"Asya, you can't get out of here on your own."

Slowly, Asya lowered the knife. She let go of the chains, and they slithered back down to the icy stone. But even as she did so, she wasn't sure she'd chosen right.

Yuliana stepped back, palms out in a gesture of appease-ment. She moved around the cage, to the small hatch on the other side. Asya's eyes darted around, alert for the slightest sound. Had the footsteps been going somewhere else? Or had something made them stop?

Even the low scrape of the bolt resonated like a bell chim-ing in the quiet. A signal to the order of what was happening.

Yuliana offered a hand to help her through the small gap, but Asya didn't take it. Touching her again would just be a reminder, a step back into that hope. One she wasn't ready to take yet. Even if Yuliana said some of it had been real, it didn't change how much of it wasn't—or that Asya had no way of knowing which parts were which.

Asya almost stumbled as she stepped away from the cage.

She'd been so used to the weight of the firestone that without it, she felt off balance.

Yuliana caught her arm to steady her, before quickly dropping it at the look on Asya's face. "You're freezing." Yuliana started to undo the top button of her coat. "Do you want—"

But Asya waved her off. The Firebird was already uncurling inside her, ready to break free again. "I won't be for much longer. Now, which way?"

Yuliana nodded, slipping back into the role of the soldier. "Through the old cloisters. They don't have anyone on watch there now, and it'll give us cover to reach the trees."

Asya pushed away the last of her misgivings as she followed the strashe into the shadows. She kept a firm grip on her knife. The Firebird prickled beneath her skin. With every step the lingering power of the firestone grew fainter. But she wasn't strong enough to take on attackers yet, especially not with the wound on her leg. It wasn't deep—not more than a scratch. But enough to leave a trace of firestone in her blood.

Yuliana led her through a crumbled archway, away from the nave and through a door that must've once led to a bishop's cloisters. They moved quickly, careful to keep the sound of their steps muffled against the hard stone.

Asya tried to focus on Yuliana's back. On forcing her muscles to move, even as exhaustion tugged at her. The slash in her leg was bleeding again, leaving a crimson trail that would make it easy for the order to track them.

Fear pounded through her, in time with the rhythm of her feet. Not just for herself now, even if she didn't want to admit it. Even if she wasn't sure. Despite the shadowed light, the stark bruise still shone on Yuliana's face, catching in the corner of Asya's vision. How much worse would the order do to her if they realized she'd helped Asya escape?

They turned another corner, into a moss-covered passage. Statues of the saints must've once lined the walls, but they'd been reclaimed by the earth. Scattered pieces of stone—just recognizable as figures—littered the ground. A cracked kokoshnik of thorns. A stone dagger that must have been Restov's.

Seeing the saints shattered at her feet made the hairs on the back of her neck prickle. Like standing in a ruined, empty place, devoid of the gods. Could this be the world if the Fading continued, if the price continued to rise?

She shook the feeling off. She had to focus. Up ahead—through a rotted door—she could see the distant branches of a forest. Once she was there, it would be easy to lose any pursuit. The forest was a home to her. She knew how to follow birds or animal tracks back to a water source, and the river would lead her away.

They'd be safe.

Yuliana was barely four paces from the doorway when a figure stepped out of the shadow of a column.

She skidded to a halt, digging rivets into the moss. Asya forced her feet to stop, catching herself on the jagged remnants of the wall.

The person stepped forward, into the pale light of the clouded sky. Asya drew in a breath. His hair was ink black, sharp cheekbones leading up to gray eyes. Storm-gray eyes.

The brother who had taught Yuliana to fight.

Yuliana stepped between them, holding out a hand to each as if she could force them back. Her gaze darted to Asya. "Don't attack."

Asya hesitated, glancing over her shoulder. Even now, someone might've found the empty cage. The trail of blood. She looked back to Yuliana, to her brother.

He made no move forward—no sign of aggression.

Asya could leap to attack anyway. Use the little of the Firebird's power she had to force him aside. But she wouldn't prove to him the order was right. Wouldn't be the monster they believed.

His eyes flicked from Asya to his sister. "Yuliana, what're you doing?"

"Dima, please—"

With those two words—the frayed desperation in her voice—her brother changed. His expression hardened. His hand jumped to the saber at his waist, pulling it free with a shriek of metal. "They were right then. You have turned against us."

Yuliana took a step back—a step toward Asya. "No, it's not that simple—"

Dima matched her movements. "This is everything we've worked for, everything we've ever wanted. And you're helping *it*."

Yuliana fumbled for her own weapon. The soldier was gone, crumbled away like this church. Replaced with the lost child again. "You have to understand. This isn't right. We can't kill her."

Dima didn't stop, prowling forward. "Just stand aside. You don't even have to get your hands dirty."

Yuliana's jaw clenched; fingers tightening on the hilt.

As he moved closer, Asya realized she was wrong. His eyes weren't the storms that Yuliana's were but hard stone. Cold and unfeeling. "What would Father think?" he spat. "What would he say if he saw you now?"

Something fractured across Yuliana's face, an old grief torn free, but she still didn't move. "Father wouldn't want us to be murderers."

Asya's heart lurched. No matter what Yuliana had done, she didn't deserve this.

Dima bared his teeth. "It's not murder to slay a monster."

Asya grasped Yuliana's arm, pulling the strashe behind her. A sudden need to keep her away from her brother—away from the words that so clearly cut down to Yuliana's core—burned through her. Asya fixed Dima with an icy glare. "We're leaving. Don't try to stop us."

She'd only taken a step toward the gaping doorway when shouts echoed behind her. Black-clad order members burst into the passageway, firestone-edged blades drawn.

Yuliana's eyes widened. "Go!"

But as they stepped toward the doorway, more people emerged to block their path. They'd been hidden by the collapsed curve of the arch. Waiting.

Asya's chest constricted as if the bars of the cage were closing over her already. Freedom was so close—only a few desperate steps away.

Fyodor pushed to the front. His eyes fixed on Yuliana, a look of deepest regret shadowing his features. "How disappointing. You are a traitor, after all."

Chapter Forty-Nine

Izaveta stared at Kyriil, and that night three years ago, when she'd first seen his true colors, flickered across her vision. His voice as he'd schemed with his father, the coldness as he examined her every flaw. Her weaknesses.

She hadn't thought he'd be able to get past her armor this time, but somehow he'd still managed it. She was still being played for a fool.

Looking away, she dug her nails into her right wrist. She wanted to tear the skin away, to wipe herself clean of that mark. Of the guilt that came with it.

But her sister would be the price.

She grasped for a logical explanation, a flaw in his plan. "And how will I control the cabinet without her?"

Kyriil shrugged. "You don't need the Firebird. Walk into the cathedral with me on your arm, make your alliance clear, and the cabinet will fall into line."

He was right. That was the most frustrating thing, the thing that made her want to scream into that gathering storm.

He took a step forward, his eyes wide and imploring. "What will it take for you to understand that I did all of this for you?"

"All of this?" she repeated. The realization hit her like a blow, the events from the past twelve days thrown into stark relief. The missing spy, the empty cabinet seat, Kyriil's convenient help.

She stared up at him, horror burrowing down to her bones. "*You* are the one who's been working against me. You had Vittaria killed to open up a cabinet seat. You got rid of the spy who was supposed to protect her. And you funded this order to get my sister out of the way. To isolate me—to make me look weak—so I'd have to turn to you."

He let out a low laugh. "You're almost right." He glanced up at her, his eyelashes sending spidery lines across his face. "But I did more than that. Gold is a marvelous thing, you know. It always surprises me the lengths people will go to for it. Some will even forsake the gods. And once one has a spy in their pocket, it's amazing the places they can reach. The information they can gather."

Izaveta's insides stilled. He'd had the first pakviye killed by one of their own—the only other person who would have known the spy's movements. Bribed them to break their oath and then used them. An informant at the heart of Izaveta's operations.

She looked up at him. "Is that the same pakviye who failed to provide the antidote on Saints' Night?"

His lips tightened, a shadow of regret crossing his features. "That was unintentional. I was meeting with them to hear

of any new information. It was too late when I learned of
your plan."

She let out a derisive laugh. "Well, as long as you only *un-
intentionally* almost caused my death."

"Izaveta, you're wrong to think I did any of this to hurt
you." He moved forward, hands reaching toward her. "I did
it all to make you strong. You will be the youngest queen in
the history of Tóurin, but also the most powerful."

Izaveta stared at him, letting the poison of his words seep
through her. There was a part of her that wanted that. Wanted
to prove who she could be—prove she could be more than
her mother. To become the queen she'd always dreamed of
being. In control of the board at last. No Firebird to hold her
in check.

When she spoke, her voice was low, no more than a whisper. But anger threaded through it, biting and visceral.
"Where is my sister?"

Kyriil held her gaze for a moment. "The order took her
to the Elmer."

The Elmer. Izaveta knew that from her research, the ruin
of one of the first churches to Dveda. A place of old magic
and ritual. Just the place to kill the Firebird.

Even with the question, Kyriil didn't look fazed. He was
so sure he knew her, knew the machinations of this political
game. "You'd better decide quickly. You'll be late for your
own coronation."

"I could just send the strashe," Izaveta said slowly, watching
his reaction. "They'd make quick work of a religious sect."

Kyriil's smile widened, as if he'd anticipated just that. "I'd be careful who you trust. How do you think the Firebird was captured in the first place?"

Izaveta ground her teeth. Everything was crashing down around her, all her carefully laid plans reduced to ashes.

What would her mother do?

But as soon as the question rose in Izaveta's mind, she realized she didn't care. She'd spent so much time fashioning herself after her mother, desperate to live up to her impossible standards, that she'd hardly stopped to wonder if that was what she really wanted.

A political move didn't matter here. Asya did. Izaveta made this mess, and she wouldn't let her sister pay for her mistakes.

She didn't need the strashe—didn't need her cabinet—to do the right thing. To make a different choice define her.

She straightened, rolling her shoulders back. She wouldn't bend to Kyriil now, to the will of a man who would discard her at the first opportunity. And she certainly wouldn't abandon her sister for a crown.

Her voice hardened as she fixed her eyes on him. "If you know what I did—*why* I'm marked—then you know what I am capable of." She turned on her heel, throwing the last words over her shoulder like a knife. "You would be wise not to be here when I return."

She strode out into the passageway, which was populated only by the strashe still on duty. The noise from the cathedral's hall reached toward her like a wave on the shore, desperate to drag her back.

She spun away from it, back toward the palace—and almost walked straight into Nikov. He wore his Amarinth robes for the formal occasion, his dark eyes picking up the purple like twilight.

"Tired of queenship already?" he asked, but his smile died as he took in her expression.

She didn't waste time with preamble. "Asya's been taken."

Nikov froze. "How?"

Izaveta shook her head. "I don't know. But I can't trust the strashe." An idea struck her—a plan forming in her mind. She couldn't rush in there completely alone, much as she wanted to in that moment. But there were still other people she could trust, at least when it came to the Firebird.

She grabbed Nikov's arm, pulling him along with her. "Go find Zvezda, the spymaster. And Tarya. Tell them Asya has been taken and she's being held in the Elmer. Tell *no one else*."

"Where are you going?"

"The Elmer," she replied, as if it was obvious. Which it was. Now that she'd managed to push her mother out of her head, the choice was clear and simple.

Nikov raked a hand through his hair. "No, you can't...the coronation—"

Izaveta was already turning away. "What kind of queen would I be if I abandoned my sister when she was in need?"

He grabbed her hand, trying to pull her back. "Izaveta, you have to be careful. If you're not crowned tonight, the consequences of this—"

She shook him off. She didn't need to hear this was a terrible idea, that she was risking everything. She already knew that. It didn't change anything. "It's time I faced the consequences of my actions."

He hurried after her, a fervor on his face that she'd never seen there. "Wait, I need to tell you something—"

She turned, grasping his hand in hers, trying to make him understand the weight of this moment. "You were right before, Nikov. It's our choices who make us who we are." She pulled her hand free, imploring him not to follow. "And I choose my sister."

Even if she might kill me.

Still wearing her coronation gown, Izaveta had startled several of the bearkeepers when she hurried in demanding Olyeta, but she hardly cared. With a last glance back at the spires of the cathedral and a wrenching tug in her gut that told her this was the wrong decision, she'd headed out into the woods.

The snow-white bear blended with the pale landscape, a beast of winter returned home. But with her fingers numb on the reins and nothing but the howling wind to keep her company, Izaveta couldn't stop her thoughts from crowding in.

Leaving Nikov to find Tarya and Zvezda was putting a lot of trust in him. A part of this hasty mess of a plan that she could not control. For all Izaveta knew, she could be riding into this completely alone. No one left to follow her.

But even as those doubts needled at her skin, as sharp as the wind, she couldn't get herself to turn back. No matter the danger, she wouldn't abandon Asya now. She couldn't.

Digging her fingers into Olyeta's fur, Izaveta tried to reach for reason. For the comforting reassurance of a logical plan. All she had to do was find a way to stall, to delay long enough for reinforcements to arrive. But her mind was refusing to cooperate. She couldn't separate herself from the chilling fear that she might already be too late. Couldn't reduce this to pieces on a zvess board when the threatened piece was her sister.

As she rode, the storm she'd seen on the horizon drew closer. It seared against the skyline, silhouetting the trees in bright gold light. By the time the sun had nearly sunk into the storm's depths, Izaveta was seriously regretting not stopping for a coat. Her fingers were already numb through the impractical velvet gloves, and her skin was tingeing blue.

She felt—rather than saw—when she reached the right place. A creeping chill at the back of her neck.

Dead starbirds littered the ground—just like the ones Asya had seen in the queenstrees. They still shone faintly, freshly killed. Their dying light illuminated the scene in a pale, ethereal glow. The sight sent nausea writhing through Izaveta's gut.

The last branches parted, and the old church loomed in front of her. Its facade was still standing, though it teetered as though it might crash down at any moment. The shell of a spire clung to the roof, surrounded by empty plinths. The colorful paint had faded, leaving dark scars along its surface. Broken windows stared out, empty as the eyes of the dead.

The whole place had the feeling of something lost. Something that was never meant to be found.

Izaveta dismounted, giving Olyeta a quick pat on the muzzle. She didn't like to leave the bear behind, but she'd give away their position in an instant. Izaveta needed all the advantages she could get.

There was no sign of people. No hint of the order acolytes she'd been expecting. But still, the hairs on the back of her neck prickled. As if someone were waiting for her. She glanced up at the dark shadow of branches, and her stomach lurched. Something *was* watching her. Yellow beaded eyes, luminescent against the sky, and oil-black feathers.

More than Izaveta had ever seen—more than she'd have even thought possible in one place. They filled the branches like feathered leaves, all their eyes on her.

Falcons.

CHAPTER FIFTY

Asya's eyes darted from Fyodor to Yuliana. Flames still crack-led around her fingers, but it was taking every drop of strength to not let them falter. To not let her foes realize how weak she actually was.

Fyodor gestured to Dima, a silent command. He leaped forward and Yuliana's eyes widened—the moment of surprise giving him the advantage he needed. He twisted her saber from her grip and spun her round, lifting his own blade to her throat.

"Dima?" Yuliana whispered.

But he didn't respond. His eyes were on Fyodor, awaiting his next order.

Asya went to lunge forward, but he pressed the blade harder into Yuliana's throat. A warning.

"Let her go," Asya growled. She dragged whatever flames she could muster to the surface, letting them coil around her fingertips, along the glinting jewel of her makeshift weapon. A show of power to make them falter.

It worked for an instant. Several of the order members flinched back, weapons lowering at the sight of her fire. One of them touched the hollow of their throat, as if to ward off her evil.

Fyodor was unmoved, watching her with that same martyred sorrow. "Don't make this harder than it has to be, Asya. Remember, we know your weakness."

They certainly did. She could still feel that strangling weight of firestone, the sudden pain of the arrowhead in her chest. Hollowing her out from the inside.

She swallowed, refusing to let it show. To let them know the terror that cage brought out in her. "You can't hope to win this. I am tasked with protecting this land—with ensuring magic cannot run rampant and destroy us. If you kill me, we all lose." Her eyes scanned along the assembled people as she spoke, hoping to break through to just one of them. To pull at one fragile link in the chain.

"You're wrong, Asya. That's what you were taught, but it's far from the truth." Fyodor lifted something from the folds of his robe. Dark rings of stone veined with red. "Just put these back on."

He held out the firestone manacles, the same ones they'd used to bring her here. She took a step back, letting her fire creep out. Helplessness squeezed around her. She was surrounded. A trapped animal again.

And she didn't even have her full power to fend them off.

Fyodor stepped closer, his low voice crawling across her skin. "You're powerful, but you can't hope to get past all of us. Surrender now—or watch as we slit young Yuliana's throat and capture you anyway."

Bile churned in Asya's stomach, bitter and caustic. The way he said that—the casual manner—was unnerving. "She's one of your people."

Manic fervor shone in his eyes again. The cause that had to be held above all else. "She betrayed us. There's no mercy for traitors here."

Asya's eyes darted to Yuliana. To the cruel glint of that blade against her neck. Dima was her brother. Surely he wouldn't go through with it?

It was a feeble hope. Even if he didn't, there were a dozen others around who would take up the task. All because Yuliana had helped Asya. Because she'd seen more than the monster.

She looked back at Fyodor. Her every muscle was tensed, screaming at her to run. To fight. "How do I know you won't kill her anyway?"

He smiled, though there was no happiness in that look. "I think I'll find she's more useful alive."

Asya looked around. There had to be another way out of this. She couldn't give up now—couldn't let them do this. But she also couldn't abandon Yuliana, even if she had betrayed her. The Firebird's flames receded, almost as if it agreed.

If she could just get Yuliana away from her brother, they might have a chance. A feeble, impossible chance—but *something*.

Asya whirled, sending out a tongue of flame. It was weak—a shadow of her full power—but the nearest order members stumbled away from her, throwing up their arms to shield themselves. But others surged forward. Their firestone-edged blades gleamed as they arced toward her.

Exhaustion clawed at the edge of her mind. The draining

power of the wound on her leg pulsed through her. She used the cover of another sputter of fire to dive toward Yuliana. But Dima anticipated her. He pulled his sister out of Asya's reach, blade perilously close to Yuliana's throat.

The dive sent Asya rolling toward another of the order members. His hand shook on his saber. Launching herself to her feet, she swung around him and lifted her own makeshift blade to his throat. The movement around her ceased in an instant. All eyes were on her, the order members still wary.

"Let us go or one of your loyal acolytes dies." She tried to push every drop of venom into those words, every last trace of her anger. To not let it show that she wasn't sure she could bring herself to kill this trembling boy, even if he was part of all this. "And I'm sure I could take more of them with me."

Fyodor glared at her, his calm demeanor shattered by the outburst. "We have you surrounded. Nothing you do will change the outcome. We will get you back in that cage, Firebird, even if it kills every one of us."

Her eyes darted around. Her sister would think of a way out of this, so why couldn't she? Every breath pulled the noose tighter around her neck. Each pounding heartbeat a ticking clock that led to the same inevitable place.

Fyodor shook his head, a flicker of regret. "I did warn you."

Yuliana struggled against her brother's grip. "Don't listen to them, Asya. *Run!*"

Asya gritted her teeth. She let out a last desperate burst of flame—more frustration than a true attempt at escape— sending Fyodor staggering back. He clutched his hand where the heat had seared his skin. His mouth contorted into a snarl. "Do it, Dima."

Yuliana's eyes strained, her mouth set in a grim line. *"Go."*

If anything, that solidified Asya's choice.

"All right!" Her voice cleaved through the air. A decision she couldn't take back.

She held up her hands, letting the glittering jewel clatter to the ground. The boy scrambled away from her, not even bothering to pick up his fallen saber in his haste. Out of the corner of her eye, she saw Yuliana's shoulders slump. Such a small movement, but it resonated through Asya's chest.

There was no way out of this one.

Chapter Fifty-One

Asya thought she had gotten used to the firestone. She knew its power, having spent time under its grasp. But returning to the cage after that brief glimpse of freedom was so much worse than before. Like finally breaking through the surface of a frozen lake, only for the current to drag her back down, paralyzing her muscles as the cold crept into her bones, water filling her lungs.

Despite her word, she still struggled as they pushed her back behind those bars. Not that it made a difference. There were too many of them, and they all knew her weakness. Her *weaknesses*, both magical and mortal.

They took no chances this time, retying the chains around her wrists and hoisting her arms up so that her toes skimmed the ground. She was left alone then, in that suffocating silence. She'd seen the forest just beyond the crumbled walls, but there was no hint of birdsong. None of the comforting sounds that should have come with its presence. Just the empty quiet.

There had to be guards watching her, standing just out of

sight. Far enough away that she couldn't do anything to try to trick them again—that she couldn't even ask where they'd taken Yuliana. The slithering fear that they might have killed her anyway was as suffocating as the firestone. It wormed its way up her throat, bitter and cloying.

She hadn't been able to watch Yuliana die, and this was the price. Asya had probably damned them both anyway.

There was one hope, one last thing she grasped at. The wait gave her leg time to heal. It must've only been a glancing blow, leaving only a trace of that poisonous mineral in her blood. And with that injury gone, if the cage was opened again, the Firebird would rise in full force. But that tiny *if* was a lot to pin her hopes on.

Fyodor returned at sunset.

His acolytes crowded in with him, their crests glittering gold against their dark robes. Some still looked nervous, giving Asya a wide berth. But others looked excited, *vindicated*. Yuliana's brother passed close by the bars, gray eyes shadowed as he shot Asya a glare. A look that spoke of revenge.

Their hushed whispers slithered around the open space, echoing against the forgotten stone. There were so many of them—more than Asya could have imagined. They filled the vast space, stretching back through the crumbled pews to the collapsed dome. All eager to see her death. To see the Firebird finally defeated.

Fyodor held up a hand, and they fell silent.

He glanced up at the burning sky, the deep oranges bleeding into crimson flames beyond the jagged edges of the fallen dome. "The coronation should have started by now. The queen is crowned, and your power is consecrated." He looked back at her, eyes bright and shining. Fanatical. "Shall we begin?"

He turned to face his people, like a performer introducing a play. "For centuries we have been held hostage by the Firebird, a creature who demands a blood price for something that should be our right as given to us by the gods." He spun, throwing his arms up to the open ceiling. "Here is where magic was first given to mortals, and here is where we shall reclaim it."

Asya's heart pounded. Her eyes jumped around, from the enraptured acolytes to the unseeing statues. Every part of her screamed to run, to find some way out. It couldn't end here. Not like this, abandoned in a forsaken church.

Fyodor's gaze snapped back to her. "We shall sacrifice the Firebird in its true form—a gift to the gods—and finally rid the world of this monster."

Asya didn't flinch at his words. *Monster* didn't cut into her flesh as it once had—certainly not from a man who would kill as soon as blink.

She glared at him, dragging up the last drops of her defiance. "The Firebird can't reach its full power with this firestone around it. Let me out. Then I can show you my true form."

His lips curled into a poisonously sympathetic smile. "I am no fool. Queens kept their Firebirds in cages just like this for years. This one is based on the design of Queen Teriya's cage. Specially crafted so the Firebird's power can rear—can take a price—without spreading beyond the bars."

Asya strained against the chains, sparks dancing along her wrist with the effort. "What do you think will happen?" she bit out, trying to keep the edge of desperation from her voice. "Without me, magic will run rampant. You saw the bane-wolf. That is the *least* of what could happen. I—"

"If the Firebird will not come out willingly," he interrupted with a patronizing air of righteousness, "then we shall have to make it."

He turned back to his people, drawing them into his narrative. His fervent belief in their glory. "I have studied the Firebird for years, dedicated my life to this order." He glanced back at Asya, his eyes gleaming. "I know there are ways to bring it out. Tempting it with a price is quickest, as the Firebird is always driven by that greed. But, as is the case with any creature, self-preservation is inescapable."

Two of the acolytes stepped forward, as if on command. Their faces were alight, matching expressions of devotion.

Asya struggled harder, tearing her skin against the rough metal. Blood trickled down her arms, but it was no use. She wouldn't be managing that trick again.

The bolt slid back, and the small hatch on the side of the cage opened. Asya strained for it, her shoulders wrenching against their sockets. But the two acolytes stepped through and it slammed shut. That small glimpse of freedom snatched away again.

The space was tiny, barely enough for three of them to stand. She could see every line on their faces, pick out every color in their irises. The two acolytes drew short daggers, their eyes on Fyodor. Waiting. These blades were not edged with firestone. Because they didn't want to subdue the Firebird, they wanted to antagonize it.

If they succeeded, these two people would die. Devoured

by the flames as soon as Asya let the Firebird free. And they didn't care. She could see it in their faces. In their blazing eyes. They believed their sacrifice would be worthy.

Her mind scrambled for words, for some way to convince them. It was like scraping the bottom of a dry well. She wasn't Izaveta, didn't have her sister's persuasion. All she had was herself.

And the grim determination closing around her. If they needed to sacrifice the Firebird at its full power, she would not let it out. Those days of suppressing it, of pushing away the faintest hint of the Calling, would prove helpful. But even the proximity of these two people made the sparks want to leap free, to give an outlet to the helpless anger that burned inside her.

Fyodor nodded. A small, decisive movement. Unyielding as the arc of the executioner's blade.

The two daggers plunged into her flesh.

Asya screamed, and the Firebird screamed with her. A terrible, bone-shattering sound that filled her ears alone. Her vision blurred to nothing but a swirl of colors. Firestone black threaded with deepest red and forgotten gray. The blades twisted, sending jagged swirls of pain across her skin.

They didn't remove them—didn't give her that respite, the chance for the Firebird to heal. Instead, two more blades dug in. One struck bone, the pain exploding through Asya's skull like a bright burst of light. It dragged a muffled sob from her chest. The Firebird pulled against her, straining to leap free. It wanted to get away from this, to fight back.

Asya wanted it too. But she couldn't let go. She tried to think of the people who needed her, who needed the Firebird to survive. Tarya. Izaveta. Even Yuliana. Their faces swirled past Asya's vision, stolen away as quickly as she conjured them.

The onslaught kept coming. Each blow resonated through her, drawing the Firebird closer to the surface. Even against the weight of the Firestone, she could feel it struggling. As desperate as she was to just end this. To consume the volley of blows in flame, even if it destroyed her too.

And then, just as Asya's world was reduced to pinpricks of glistening light, it stopped.

Flames leaked from the wounds like blood. They slithered away eagerly, reaching for the two acolytes. But Asya clamped down. Folded in on herself, into that dark core of pain and silence.

Tears ran down her cheeks, sizzling to vapor as the Firebird clawed beneath her skin.

Fyodor watched her, eyeing the trailing sparks. "You can sacrifice yourself to this, Asya. Don't let the Firebird make a monster of you too."

She coughed, her chest heaving. She looked up at Fyodor. "I *am* the Firebird. And I have survived centuries." Her voice came out hoarse, her throat coated in ash and bile. "You think it can be broken by a few daggers?"

"No, I suppose it can't." Something shifted on his face, a realization. It sent a plunging fear through Asya's stomach. "But you can." His eyes flicked to Dima. "Fetch your sister."

Chapter Fifty-Two

The moonlight arises in the east, by conjuring of the falcon.

At the sight of those assembled falcons, eerie witnesses standing on ceremony, that line of ancient Versch played through Izaveta's mind. She thought of the strashe who'd been killed by a falcon because of the imbalance.

Did they know? Did they know somehow that Izaveta had not paid the price?

A scream rent the air, cutting off her questions. She froze, frost crystallizing through her insides, turning them to ice.

She knew that voice.

She hurried forward, hardly noticing the snap of twigs and dry leaves underfoot. Ducking through a cracked hole in the church's outer wall, she stepped into what would once have been its porch. The wall separating it from the main hall was all but gone, just a trace of wooden frames left, so Izaveta could see straight through to the altar at the far end.

A cage sat atop it, bars gleaming red in the dying light.

Izaveta's breath caught in her lungs, as trapped as her sister.

Her own words from the night before came echoing back, a vicious irony. *Queen Teriya used to keep her Firebird in a cage.* She hadn't meant it, not really. Her only weapons, thrown out in anger and fear. But that didn't change this, didn't change that exactly what Izaveta had threatened had come to pass.

People dressed in black wool surrounded the cage, their dark profiles mingling with the oncoming shadows. Their eyes were all on Asya as well, fortunately for Izaveta. Otherwise they would have spotted her at once. She crouched down, hiding behind the decayed remains of a statue.

She scanned the assembled people, her heart sinking lower and lower as she counted. Some of them were vaguely familiar, perhaps traitorous strashe or courtiers. All of them were armed. She silently cursed her recklessness. What had she expected? The Firebird to be taken by a wizened old man that Izaveta could outsmart and then save the day?

Another scream split the air. Izaveta's fingers dug into the soft stone of the statue, the cry resonating in her bones like a blow.

All she'd achieved was arriving in time to watch them kill her sister.

Svedye. What could she do? She needed time, needed a way to get them away from Asya until Tarya and Zvezda could arrive. Assuming they were coming. That was the other lingering doubt, the question of whether Nikov would succeed in convincing them. Or if they'd already been turned against her.

She swallowed that thought, casting her eyes around for something that could help. Izaveta schemed and plotted, she didn't fight. She wasn't the Firebird—she wasn't even a queen. Even if she had a weapon, she'd be useless with it.

CHAPTER FIFTY-THREE

A stuttering gasp fell from Asya's lips as Dima pushed Yuliana into the circle of candlelight. At least they hadn't killed
her yet.

The brief flash of comfort at seeing Yuliana alive was short-
lived. A fresh bruise blossomed along her jaw, matching the
fading one at her temple. Dark blood trickled down her neck.
Asya's stomach twisted. Her grip was slipping already, the
Firebird's wings beating against her ribs.

She pulled against the chains, her words tumbling over
each other. "The Firebird has no mortal connections. Why
should it care what you do?" She'd meant for it to come out
cold, the biting remark of the monster, but she couldn't hide
the tremor in her voice.

Fyodor tugged on his sleeves, straightening. "This seems
as good a moment as any to test that theory."

Dima still held Yuliana's arm in his, but a slight flicker
broke through the stone-cold certainty in his eyes.

Asya grasped at it, a final attempt. "That's your *sister*. Whatever you may think of me—of the Firebird—what you're doing is far worse." She drew in a deep breath, her lungs scalding. "Your father wouldn't want you to hurt her."

As soon as the words left her lips, she realized she'd said the wrong thing. The uncertainty vanished, his expression hardening. "I suppose we'll never know," he growled. "Because of you."

Fyodor held up a hand, quelling the discussion. "It is an honor, even if the girl is a traitor. She is the catalyst for this glorious event." He jerked his head, and two more acolytes slipped forward, grabbing Yuliana's arms and forcing Dima back.

Yuliana kicked, trying to wrench herself free. "Asya, don't—"

The acolyte's hand flashed out, cracking across Yuliana's jaw. She would have staggered back, but those arms held her in place. The Firebird crashed against Asya's chest. Her power could end this, could destroy all these people, if it weren't for these bars.

Fyodor drew a curved knife from the folds of his tunic. A svash, the sacred knife used in church rituals. Made of enchanted metal, it was sharper than any sword. The same one that had left the scar on Asya's palm all those years ago, destining her for this.

Surely this could not have been what the gods intended when they chose her as Firebird? When they'd let moonlight run in her veins? Or perhaps they had not anticipated how she would fail them. Fail everyone.

Fyodor took Yuliana's hand in his, splaying her fingers. Her face paled even as her jaw set, the unwavering soldier through and through. He glanced up at Asya, a final unspoken question.

Tears burned behind Asya's eyes. Or perhaps that was flames. Everything burned. All her emotions—her guilt— a rising tide of fire inside her. But she couldn't let the Firebird go. Couldn't let them do this.

She caught Yuliana's eye through the bars, vibrant and blazing in the fading light. Something silent passed between them in that instant, as tangible as lightning. An apology for mutual damnation. An understanding that, at least, these two lost girls were not alone in their last moments.

The blade lifted. A gleaming star against the darkening sky. It was useless, but Asya tried to throw herself forward. To do anything that could stop this spinning nightmare.

"Don't!" The scream tore from Asya's chest, dragging flames with it. Even Dima lunged toward his sister—too late.

There was a sickening scrape of metal against bone, and the finger fell to the stone.

Asya couldn't stop it. Couldn't hold back the visceral reaction as Yuliana's cry tore through the hall.

A bright burst of flame—like taking a breath after being held underwater—and the Firebird spread its wings.

CHAPTER FIFTY-FOUR

The storm was drawing closer now. Its bright lightning, almost blue against the sky, illuminated the treetops. Izaveta could hear distant thunder, like the nearing battle of ancient gods. The wind was picking up too, snapping through her hair. But the sound—and Asya's heart-wrenching screams— gave Izaveta the cover she needed.

She ran back to the forest, to where Olyeta still stood waiting. She kept her eyes firmly on the ground, on the scattered starbirds rather than the watching falcons. Pushing off Olyeta's saddle, Izaveta led the bear forward while stooping to grasp several of the fallen starbirds that still glowed with magic.

It was slow moving over the jagged ground that surrounded the Elmer. Olyeta wasn't trained for subtlety, and her white fur shone against the darkened trees. Not to mention the clashing storm was already making her ears twitch uneasily—she might flee upon seeing the flames inside.

But Izaveta managed to maneuver the bear behind a crumpled wall, one just tall enough to hide her bulk. She tore off the pearled cape that hung from her shoulders, the ripping of the fabric buried in another clash of thunder.

As gently as she could, keeping her movements slow, she tied the fabric around Olyeta's head. She tore at the velvet, trying to form it into the right shape. It just needed to resemble Dveda's kokoshnik, even if it fell apart under closer examination.

It was a fragile plan, no denying that.

For one thing, Olyeta was the wrong color. Her snow-white fur was a pale gleam even in the dark, clearly not the rich brown of Dveda's. But if Izaveta could manage to silhouette her enough, it should work. She only needed a brief distraction. And this was all she had.

Her fingers scrambled through her hair—hands shaking—searching for the pin that kept it in place. It was blunt, but it would have to do. Her stomach turned as she looked down at the starbirds. Their magic came from their core, so if she wanted to use their bursting light, that was what she needed.

She squeezed her eyes shut, trying to lose herself in the darkness behind her lids. This was just another move in a game, nothing more. She clung on to that cold detachment and plunged the pin into the first starbird. It was difficult work, their silvery blood running over her hands like rain, tiny bones snapping beneath her fingers. But she reached the first one's heart, and glistening light spilled from it. A star captured in her palm.

She made quicker work of the other two, but she had to move fast now. Before their light faded—before Asya's light faded. Grabbing Olyeta's reins, she led the bear toward the hollow doorway. The perfect framing for her illusion.

Keeping well back, Izaveta peered around the corner just enough to tell when she should throw the starbirds' hearts to maximize the effect. But she couldn't keep her eyes from straying to Asya. Blood seeped down her front from more wounds than any mortal could bear. It mingled with a trail of sparks, as if Asya bled fire too.

Izaveta's heart punched against her ribs. She'd never been in a situation like this. For all the games of politics in court, she'd never stood in an instant where death felt so present. All she'd have to do was stretch out her hand to brush its shadow, so eager was it to clamp down on her sister.

Part of her wanted to run in there and scream at them to stop, and that part pressed down on her like a crushing weight. But she couldn't be irrational. That wouldn't help Asya.

Olyeta's head turned, her wide nose sniffing the air. Then she caught sight of the assembled people, the cage. Olyeta was not a bear trained for battle, but she knew how to sense danger. How to tell when something was a threat.

And this was clearly a threat.

She reared up onto her hind legs, letting out a roar as loud as the approaching thunder. Izaveta pulled her head back from the opening and threw the starbirds' hearts at the bear's feet, their glow bursting beneath her like a divine illumination.

An unfamiliar voice screamed, "Dveda!"

At that exact moment, the Firebird blossomed out of Asya. The dazzling light seared across Izaveta's vision. Chaos splintered through the room. People scattered, some recoiling from the Firebird, some staring at the silhouette in awe. Shouts crashed over them, a high voice trying to call them back to order.

Izaveta didn't wait to see if she had enough cover, she just threw herself through the archway. The light of the starbirds shone behind her, while the burning Firebird drew away any further attention. Her feet slipped over the loose stone—one acolyte nearly charged into her in their haste to follow the bear. People ran in all directions, unloosed from their leader, and pulled away on the tide of hysteria.

Her eyes darted around as she moved through the people, her black dress giving her momentary cover amongst their dark clothes. She ducked low when she reached the cage. The Firebird loomed above her, its dancing flames hissing as they met the firestone, so bright she had to shield her eyes.

Several acolytes lunged forward, blades drawn, desperate to complete whatever ritual it was they were enacting. But the blinding light of the Firebird disoriented them, sending them tumbling over each other.

Izaveta hurried for the side of the cage. She wanted to speak, to reassure her sister that she was there, but smoke clogged her throat. Her fingers dug into the burning metal, eyes watering at the heat that radiated from Asya. Izaveta pulled down the sleeve of her dress, trying to give herself some protection from the scalding bolt. It still seared through her flesh as she grasped it, but she gritted her teeth, wrenching it free.

The cage door swung open, the Firebird's flames leaping with it. But Asya was still chained, still tied and ready to slaughter. Izaveta scrambled up onto the altar, ignoring the clawing flames as she reached for the chains—when hands dragged her back.

"Let go of me!" she spat out, words coated in ash.

But the acolyte didn't relent, fingers digging into her arm as he pulled her away from the flames. He threw her against a crumbled pillar—her head snapping back against the stone in a bright burst of pain.

"You shouldn't be here. It's not time yet."

That voice—the desperate undertone to it—cut through her whirling head. She blinked, trying to focus. "Fyodor?"

He stepped closer, grabbing her arm. "You have to go back. The coronation—"

Izaveta struggled to pull free, her mind still sluggish. "But Asya—"

Fyodor didn't stop. His voice was low, almost manic. "You won't understand now, but you will. When this works, you will."

She finally wrenched her arm free, staggering back as she stared at her tutor. His words replayed in her head. Her eyes snagged on the gold crest around his neck. The same crest from Nikov's book. "You—you're a member of the order."

"I'm more than that," Fyodor said. "I'm its leader."

She was sure she should have felt that betrayal. Should have felt the knife sliding into her back, the way her world tilted on its axis as she realized one of the few people she trusted was a traitor. But there was no room for that now. Not with her head spinning and her sister trapped.

"Let me past," she bit out, voice coated with smoke.

"I know I should have told you, but you wouldn't have understood. You're too young." He held his hands out to her, imploring. "I dedicated my life to this, Izaveta. Years—*decades*. You have seen the work. It's hopeless. There is no other way. We cannot allow a monster to reign over us."

Izaveta almost laughed—she must've hit her head harder than she'd realized. The irony that he thought destroying the Firebird would save them, when Izaveta was the true monster.

He was so focused on Izaveta in that instant that he didn't see what loomed up behind him. Didn't see that the creature had escaped from its cage. She probably could have warned him. Could have drawn in a breath and yelled—or tried to push him aside.

But she didn't.

The Firebird devoured him in a single blow. A rush of orange and red, and then her tutor was reduced to ash.

Only a hint of sadness echoed through Izaveta's chest. But it was smothered by the memory of Asya's screams. The desperate cries that had torn through the air. All because of Fyodor—because of someone Izaveta had trusted.

The Firebird turned to the remaining acolytes. Its eyes rose above Asya's, matching expressions of ruthless vengeance. There was no forgiveness there. Those who hadn't already run, burned. Just like the banewolf, consumed by remorseless fire in an instant. The Firebird's wrath was terrible. A living thing, as scorching as its flames.

Izaveta slid down the pillar as she watched, her legs finally giving in. But even with her head pounding and corpses burning, relief coursed through her. Asya was safe now.

And then there was no one left. Just a terrible silence, Izaveta's rushing heart, and the lingering scent of blistered flesh.

Those cold eyes turned to Izaveta. It moved so quickly—one instant in front of the acolyte's ruined body, the next it was above her. Its burning face, the serrated hook of its beak, all but obscured her sister. There was no mercy in that face.

Chapter Fifty-Five

Asya scorched through the hall, uncontrollable and unstoppable as any fire. But even though the people who had wronged her were gone, those flames still wanted to devour. To take what they were owed.

That was when it hit her. As bright and piercing as it had been that first night, but this time she could hear the melody beyond it. Feel the perfect rightness of this Calling in every fiber of her being. She turned from the charred bodies—they didn't matter anymore. She needed to find who was singing, who was drawing the fire toward them in this beautiful maelstrom of sound.

She halted as she reached the crouched figure. The Calling emanated from them in waves, urging the flames forward. And who was Asya to stop them? This was what they wanted. What they were owed.

This was the person she'd been hunting all this time, the person who killed her mother.

A spark of recognition flashed in her mind, a familiar curve to the figure's face. The realization crashed into Asya like a tumbling rock. Her vision cleared, understanding echoing through her. Still the Firebird reached out. It had been submerged for too long. Now it had to devour.

Asya let out a shuddering gasp, staggering back as she folded her wings. Forced the fire to recede from her veins, to pull back the tongues of flame that reached for her sister.

She had to steady herself against the crumbled altar, fingers digging into the stone to stop the Firebird from rearing again. She stared at Izaveta, at the face that was almost as familiar as her own. "It's you?"

Asya half expected a denial, an explanation that would set the world right again. But instead, Izaveta pulled off her glove. The stratsviye was unmistakable against her pale skin.

"You're the one who—you—" Asya couldn't form words, couldn't get her mind to process what she was feeling. Everything had fallen off balance. The colors muted, poisoned and bitter, by this thing that couldn't be possible.

But it was. Asya felt it in her very core, in her heart that beat not just blood but flames. She pushed herself back, expanding the distance between her and Izaveta. "You have to get out of here." Her voice was urgent—pleading. When Izaveta didn't move, Asya yelled, hoping to jolt her to action. "Go, Iza. *Run!*"

But Izaveta just shook her head. Tears slid down her cheeks, shining and out of place. "I can't keep running, Asya."

"I don't know how long I can keep it back." Even as she said the words, the Calling echoed in the back of her mind. So clear now, she didn't know how she hadn't seen it before.

Izaveta stared up at her, an odd smile twisting her lips. "Don't you want to know what I did?"

Asya shook her head. She didn't want to hear any of this. Couldn't process any of this. It was too much, a bonfire ignited inside her that burned everything away. Feelings, thoughts, understanding. All scorched to ash.

Izaveta rose, reaching out to grasp Asya's hands. She recoiled, but her sister held firm. "You don't have to understand. But you have to know I didn't want it to end like this. I didn't mean for—" Her words choked. "For mother—"

Asya wrenched her hands free. The Calling was thrumming in her ears, too loud. Everything was too loud. How could it be Iza? How could Asya have missed so much? She and Izaveta had been inseparable, they could read each other's thoughts better than their own.

So how could Asya not have seen this?

But as soon as she thought about it, the pieces all fell into place. Izaveta's gloves, the way the Firebird had felt agitated around her. The familiar scent of magic in the queenstrees. The flames that had tried to leap from the banewolf to her.

Asya looked over at Izaveta, at the person at once so familiar and so unknown. "Why?" The word was tiny, pathetic in the vast space of the church. Almost swallowed by a rumble of thunder.

Izaveta looked so helpless in that moment. Staring at Asya with an expression of emptiness, a person carved out from the inside by their deeds. "I didn't want you to think differently of Mother. But she was planning something. Planning to use the Firebird for its magic." She looked away, as if she couldn't bear to see Asya's reaction. "To strip it down to its bones if necessary. It could have destroyed Tóurin—it would have destroyed you. And she wouldn't listen to me. I didn't know what else to do."

The revelation resonated through Asya like a remembered pain, swallowed by the bright burn of the Calling in her ears. It didn't even surprise her that the mother who used them all in her games would sacrifice one of her own daughters to further her power.

"I—" Izaveta swallowed, still trying to compose herself. "I didn't mean for her to die." The last sentence came out like a gasp, a whispered confession dragged from the depths of Izaveta's soul.

Before Asya had a chance to respond—to try to comprehend what her sister was saying—a blinding flash of light splintered the air, sending stone tumbling around them.

Chapter Fifty-Six

Rubble fell like rain, the remnants of the dome shattering at their feet. The sky above them had turned a violent red, lightning streaking through it in bright bursts of light.

Izaveta threw up her arms to shelter herself as the wind cut through the hollow room. It whipped around them, unnatural. She'd been right, this was no ordinary storm.

It was magic, unbridled and wild.

Brought on by her, by the price still unpaid.

She turned back to her sister, contorting her expression into something cold. "You should want to do it," she yelled, words buffeted by the gale. "I deserve to pay this price." She took a step toward Asya, their tattered dresses whirling around their feet. "I caused all of this. The banewolf, that village, the strashe. Even this storm. All of that was me. I watched it happen while I stood back and did nothing."

Asya's expression was unreadable, bloodred hair snapping around her face.

"If not for me, you'd have had more time as a mortal," Izaveta pressed. Reaching for the offensive, goading Asya toward the destruction Izaveta deserved, was so much easier than watching the sadness fracture at the corners of her sister's eyes. "So do it, Firebird. Fulfill your duty."

Asya shook her head. "Don't do that, Iza. Don't play that game with me."

The fight bled out of Izaveta at those words. Her sister could always see through her. Izaveta's voice softened to no more than a whisper, barely audible over the growl of thunder. "You *should* hate me for it."

Asya stepped forward this time, hands tentative as they reached out. Her skin was warm against Izaveta's, but no longer scalding. "I could never hate you. You were trying to help."

A painful lump rose in Izaveta's throat, her heart clenching. She didn't deserve this, didn't deserve the sister who could forgive her. "That doesn't change what has to be done."

Lightning struck again, a bright purple streak that sent up a spray of stone. The two of them moved in unison, diving toward a pillar. The stone scraped the skin of Izaveta's forearm, a jagged pain that pulled her firmly into this moment.

Asya righted herself first, grasping Izaveta's hands again and pulling her under the shelter of a fallen pew. "No," Asya said, even as another bright streak of magic crested the sky. "We can find a way. There's always a way. You have all those books, the—"

"It's too late." The words fell heavy from Izaveta's lips, but they were true. She was finished running from what she'd done. "I've dragged this out enough as it is. I've hurt people already. People have died, Asya. What kind of queen allows that to happen to her people?"

Asya's eyes were shimmering, her lip trembling. "We could—"

"I don't want to be that person." Izaveta's voice cracked, but she didn't care. She was done playing these games, done being the perfect little imitation of her mother. "For once, Asya, let me do something good."

CHAPTER FIFTY-SEVEN

Asya's world was falling away from her. Piece by piece the ground beneath her feet was wrenched away. Even the Calling was fading, a distant ringing in her ears. This couldn't be happening. She must still be trapped in the cage, Fyodor concocting some elaborate spell to torture her.

Or perhaps she'd never woken up after the queenstrees, and now she was trapped in this strange In-Between. This place where nightmares roamed, and nothing made sense.

"You're still my sister," she breathed. "I'm not giving up on you."

A terrible sadness rose in Izaveta's eyes. The expression of someone who knew they were right, but wished they weren't. "It's not giving up. It's accepting."

But Asya shook her head, blinking tears from her eyes. "We only just found each other again." The unfairness of it all sharpened inside her like a blade. This twisted situation, the perverse path destiny had set before her. She thought of Fyodor, of his zealous certainty that the price was wrong.

It had been so easy to ignore when it wasn't personal to Asya. When it wasn't her sister.

On their knees facing each other like this, they were two halves of the same person. Two sides of the same coin. One could not exist without the other.

"You can't ignore your duty," Izaveta said. "Just as I cannot ignore mine."

A streak of bright red struck the altar, cracking it in half with enough force to send a shudder through Asya's bones. A piece of stone spun off, shattering the pew above their heads. Asya grabbed her sister's arm, pulling her from the path of the debris. Smoke and ash and the tang of magic filled her mouth—so strong it was almost choking.

Izaveta coughed. "This won't end otherwise, Asya. This storm—none of it. It won't just be here. It'll be all of Tóurin." She looked up at her, dark eyes pleading. "I can't be responsible for that."

A painful lump rose in Asya's throat. She knew that feeling. Understood the crushing weight of that guilt.

Izaveta reached forward gently, pushing Asya's hair from her face. "What happens now isn't your fault. I'm asking you to do it."

"It's not your fault either," Asya whispered. All this power, and she was just as helpless as she'd been inside that cage. "I can't lose you again." Her voice came out like a child's cry, the desperate little girl who'd fought the day Tarya had come to take her away.

But Asya wasn't that little girl anymore.

She looked up, meeting her sister's eyes in the midst of the churning storm. Of the turmoil of magic and fire. In that moment she knew what she had to do. They both had to uphold this duty, this responsibility. It wasn't something either of them had asked for, but it was something they couldn't run from.

It wouldn't be Asya taking from Iza. It wouldn't be the monster stalking her in the night. This was their sacrifice. The decision made together, as sisters.

Asya swallowed hard, a sob wrenching through her chest. "I love you."

Izaveta squeezed her eyes shut, pressing her forehead to Asya's. "I love you too."

They stayed like that, huddled together in the center of the ruined space, as Asya let go. The storm still blew around them, but it was suddenly very distant. Separate.

The Calling rushed in Asya's ears, the perfect notes jarred by the crushing ache inside her. The burning wings spread, curling around the two of them—almost protective. Hiding them from the storm.

The flames curled out, wrapping tight around Izaveta's arms. They snaked up, golds and reds illuminating her face. Asya's last, fragile hope fractured. The quiet whisper that perhaps the price would not be too high. But she could feel it, could feel what the fire demanded.

Her grip on Iza's hands tightened, as if by sheer strength of will Asya could keep her there. Could stop herself from being ripped irreparably in two.

But Izaveta was unwavering, her grasp firm in Asya's. Just as she had been the day of the ceremony. The day that had sent them on this colliding path. Desperate to wrench them apart, right to the end.

The flames looked beautiful as they curved down Izaveta's

neck, illuminating her shining eyes. The fire surged on, eager as it devoured. As it clamped around her heart.

One last, brilliant image of Izaveta surrounded by flames. An old painting of a star falling from the sky, ignited in brightest gold.

And then—no matter how Asya's fingers struggled to hold on—Izaveta was gone.

Chapter Fifty-Eight

The library was colder than the frostbitten night beyond. Darkness had settled around Asya, and she hadn't bothered to stand to light the fire or scattered candles. Now the space was illuminated only by the pale moons beyond the windows. They carved deep shadows into the room, spindled fingers desperate to claim Asya for their own.

Books lay around her in haphazard piles, parchment littering the floor. But there were no scholars to reprimand her, no Izaveta to sort through the mess. Fyodor was ashes in a ruined church. And Izaveta…

Asya swallowed hard, her eyes stinging.

She wasn't sure what had made her come here, not at first. She just knew that she couldn't sleep. Couldn't spend one more moment in that suffocating room. And the place that had once been her refuge—the forest, the comforting canopy of trees—had been poisoned.

Because now it just made her think of the previous night. Of stumbling into the dark branches. Sobs heaving through her as she ran blindly. Running from what she'd done. Fractured images from the day before fluttered behind her eyes, refusing to leave. The heavy bars of the cage. The bright pain of the knives. Yuliana's hand, blood spurting from it like fire.

And her sister. Kneeling in front of her, dark eyes wide and pleading.

The storm had dissipated almost as quickly as the flames. Sweeping away just like Izaveta, gone as if it had never been there at all. Though the storm had left scorch marks, vibrant fires that still burned in its wake.

But there was nothing left of Iza. Not even ash.

Yuliana had vanished too. The remaining strashe had searched the surrounding woods for any survivors after looking over the bodies. But neither Yuliana nor her brother were anywhere to be found.

That was a different kind of loss. Not the pain of her heart torn in two, but a hollow sadness. Asya couldn't blame Yuliana for leaving. Not after what had happened to her. Not after she'd seen Asya murder her own sister.

The words on the page before her were blurring together, her sleep-deprived mind hardly making sense of them anymore. She leaned forward, cupping her face in her hands. At least the library gave her a respite from the stares. From the constant questions and the dark looks.

They'd been incessant ever since Tarya had found her, wandering and freezing in the woods. What had happened? How had she escaped?

Where was her sister?

Telling everyone was almost worse. Watching the realization break across their faces, the shock, the veiled judgment.

Only Tarya had offered her comfort, had murmured that she'd done the right thing.

But Asya wasn't so sure anymore. Without Izaveta at her side, she wasn't sure of anything.

Most in the court didn't know the full story, of course. But that didn't stop the whispers. The venomous words that followed Asya as she waited outside the cabinet room while they discussed her, still trying to decide if she should be tried as a traitor or crowned the next queen.

She wasn't sure she cared which they chose.

But there was one thing Asya could hold on to. One last hope she wouldn't let go of in the midst of this vast, empty night she was left in. The question that had prickled at the back of her mind before, only to be dismissed. It was ephemeral, half-formed in her head.

The question that had drawn her to this place, the only place that might hold an answer. Because that same scene replayed over and over in her head—the Firebird's flames reaching out, claiming each of the acolytes. The acrid scent of their burned flesh.

But when the flames took Izaveta, they left no residue. No body, no scattered ashes.

It was a desperate hope, the unanswered prayer of a child. But Asya knew it as certainly as fire ran in her veins: she wasn't giving up on her sister yet.

★ ★ ★ ★ ★

Pronunciation Guide

Adilena Karasova: ah-dih-len-ah KA-ra-so-vah.

Amarinth: am-ah-rinth.

Amyeva: am-YEH-vah.

Araïse: ah-raise.

Arille: ah-ree.

Asya Karasova: az-yah KA-ra-so-vah.

Basbousa: bass-boa-sah.

Bazin: bah-zin.

Conze: con-zay.

Demonya: deh-mon-yah.

Demonye: deh-mon-yeh.

Demonyesha: deh-mon-yeh-sha.

Dima Vilanovich: dee-mah vih-lan-oh-vich.

Diye meshok: dee-yeh meh-shok.

Dveda: d-veh-dah.

Dyena: d-yeh-nah.

Estava: ess-TA-vah.

Fyodor Alyeven: fee-yo-dor al-YEH-ven.

Hunte Rastyshenik: hoo-n-teh RASS-ti-yeh-she-nik.

Ilyova: ee-lee-OH-vah.

Iveshkin: IH-vesh-kin.

Izaveta Karasova: EE-zah-veh-tah KA-ra-so-vah.

Kaizer: kai-zer.

Karaznoi: kah-razz-noy.

Katvesha: kat-VESH-ah.

Kessek: kess-ek.

Kharur: ka-rur.

Kharuri: ka-rur-ee.

Kirava: kee-RA-vah.

Kokoshnik: ko-kosh-nik.

Korona: koh-ron-ah.

Korovai: koh-roh-vai.

Koschei: ko-shey.

Kyriil Azarov: kih-reel ah-za-rov.

Leonhar: lee-yon-har.

Liljendaär: leel-yen-dar.

Liljendaän: leel-yen-dan.

Lirina: LIH-ree-nah.

Lyev: lee-YEV.

Lyoza: lee-oh-zuh.

Matryoshka: mat-ree-osh-ka.

Meshnik: mesh-nik.

Mira: meer-a.

Mishka: meesh-kah.

Mosovna: moss-ov-nah.

Nikov Toyevski: NEE-kov TOY-ev-skee.

Nisova: ni-SOH-va.

Noteya Svedsta: not-ey-a s-ved-stah.

Olyeta: oll-ye-tah.

Onishin: on-yee-shin.

Oravin: or-ah-vin.

Orlov: orr-lov.

Oryaze: ORR-yazz-ey.

Ozya Kerivnei: ozz-yah keh-riv-nay.

Pakviye: pak-VEE-yey.

Parakov Evanova: PA-rah-kov ee-va-no-va.

Pelmeni: PEL-men-ee.

Petrik: peh-TREEK.

Raslava: rass-LAV-ah.

Restov: ress-tov.

Sanislav: san-ih-slahv.

Saveya: sah-vey-ah.

Shashka: SHASH-kah.

Shzuba: zjoo-bah.

Stavoye verenish: STA-voy-eh ver-EH-nish.

Strashe: strah-shey.

Strashevsta: stra-shev-stah.

Stratsviye: stratz-VEE-yeh.

Stravínžk: strah-vinsk.

Stroganov: stro-gah-nov.

Svash: s-vash.

Svedye: s-ved-yeh.

Syrnyki: SEER-ni-kee.

Tarya Karasova: TAH-ya KA-ra-so-vah.

Täusch: tau-sh.

Teriya: te-ree-yah.

Tóurensi: tuh-ren-zee.

Tóurin: tuh-rin.

Trozye: trozz-yeh.

Tsvestov: z-vez-tov.

Uchev Saravne: oo-chev sa-rah-v-ney.

Vada: vah-da.

Valerii: vah-LERR-iy.

Vasha: vah-sha.

Vasilisa: vass-EE-lee-sa.

Vas Tiraviya: vass teer-AH-vee-yah.

Vas Xekiva: vass ze-KEE-vah.

Versbühl: vers-bool.

Versch: ver-sh.

Vetviya: vet-veeya.

Vibishop: vai-bi-shop.

Viila: vee-lah.

Vilanovich: vih-lan-oh-vich.

Vittaria: vih-TA-riya.

Voda Svediye: voh-da s-ved-EE-yeh.

Volke otrava: voll-keh oh-tra-va.

Voya: voy-ah.

Voye: voy-eh.

Vrostav Zev: vross-tahv zehv.

Xishin: zji-SHIN.

Yuliana Vilanovich: YU-lee-yah-na vih-lan-oh-vich.

Zmenya: zuh-MEN-yah.

Znaya: zuh-NAI-yah.

Zvess: zu-vess.

Zvezda: zveh-z-dah.

ACKNOWLEDGMENTS

So many people have played a part in making this book what it is that I almost don't know where to start! But first I have to thank Natascha Morris. You believed in me even when I didn't and pushed me to be a better writer every day. Without you, this book really wouldn't exist. Thank you also to the whole team at BookEnds Literary for your tireless help and support, especially James McGowan and Naomi Davis. And thank you to the team at New Leaf for stepping in to support me, especially my agent Patrice Caldwell and the amazing Meredith Barnes.

A huge thank-you to my wonderful editor, Connolly Bottum, who saw a spark in this book and helped me to shape it into something magical. Your guidance has truly been invaluable. I can't thank you enough for taking a chance on me and my angsty girls and for all your support along the way. And thank you as well to the whole team at Inkyard Press: the amazing copyeditors, Stephanie Van de Vooren and Anne Sharpe. Bess Braswell, Brittany Mitchell, and Laura Gianino, who all championed this book and helped it get out into the world, and everyone else who had a hand in making this book what it is.

I also have to thank the amazing art director, Kathleen Oudit, for the cover and beautiful map, and Marisa Aragón Ware for the absolutely stunning cover illustration. They truly managed to bring this book to life! Thank you as well to Tara Spruit for the brilliant character card art.

I would never have come this far in my writing journey without the truly amazing writer friends I've made, and I thank all of you from the bottom of my heart. Katie Passerotti, the most glorious starbeast and my one true soulkin: I don't know what I'd do without you. You've been there with me from the beginning, listened to me through all the ups and downs, and always pushed my writing to be better. You're beyond amazing, and I don't know what I did to deserve you.

Huge thank-you to Briston Brooks, my Slytherin heart twin. Thank you for answering all my anxious DMs and making my words so much better. To Tara Gilbert, your support and encouragement have helped me through so much. Thank you for being my romance guru, sharing in all my obsessions and always being there for me. To Tamara Mahmood-Hayes: the publishing gods smiled on us the day we met in that signing line, and I'm so lucky to have you in my life. To Zabé Ellor, my fellow resident of submission hell: we did it! Thank you for the shared screams and all your support. To Laura Taylor Namey for answering my constant stream of questions.

A special Bulbasaur-filled thank-you to Tiffany Lea Elmer for being the best dragon mum there is and welcoming me into your group all those years ago. And to all of the amazing Dragon Hatchlings: thank you for listening to my endless rambling and supporting me through every crisis. To the sisterhood: Sarah, Katie, Katie Two, Briston again. DP forever. To my P2P ladies, who first brought me into the writing community and have been such steadfast support ever since: you are all amazing, and I can't wait for your books. To all the wonderful Team Nat authors: I'm so grateful to have you all at my side. And to all the other writers who made me feel so welcome in the online writer community.

And a huge thank-you to everyone else who has had eyes on this book and had a hand in making it what it is: Delara Adams, Elayne Becker, Lindsey Hall, Natasha Hanova, Kat Howard, Kalyn Josephson, Felice Laverne, Katherine Locke, Fadwa, Aneeqah Naeem, Mara Rutherford, Elsa Sjunneson-Henry. Your critiques, guidance, and support made a world of difference.

Thank you to my real-world friends who had to put up with this whole writing lark where I lock myself away for months at a time and only come out for ice cream. Especially to Eloise Orton, Allie Delanois, Lila Victor, Marisa Goff, Gabrielle Gorman, and Kianna Shore. You are all magic, and I couldn't do this without you. A special thank-you to Christa Fassi and everyone at TSPC for always being there for me.

Very important thank-you to both *The Great British Bake Off* and Nutella for getting me through the hard days. Plus, my cats, for not *succeeding* in deleting half my book, even if you tried.

And finally I have to thank my expansive, hectic family. I'd need a whole other book to list you all here, but you know who you are. Special thanks to my grandparents for being my tireless supporters and letting me see that there's value in creativity. To my dad for supporting my book-buying habit from a young age and encouraging my love of writing. To my mum for getting me through the ups and downs and making all this possible.

To my sister, Clemmie, because I know you'd want to be last. You're a poophead, but you're *my* poophead. Thank you for the endless texts and phone calls, and for always seeing something in my writing—even when I didn't.

And a final thank-you to you, the reader. Thank you for going on this journey with me and taking a chance on Asya and Izaveta. Don't be afraid to let your fire burn.